MRS. JEFFRIES SERVES TWO

MRS. JEFFRIES
AND THE BEST LAID PLANS

MRS. JEFFRIES
AND THE FEAST OF ST. STEPHEN

EMILY BRIGHTWELL

BERKLEY PRIME CRIME, NEW YORK

Contents

MRS. JEFFRIES
AND THE BEST LAID PLANS

INSPECTOR WITHERSPOON ALWAYS TRIUMPHS . . . HOW DOES HE DO IT?

Even the Inspector himself doesn't know—because his secret weapon is as ladylike as she is clever. She's Mrs. Jeffries—the determined, delightful detective who stars in this unique Victorian mystery series. Be sure to read them all.

The Inspector and Mrs. Jeffries
A doctor is found dead in his own office—and Mrs. Jeffries must scour the premises to find the prescription for murder.

Mrs. Jeffries Dusts for Clues
One case is solved and another is opened when the Inspector finds a missing brooch—pinned to a dead woman's gown. But Mrs. Jeffries never cleans a room without dusting under the bed—and never gives up on a case before every loose end is tightly tied.

The Ghost and Mrs. Jeffries
Death is unpredictable . . . but the murder of Mrs. Hodges was foreseen at a spooky séance. The practical-minded housekeeper may not be able to see the future—but she can look into the past and put things in order to solve this haunting crime.

Mrs. Jeffries Takes Stock
A businessman has been murdered—and it could be because he cheated his stockholders. The housekeeper's interest is piqued, and when it comes to catching killers, the smart money's on Mrs. Jeffries.

Mrs. Jeffries On the Ball
A festive Jubilee celebration turns into a fatal affair—and Mrs. Jeffries must find the guilty party.

continued on next page . . .

Mrs. Jeffries on the Trail
Why was Annie Shields out selling flowers late on a foggy night? And more importantly, who killed her while she was doing it? Mrs. Jeffries must sniff out the clues.

Mrs. Jeffries Plays the Cook
Mrs. Jeffries finds herself doing double duty: cooking for the Inspector's household and trying to cook a killer's goose.

Mrs. Jeffries and the Missing Alibi
When Inspector Witherspoon becomes the main suspect in a murder, Scotland Yard refuses to let him investigate. But no one said anything about Mrs. Jeffries.

Mrs. Jeffries Stands Corrected
When a local publican is murdered, and Inspector Witherspoon botches the investigation, trouble starts to brew for Mrs. Jeffries.

Mrs. Jeffries Takes the Stage
After a theater critic is murdered, Mrs. Jeffries uncovers the victim's secret past: a real-life drama more compelling than any stage play.

Mrs. Jeffries Questions the Answer
Hannah Cameron was not well-liked. But were her friends or family the sort to stab her in the back? Mrs. Jeffries must find out.

Mrs. Jeffries Reveals Her Art
Mrs. Jeffries has to work double-time to find a missing model *and* a killer. And she'll have to get her whole staff involved—before someone else becomes the next subject.

Mrs. Jeffries Takes the Cake
The evidence was all there: a dead body, two dessert plates, and a gun. As if Mr. Ashbury had been sharing cake with his own killer. Now Mrs. Jeffries will have to dish up some clues.

Mrs. Jeffries Rocks the Boat
Mirabelle had traveled by boat all the way from Australia to visit her sister—only to wind up murdered. Now Mrs. Jeffries must solve the case—and it's sink or swim.

Mrs. Jeffries Weeds the Plot
Three attempts have been made on Annabeth Gentry's life. Was it due to her recent inheritance, or was it because her bloodhound dug up the body of a murdered thief? Mrs. Jeffries will have to investigate.

Mrs. Jeffries Pinches the Post
Harrison Nye may have been involved in some dubious business dealings, but no one ever expected him to be murdered. Now, Mrs. Jeffries and her staff must root through the sins of his past to discover which one caught up with him.

Mrs. Jeffries Pleads Her Case
Harlan Westover's death was deemed a suicide by the magistrate. But Inspector Witherspoon is willing to risk his career to prove otherwise. And it's up to Mrs. Jeffries to ensure the good inspector remains afloat.

Mrs. Jeffries Sweeps the Chimney
A dead vicar has been found, propped against a church wall, and Inspector Witherspoon's only prayer is to seek the divinations of Mrs. Jeffries.

Mrs. Jeffries Stalks the Hunter
Puppy love turns to obsession, which leads to murder. Who better to get to the heart of the matter than Inspector Witherspoon's indomitable companion, Mrs. Jeffries.

Mrs. Jeffries and the Silent Knight
The yuletide murder of an elderly man is complicated by several suspects—none of whom were in the Christmas spirit.

Mrs. Jeffries Appeals the Verdict
Mrs. Jeffries and her belowstairs cohorts have their work cut out for them if they want to save an innocent man from the gallows.

Visit Emily Brightwell's website at
www.emilybrightwell.com

Also available from Prime Crime:
The first three Mrs. Jeffries Mysteries in one volume
Mrs. Jeffries Learns the Trade

MRS. JEFFRIES

AND THE BEST LAID PLANS

EMILY BRIGHTWELL

BERKLEY PRIME CRIME, NEW YORK

THE BERKLEY PUBLISHING GROUP
Published by the Penguin Group
Penguin Group (USA) Inc.
375 Hudson Street, New York, New York 10014, USA
Penguin Group (Canada), 90 Eglinton Avenue East, Suite 700, Toronto, Ontario M4P 2Y3, Canada (a division of Pearson Penguin Canada Inc.)
Penguin Books Ltd., 80 Strand, London WC2R 0RL, England
Penguin Group Ireland, 25 St. Stephen's Green, Dublin 2, Ireland (a division of Penguin Books Ltd.)
Penguin Group (Australia), 250 Camberwell Road, Camberwell, Victoria 3124, Australia (a division of Pearson Australia Group Pty. Ltd.)
Penguin Books India Pvt. Ltd., 11 Community Centre, Panchsheel Park, New Delhi—110 017, India
Penguin Group (NZ), 67 Apollo Drive, Mairangi Bay, Auckland 1311, New Zealand (a division of Pearson New Zealand Ltd.)
Penguin Books (South Africa) (Pty.) Ltd., 24 Sturdee Avenue, Rosebank, Johannesburg 2196, South Africa

Penguin Books Ltd., Registered Offices: 80 Strand, London WC2R 0RL, England

This is a work of fiction. Names, characters, places, and incidents either are the product of the author's imagination or are used fictitiously, and any resemblance to actual persons, living or dead, business establishments, events, or locales is entirely coincidental. The publisher does not have any control over and does not assume any responsibility for author or third-party websites or their content.

MRS. JEFFRIES AND THE BEST LAID PLANS

A Berkley Prime Crime Book / published by arrangement with the author

Copyright © 2007 by Cheryl Arguile.
Cover art by David Stimson.
Cover design by Annette Fiore.

ISBN: 978-0-7394-8880-5

BERKLEY® PRIME CRIME
Berkley Prime Crime Books are published by The Berkley Publishing Group,
a division of Penguin Group (USA) Inc.,
375 Hudson Street, New York, New York 10014.
The name BERKLEY PRIME CRIME and the BERKLEY PRIME CRIME design are trademarks belonging to Penguin Group (USA) Inc.

PRINTED IN THE UNITED STATES OF AMERICA

For Nanette Caldararo, with love and appreciation
for all the years of inspiration and support.
Thanks, Nanny; you helped me to live my dream.

CHAPTER 1

"I don't think we'll ever get this wedding planned." Betsy sighed and closed the cookbook. "Worrying about all the details has me so muddled that I can't even think of what to serve at the reception."

Mrs. Jeffries, the housekeeper for Inspector Gerald Witherspoon, smiled sympathetically at the pretty blonde-haired maid. "You're doing fine, Betsy. We've still almost a month before the big day. That's plenty of time to decide on the menu."

"It feels like it's happening tomorrow and I'm not near ready. I can't even decide on what kind of dress I want."

"You'll get it all done," said Mrs. Jeffries, glancing at the maid. Betsy was staring morosely at the closed cookbook. The poor girl was going to make herself ill over a few simple wedding plans. This wasn't at all like her. Betsy was normally a strong, rather decisive young woman who could make the hardest decisions, some of them involving life and death, with the greatest of ease. Yet planning her own wedding had turned her into a nervous Nellie of the worst sort. There was nothing that the housekeeper could say that would allay her fears, either. The girl had to fight these demons on her own.

Betsy was afraid she was going to fail, that she was going to embarrass herself or even worse, her fiancé, Smythe, by doing something wrong on the most important day of their lives. She'd come from a poverty stricken family in the East End of London and she'd ended up as a maid here at Upper Edmonton Gardens by collapsing on their doorstep. She was having a proper wedding and an elegant reception. Unfortunately, she had little confidence in her own social skills, and she was terrified that something would go wrong.

"But I don't want to inconvenience Luty, and it's her staff that's doing all the work," Betsy cried. "I'm going to make up my mind. Gracious, it's only a little reception."

"Take your time, child," Mrs. Jeffries said kindly. "Luty won't mind in the least." Luty Belle Crookshank was an American friend of the household. She had insisted on hosting Betsy's wedding reception at her elegant home in Knightsbridge. To anyone outside their immediate circle, it might seem an odd state of affairs for a wealthy woman to host a reception for a poor housemaid. But the bonds between the household of Upper Edmonton Garden and Luty Belle Crookshank were special enough to overcome the rigid class structure of socially conscious London.

"I know she won't mind, but I want to get it done. It's important that everything is planned properly, you know what I mean?" Betsy flipped open the cover of the huge red book. "Mind you, I wish Smythe would tell me what he's got up his sleeve for us. I don't even know where we're going to live."

"Have a little faith, girl," Mrs. Goodge said as she came in from the hallway. The cook had been in the dry larder and she carried a tin of baking powder in one hand and a bag of currants in the other. She was a plump, elderly woman with wire-framed spectacles, white hair tucked under her floppy cooks cap, and a pristine white apron over her pale blue work dress. A big, yellow tabby cat followed at her heels. "Smythe will do right by you. He's got everything arranged."

"Well, it wouldn't hurt him to tell me a few bits and pieces, would it," Betsy declared. "Don't get me wrong; I'm happy to be getting married and I love him with all my heart, but it's going to change things. It's going to change everything, and that scares me a bit. I don't think I'm ready to give it up yet."

"Who says you have to?" Mrs. Jeffries understood exactly what "it" was. "Our investigations are just as important to Smythe as they are to you. I'm sure he's thought of a way for you to live together as man and wife and still work with us. He's not ready to give it all up yet, either."

Hepzibah Jeffries was the widow of a Yorkshire policeman. After her husband's death, she'd sold her property and come to London. She'd intended to spend her days doing charity work, going to museums, and perhaps traveling on the Continent as a companion to a gentlewoman. Instead, she'd seen an advertisement offering a position as a housekeeper for a policeman. She soon found herself working for Inspector Gerald Witherspoon of the Metropolitan Police Force.

Witherspoon had been in charge of the records room, but soon after her arrival in his life, his world had changed when she and the rest of the household had begun investigating the horrible Kensington High Street murders. Naturally, he was unaware of their involvement. By the time the case was solved and he'd caught the killer, he was no longer in charge of the records room. By now, their inspector had solved over twenty homicides and was by far the most famous detective in the city.

"I suppose not." Betsy sighed again. "I just wish he'd tell me. But all he says is that it's a secret and I'll love it."

"Then take him at his word." Mrs. Goodge took off her apron, draped it over the back of the chair, and then sat down. She pushed back from the table and patted her lap. The cat, Samson, jumped up and curled into a ball. After giving the other two women a good glare, he settled down and began to purr. "And quit worryin' so much. It'll all come out in the wash. It's only a simple reception. What could possibly go wrong?"

"What if I serve the wrong thing?" Betsy asked worriedly. "Wedding breakfasts have very strict etiquette."

"Don't be silly. I've cooked in some of the finest houses in this land. Do you think I'd sit idly by and let you serve anything that isn't right?" Mrs. Goodge had had enough of the girl's foolishness. She wasn't going to allow her to ruin the best day of her life by fretting over every little detail.

"Yes, I know," Betsy protested. "But it's not just the food. What if I do something or say something—"

"You'll be just fine," the cook said firmly. "You're an intelligent young woman who knows what's what. Now, take a good gander at that cookbook and decide what you'd like served at the reception. We want to have all the details of your wedding planned just in case we get us another investigation."

"Another murder," Betsy wailed. "Oh dear, I'd not even thought of that." This was an out-and-out lie. She'd thought of nothing else. She'd love to have a good investigation to think about; anything would be better than planning this wedding. Dashing about London talking to shopkeepers and tradespeople would be so much easier than trying to figure out whether to have the reception at eleven or eleven thirty or whether to serve roast beef or chicken cutlets or whether to have pink roses or yellow ones. Or maybe she shouldn't use roses at all; perhaps using flowers as the center-pieces at a wedding reception was completely inappropriate.

She loved Smythe so much, and her dearest wish was for him to be proud of her on that special day. She was so scared she wasn't up to this task. Why couldn't they have just gone off to Gretna Green and gotten married? "For once, I hope that doesn't happen. I couldn't do both."

" 'Course you could," the cook said stoutly. "You're young and spry. You can do anything you set your mind to do." Mrs. Goodge had worked for some of the wealthiest families in England, but there was no household she'd rather be in than this one. When her last employer had let her go, she'd accepted this position thinking she'd taken a step down in the world. She, who had worked for England's oldest, most aristocratic families, had been forced to take a position with a common policeman. But it was the only position she could find. After a lifetime of keeping everyone in their proper place and staying firmly in her own, once she'd come here, the bounds she'd set between herself and others withered and died. These people had become her family. Mrs. Goodge wasn't sure exactly how that had happened. Certainly the murder investigations had helped strengthen the bonds between them all, but it had been more than that. They'd come together because they were each of them alone in the world, and everyday, Mrs. Goodge thanked God he'd guided her here and not to the home of some dissolute baron or count.

Since she'd first walked in the back door of Upper Edmonton Gardens, she'd changed a great deal. Who said you couldn't teach an old dog new tricks? She smiled and stroked Samson's back. She'd certainly learned a few tricks these past years. She'd discovered she could loosen every tongue that passed through this kitchen by plying them with tea and treats.

Mrs. Goodge did all her investigating without ever leaving the comfort of this cozy room. She had a huge network of tradespeo-ple, gas men, delivery boys, street vendors, and old colleagues that she called upon when they had a case. Gossip was her stock and trade, and she'd gotten very good at gleaning every morsel of information there was to be had about a victim or a suspect in one of their murders. But interesting as their investigations might be, she was most proud of the fact that in the twilight of her life, she'd had, through God's grace, the chance to contribute to the cause of justice. Their investigations had brought vicious killers to their just rewards and, more important, had kept the innocent from hanging.

"Mrs. Goodge, are you all right?" Betsy stared at her anxiously.

"Oh, yes, sorry. I was woolgathering. Did you say something?" She shifted in her chair and the movement caused the cat to let out a tiny meow of displeasure. "There, lovey, it's fine," she soothed.

"I asked if you think we ought to have roast chicken or the rolled beef," the maid replied. "What do you think?"

"Have both," the cook replied. "It might be called a wedding breakfast, but it's really more of a luncheon. Your guests will expect a nice feed."

"But I don't want to put Luty's staff to too much trouble," Betsy said. "I don't want to overstep my bounds."

"Don't be silly," the cook replied. "Luty's your friend. She wants to do this for you. You're not taking advantage of her in the least."

"Of course you're not," Mrs. Jeffries added. "Luty and Hatchet are absolutely thrilled to host this for you." Hatchet had also insisted on being a part of the festivities. He was Luty Belle's butler, but from the way the two of them related to one another, he was far more than just a servant. He was Luty's most trusted friend.

The two households had met during the second of the inspector's murder investigations. Luty had been a witness. But though she was elderly, she'd figured out soon enough what they were about, and after that case was solved, she'd then come to them with a problem of her own. She and Hatchet had helped in that investigation, and ever since, they'd insisted on helping with all of them. Their connections had proved very useful as Luty was no stranger to homes of the rich and the powerful. Though Hatchet was a bit reticent about his past, his circle of acquaintances had proved helpful on more than one occasion.

"All right then, we'll have both the roast chicken and the beef. What do you think about the soup?"

"Leek and potato soup is always good," the cook replied. "It's hearty without being overpowering."

"I like leek and potato soup," Wiggins, the footman, declared as he strolled into the room. He was a cheerful lad in his early twenties with a ready smile, rosy round cheeks, and brown hair that had a tendency to curl when he went too long between trips to the barber. He carried a tin of brass polish in his hand. Fred, the household's black-and-brown mongrel dog, trotted at his heels.

Samson took one look at Fred, hissed in his direction, and then leapt off the cook's lap and charged for the sanctuary of Mrs. Goodge's room. Wiggins laughed. "I'm glad Fred finally learned how to handle your cat, Mrs. Goodge," he said. He knelt down and pulled open the cupboard under the sink and shoved the tin inside.

"It took him long enough," Mrs. Jeffries murmured. Poor Fred had skulked about in fear of Samson for weeks after Wiggins had brought him home. He'd rescued the animal from certain starvation. Samson had been the pet of a murder victim, but he'd such a miserable disposition that he'd have been destroyed if Wiggins hadn't taken pity on him. Samson repaid this kindness by biting and scratching his benefactor and everyone else in the household, especially if they went too near his food dish. Yet the cat had taken one look at the cook, and it had been love at first sight.

"I don't know why everyone thinks Samson is so mean," Mrs. Goodge complained. "He's a sweet old boy if you treat him right."

No one had the heart to argue with her. They all just kept their fingers away from Samson's food dish.

"The brass polish is almost gone," Wiggins said to Mrs. Jeffries. "And I saw Smythe coming down the road. What are we havin' with mornin' tea? Are we 'avin' them little sweet buns you was bakin' yesterday?"

"Those are for supper," Mrs. Goodge replied. "I've got a nice loaf of bread and a plain seed cake for tea. If Smythe is almost here, we can sit down on time for once."

"I'll put the kettle on the boil." Betsy closed the cookbook and got up.

"It's startin' to rain out there," Smythe announced a moment later as he walked into the kitchen. He was a tall, muscular man in his late thirties. He had a headful of black hair, thick eyebrows, and harsh, heavy features. He shrugged out of his jacket and hung it on the coat tree.

"It's been a very wet spring," Mrs. Jeffries commented as she laid a stack of plates in the center of the table.

"I hope it won't rain on our wedding day." Betsy pulled the big brown teapot down off the shelf and reached for the tea tin. "That would really be awful."

Smythe walked over and put his hands on her shoulders. "Now, love, I've told ya a dozen times. Stop frettin' about the wedding. It's all goin' to come right. Even if it rains, the church roof doesn't leak."

"Yes, but I don't want it to rain. It's our wedding, Smythe, and I want everything to be perfect." She looked at him over her shoulder. "Where have you been this morning?"

He laughed and dropped into his chair. "Now that would be tellin', wouldn't it? You'll know soon enough."

Betsy gave him a good glare and then went back to making the tea.

Years ago, Smythe had worked as a coachman for the Inspector's late aunt, Euphemia Witherspoon. Then he'd gone to Australia to seek his fortune. He found the fortune and came home to England. As a courtesy, he stopped in to say hello to his former employer. He discovered her dying and surrounded by a houseful of servants, all of whom were taking terrible advantage of the poor woman. Wiggins, who was really just a lad at the time, was the only one tending to the poor lady's illness.

Smythe had sent the servants packing, called in a decent solicitor to handle the woman's affairs, and then prepared to take his leave. But Euphemia knew she wasn't long for this earth, and she'd begged him to stay on in the house and see her nephew, Gerald Witherspoon, settled in properly. She didn't want people taking advantage of him the way she'd been used. Smythe had come back from Australia as rich as sin, but he did as Euphemia asked and stayed on in the household, telling himself he was simply making sure the newest servants, Mrs. Jeffries and Mrs. Goodge, were both decent people. Then Betsy had collapsed on their doorstep, so he'd stayed a bit longer, and before you could say "Blast a Spaniard," they were investigating murders and becoming a family. By then, of course, he was madly in love with Betsy.

The problem then became how could he tell them he was rich? People didn't like to think you'd been deliberately trying to fool them, and after so much time had passed, he was afraid that was how they might feel. But Mrs. Jeffries had figured it out on her own, and when he and Betsy had gotten serious, he'd told her. But the others still didn't know his true wealth.

"I wish we 'ad us another murder," Wiggins said as he took his place at the table. "All this wedding plannin' is enough to drive a fellow mad."

"It's got nothing to do with you, lad," Mrs. Goodge chided. "It's us women that are doin' all the work. But that's always the way of the world, isn't it? A woman's work is never done."

"I'm doin' my part." Smythe slipped into his chair. "I went to see the vicar today about the banns."

"That's not exactly hard work," Betsy said.

"It is too 'ard work," the coachman argued. "Fellow likes the sound of his own voice. I spent an hour and a half listening to him go on and on about the need for Portuguese prayer books for the mission in Brazil. I 'ad to given him a couple of shillings to escape when I did."

Lawrence Boyd stepped back from the easel and studied his work critically. The light streaming in from the large windows let him see every imperfect detail of the painting. He frowned, not liking the look of the cat. He'd taken a bit of artistic license here with the color, but so what. That was his right; he was an artist. The color was fine, but there was something about the shape of the head that didn't look right. He could fix that. He laughed to himself as he reached for the tin of turpentine on the little table next to the easel. This was going to be a wonderful day. He reminded himself to periodically check his pocket watch. He wanted to allow plenty of time to get ready for luncheon. But he had a few minutes left before he had to stop.

There was a soft knock on the studio door.

"Come in," he called. He put the turpentine back on the table, leaving it open so he could clean his brushes.

"Sorry to disturb you, sir." James Glover, his chief clerk, hovered in the doorway of the small studio. "I've brought you the files you asked for, sir."

"Bring them in man. Don't just stand there. I expected you twenty minutes ago."

"The traffic was dreadful, sir." Glover, a fat man of forty with thinning blond hair and a handlebar mustache, stepped into the studio. He wore a dark blue suit, white shirt, and old-fashioned maroon tie. Sweat darkened the hair around his temples, and his face was flushed, as though he'd been running. In his arms, he carried a stack of folders. "There was a terrible accident on the Uxbridge Road. I finally got out of my hansom and walked the half mile."

"Yee Gods, man, you can walk the entire distance in twenty minutes." Boyd waved off his excuses. "Did you bring the Pressley file?"

"Yes, sir." Glover swallowed nervously. "It's right here."

"Put them on the table by the door," he said, staring at Glover. "Good Lord, Glover, you're sweating like a pig. What on earth is wrong with you?"

"I'm fine, sir." Glover smiled weakly. "The rain has made everything a bit sticky. If it's all the same to you, sir, I'll go tidy myself up a bit."

"There's a bathroom off the hall you can use," Boyd replied. "Then I'd like you to peek into the study and check that Miss Clarke is working. Don't let her see you. She seems to know what she's about, but it never hurts to keep an eye on people. Even the most trustworthy staff can disappoint you." He stared hard at Glover as he spoke and was rewarded by seeing the man's cheeks turn deathly pale.

"Yes, sir." Glover's voice was barely audible. He looked as if he were going to be ill. "I'll see you at the luncheon, sir. Thank you very much for inviting me."

"I want to speak to you afterward." Boyd smiled, "Come into my study after the others have left."

"You want to speak to me?" Glover's voice was now a high-pitched squeak. "Really? About what sir?"

"We'll discuss it then," Boyd replied. "Go along, now. I want to work for a little longer"

"Yes, sir." Glover backed up toward the door as he spoke, then whirled about and hurried out.

Boyd watched him through the small window that overlooked the back garden. Glover's head was bowed and his shoulders slumped as he trudged across the wet lawn to the main house.

"You've reason to look worried," Boyd muttered. But he was determined not to let the ugliness of what was coming ruin his perfect day. He could deal with Glover after the luncheon, after Gibbons made everything nice and official. He picked up his cigar from the ashtray on the small table, struck a match, and lit the end. He turned back to the painting and studied it as he smoked. It was very good, but there was a detail or two that he still thought could use a bit more work.

He put the cigar down and picked up his brush. He had enough time to correct the shape of the cat's head. For the next twenty minutes, he concentrated on making the delicate brush strokes that would perfect the painting. He heard the door open again, but he didn't bother looking away from his work. "I told you I'd see you after luncheon, Glover. Now take yourself out of here and leave me in peace. I've got another ten minutes more work to do."

But there was no reply, merely the sound of footsteps crossing the hard wood floor. Alarmed now, Boyd tore his gaze away from the painting and whirled around. His eyes widened in surprise and his mouth gaped open in shock. But before he could speak, something hard and heavy crashed into the side of his head. Moaning, he slumped to his knees. The assailant raised his hands and hit him again, this time harder, landing the blow smack in the back of his victim's skull.

Boyd swayed to one side, but his attacker grabbed him by the back of his smock just as he toppled to the floor and maneuvered him toward the settee. Working swiftly, the killer managed to shove, push, and pull Boyd until he was lying on the settee with his feet hanging over the end and his head at the other end, battered side down.

Working quickly, the assailant checked for a heartbeat, but there was nothing. Lawrence Boyd was well and truly dead.

The murderer stood up and grabbed the tin of turpentine off the table, pausing for a brief moment to look at the painting before continuing on with the grim task of pouring the paint remover on the dead man. It was important to make sure it soaked Boyd's smock and the settee. The tin was almost full, so the liquid splashed everywhere as it dispersed, dousing the muslin table runner, the floor, and the bottom of the easel.

Then the assailant picked up the cigar and tucked it neatly between Boyd's now lifeless fingers, reached for the matches, struck one, and tossed it at the muslin runner.

The killer tossed the remainder of the turpentine about the room, soaking the old carpet remnant by the side table and splattering the limp curtains on the little window by the door. The killer struck another match, and within moments, the curtains were blazing and the carpet smoking.

The killer moved to the doorway, took one last look around, and smiled in satisfaction before opening the door and stepping outside. By the time help arrived, it would be too late; the entire studio would be up in flames and with it, the evidence that murder had been done. This would simply be an unfortunate accident.

That was exactly the way the murderer had planned it.

"Oh dear, the guests should be arriving any moment now. I suppose the luncheon will have to be cancelled." Leeson, the butler to Lawrence Boyd, looked anxiously toward the main house. He was standing on the gravel pathway leading to the studio. A fireman stood at the front door and another two were on the roof of the small building, checking that the fire hadn't spread to the rafters. Tendrils of smoke drifted on the wind and the air smelled like burning wood, but the fire itself had been put out before it could do too much damage.

Leeson sighed and wished he didn't have to deal with this mess. It simply wasn't fair. He was a butler, for goodness sake. Now he was going to have to go and tell the guests that Mr. Boyd was dead and the luncheon cancelled. He wondered if he ought to invite them to eat before they left. What did etiquette dictate in these circumstances? They had been invited and there was plenty of food. Perhaps Mrs. Rothwell would know what they ought to do. After all, she wasn't just the housekeeper; she was a distant relation to Mr. Boyd. Yes, that's what he'd do. He'd let her make the decision.

He breathed easier and turned his attention to the clump of people standing on the small terrace by the back door of the main house. Miss Clarke, the typewriter girl, was speaking to one of the maids, and Mrs. Rothwell was standing next to the cook. Leeson moved toward the fireman standing by the studio door.

"We're almost finished here," the fireman said as he approached.

"Poor Mr. Boyd. What a terrible thing to have happened, but I suppose if Miss Clarke hadn't seen the smoke and raised the alarm, it might have been much worse. We were all gone."

"If she'd not raised the alarm, the building would have been completely burned." The fireman adjusted the chin strap to his helmet. He glanced through the open door of the studio to the body lying on the settee. "But before you do anything else, you'd best get a policeman here and be quick about it."

"A policeman?" Leeson was dreadfully confused. "But you said the fire was out. Why do we need a policeman?"

"Because your Mr. Boyd is dead, but it wasn't the fire that killed him."

"At least this one is in your district, sir," Constable Barnes said to Inspector Gerald Witherspoon as their hansom cab headed for Bayswater. Barnes was a smart old copper with steely gray hair, a ruddy complexion, and weak knees. He'd been on the force for more years than he cared to recall but now found himself in the enviable position of working almost exclusively with Inspector Gerald Witherspoon. "That's a bit of a relief."

Witherspoon had a pale, bony face, thinning brown hair, and deep-set blue eyes. He pushed his spectacles up his long nose and looked at Barnes. "Why is it a relief? Is there something about this case that I ought to be concerned about?"

Barnes tried to think of a diplomatic way of putting the situation. "Well, sir, I only meant that Inspector Nivens can't grouse that you've stolen this one from him. It's in your division, sir, so by rights you should be the one to take it."

"He'll still complain." Witherspoon shrugged philosophically. "But there's nothing I can do about that."

Barnes grabbed the handhold as the cab lurched forward. "You can get there first, sir. I know you don't like running to the chief inspector and telling tales, but you could let him know that Nivens has threatened to ruin you. If you get that established right away and make sure a formal complaint is lodged in his record, it might make Nivens think twice before he tries making any mischief."

Witherspoon waved his hand impatiently. "We mustn't blow it out of proportion, Constable. He was very upset about the Odell matter and if you look at it from his point of view, we did interfere in the case."

"We kept an innocent man from hanging," Barnes protested.

"Of course we did and we acted properly in doing so, but our proving Odell innocent meant that Inspector Nivens lost his only homicide conviction."

Barnes realized that being diplomatic wasn't going to be very useful. "He's out for blood, sir. Take my word for it; Nivens is going to do everything he can to ruin you and your reputation. You must take care."

The inspector said nothing for a moment. "I appreciate your concern, Constable, but I won't complain against the man. Not until he actually does something to me."

"By then it might be too late, sir," Barnes said earnestly. He had to get Witherspoon to understand how much damage Nivens could and would do.

"We've no time to worry about Inspector Nivens at the moment. Tell me what you know about *this* murder." The inspector was tired of both his constable and even his household constantly warning him about Nivens. Why just this morning his housekeeper had mentioned watching out for the fellow. Honestly, they were all making far too much of a few idle threats made in the heat of the moment.

Barnes knew when to shut up. He whipped out his little brown notebook and flipped it open. "The name of the victim is Lawrence Boyd. He's a banker."

"How was he killed?"

"The report didn't say. It only gave his name and address: 14 Laurel Road, Bayswater." Barnes looked out the window. "This is a posh neighborhood, so I expect he's someone with either money or connections, probably both. Oh good, we're almost there. We've turned onto his street."

Lawrence Boyd lived in a large four-story house made of white stone and red brick. There was no fencing between the house and the road, merely a strip of lawn with newly dug flower beds at each corner. On each side of the black doorway, there was a large brass lamp. A police constable stood guard by the front door. He hurried toward them as they climbed out of the hansom.

"I can see why they called us in so quickly," Barnes muttered. "Rich people hate murder. It's so very inconvenient for them."

"Yes, I daresay, you're right," Witherspoon murmured. Murder amongst the wealthy was always very tiresome. It had been his experience that the more money people had, the less inclined they were to cooperate with the police.

"Good day, sir." The constable directed his remark to the inspector and then nodded respectfully at Constable Barnes. "I'm Constable Tucker. We're very glad you've arrived. If you'll come this way, I'll take you around to the body." He started toward the side of the house.

"I'm Inspector Witherspoon and this is Constable Barnes," the inspector said as they trailed after the constable.

"I know who you are, sir, and in keeping with your methods, Constable Maxton and I have made sure that nothing has been touched," Tucker said eagerly. "Once we got here and saw the body, we didn't even let the fire brigade muck about any more than was necessary to insure the fire was out. But actually, they had the fire already out, so it wasn't so much a matter of them mucking about as it was picking up their equipment and leaving. But we made sure they were careful not to move things about any more than they had to, sir." Tucker smiled proudly at the inspector.

"Er, yes, that was very good thinking on your part," Witherspoon murmured. By now, they had rounded the building and come to the back garden. By London standards, it was huge. The lawn was ringed by flowers beds and thick bushes, behind which was a wood fence that stood at least eight feet high. At the far end of the garden was a small wooden structure that was larger than a shed but smaller than a conservatory. Two policemen were standing by the open door. Tendrils of smoke drifted up from the small open window. Witherspoon wrinkled his nose as an ugly, burning scent assaulted his nostrils.

"Ugh, that's not very pleasant." Barnes made a face. "It smells like burning carpet mixed with roasted pig."

"It could have been a lot worse, sir," said Constable Tucker as they continued across the garden. "If the body had been burnt, it would really stink the place up to high heaven. That's what the fire captain told us."

"You were called here by the fire brigade?" Witherspoon asked.

"Yes, sir. As soon as they saw the body, they sent for us straightaway."

They reached the structure, and Witherspoon nodded at the two constables.

"The body is just in here, sir," one of the lads said helpfully. "We've not touched anything."

Witherspoon hesitated. There was still smoke rising from the roof, and now that he was this close, he could see scorch marks on the door and window. "Is it safe?"

"Oh, yes, sir," Constable Tucker said eagerly. "The fire brigade assured us the fire is completely out. It'll smoke for awhile, but it's quite safe to go inside."

Witherspoon nodded dully. "Uh, is the body badly burnt?" He swallowed heavily, telling himself he must do his duty. He mustn't be so squeamish. Looking at corpses was part and parcel of his position.

"No, sir. It's hardly been touched. Which is a bit of a luck if you ask me," Tucker replied. "See for yourself, sir."

Barnes stepped through the door. Witherspoon steeled himself and followed.

Once inside, they stopped and gaped in amazement. On the right side of the room, most of the wall had been removed and the wood replaced with three very large windows. At the far end of the room behind the settee, there was a row of built-in cupboards. The body was on the settee, looking for all the world like a man asleep.

Witherspoon crossed over to the table on the far end of the settee and looked at the painting on the easel. It was singed a bit about the edges, but otherwise it appeared intact. Near the door, there was an old faded carpet remnant, now badly burnt and soaked with water, and beyond the rug, another smaller table with what looked like files piled atop it. He was surprised at how nothing appeared to be badly damaged. If it wasn't for the water soaking everything, one would not even notice there'd been a fire.

Witherspoon stiffened his spine and turned to the body. He stood looking at for a long moment. "The body's hardly been touched."

Barnes eased in on the other side of the settee, directly across from the inspector. He reached down and grasped Boyd's chin, gently turning the head to afford a better view of the back of the skull. "I can see why they called us so quickly, sir. His head's been bashed in. That's probably what killed him."

Witherspoon swallowed the bile that rose in his throat. He took a deep breath and then wished he hadn't as his nostrils filled with air smelling of harsh chemicals, smoke, and now, blood. He knew he was being fanciful; it was far too soon for the corpse to begin to smell, but nonetheless, he was certain he could sense it. He sniffed again, this time concentrating and trying separate out the different scents. "Do you smell that, Barnes?"

"Smell what?" Barnes sucked up air through his nose and then shook his head, his expression rueful. "I can't smell much of anything, sir. I never could. The missus claims I couldn't smell a dead skunk if it was lying two feet from my big toe."

"It's a chemical smell." The inspector frowned. "You know, like creosote or lime water."

Barnes noticed the tin of turpentine lying on the floor beneath the small window. "It's turpentine." He pointed at the tin as he came out from behind the settee. "The cap is off, sir."

Witherspoon glanced around the room and spotted the cap on the table. "Someone deliberately took the lid off and spilled it about the room," he concluded. "That tin didn't fly from the table to the floor on its own. I expect the killer used the turpentine to try and spread the fire. Perhaps even cover up that the poor fellow had been murdered."

"Surely no one could think this would be thought of as an accident?" Barnes said. "The poor man's head has been bashed all to bits."

Witherspoon thought for a moment. "Yet why bash his head in and then try to make it look like an accident? Why start a fire at all? No, the killer either started a fire to draw attention to the body, which I highly doubt as most people tend to want to avoid drawing attention to people they've just murdered, or the murderer wanted to cover up the fact that it was murder. If the fire had spread and the walls had collapsed, then the entire ceiling would have caved in. In which case, there wouldn't have been enough of the victim left to give us any indication of how he'd really died."

Barnes wasn't so sure, but he said nothing. He didn't have any better ideas himself.

Witherspoon moved over to the small window and turned to survey the room. He noted the position of the corpse, and on the floor, just below where the man's fingers rested, he saw the burnt remains of a cigar. "And in case the roof didn't cave in and only the interior of the room and the body were burned, the murderer tried to make it appear as if Mr. Boyd had fallen asleep while he was smoking," he said, speculating. "That's what the killer wanted us to think."

"If the killer was trying to make it look like an accident, he botched it badly." Barnes pointed at the burnt cigar stub. "The first thing that would burn in a fire is that bit there. There'd have been nothing there but ash."

"True." Witherspoon turned his head and glanced out the small window. Constable Tucker was trudging across the lawn. He carried a pair of scissors and a ball of twine and had a roll of brown paper tucked under his arm. "What's more, people are afraid of fire. When they see smoke, they call the fire brigade. Surely the murderer must have known someone would get help and the ruse would be discovered."

Constable Tucker popped his head into the studio. "May I come in, sir? I'd like to wrap up the evidence and take it down to the station." He waved the roll of brown paper and grinned triumphantly. "I know all about your methods, sir, so I said to myself, 'Tucker, what would the inspector do?' So I marched right into the kitchen and asked the cook if I could borrow a few things. She was quite happy to oblige, sir."

Witherspoon wasn't sure what Constable Tucker wanted to do, but he didn't wish to discourage the young man. "Certainly, Constable, come right on in. We're almost through here."

Tucker dashed across the wet floor, almost slipped, and then righted himself.

"Take care, Constable," Witherspoon warned. His gaze shifted to the floor. Most of the water had seeped through the floorboards, leaving bright puddles and splashes of color, especially under the easel. "We don't want you breaking a leg." He turned back to Barnes and left Tucker to his evidence gathering, which looked to consist mostly of wrapping up Boyd's painting. Witherspoon didn't particularly see that as any sort of evidence. It wasn't as if the man had written the name of the killer on the painting, but he didn't wish to make Tucker feel like his efforts were unappreciated.

"Er, excuse me, Inspector, may I have a word with you?" The voice came from the open window.

Witherspoon turned and peered out between the remnants of the burnt curtains. A tall, gaunt-faced man dressed in an old-fashioned butler's uniform stared back at him. "I take it you're the butler," he said.

"Yes, sir, I'm Leeson. I'm sorry to bother you, but the guests were wondering if they might leave. They've been here for several hours now and they want to go home." Leeson struggled to keep his gaze on the Inspector and not the body lying on the settee.

"Guests? Mr. Boyd was having guests today?"

"Yes, sir, I tried to get word to all of them that the luncheon was cancelled, but they all arrived just as the fire brigade was leaving and then insisted on staying until they heard what had happened. But now they'd like to leave. Especially Mr. Glover. He'd like to go back to the office and let the others know about Mr. Boyd's death."

"No, I'm afraid the guests can't leave," Witherspoon said quickly. "Tell them we'll be up directly to have a word with them."

"But they weren't even here when the fire started," the butler protested. He knew that none of the guests were going to take kindly to being trapped here any longer. Besides, if they stayed much longer, they'd want tea and cook was already in a horrid mood. "No one was here but Miss Clarke and Mr. Glover."

"What about the servants?" Barnes walked over to stand beside the inspector. "Weren't they here when the fire started?"

"We were all at a funeral," Leeson explained. "One of the house-maids died of pneumonia. Everyone except Mr. Boyd went to the funeral. The fire brigade was here when we got back."

"But you were having guests for luncheon today?" Barnes pressed. "Who was doing the cooking?"

"It was already prepared," Leeson explained. He looked nervously over his shoulder at the house, as though he were expecting a horde of angry guests to come streaming out the back door, demanding to be either fed or let go. "Mr. Boyd knew the staff wanted to go to Helen's service, so he told cook to prepare a cold luncheon. Everything else was done; the table was set and the serving trolleys at the ready, so all we had to do was serve."

"What about this Miss Clarke and Mr. Grover?" Witherspoon interjected. "Why didn't they go to the funeral?"

"They're not part of the household. Miss Clarke is a typist. She's from one of those agencies. She came along to help Mr. Boyd catch up on his work. Mr. Glover brought some files over from Mr. Boyd's office. Please, sir, can I go back to the house and tell the guests that they've got to stay for awhile longer? I do believe that some of them are going to leave with or without your permission."

Witherspoon glanced at Barnes. "Constable, can you go along with Leeson and insure that no one leaves just yet. I'll be in as soon as I've given the police constables their instructions."

Barnes grinned broadly. "Certainly, sir. Come along, Leeson. Let's go and take care of your guests."

As soon as the two men had gone, Witherspoon forced himself to go back to the body. Tucker was putting another sheet of brown paper around the painting, but he stopped what he was doing and watched the inspector.

Witherspoon went behind the settee and gazed down at the back of the skull. He wasn't sure what he was looking for, but he knew it was important to absorb as much detail as possible. Unfortunately, the ugly mangle of matted hair, blood, and bone told him only that the poor fellow had been hit with something very hard.

"Excuse me, sir, but what are you looking for?" Tucker asked.

"Anything that may help us solve the crime," he explained. "I think our victim was hit with something very hard, something that killed him very quickly and that might become important evidence."

Tucker reached for the ball of twine. "I don't see anything in here that could be a murder weapon."

"Let's have a good look at the place before we make any assertions, Constable." He surveyed the small room again. "The weapon would have to be something heavy, something that could be easily lifted by the killer and used to hit hard enough to break through hair and bone."

"Right, sir." Tucker wound the ball of twine around the painting. "There's no metal doorstops or big brass candlesticks."

"Let's have a look at what's in the cupboards." Witherspoon opened the one nearest him and looked inside. The cupboard was wide and deep with two shelves. On the top shelf there were two fat sketchbooks and a box of charcoal. On the bottom shelf were three canvases stored sideways. Witherspoon pulled one out and saw that it was simply a painting of the sea.

"Did you find anything, sir?" Tucker asked eagerly.

"No, just art supplies and more paintings." He shoved the last one back into the cupboard and continued his search. In the other cupboards, he found more paints and another tin of turpentine. But he found nothing that could be used as a weapon. "I'm afraid, Constable, that the murder weapon isn't here. That's going to make finding the killer much more difficult."

"Not to worry, sir. You'll catch the murderer." Tucker lifted the painting off the easel. "You always do."

Witherspoon wasn't so sure. He was beginning to think that living up to his own reputation was becoming harder with each and every case.

CHAPTER 2

"How much longer are we going to be kept waiting?" Walter Gibbons demanded. He glared at Constable Barnes, who stood solidly by the drawing room door, making sure that none of them actually managed to leave.

"I'm sure the inspector will be here shortly, sir," Barnes replied easily. He stared at Gibbons curiously. He wasn't an old man; judging from the smooth skin on his face, the constable would put his age in the mid-forties. Yet Gibbons's hair was completely white.

"This is outrageous." Gibbons, his hands behind his back, stomped back and forth in front of the fireplace and glared at Barnes. "Utterly absurd. You've no right to restrain any of us from leaving. I shall speak to your superiors; you can rest assured about that."

"The constable was acting upon my instructions." Witherspoon strode into the room. "So kindly direct your comments to me. If you'd like to lodge a complaint, the name of my superior is Chief Inspector Barrows. His office is at New Scotland Yard."

"Humph," Gibbons snorted. "Rest assured that I shall. Now, may I go?"

"No, I'm sorry, but you may not." The inspector surveyed the small group of people in the drawing room. A well-dressed couple was sitting on the settee, and a lone young woman wearing a long-sleeved white blouse and a dark green skirt was standing by the window. A heavyset fellow was sitting next to a small table by the door at the other end of the drawing room, staring morosely at the floor. He had barely looked up when the inspector had come into the room. Witherspoon wondered if these were the only guests that had been invited for lunch or if some of the others had managed to slip away.

"I'm Inspector Witherspoon," he said. "I'm sorry to have inconvenienced you, but we do have some questions for all of you."

"Questions?" The man who'd been sitting on the settee rose to his feet. "What kind of questions? We had nothing to do with the fire, so I don't see how we can be of any use to you, sir. When my wife and I arrived, the fire brigade was already here." He was of medium height with brown hair, a square jaw, small gray eyes, and a stocky build. He wore a dark gray suit with a maroon waistcoat and a black-and-white striped cravat.

"It's not about the fire," Witherspoon said softly. He glanced at Barnes, who gave a barely perceptible nod. The constable hadn't told them there was a murder. "Mr. Boyd's death wasn't an accident. It was murder."

"Murder?" the woman on the settee gasped.

"That's ridiculous," Gibbons snapped. "The butler said he died in a fire."

"Oh dear," the fellow sitting at the table murmured.

The young woman by the window simply sighed.

"Please explain yourself, sir." Gibbons stomped over and stood directly in front of Witherspoon.

The inspector briefly wondered how much clearer he could be, but he'd give it another try. "I know this must be a shock to all of you, but as I said, Mr. Boyd didn't die as a result of the fire. He was murdered. Now, I'd like to ask you a few questions and then you can be on your way. But before you go, can any of you tell me if you were the only guests that came here today?"

For a moment, no one spoke, then Gibbons said, "Yes, it was just myself and the Sapingtons."

"Uh, I was invited as well," the chubby fellow said. His voice was so low it was barely audible. "Mr. Boyd invited me this morning."

"So it was just the four guests." The inspector scanned their faces. "No one else, no one who might have slipped off before making a statement?"

"I've no idea if Boyd invited anyone else," Gibbons snapped. "And I've no idea why he thought he had the right to invite anyone else. This was an official luncheon of the Bankers Benevolent Society. That's the only reason that I'm here. I had business to conduct with Lawrence Boyd. Now, can we please get on with your questions. I'm a busy man."

"Constable Barnes, please take this gentleman," Witherspoon nodded toward Gibbons, "into the reception room next door and get his statement."

"This way, sir." Barnes pulled open the door and stepped into the hall. Gibbons looked as if he wanted to argue, but he clamped his mouth shut and followed the constable.

Witherspoon trailed after the two men, stuck his head into the hallway, and called out, "Constable Tucker, can you step in here, please?"

Tucker, who'd been at the front door ensuring that no one left, hurried toward Witherspoon. "Yes, sir," he said.

"Can you please take this gentleman," the inspector said, nodding at the man sitting at the table.

"My name is Glover," the fellow said glumly.

"And this lady," Witherspoon continued, indicating the young woman by the window.

"I'm Eva Clarke," she said.

"Thank you, that helps a great deal," Witherspoon said. He turned back to the constable and wished this wasn't so difficult. Egads, simply getting people apart long enough to take their statements was an ordeal, let alone trying to find out how many of them were actually supposed to have been having lunch with the dead man. But perhaps it was his fault. He really ought to have asked them to introduce themselves as soon as he'd come into the drawing room. "Can you please take Mr. Glover and Miss Clarke out to the hallway? Ask Constable Maxton to take Mr. Glover into the dining room to get his statement, and you take Miss Clarke into the study for hers, please."

"Yes, sir." Tucker beamed proudly and scurried for the door, glancing over his shoulder to make sure his charges were following after him. He ushered them out into the hall and shut the door softly.

Witherspoon turned to the two people left in the room. "May I ask your names?"

"I'm Arnold Sapington and this is my wife, Maud," the man replied. "But I don't think we'll be of much help to you. As I've already said, the fire brigade was here when we arrived for luncheon."

Maud Sapington smiled slightly at the introduction. She was a dark-haired woman with a jawline almost as sharp as her husband's, a wide mouth, and blue eyes. She wore a high-collared pink dress overlaid with a plum-colored vest trimmed in pink piping and a pair of cream-colored gloves. She carried a matching pink-and-plum striped parasol with a pink-frilled edge. On her head was a plum-colored bonnet with small cream and pink feathers on the side.

"What time was that, sir?" Witherspoon asked. He wondered if it would be uncivil of him to sit down. His knee was bothering him again.

"One o'clock," Sapington replied.

"But we were a few minutes early," his wife supplied. "It was ten to one when we knocked on the door."

"Who answered?" Witherspoon thought it might be useful to establish who was actually here at what time. He edged closer to an uncomfortable looking chair next to the settee.

"The housekeeper," Sapington said.

"That's not quite true," Mrs. Sapington interjected. "Mr. Glover actually answered our knock."

Arnold Sapington gave his wife an irritated glare. "For goodness sake, Maud, Mrs. Rothwell was right behind the fellow."

"Sorry, dear," Mrs. Sapington murmured.

Sapington sighed. "Mr. Glover answered the door, but only because he appeared to be leaving just as we arrived. The housekeeper was right behind him."

"Mr. Glover was leaving?" Witherspoon pressed. That was very interesting.

"Well, he said he really ought to get back to the office, but then he was prevailed upon to stay," Sapington replied.

"Are you his employer, sir?" Witherspoon asked.

"No, he's employed by Mr. Boyd."

"So he stayed at your request?" The inspector wanted to make sure he understood every single detail.

"Not really. It was Miss Clarke who suggested he might want to stay," Sapington replied. "By that time Walter Gibbons had arrived, so he put his briefcase down and came into the drawing room with us."

Witherspoon made a mental note to ask Miss Clarke why she suggested Glover stay at the house. "Er, Mr. Sapington, I got the impression from the other gentleman that today's luncheon was some sort of official function for this society he mentioned. Is that correct?"

"I don't know that it was all *that* official," Sapington replied. "It was just a luncheon."

"That's not quite true, dear," Mrs. Sapington said. "We expected Walter to tell us who was going to be this year's chairman of the Bankers Benevolent Society." She smiled broadly at the inspector. "It was going to be either Lawrence or my husband." She looked at her husband. "I suppose now it'll go to you by default."

"Maud, I don't think it's appropriate to comment on such matters with poor Lawrence dead." He pursed his lips in disapproval and then turned his attention back to Witherspoon. "The luncheon was Lawrence's idea. He thought it would be amusing and I agreed. The chairmanship is a friendly sort of rivalry. But I'm sure you're not interested in that. No doubt you'd like a few more details about today. My wife and I arrived at about ten to one. When the hansom let us off, we noticed the fire wagon out front, and of course, we were concerned. When Mrs. Rothwell told us what had happened, that there had been a fire and Mr. Boyd was dead, we were shocked."

"So it was Mrs. Rothwell who gave you the news?"

"That's correct," he continued. "We came in here with the others, as I said. By that time, Walter had arrived. A few minutes later, a constable stuck his head in and asked us to wait. That was hours ago, sir, and frankly, that's really all I can tell you."

Witherspoon wasn't going to keep them any longer. He had no grounds for holding people against their will, and all in all, they'd been fairly cooperative by waiting as long as they had. "If you'll leave me your address, sir, you and your wife are free to go. I might have more questions for you as the investigation progresses."

Sapington nodded. "We live at number 34 Parrington Street in Mayfair." He extended a hand to his wife and helped her to her feet. They walked to the door. Sapington looked back at the inspector. "You're sure it was murder?"

"Oh, yes, there's no doubt about that. Uh, before you go, I do have one more question. How well acquainted with Mr. Boyd were you or your wife?"

"We're business acquaintances." Sapington reached for the

doorknob and pulled the door open. "I'm the managing director of Reese and Cutlip on Broad Street."

"You could say they were competitors." Maud Sapington smiled at her husband. "But only in the most gentlemanly sort of way."

In the room next door, Constable Barnes wasn't having much luck getting information out of Walter Gibbons. "I've already told you," Gibbons said as he began to pace again. "I arrived right after the Sapingtons. Mr. Glover and Miss Clarke were already here."

"And you were invited to luncheon, sir?" Barnes probed.

"Yes, luncheon was to be at one o'clock," Gibbons said impatiently. "I've already told you all this."

"From your earlier comment, Mr. Gibbons, I take it you and Mr. Boyd weren't friends." Barnes watched him carefully as he asked the question. But Gibbons didn't so much as bat an eyelash or do anything else to indicate he might be uncomfortable.

"Hardly. As I said before, I'd have never set foot in the man's house if I hadn't had to come here in my official capacity as the president of the Bankers Benevolent Society."

"And the reason you had to come, sir?" Barnes pressed.

"Because Boyd sweet-talked our board into making him this year's honorary chairman—a most presitigous position, I might add. Boyd and Sapington were our two final candidates for the honor, and this luncheon was to officially let Boyd know he'd got the prize. Poor Sapington. He's worked very hard for the society, but that didn't seem to make any difference to the board. All they could see was the huge donation that Boyd was prepared to make. Sapington can't or couldn't compete with that sort of thing. He's quite willing to work for charity, but he doesn't give much in the way of actual cash."

"Did Mr. Sapington know that he wasn't going to get the chairmanship?" Barnes wondered if these sort of people ever did any work.

"I don't see how he could." Gibbons sighed. "The board only made their final decision yesterday, and the luncheon's been planned for a long time."

"When you arrived, did you notice anything unusual—I mean, other than the fire wagon?"

Gibbons shook his head. "Just the fire brigade."

"Who told you Mr. Boyd was dead?"

"Mrs. Rothwell, the housekeeper. She said luncheon was cancelled and that there had been a terrible accident."

"Then why didn't you leave immediately?" Barnes asked.

"Because by then the police had arrived, and before we could go, a constable had sent the butler in to ask us all to remain."

"So you sat in the drawing room waiting?"

"Oh, no, Mrs. Rothwell insisted we eat. After all, luncheon was already prepared, so it was a shame to let the food go to waste."

"The inspector's late this evening," Mrs. Jeffries said to no one in particular as they milled about in the cozy kitchen.

"Not to worry," Mrs. Goodge said. "His supper is staying nice and warm in the oven. The longer it sits, the better a beef stew tastes, that's what I always say."

"It tasted good tonight." Smythe sank into his seat and reached for Betsy's hand under the table. They'd had their supper earlier and even done the clearing up.

Mrs. Jeffries frowned. "It's past seven. He's always home by now unless he's on a case."

"Maybe he's got a murder," Wiggins said eagerly.

Under the table, Smythe squeezed Betsy's hand. She smiled at him, trying to let him know without words that she trusted him to find a way for them to continue their investigations. She wasn't worried about their future together. They could have their marriage and their home, and do the work that was so important to both of them. She trusted he had a plan.

Mrs. Jeffries glanced at Betsy and noted with some relief that the girl didn't look as if the idea of a murder was going to cause her a flurry of nerves. The wedding was taking a lot of planning time, but the housekeeper was sure the lass could cope. Betsy was strong. She looked up at the clock again and told herself not to jump to conclusions; there were many reasons why the inspector might be late getting home.

Fred, who'd been sleeping peacefully on the rug near the cooker, suddenly shot to his feet and charged for the back stairs. "That'll be the inspector," Wiggins muttered. He looked morosely in the direction the dog had disappeared. Fred had gotten a tad more attached to the inspector since Mrs. Goodge's Samson had taken over below stairs, so to speak, and the footman's feelings were a bit raw on the subject. But he didn't begrudge the inspector; no, he wasn't the sort to act like a jealous old tabby. He cast a quick glare at Samson, who was curled up on a little stool near the cook's chair. Samson twitched his tail and glared right back.

Mrs. Jeffries was already on her feet and moving to the back stairs, not quite as fast as Fred, but hurrying none the less.

Fred bounced wildly up and down as the front door opened and the inspector stepped inside. "Gracious, old fellow, don't make such a fuss," the inspector said, but he was beaming broadly as he spoke. Fred's tail wagged madly and he tried, unsuccessfully, to lick the inspector's face.

"Good evening, Inspector," Mrs. Jeffries said. "Fred, get down now so the inspector can take off his hat and coat."

The dog settled immediately, and Witherspoon took the opportunity to slip off his coat. "It's nice to be so warmly greeted, especially after the day I've had."

"Tiring was it, sir?" she held her breath, hoping that she wasn't wrong; then she immediately felt guilty. If there was a murder, it meant some poor soul had died. Really, she mustn't allow herself to be so hopeful about such wickedness.

"Exhausting." He handed her his bowler hat. "I got called out for a murder at a house in Bayswater. I don't suppose we've received any word from Lady Cannonberry?"

Ruth Cannonberry was their neighbor and a special friend of the inspector's. But their relationship was having a difficult time making any progress as Ruth kept getting called out of town to play nursemaid to her late husband's relations, most of whom seemed afflicted with one ailment after the other, both real and imaginary. This time she'd had to go all the way to Northumberland to stay with her sister-in-law.

"Nothing yet, sir, but she only left yesterday morning. You'll probably get a letter tomorrow." She took his hat and hung it up next to his coat. "I'm sorry your day was so awful, sir. No wonder you're home so late." She was thoroughly ashamed of herself for the feeling of elation that swept through her. "Who was murdered?"

"Fellow by the name of Lawrence Boyd. He's a banker." Witherspoon sighed. "I don't wish to inconvenience the household, but do you think Mrs. Goodge would be put out if I had a sherry before dinner."

"Not to worry, sir." Mrs. Jeffries started down the hall toward the drawing room. "The household won't mind in the least. Mrs. Goodge has laid on a nice beef stew. It's in the oven and I'll serve it whenever you're ready."

She was so very grateful that the inspector hadn't been raised with servants. He'd never learned to treat them as objects for his own convenience.

She swept into the drawing room and headed for the sideboard. Opening the lower cupboard, she pulled out a bottle of Harvey's and then reached for the glasses. The inspector, now minus Fred, who'd wandered back downstairs, sank into his favorite chair.

"I've so looked forward to this," he admitted as she handed him a glass of sherry. "It's been a very busy day. Do pour one for yourself."

"Thank you, sir," she replied. She took her drink and sat down in the chair opposite him. "What happened, sir?"

"Well, I was working away at Ladbroke Grove station, and we were getting ready to go have lunch when the duty officer came in and said they'd had reports of a murder at number 14 Laurel Road in Bayswater. As it was in my district, I was up for it, of course."

Mrs. Jeffries had no doubt that even if he hadn't been the detective on duty, they'd have sent for him anyway, but she said nothing.

"Constable Barnes and I took a hansom, and we were there very quickly. It's amazing how fast one can travel about London these days, isn't it." He took a quick gulp of his drink. "Apparently, Mr. Boyd, the victim, was in the studio behind his house working on a painting when his assailant murdered him. The killer then set the place on fire, probably trying to hide the fact that a murder had taken place at all."

She forced herself to give him an encouraging nod instead of blurting out one of the many questions that had sprang into her mind.

"Luckily for us, there was a young woman on the premises who saw the smoke and took immediate action. The fire brigade got there very quickly and put the fire out."

"So the body wasn't burnt?" she ventured.

"Oh, no, though there was enough turpentine splashed about the room that it should have gone up quickly, but I suspect the wet weather we've had recently worked to our advantage. Even wood doesn't burn very quickly when it's so damp out."

"How was Mr. Boyd actually murdered?"

"He was bashed on the back of the head with something very heavy," Witherspoon replied. "There was nothing in the studio that looked as if it could be used as a weapon, so I had the police constables do a thorough search of the grounds and the house. We found nothing, so I've expanded the search to the neighborhood around the home, not that I think we'll have much luck."

"Had the servants seen anything?" she took a sip of her drink.

"No, they weren't there." He frowned. "It was the oddest situation, Mrs. Jeffries. Apparently, they were all at a funeral when the fire started. If it hadn't been for Mr. Boyd's typewriter girl—or are they called Remington Girls? I can never remember which it is, but that's not really pertinent. What is pertinent is that other than Miss Clarke, the house was empty. Except, of course, for Mr. Glover, who I believe brought along some files and then stayed as he'd been invited to luncheon."

"He was invited to the luncheon as well?" she queried. She wanted to keep all the facts straight.

"Yes, but I gather it was a last minute invitation."

"I'm not sure I understand," Mrs. Jeffries murmured. "How could there be a luncheon planned if there were no servants?" She knew that if the house was in Bayswater and the victim a banker, it probably meant the household was wealthy. In her experience, the rich rarely served themselves.

"It was a cold luncheon," Witherspoon replied. "Everything was laid out and ready for when the guests were to arrive. Of course, when the servants got home, they found the fire brigade there and the master of the house dead." He finished off his sherry and got to his feet. "I better not keep Mrs. Goodge's dinner waiting any longer."

Mrs. Jeffries finished her own drink and stood up as well. "I'll serve you, sir. Do go into the dining room and make yourself comfortable. I'll be right up with your supper."

"That sounds wonderful. What does Mrs. Goodge have for pudding?"

"Apple tart with custard," Mrs. Jeffries replied. The inspector did enjoy his sweets. "It's especially good this evening." She hurried out and flew down the hall to the back stairs. The only thing that kept her from a flat out run was fear that she'd fall and break a bone.

The others were still in the kitchen. Mrs. Goodge had put the inspector's supper on a large wooden tray.

"Don't any of you go to bed." The housekeeper grabbed the tray and hoisted it effortlessly. "We've got a murder. As soon as the inspector finishes his meal, I'll be down to tell you everything."

"Learn as much as you can," the cook said bluntly. "If he got it today, we're already behind."

On several of their last few cases, Witherspoon had been summoned from home instead of the station. The household had gotten quite used to starting their investigations almost from the moment the inspector began working.

Mrs. Jeffries disappeared down the hall with the inspector's dinner. They rest of them kept busy by doing small chores to pass the time. Betsy filled the sink with soapy water, Wiggins topped up the fuel in the cooker, Smythe moved some provisions off the top shelf in the dry larder into the kitchen cupboards, and Mrs. Goodge wrote up a list of provisions. Finally, after what seemed hours but was in reality less than thirty minutes, they heard Mrs. Jeffries footsteps coming down the backstairs. Betsy leapt to her feet. "I'll go clear up the dining room."

"No need." The housekeeper swept into the kitchen carrying a tray piled high with dirty dishes, a wrinkled serviette, and an empty water glass. "I've got it all. If there's any crumbs left on the dining table, we'll get them tomorrow morning before the inspector eats his breakfast." She handed the tray to Betsy, who took it over to the sink and began putting the crockery in the pan of soapy water.

"The inspector is going directly up to his room," she continued. "He's very tired. I told him that Wiggins would take care of giving Fred his walk."

"'Course I will," Wiggins said. Fred, hearing his name, rose from his spot near the cooker and came over to the footman. "You 'eard the word, didn't ya, old boy? Well, you've got to wait till we 'ave our meetin', then we'll go out."

Ten minutes later they had the last of the dishes washed and were taking their usual spots at the dining table. Mrs. Jeffries had slipped upstairs and made sure the inspector had actually retired for the night. It wouldn't do to have him coming down while they were in the midst of talking about his latest murder.

"Who was murdered?" Mrs. Goodge asked bluntly.

"A banker by the name of Lawrence Boyd," the housekeeper replied. "He lives in Bayswater. He was murdered in the studio behind his house while he was painting a picture." She repeated the details she'd learned from the inspector, taking care to stress the circumstances and making sure she didn't forget anything. "Boyd was the general manager of Boyd, Stanford, and Sawyer, Merchant Bankers."

"I've heard of them," Mrs. Goodge muttered. She was somewhat relieved. The further up the social ladder a murder victim was, the easier it was for her find out what she needed to know. There was generally far more gossip to be had about the rich and the famous than there was about the poor and obscure. "They've offices just off Chancery Lane."

"That's good," the housekeeper said. "I've a feeling this case is going to be very odd, and it's going to take all our resources to get to the bottom of it."

"Seems to me the inspector's cases are always strange," Wiggins muttered. "But this one takes the cake. Imagine trying to kill someone by burnin' down a building."

"Actually, when you think about it, it was quite clever," Betsy replied thoughtfully. "I mean, if the killer knew the victim was going to be alone, then a fire might have destroyed the evidence of murder and everyone would think it an accident."

"But Mr. Boyd wasn't on his own," Wiggins pointed out. "There was the typewriter lady and that fellow from his office."

"But the murderer probably didn't know that," Smythe interjected. He agreed with Betsy's assessment. "Look at it this way: if the killer wanted to do this Mr. Boyd in and he heard that all the Boyd servants were going off that morning, then he probably thought he could get away with it."

"We're getting very much ahead of ourselves," Mrs. Jeffries interrupted. "Until we know more facts, this sort of speculation is very dangerous. I suggest we proceed as we usually do and see what we can learn."

"That's too bad. I was quite enjoyin' myself." Smythe grinned broadly.

"Me, too." Betsy laughed. "But Mrs. Jeffries is right. We'd best find out a few facts before we come up with any ideas. We know how easy it is to make a mistake when you let your imagination run wild. I'll start with the local shopkeepers tomorrow and see what kind of gossip I can find about our poor Mr. Boyd."

The housekeeper nodded in agreement and turned to Wiggins. "I'd like you to find someone from the Boyd household and see what you can learn. Find out how long the servants had known they would be going to a funeral that morning."

"Surely it couldn't have been too far in advance." Mrs. Goodge pursed her lips disapprovingly "According to the inspector, the girl's death wasn't unexpected, but no one could have known for certain when she was actually going to die."

"But you have to give the undertaker and the priest a bit of notice," Wiggins pointed out. "You can't just show up at the church with the body and 'ave a funeral. You've got to talk to the vicar, and that's got to take a day or two."

"Maybe the killer didn't need much time," Smythe suggested. "Besides, I thought we agreed we'd not do anymore speculatin'. Just get us some facts, lad."

Wiggins didn't take offense at the gentle chiding. "I'll do my best," he promised. "If I don't 'ave any luck with the Boyd servants, I'll try and chat with a servant from one of the neighbors' houses."

"Excellent idea." Mrs. Jeffries beamed approvingly. She was so proud of them all. They certainly didn't need to be told what to do.

"I'll get up extra early and get the baking done," the cook said. "The laundry is going be picked up at nine, and Mr. Miller is coming by at ten to repair the shelves in the wet larder." Mrs. Goodge mentally began to calculate how many people were going to be in and out of her kitchen tomorrow. After a moment, she realized it wasn't near enough. "I'd best send out an invitation or two," she said. "Surely one of my old colleagues will know something about someone involved with this case."

"Speaking of which, what about the others that came to the house that day? The luncheon guests and the typewriter girl," Betsy asked. "Shouldn't we look at them as well?"

Mrs. Jeffries thought for a moment. "The guests supposedly got there after the fire and the murder had already happened. But as they're the only names we've got so far, we might as well see what we can learn about them."

"What were their names again?" Mrs. Goodge asked. "I know the typewriter girl was a Miss Eva Clarke."

"Arnold and Maud Sapington." Mrs. Jeffries tried her best to recall everything the inspector had said. "I believe the inspector said Mr. Sapington is also a banker, but I don't think he mentioned the name of any bank. A gentleman named Walter Gibbons was present, and of course, Mr. Glover, the chief clerk from Boyd's office. Mind you, I've no idea where any of these people might live. But when Constable Barnes comes by tomorrow morning to fetch the inspector, I'll have a quick word with him and see if he has any further details."

Barnes was one of the few people who knew what the household did for the inspector. It had taken him a goodly number of cases before he'd put it together, but once he had, he'd made sure to let Mrs. Jeffries know he approved.

"What about Luty and Hatchet?" Smythe asked. "We'd best include them right from the start. They missed the last one."

"Oh dear, you're right." Mrs. Jeffries agreed. "We must include them."

"It's not that late. Why don't I go along to Knightsbridge and tell them what's what," Wiggins suggested. "Then they can be here for our morning meetin'. I can take Fred with me . . ."

Mrs. Jeffries interrupted him. "That's a very good idea, but you must take a hansom cab. Otherwise you'll be gone all night." She wasn't an unduly cautious person, but she did realize that they worked for the famous Inspector Gerald Witherspoon who had sent over twenty murderers to the gallows and not everyone in London appreciated his efforts. Mrs. Jeffries was fairly sure there wasn't any immediate danger, but it paid to be careful. "Don't worry about the cost. I've household money set aside for situations like this."

Wiggins looked doubtful. "Will the driver let Fred ride in the cab?"

"He will if you give 'im this." Smythe handed the lad a sixpence and two farthings. "Just be sure to tell 'im that Fred's a good dog and you'll not let him climb on the seats."

"Cor blimey, this is workin' out well. I'll nip upstairs and get my jacket. Betsy, can you put Fred's lead on 'im. This is goin' to be a right old adventure."

Luty Belle Crookshank's Knightsbridge home was ablaze with light from top to bottom. Even from the pavement, Wiggins could hear the tinkle of glasses and the sound of laughter. He looked down at Fred. "Cor blimey, Fred, what should we do? Luty's 'aving some sort of fancy do. Listen, you can even 'ear music."

Fred plopped down on his hindquarters and began scratching his ear.

"But if we don't tell 'em, they'll be upset, especially Luty. Come on, Fred, whatever's goin' on, we'll just 'ave to interrupt." He tugged gently on Fred's lead, and together they bounded up the short walkway to the front door. He knew better than to go to the servants' entry because the one time he'd done that, Luty had given him a stern lecture. She had told him he was a friend and she didn't want him or anyone else, even her own servants, to use that entrance. The servants door was to be used only for deliveries and then only because it made life easier for the delivery lads. Luty had some very strange ideas, but that was to be expected. After all, she was an American.

Keeping a firm hold on Fred's lead, he raised the heavy brass door knocker and let it drop. A moment later, the door opened and Hatchet, Luty's white-haired butler, appeared. He smiled broadly. "This is a very pleasant surprise. Do come in Wiggins."

"Let me tie Fred's lead to the fence," Wiggins replied.

"No, no, bring him inside. His manners are probably better than most of madam's guests." Hatchet opened the door wider and motioned them inside. "I'll tell madam you're here."

Wiggins began to have second thoughts. Maybe this could wait for tomorrow. Maybe he should just leave word with Hatchet and get back home. The place was filled with people. "Cor blimey, do you think I should? It sounds like you've got a 'ouseful."

"Of course we do," Hatchet replied cheerfully. "But that doesn't matter. It's only one of madam's charity functions."

Wiggins hesitated. He really did feel odd about interrupting a big do like this. But Fred had no such qualms; his tail wagging wildly, he strained forward and butted his nose against Hatchet's hand.

"Oh, come on, lad." Hatchet reached across the threshold and pulled Wiggins inside. He petted Fred and then shoved them gently in the direction of the library. "I do hope you're here because of that murdered banker, and believe me, if you think the madam wouldn't throw the whole lot of them out the front door so she could hear what you've got to say, you're sadly mistaken." He jerked his head toward the sound of the festivities. "Now get into the study lad. I'll send Julie in with some food and drink for you and the pup. It might be a few minutes before madam can extricate herself from Lord Dinsworthy. He does rather love the sound of his own voice."

Wiggins laughed and started down the hall. "Right then, I can always eat."

The house was elegantly furnished and very beautiful. In the foyer, a huge Chinese ceramic vase containing an artistic display of fresh flowers stood on a round mahogany claw-foot table. The hallway was lined with ornately framed portraits, pastoral scenes, and seascapes. Gas lamps in polished brass sconces blazed brightly, showing off the pale cream walls and intricately detailed white molding on the high ceiling.

He stepped through the big double oak doors and into the library. As always, he stood for a moment staring at the huge room with its wall-to-ceiling bookcases. Wiggins loved to read. "Cor blimey, Fred, I'd not mind being stuck in here for a few days." It wasn't the first time he'd been in the room, and Luty had always told him to come along and borrow any book he wanted. But he was still a bit too shy to do such a thing. Besides, the lending library near Upper Edmonton Gardens was perfectly fine for his needs. But this was a treasure trove. He dropped Fred's lead and wandered over to the nearest shelf. He spotted a copy of Mark Twain's novel, *Tom Sawyer*. It was one of his favorite books. He pulled it out, flipped open the cover, and began to read. Within moments, he was so engrossed in the story he didn't even hear the door open.

"Get off, you silly pup," Julie said with mock severity. "You're going to make me drop your treat."

Wiggins turned. "Hello, Miss Julie. Fred, leave off. She's got her hands full." The young, dark-haired maid was carrying a tray with two plates piled high with food and a glass of lemonade. She put the tray down on the top of a small end table.

"The pup's no trouble." Julie reached down and stroked Fred's back. "He just gets a bit excited. Madam will be here in just a moment. Last I saw of her, she was trying to get away from Lady Dinsworthy."

"I thought she'd been trapped by Lord Dinsworthy." Wiggins put the Twain book back in its place and moved toward the food.

"It's both of them." Julie laughed. "Even madam has a hard time outtalking those two, but I've no doubt she'll do it. She's a very determined—" Julie broke off just as the double doors opened and Luty Belle Crookshank flew into the room.

Luty was wearing a bright red taffeta evening gown with a high lace collar and long sleeves. It rustled as she charged across the room. A concoction of feathers and ribbons were wound in her gray hair, and there was a sparkling diamond necklace around her neck. Matching earrings dangled from her ears.

"Did the inspector get it?" Luty asked. "And don't pretend you don't know what I'm talking about, boy."

Wiggins glanced at the clock, noted the time, and decided he'd better eat while he had the chance. He reached for a slice of roast beef. "He got it all right. The victim was a banker named—"

"Lawrence Boyd," Luty interrupted. "I know. I've already got my feelers out asking about him. Go on and tell me the rest of it."

"Mrs. Jeffries wants you to come to the morning meeting," Wiggins said around a mouthful of succulent beef. "There's all sorts of bits and pieces you need to know." He didn't want to stay too much longer.

"Don't you worry; we'll be there. But I've got half of London in my parlor"—she jerked her thumb toward the double doors—"and I ain't missing this chance to ask a few questions. Come on, give me a few facts, something I can inquire about. Everyone's already heard the news, and they're jawin' about it something fierce. There are more bankers in my parlor than there are fleas on a barnyard cat."

Wiggins understood her point. "I'll tell you what I know. Boyd was bashed in the 'ead, and the killer tried to make it look like an accident by settin' the place on fire, but it didn't work."

"Who else was there?"

Wiggins took another bite and tried to recall all the names. "Uh," he swallowed, "I believe one of them was named Arnold Sapington. He and his wife Maud were both there."

"Don't eat so fast, lad, you're going to choke to death. Give Fred a few bites; he's hungry, too," Luty admonished.

Julie snickered. "I'll feed Fred."

"I can't stay too long. The women'll 'ave my 'ead if I'm too late. You know 'ow they worry," he protested.

Luty waved her hand dismissively. "Don't be daft. The carriage is right outside. I'll send you home in that. Now, who else was at Boyd's house."

Wiggins tried to remember. "The typewriter lady was there. Her name is Eva Clarke. She's the one that called for help. The household was out at a funeral, and so none of the servants were about the place. There was another man there, too. I think his name was Walter Gibbons."

"Good, good." Luty nodded encouragingly. "Go on. What else can you recall?"

"The inspector said they didn't see anything in the studio that could 'ave been used as the murder weapon. No brass candlesticks or doorstops or anything like that. He's got police constables searching the Boyd house and the neighborhood for the weapon."

Luty snorted. "He'll not have much luck finding it, not unless the killer's a real fool. Most likely the murder weapon is at the bottom of the Thames."

Hatchet stuck his head into the room. "Madam, your guests are asking for you. Your absence has become quite noticeable. Miss Teasdale and Lord Dinsworthy are making quite a fuss."

Luty's eyes narrowed suspiciously. "How long have you been listening at the door?"

Luty and Hatchet were very competitive when they were on one of the inspector's cases. Wiggins picked up the glass and took a drink of the lemonade. He might as well enjoy himself a bit. These two could squabble worse than Samson and Fred as they vied for clues and the upper hand.

Hatchet contrived to look offended. "Really, madam, that is an outrageous slander. I'm hardly in the habit of eavesdropping." As he had been listening at the door, that was also an outrageous lie, but he didn't care in the least. Madam would pretend to tell him all the details she'd learned from Wiggins, but he knew that she was quite capable of leaving one or two pertinent facts out of her recitation. And she wasn't the only one with sources here tonight.

"Slander my foot," Luty snorted. "You just don't want me gettin' the drop on you."

"I've no idea what you're talking about." He turned his head and looked down the hall. "Lord Dinsworthy is coming this way, madam. I suggest you come out and meet him." Hatchet smiled wickedly. "I'll be happy to take your place and get the rest of the details from Wiggins."

From outside the room, they heard a voice bellow, "Luty, where the deuce are you?"

"Blast." Luty stamped her foot and headed for the door. She glared at Hatchet as she swept out into the hall. "I know you told him where I was," she hissed.

As he had, Hatchet didn't bother to deny it. He simply came into the library and smiled at Wiggins. "Now, what else is there to hear?"

CHAPTER 3

The next morning, Luty and Hatchet arrived at the back door of Upper Edmonton Gardens at almost the same time the inspector and Constable Barnes were leaving by the front door. "We're here," Luty announced as they came into the kitchen. "And I for one am rarin' to go. I found out some good bits last night."

"Really, madam, do contain your enthusiasm. You've no idea if what you learned is going to be useful or not," Hatchet sniffed disapprovingly. Despite his best efforts, he'd not been able to get her to say a word on the way over here.

"I'm sure you'll both have much to contribute in the coming days," Mrs. Jeffries said quickly. "Do take a seat and we'll get started." She slipped into her chair at the head of the table. "I think we've quite a bit of ground to cover this morning."

"Why don't you give us a brief summary of what you know thus far," Hatchet suggested. "Wiggins told us a few details, but I'm sure there's more." He was also sure she'd managed to have a quick word with Constable Barnes this morning, which meant there might be even more information to be had.

"And we've got some bits to tell," Luty declared as she smiled wickedly at Hatchet. "The murder was all people could talk about last night, and I got an earful."

"As you know, the victim was a banker named Lawrence Boyd," Mrs. Jeffries began. "The presumed cause of death is multiple blows to the head, and the killer or killers then set the room on fire. But luckily, the fire didn't spread."

"Killer musta been a fool," Luty muttered. "This is the wettest spring we've had for years."

Mrs. Jeffries nodded and continued on with her recitation. She went over the facts they had thus far and even added an idea Constable Barnes had shared with her earlier. "The guests don't appear to be overly fond of Boyd, so we must have a good look at them as well." The inspector hadn't been clear about that point last night, and she was glad she'd had the chance to talk to Barnes.

"But the guests came after the fire was started," Mrs. Goodge mused. "So I expect we'd best try to find out where they were that morning, see if any of them can account for their whereabouts during the time the murder was happening."

"That's a very good idea," Mrs. Jeffries agreed.

"And I think it's tellin' that the killer tried to make it look like an accident," Wiggins said. "Means whoever did it might 'ave planned it out in advance."

"Boyd was supposedly alone in the house?" Luty asked.

"That's right." Mrs. Jeffries picked up her tea cup. "The servants were at a funeral. Boyd had taken the day away from his office to work on a painting. Constable Barnes told me Boyd was quite an accomplished amateur artist. He always entered a painting for the summer exhibit at the Royal Academy."

"But there was the typewriter girl there, a Miss Clarke," Hatchet mused. "I wonder how many people knew she was going to be in the house."

"And that Mr. Glover was there as well," Wiggins added. "He brought Mr. Boyd some files from his office."

"I think the question is whether or not the killer thought Boyd was on 'is own," Smythe said. "But we'd best not get too far ahead of ourselves. We've come a cropper a time or two with speculatin' too early in a case on what was what."

"That's certainly true." Betsy nodded in agreement.

"What did you hear last night?" Mrs. Jeffries looked toward Luty and Hatchet, who were sitting next to one another.

Luty spoke first. "The gossip I heard was that Boyd was a pretty ruthless character. He had a mean streak, and considerin' I heard this from a banker, then Boyd musta been pretty bad. Them money men usually hang together."

"Was he ever married?" Betsy asked.

"I didn't hear anyone mention a wife," Luty replied. "But then again, all they could talk about was who mighta wanted him dead. Apparently, it's a pretty long list. He's sacked a few clerks and called in a fair number of loans in his time. As it's a merchant bank, when he called a note, lots of people might have lost their jobs."

"Why is that?" Wiggins asked. He wasn't sure what the difference was between a merchant bank and an ordinary one.

"Because merchant banks lend money to businesses, not individuals," Luty explained. "So when Boyd called in a loan on a business, he'd probably force it to close, and if there were employees, they'd be out of a job." Since her husband's death many years earlier, Luty had managed her own business affairs. She knew more about banking and money than most men.

"Boyd was also considered a very competitive individual," Hatchet added. He'd picked up a tidbit or two of information, but he was saving them until later. Truth was, some of what he'd heard didn't make much sense at this point. But he'd learned to be patient. One never knew when a stray fact or two might become very relevant.

"I expect bein' competitive would be useful if you were a banker," Mrs. Goodge commented. She looked at Luty. "Do you remember which of your guests seemed to know the most about Boyd?"

"Oh, everyone had heard of him." Luty grinned. "He's got his fingers in a lot of pies, not just banking. He's on the board of half a dozen charities, serves on a couple of local political committees, and he has the ear of the chancellor of the exchequer."

"So he's quite well known," Mrs. Jeffries murmured. Drat, that might make things difficult for Inspector Witherspoon. If their inspector didn't get results quickly, she had no doubt that Inspector Nigel Nivens would try to horn in on the case.

Nivens was politically well connected and ethically underhanded; in short he was a boot licking dog. He was desperate to rise in rank, and he let nothing, including justice, stand in his way. He loathed Witherspoon and would do everything in his power to ruin him. Nivens was a worry, but she couldn't think what to do about him.

Hatchet, not wanting to be outdone by Luty, blurted out a few of the tidbits he'd been saving. "I overheard Lord Dinsworthy comment that Boyd's paintings were considered top quality, but he never sold them."

Luty grinned slyly. She knew it was just killing Hatchet that she had found out more than him. "'Course he didn't sell 'em. He gave 'em away to charities and institutions. Lady Dinsworthy claimed that was how he got on so many prestigious boards."

Mrs. Jeffries forced her concern about Inspector Nivens to the back of her mind. She needed to concentrate on the task at hand. "Did you hear anything else?"

"Not really, just people jawin' over the murder," Luty replied. "Oh, I did hear Eudora Higgleston makin' some comment about who would get Boyd's paintings. But when I pressed her on the matter, she didn't really know anything."

"His paintings are that good?" Smythe asked. "I mean, good enough that people are already speculating on who will inherit them?"

"Sounds like it." Luty shrugged. "He's exhibited at the Royal Academy, and from what I hear, every amateur in England would sell their grandmothers for a chance to have their work hanging on those walls. But like I say, there was a lot of talk last night and it's hard to tell what's true and what ain't. You know how people are: everyone wants to pretend they know more than they do."

"That's certainly true," Hatchet said with a sideways glance at Luty. "I, on the other hand, only repeat information I know to be factual."

Luty grinned at her butler but didn't rise to the bait. She turned her attention to Mrs. Jeffries. "I thought that if it was all the same to you, I'd see what my sources in the city have to say about Boyd."

"That's an excellent idea," Mrs. Jeffries replied. Luty's access to the financial community in London was unsurpassed.

Hatchet leaned forward and said, "I've a number of sources in the art community that I can tap for information, if, of course, you think that line of inquiry would be useful."

"At this point, all lines of inquiry are useful," Mrs. Jeffries replied. "And if his work is as good as we've heard, perhaps his death is connected to his painting."

"But that was just a hobby," Mrs. Goodge protested. The one area she was sadly lacking in sources was the art community. None of her previous positions had been with anyone connected with the creative world. She'd mainly worked for aristocrats or the wealthy, and none of that lot was remotely artistic. "Surely no one would go to the trouble of murdering someone over a painting!"

"But we don't know that," Betsy said. "And according to what we do know, he was in his studio working on a painting when he was killed."

"That's true." The cook frowned. "I wonder what happened to the painting. I mean, maybe the fire was set to destroy it, not hide the fact Boyd had been murdered."

They all stared at her. Finally, after a long moment or two, Mrs. Jeffries said, "That's a very interesting idea, Mrs. Goodge. We really must find out. I'll ask the inspector tonight. But really, we mustn't get ahead of ourselves. We've much to learn, and I've a feeling we'd best learn it as quickly as possible."

"What's wrong?" Smythe asked. "Why do we have to be quick about this? It's not like our last case. No one's life is at stake."

"No, but the victim was apparently a very prominent person, which means the Home Office will be watching it closely and pressing the police for results." Mrs. Jeffries sighed heavily. "I suspect that Nigel Nivens will do everything he can to get the case taken away from our inspector, especially after what happened with Tommy Odell."

"Nivens won't forgive or forget the fact that our inspector overturned his one and only murder conviction," Wiggins muttered. "'E'll be out for our inspector's blood. We'd best be on our toes on this one."

"I say we'd best watch our backs as well," Smythe warned. "I wouldn't put it past the fellow to sneak about and try to suss out what our inspector is doin'."

"Surely he'd not go that far," Betsy said.

"Nivens was willing to let an innocent man hang," Luty exclaimed. "So I'd not put anything sneaky or underhanded past him. Smythe is right; we'd best all watch our backs."

"And what do we do if we see somethin' odd?" Wiggins looked at the housekeeper. He'd not wanted to say anything, but last night when he'd come home in Luty's carriage, he thought he'd felt someone leap off the back just as the carriage pulled up and stopped. But street urchins sometimes hitched a ride by leaping on the back of a carriage, so he'd put it out of his mind. He'd even done it a time or two when he was younger and more willing to risk breaking a leg or getting a thrashing from an irate coachman.

"I'm not sure," she mused, "but rest assured, we'll do something. I thought I'd go see Dr. Bosworth today."

"Going to see if he can get a copy of the postmortem report?" Betsy asked.

Mrs. Jeffries nodded. "Yes, he might have some idea of what the murder weapon might have been. I think that information would be very useful."

"Maybe the inspector or one of his lads will discover something," Wiggins suggested. "I mean, they didn't find the murder weapon, so the killer must 'ave took it with 'im. Seems to me, carryin' something covered in blood about London is a bit risky. I'll see if I can find a scullery maid or a tweeny who's heard something."

"But they weren't there," Betsy pointed out. "They were at a funeral."

"True, but they might still know something. If the killer used an object from the 'ouse to bash Mr. Boyd's 'ead in, it would 'ave to be cleaned off before it could be put back. Someone might 'ave noticed something out of place or wet, and I'll see what else I can learn as well."

There was a knock on the back door just as the clock struck the hour. "That'll be the grocer's lad." Mrs. Goodge got to her feet. "I doubt he knows anything, but he might." She looked pointedly at the others. They quickly got out of their chairs.

"We'll meet here this afternoon around half past four," Mrs. Jeffries said as she headed for the coat tree to get her hat and spring jacket.

Smythe grabbed Betsy's hand. "Walk me to the back door, love."

"I've got to get my hat and gloves," she protested. "I want to get out and about as well. There are shopkeepers out there with all sorts of useful information."

"Here's your bonnet." Mrs. Goodge handed the pale gray hat to the maid. "And your gloves are tucked neatly inside. Now be off with all of you. I need this kitchen for my sources."

"May we speak to Miss Clarke, please?" Witherspoon smiled at the young maid who answered the door of the small lodging house. "She's expecting us."

"Miss Clarke's in the sitting room." The maid opened the door wider and pointed at a door just off the small foyer. "It's just through there."

Eva Clarke nodded politely as the two men stepped into the

small room. She was seated on a maroon sofa. "Hello, Inspector, Constable. I appreciate your punctuality. I've an interview for another position later today and I shouldn't like to be late. Please sit down." She gestured toward two matching horsehair chairs opposite the couch.

Witherspoon took off his bowler and Barnes whipped out his notebook as they took their seats. She sank back to her spot on the settee. Eva Clarke was an attractive young woman with red-gold hair, a porcelain complexion, and brown eyes. She wore a gray skirt and a crisp white blouse with a high neck and long, narrow sleeves. Lying next to her on the settee was a plain gray jacket, black gloves, and a sensible gray hat decorated with a small, wispy veil on the crown.

"We'll try to be as brief as possible," the inspector said. "First of all, can you tell us what time you arrived at Mr. Boyd's home?"

"Ten o'clock," she replied. "Mr. Boyd had sent a messenger to the agency that morning, requesting my services. Luckily, the agency is just around the corner from here, so they contacted me immediately and I went straightaway."

"What's the name of the agency?" The inspector shifted slightly. The seat of the chair was quite rough, and he could almost feel the horsehairs poking through his trousers.

"Croxley and Gills," she replied. "They're a secretarial agency."

"What the address, please?" the constable asked.

"They're at number 54 Potter Road," she replied. "As I said, they're just around the corner."

"Mr. Boyd requested you specifically?" Barnes looked up from his notebook.

"Yes, I'd worked for him on several previous occasions. Usually I worked at his office, but this time he specifically requested I come to his home."

"You were comfortable doing that?" Barnes asked.

"Oh, yes." She smiled easily. "I'd been there before, and I knew Mr. Boyd had a full staff. Mind you, I didn't realize none of them would be there yesterday. I was a bit concerned when he answered the door instead of the housekeeper, but I needn't have been worried. Mr. Boyd simply gave me my instructions and then went off to paint in his studio."

"Yes, I see." Witherspoon understood what she meant. A young woman alone in a man's home could easily be a cause of concern.

"I'd never have taken the assignment if I'd known he was there alone," she explained. "But once I got there, it seemed silly to make a fuss, especially with Mr. Boyd. He's only interested in how fast I could get the work done."

"You operated a typewriter." Witherspoon looked at her curiously. He'd seen typewriters, of course. They had several of them at the Yard, and some of the younger lads claimed they were exceedingly useful in writing reports. But the actual operation of one seemed like magic. Why, one's fingers seemed to be actually operating independently of one's eyes.

"That's correct." She smiled brightly. "I went to business college in the United States, in Chicago. Typewriting is a most useful skill to acquire. Take my word for it, Inspector, within a few years, all offices will use typewriters. They are so much more efficient than writing by hand."

"Yes, I'm sure you're right," Witherspoon replied. "How did you come to be acquainted with Mr. Boyd?" He'd no idea why he asked that question, but it had popped into his head so he supposed it must be important. He'd learned to trust his "inner voice." As Mrs. Jeffries always told him, that "inner voice" of his had led to success in numerous cases.

"Through the secretarial agency." She smiled again. "Mr. Boyd acquired a typewriter for this bank, and then he realized there was no one who knew how to operate it properly. So he contacted the secretarial agency, and they asked if he would consider a woman. He said he would. He never offered me a permanent position, but he'd call me in whenever he wanted typewriting done."

"I see." Witherspoon wanted to ensure that Miss Clarke's relationship to the victim was a business one and not personal. Miss Clarke looked like a perfectly nice young woman, but he'd seen other perfectly nice-looking young ladies turn out to be ruthless killers, especially in matters of the heart. Just to be on the safe side, he'd have a chat with the servants at the Boyd household and see just how well Miss Clarke and victim were acquainted. He'd also have a word with the secretarial agency. "So you went there yesterday morning and he gave you your assignment. I take it he had his own typewriting machine?"

She frowned thoughtfully. "I'm not sure. I think whenever he wanted personal typewriting done, he brought the one from the bank home. But I can't be certain. Remingtons all look alike."

"You weren't doing work for the bank?" the inspector asked.

"Oh, no, I was typing his acceptance speech." She grinned. "It took quite awhile. He'd written it out in longhand, and deciphering his scribbling wasn't the easiest task I've ever had. But I managed. I did feel a bit of sympathy for the poor souls who were going to be at the Bankers Benevolent Society dinner; it's a very long speech." She sobered. "But I suppose now, no one will hear it. That's very sad. Mr. Boyd was always nice to me."

Witherspoon nodded. "You worked in Mr. Boyd's study at the back of the house, correct?"

"That's right. As I said, it wasn't easy to decipher his handwriting, so actually typing the speech took longer than I'd originally thought it would. As a matter of fact, I was quite surprised when I finished and realized how late it had gotten."

"Was that when you saw the smoke?" Barnes glanced up from his notebook again.

"Yes, I wanted Mr. Boyd to know that I was done. I was going to take him the pages, but then I looked out the study window and I saw smoke coming from the studio. I ran out to the hallway, toward the back of the house, and raised the alarm. You know the rest."

"Did you actually go to the studio and see the fire?" Witherspoon asked.

She shook her head. "Oh, no. Mr. Glover, who I didn't even know was in the house, came rushing out as well. I must have made some sound of alarm when I saw the smoke. He's the one who ran to the studio. He shouted for me to get the fire brigade."

Witherspoon gave an encouraging nod. "And is that what you did?"

"Yes, there's a fire station two streets over from the Boyd house, so I ran as fast as I could to fetch them. They came straightaway," she replied. "When I got back, Mr. Glover was beating at the flames with a rug through the open door, but as the fire brigade was right on my heels, they pushed him aside and took over."

"Could you see flames when you returned?" Barnes asked. "Or just smoke?"

She thought for a moment. "Now that I think about it, it was mainly smoke billowing out of the building, but I do recall seeing fire through that little front window. It was very frightening."

"You weren't aware that Mr. Glover was in the house." Wither-spoon looked at her curiously. "Isn't that a bit odd?"

"I suppose it must seem so." She smiled hesitantly and shrugged. "I did ask him about it. He said he'd come by at Mr. Boyd's re-quest to bring him some files and that he'd been invited to stay to luncheon."

"Where was he waiting?" Witherspoon asked.

"In the drawing room," she replied. "He said he was waiting for everyone to arrive. Then he heard me cry out and came running down the hall, when I saw smoke. He said that's when he knew something was wrong."

Witherspoon looked doubtful. "So that means you hadn't let him into the house earlier and that you had no idea he was in the house at all?"

"That's correct." She frowned. "That is very curious, isn't it? I guess this is the first time I've thought about it with any clarity. If Mr. Glover had come to the front door and knocked, I'd have had to have been the one to let him into the house. The servants were all gone and I was there alone." Her brow furrowed as she looked at the inspector. "I wonder how he got in."

That was precisely what Witherspoon intended to find out.

Wiggins surveyed his surroundings with care as he walked down Laurel Road. There was a very good chance the inspector might be about the area. Wiggins had overheard him telling Mrs. Jeffries they still had to interview the servants, and the house-to-house task of looking for witnesses wasn't finished as yet either, so he kept a sharp eye out.

The street was quite lively. Farther up the road, he could see a woman wearing a brown housekeeper's dress sweeping the front steps of a huge, elegant house, and coming around the corner was a lad pushing a grocer's delivery cart. On the far side of the street was a laundry wagon making the morning stops. He came abreast of number fourteen and stopped, dropped to his knees, and pre-tended to tie his shoes. Cor blimey, this was going to be his lucky day: the woman was sweeping the steps of the Boyd house.

He cast a quick glance in her direction, trying to decide how best to approach her. She was a middle-aged woman with brown hair tucked under a black cap, a pale complexion, and a thin, dis-approving mouth. Wiggins could see her quite clearly as she had turned and was staring straight at him. She didn't appear to like what she saw. "What do you want, boy?" she said harshly.

"Beggin' your pardon, ma'am," he said, "but I was just tyin' my shoe."

"Then move along and tie it elsewhere." She glared at him. "Go on, get off with you, boy, before I set the law on you."

As this was precisely the sort of reception Wiggins hadn't been expecting and certainly didn't want, all he could think to do was stumble to his feet. "Sorry, ma'am, I didn't mean to cause any offense." He wondered why on earth the woman was in such a foul temper. But before he could say another word, she'd turned her back on him and resumed her sweeping. He watched her covertly as he walked away, noting that she appeared to be moving the broom back and forth in the same spot over and over. He reckoned if she kept that up much longer, she'd be taking the paint off the steps.

Wiggins went up the road and around the corner. He spotted a café and decided to have a cup of tea. He went inside. It was a very small room with a counter and three tiny tables, all of which were empty. The only person in the place was a young girl standing behind the counter with her back to him. She turned as he stepped through the door. "Good morning," she said. "What can I get you?"

"Tea, please," he replied.

"Would you like a bun as well?" she asked. She was about his age, with dark hair, thick eyebrows, blue eyes, and a tiny rosebud of a mouth.

"No thanks, just the tea. You're not very busy, are you?"

"Not now." She grinned and picked up a huge brown teapot. "We were earlier, of course. We're always busy early in the morning, but then it dies down until midmorning when people start drifting in for a cuppa." She poured his tea into a tall gray mug and added milk. "Sugar?"

"Yes, please," he replied. He decided to try his luck here; at least she seemed like a talker. "I hear there was a murder around here yesterday." That was always good to get a conversation started.

Her eyes widened in surprise. "Really?"

"You mean you haven't 'eard?" he said. "There was a fellow that was bashed in the 'ead just up the road." He gestured in the direction of the Boyd house. "He died. Surely you've 'eard about it."

She stared at him blankly. "Was it in the newspapers?"

Wiggin's heart sank to his toes. His day just kept getting worse and worse.

Lawrence Boyd had worked at Boyd, Stanford, and Sawyer on Blakely Street near Chancery Lane. The bank took up the street floor of an old, two-story redbrick building.

Witherspoon and Barnes walked through the door and into a large room. Wooden shelves filled with ledgers lined three of the walls, and two doors, both of them open to reveal private offices, were on the fourth wall. A small wooden divider ran down the length of the room, behind which half a dozen men sat working at desks.

"We'd like to speak to Mr. James Glover," Witherspoon told the clerk closest to them. He was a young man with ginger hair and freckles. He'd risen to his feet when they'd entered and was now staring at them with his mouth slightly open, as though he'd never seen a policeman before. "I'll go get him," he said as he turned and hurried toward one of the private offices. "He's in Mr. Boyd's office."

"This doesn't look like any bank I've ever seen," Barnes muttered. "But then, it's not for people, is it. It's for businesses and that sort of thing. There's nothing here but desks and clerks."

Witherspoon wasn't really sure, but he didn't want to admit to his ignorance. "I believe you're correct. I don't think merchant banks cater to the general public." He noticed that on each desk there were ledgers and files. Everyone had stopped working and the room was deadly quiet. Every clerk in the room was staring at them openly.

"I don't see a typewriter anywhere, sir," Barnes muttered.

The door to an office opened and the ginger-haired clerk stuck his head out. "Mr. Glover will see you now." He waved the two policemen over.

James Glover was sitting behind a large desk. "You may go back to your post, Watkins," he said to the ginger-haired clerk before turning his attention to the two men.

The clerk scurried out, taking care to close the door behind him.

Glover stared at them for a moment. "What do you want, Inspector? I've already made a statement."

"We need to ask you some questions," Witherspoon said politely. He was a bit irritated. There were two perfectly good chairs in front of the desk; the man could ask them to sit down.

"As I said, Inspector, I've already made a statement and I think that ought to suffice." He started to get up.

"It won't suffice, sir," Barnes said harshly. "Your statement doesn't quite match what we've heard from other witnesses, so we'll either ask you a few questions here or we can do it down at the station. It's your choice, sir." The constable had taken the man's measure and decided to take the upper hand. James Glover reminded the constable of a bully boy from his school days. He'd terrorized the other boys until Barnes had stood up to him.

Glover seemed to wilt before their very eyes. He slumped back in the chair, his mouth gaping for words that wouldn't come. Finally, he said, "Well, er, one does want to cooperate with the law."

"Yes, I expect one does." Barnes pointed at the empty chairs. "If it's all the same to you, we'll sit down and take care of this properly."

"Certainly, certainly." Glover nodded eagerly. "Of course, do make yourselves comfortable. Sorry. All this horrible business with poor Mr. Boyd has made me forget my manners."

They sat down, and Barnes whipped out his little brown notebook.

Witherspoon said, "Mr. Glover, what time did you leave the office yesterday?"

"What time did I leave?" Glover looked confused by the question. "You mean here?"

"That's correct."

He thought for a moment. "I'm not sure."

"Perhaps one of the clerks would remember," Barnes suggested as he started to rise to his feet. "Shall I . . ."

"No, no, that's all right, I believe it was about half past ten," he replied. "But it might have been closer to eleven. I'm not certain."

"You took some files to Mr. Boyd's residence, is that correct?" Witherspoon asked.

"That's right," Glover replied. "But I don't see what that has to do with Mr. Boyd's death. They were just files. He'd seen them dozens of times."

"Mr. Boyd was working from his home, is that correct?" Barnes looked up from his writing.

"Yes, he'd been working from home all week," Glover said. "He was a painter, you see. He'd have much rather been an artist than a banker, but his family owns a big portion of the bank and he was the only son, so he joined the firm. He had no choice, really. It was his duty."

"Who let you into the Boyd house yesterday?" Witherspoon watched Glover's face as he asked the question.

"No one," Glover replied easily. "I went around the back to the studio. I never even knocked on the door."

"You knew he'd be alone?" Barnes asked.

"No, I knew he was working in his studio. He'd instructed me to come directly there."

"You came around the side of the house directly to the studio," Witherspoon clarified. "Is that right?"

"That's right. There's a passageway between the kitchen and the house next door. It's a service yard that opens onto the street, but the gate is behind a hedge so you've got to know where to look to find it."

"Which files did you bring to Mr. Boyd?" Barnes asked.

Glover rubbed a fat finger against his cheek. "Let me see. He wanted the Simpson file, Bertram's, and oh, yes, the Heddington file. I do hope they aren't too badly damaged. Those are very important papers. When do you think we might have them back?"

"Are you in charge now that Mr. Boyd is dead?" Witherspoon asked.

Glover shrugged. "I'm the chief clerk, Inspector, so until the partners appoint another managing director, I'm the one who will be responsible for the office. Now, I ask you again, when can I get my files?" He'd regained some of his confidence.

"When we're through with them," Barnes replied. "Will you be a candidate for managing director?" he asked quickly.

"I expect so." Glover's chest expanded proudly. "None of the partners want the burden of the day-to-day running of the place, and none of the other clerks are up to the task. I'm the most experienced person here."

"So Mr. Boyd's death means you'll get a nice chance to have a promotion," Barnes said. "I imagine there's a substantial salary increase with such a change in position."

Glover gasped. "That's absurd."

"You mean there isn't an increase in pay?" Barnes asked innocently.

"That's not what I meant at all." Glover wiped at a bead of sweat that had suddenly rolled down his forehead. "It was your implication that I find offensive."

"Constable Barnes implied nothing," Witherspoon said calmly. "He merely asked some legitimate questions. But let's go back to the issue of you just walking into Mr. Boyd's home unannounced."

"I've told you, he instructed me to come directly to the studio," Glover insisted. He pulled a white handkerchief out of his coat pocket and dabbed at his neck, mopping up the layer of sweat that had suddenly appeared. "If you don't believe me, you can ask Bingley. He was here with me when the note from Mr. Boyd arrived yesterday morning."

"Mr. Boyd sent you a note telling you to bring the files straight to the studio," the inspector clarified. "What time was this?"

"At nine, just after we opened."

"And Mr. Bingley saw the note?" Barnes pressed.

"Of course he did. I gave it to him so he could get the files Mr. Boyd had listed, the ones he wanted me to bring to him. Bingley can also verify I'd been invited to luncheon." Glover sat up straighter. "So I took the files over to Mr. Boyd's straightaway. I put them on the little table next to the door and went back to the house. It was quite warm and Mr. Boyd suggested I may want to tidy myself up before the luncheon. There were going to be some important guests and I wanted to look presentable."

Witherspoon nodded. "Did you speak to Miss Clarke when you went back to the house?"

Glover hesitated. "No, I should have, but I didn't. Mr. Boyd had asked me to check her work, but frankly, I . . . uh . . . well, I'm not used to dealing with young women in business circumstances. Really, I found it quite absurd that Mr. Boyd had engaged her services in the first place."

"So you said nothing to her; you simply went into the drawing room and sat down?" Witherspoon pressed.

"That's correct."

"How is it she didn't hear you walking down the hall?" Barnes smiled slightly as he asked the question. "You obviously heard her quite clearly when she raised the alarm about the fire. How is it she didn't hear you?"

Glover looked down at the desk. "I walk very softly."

"Were you deliberately staying quiet?" Barnes pressed.

"Certainly not," Glover snapped. "That infernal machine makes such a racket a herd of goats could have been dancing in the hallway and she'd have not heard it."

Witherspoon shifted in the chair. "What time was this?"

"I've already told you that," Glover dabbed at his neck again. "It was close to eleven o'clock."

"And the luncheon was scheduled for one o'clock," Barnes said softly. He leaned closer to Glover. "Tell me, Mr. Glover, were you going to sit quietly in Mr. Boyd's drawing room for two hours when your office is only a twenty-minute walk away. Why didn't you go back to work?"

"Of course not," Glover snapped. "After I tidied myself up, I fully intended to come back to the office." His pale face flushed red. "But I was tired and my feet hurt so I went into the drawing room to have a bit of a rest. The latest edition of the *Illustrated London News* was on the table, so I picked it up and sat down to have a quick glance at it. Reading always makes me sleepy, Inspector, and the room was exceptionally warm. I must have dozed off because all of a sudden, I was awakened by Miss Clarke. She'd shouted something, made some sort of call of distress. I leapt to my feet and saw her in the hallway running for the back door. She yelled that the studio was on fire." He paused and took a breath of air. "We both ran out to the back garden. We could see the flames through the front window of the studio, so I told Miss Clarke to fetch the fire brigade."

"And what did you do?" Barnes asked.

"I looked around for a bucket or something to use to try and put the flames out, but there was nothing that I could see that would be of any use." He sighed. "I finally grabbed the rug off the floor in the hall and tried using that to beat the flames out, but frankly, fire frightens me so I didn't want to get too close." His eyes filled with tears. "The truth is, I was so scared I didn't have the courage to even stick my head through the studio door. I kept calling Mr. Boyd's name, but he didn't reply. I think I must have known something awful had happened. I know it makes me sound a dreadful coward, but I'm terrified of fire."

"Fire frightens most people," Witherspoon said kindly. "What happened then?"

"A few minutes later, the fire brigade arrived and I got out of the way. It didn't take long to get the fire out." He broke off and laughed harshly. "It wasn't much of a fire in the first place. Yet I'd been too frightened to go through that wretched door. I'll never forgive myself; if I'd had the courage to go inside, Mr. Boyd might have been saved."

"I doubt that sir," Witherspoon said softly. "At what point did the servants come back?"

Glover tapped a finger against his lips. "I'm not sure. One moment I looked around and they were all standing near the back door looking frightened and shocked. But I've no idea how long they'd been there. Perhaps Miss Clarke will remember."

"Did you see or hear anything unusual after you gave Mr. Boyd the files?" Barnes asked.

"No, Constable." Glover shook his head. "As I said, I dozed off. I couldn't have heard anything in any case. The typewriter makes a very loud noise."

"Yet you dozed off?"

"It's noisy but very rhythmic," he explained. "A bit like riding on a train. One moment you're awake and the next, you're nodding off to the clackety clack of the wheels against the rails. I can't explain it, but that's what happened."

"Can you tell Mr. Horace Maitland that Luty Belle Crookshank is here to see him," Luty said to the young man in the reception office of Maitland, Warner, and Stutts, Merchant Bankers.

The clerk, who hadn't heard the door open, looked up. His eyes widened in surprise. An elderly woman wearing a bright emerald-green-striped day dress and an elegant hat and holding a frilly parasol, stood grinning at him. "Do you have an appointment, ma'am?" he asked.

"I don't think I'll need one," Luty replied easily. "You just skeedaddle on in there and tell him Luty Belle Crookshank is here to see him and it'll be fine. Go on now, git up off yer backside and git on in there." She waved her hand at him.

He leapt to his feet, frightened she might start waving her parasol next. "Uh, yes, ma'am, I'll just see if Mr. Maitland is available."

"Don't you fret, boy." Luty laughed. "He'll be available."

The young man disappeared into the office. A few moments later, Horace Maitland stepped into the reception room. The young man peered out from behind him. "Luty, this is a pleasure. Do come in. I'd heard you were ill."

Maitland was a clean-shaven man of medium height. He had brown hair and hazel eyes, and was dressed in a dark navy blue suit with a white shirt, blue waistcoat, and maroon tie. He took her arm. "See that we're not disturbed," he instructed the clerk as he led Luty into his office.

"I was, but I'm better now," Luty said. "I'm sorry to barge in on you like this, but I was hopin' you could help me with a problem I've got."

"Of course, of course, I'll do anything I can. Would you care for some tea?" He asked as he closed the door.

"No, thank you, Horace." Luty shook her head. "I'll not take up that much of your time. I know you're busy."

Maitland waved her into straight-backed leather chair opposite his desk. "Do sit down."

Luty sat and took a moment to gather her thoughts. It had been a good while since she'd been out "on the hunt" as Mrs. Jeffries would say, and she was raring to go. But she wanted to make sure she didn't frighten off her quarry. She was rich as sin and her American companies did plenty of business with Maitland's bank, but he was a banker and they tended to be more tight-lipped than lawyers. She knew she had to be careful.

"Now, what can I do for you?" Maitland leaned back in his chair and watched her curiously.

"I've got a little problem and I'm not sure what I can do about it." She smiled brightly. "You see, a good friend of mine has put a heap of money into a project that's goin' to be funded by Boyd, Stanford, and Sawyer, the merchant bank over on Blakely Street."

"I know who they are," he said.

"Well, I reckon you've heard what happened to the general manger, Lawrence Boyd . . ." She trailed off, hoping he'd jump into the conversation at this point, but he simply stared at her like a fish-eyed poker player, so she continued. "He went and got himself murdered. Now I'm stuck with my friend wonderin' whether or not he ought to pull his business from the bank."

Maitland stared at her for a long moment, and Luty was almost sure he didn't believe a word she was saying. Finally, he said, "Why didn't your friend come to us?"

"I told him to," she exclaimed. "But he's a stubborn cuss and he'd already started doin' business with Boyd's by the time he talked to me."

"So what you're asking is whether or not the bank is sound?" Maitland asked. "I should think that Mr. Boyd's death wouldn't have any bearing on the soundness of the enterprise."

"Don't take me for a fool," Luty said impatiently. "Of course the murder of a general partner is goin' to have a bearin' on the bank. My friend wants to know if the man's death means there's something bad goin' on. You know, hanky-panky with money, double dealin', that sort of thing. Have you heard anything?"

Maitland smiled. "Luty, tell your friend not to worry. There's nothing that suggests that Boyd's death has anything to do with any irregularities."

"But how can you be so sure?" Luty asked. This wasn't going as she had hoped. She'd forgotten how tight-lipped Maitland could be. She wasn't getting anywhere.

"You can't be certain, of course," he said. "But Lawrence Boyd had many enemies, and most of them had absolutely nothing to do with his business."

"Enemies," she repeated. "What do you mean?" Now they were getting somewhere.

Maitland glanced at the closed door of his office and then leaned closer. "Don't repeat this Luty, but the fellow wasn't very well liked."

Luty smiled eagerly and waited for more.

Maitland leaned back in his chair. "Are you sure you wouldn't like some tea?"

CHAPTER 4

"This is very nice but not very comfortable looking," Barnes murmured as he turned and surveyed the room. "I'd not fancy anyone could fall asleep on that settee. Thing looks as stiff as a plank board and so do those chairs. As a matter of fact, there's not a stick of furniture in here that looks like you could sit more than a few minutes without your backside going numb."

Witherspoon and Barnes were at the Boyd household. As they stood in the drawing room, waiting to speak to the housekeeper, the constable was studying the furnishings like a general surveying a battlefield. The inspector followed his lead and took a closer look at the furniture.

The room was done in the Empire style. The settee and the matching chairs had ornately carved backboards of heavy, dark wood and were upholstered with stiff green-and-white brocade fabric. The width of the seat on both the settee and the chairs was very shallow.

"I can't see Glover catching a catnap on anything in here," Barnes muttered. "He's too big and the seats on all the furniture too small."

Witherspoon continued his survey of the room. There was a green brocade loveseat in front of the fireplace, but it was upholstered in the same stiff brocade as the settee and had a very low back; certainly that didn't look inviting enough to sleep on. The other chairs in the room didn't look any better. "I can't imagine how Glover managed it. There's nothing in the room that looks at all comfortable, but perhaps he was really tired."

"Or perhaps he was lying," Barnes said.

"Did you sense that?" Witherspoon looked at the constable. He respected Barnes opinion as he wasn't given to rushing to judgment or assuming that everyone was guilty.

"I sensed he wasn't being completely candid," the constable replied. "But I can't put my finger on what's bothering me. Miss Clarke verified much of his story, and the clerk, Bingley, verified the note had arrived and that he'd been invited to luncheon."

The door opened and a tall, brown-haired woman wearing a gray bombazine dress stepped into the room. "I'm Hannah Rothwell. I understand you wish to speak to me."

"I'm Inspector Gerald Witherspoon and this is Constable Barnes," he began. "I'm sorry we didn't get a chance to speak with you yesterday. There are some questions we'd like to ask you."

"I had to go to the shops and order provisions for the staff. The larders were empty. Even if there's been a death in the household, people need to eat." She stared at them for a moment. "Will this take long? I've a number of tasks to do this morning. Mr. Boyd's solicitor and the vicar will be here soon."

"Are they meeting Mr. Boyd's family here?" Witherspoon asked curiously. That was a bit of luck; he'd been planning on speaking to the victim's lawyer.

"They are coming to see me, Inspector. I'm Lawrence's cousin as well as his housekeeper. We've got to arrange the funeral." She walked to the settee, sat down, and gestured at the two chairs. "Please take a seat."

They seated themselves and Barnes took out his notebook. Witherspoon wasn't sure where to begin. It hadn't occurred to him that the housekeeper might be the victim's kin. "You're Mr. Boyd's cousin?"

"I just said I was," she replied.

"Did he have many relatives?" Barnes asked. Finding out how many heirs were left to squabble over the spoils was always a good place to start a murder investigation.

"He had some cousins in Scotland, but he hasn't seen or spoken to them in years," she replied. She smiled faintly at Barnes. "But I'm not the sole heir, believe me. If I know Lawrence, and I did, I suspect he's left his estate to some ridiculous charity or an art museum."

"Mr. Boyd was a generous man, I take it," the inspector commented.

"Gracious no." She laughed heartily. "Lawrence was a mean-spirited, nasty excuse for a human being. But he did love getting his name put about on everything. That's why he was always giving charities and societies money." She leaned slightly forward. "So far, he's got his name on a park bench, a plaque at Clapham Foundling Home, and at least three annual prizes at the Amateur Artists Guild. There's the Lawrence Boyd Prize for the best pastoral watercolour, the Lawrence Boyd Prize for the most outstanding cityscape done in oils, and . . . oh, bother, I can't remember what the third one was, but it was something equally silly. I think some of the groups he belonged to simply made up prizes so they could get a bit of cash out of him."

"I see." Witherspoon took a deep breath. Sometimes, he was glad he had so few relatives. At least no one of his own blood hated him. "Er, can you give us an account of the household's movements yesterday?"

"We went to a funeral, Inspector." She looked at him as though he were a half-wit. "I believe you were informed of that fact yesterday. Have you forgotten?"

"No, ma'am, I haven't forgotten. What I'm asking for is more detail," he explained patiently. "I'd like an accounting of everything that happened yesterday from the time the household awoke until you all returned from the funeral."

Her lips pursed disapprovingly, but she shrugged. "All right, well, let's see. I got up at half past five, which is an hour earlier than usual."

"Why was that?" Barnes asked.

"I knew we were going to the funeral, and as there was also a luncheon planned, we had to take extra time to get everything ready."

"Mr. Boyd didn't mind his staff leaving on the day he had a social engagement?" Witherspoon asked.

"He was furious." She smiled broadly. "But there wasn't anything he could do about it. Helen had worked here, and we were all very fond of the girl."

"Helen was the person who died?" Witherspoon interrupted. He wanted to keep everything straight in his own mind. These were the sort of details that might turn out to be important.

"Yes." She nodded. "Helen Cleminger. She was a housemaid here for four years. She was from a small village outside St. Albans, and when she took ill, she went home. Unfortunately, she didn't recover. She caught pneumonia this winter, and it kept getting worse and worse. It finally killed the poor girl. She was only twenty-two. But as I was saying, he could hardly object to the staff wanting to pay their last respects. Oh, he tried to bully us into not going. But these days, servants have more choices. No one has to work here. There are plenty of positions about." She laughed. "Cook flat out told him if she couldn't go to Helen's funeral, she'd be moving on, and so did the tweeny and the upstairs maid."

"So Mr. Boyd relented and gave you permission," Barnes pressed. "Was he angry about it?"

"He wasn't happy, but he had a difficult time hanging onto servants in the first place so he'd not much choice. Cook came up with a menu for a cold luncheon that let him salvage his pride and act as if he were being generous in saying we could go, but I'm sure he planned on making everyone's life miserable for having the nerve to challenge his authority." She laughed again. "What he didn't know was that all of us were still planning on leaving."

"Including you?" Witherspoon watched her closely.

"Including me, Inspector," she admitted. "I'm going to Australia. I've got enough money saved to open a business and build a life for myself. Cook's going to retire, and the upstairs maid is getting married. The tweeny and the downstairs girl won't have any problem finding work as they're both fully trained."

"What time did you leave the house that morning?" Barnes asked.

"Early," she replied. "The food was all ready and in the wet larder. I'd made sure that Mary—she's the downstairs girl—had set the table properly, and I'd left Mr. Boyd's breakfast on a warming plate in the dining room. We left at half past seven; the funeral was set for ten o'clock, but it was in Helen's village church so we had to get to Paddington Station in time for the 8:10 train."

"So you went to the funeral and then came back. Can you tell us what you saw when you arrived home?" Witherspoon shifted in his seat, his backside had gone quite numb. If the rest of the furniture was this uncomfortable, he knew Glover had to be lying. Napping on one of these chairs would be like trying to sleep on a bed of rocks.

"Mr. Boyd had insisted we return in time to serve luncheon, so we came back straightaway after the funeral." She sniffed disapprovingly. "You'd have thought he and his guests could serve themselves, but oh, no, we had to come back. We barely had time to pay our respects to Helen's family. But I digress. We arrived home to find the fire wagon outside and the fire brigade all over the place."

"Were Mr. Glover and Miss Clarke here?" Barnes asked.

"Yes, it was Mr. Glover who told us that Mr. Boyd was dead." She shrugged. "I know I sound heartless, but he wasn't a very nice person. I was one of the few relatives the man had, but do you think he'd let me live here as family? He did not. He put me to work as his housekeeper and insisted I call him Mr. Boyd."

"You said he had a problem keeping staff," Witherspoon said. "What exactly did you mean?"

"People wouldn't stay," she replied. "When one is in service, taking care of a single man rather than an entire family is supposed to be one of the easier situations. But he was as hard to please as a houseful of maiden aunts. Good gracious, if there was a speck of dust on the furniture he'd scream like a banshee. If cook was a minute late getting food on the table, he'd go into the kitchen himself and humiliate the woman, and he made the poor butler's life a living hell."

"Did Leeson plan on leaving as well?" Barnes looked up from his notebook.

"He was going to retire." Hannah Rothwell grinned broadly. "The poor man deserves some peace and quiet after what he's been through with my cousin."

"Why did he stay?" Witherspoon asked curiously.

"Lawrence paid well," she replied. "That's the only reason any of us stayed. But even decent wages don't make up for being treated badly. Not these days."

Witherspoon thought about asking if Boyd had enemies and then changed his mind as the question had already been answered. Instead, he said, "Had Mr. Boyd recently sacked anyone who might want to extract revenge against him?"

Mrs. Rothwell shook her head. "Lawrence didn't sack staff. They always left on their own. At least in the time I've been here, which is ten years. Before that, I couldn't say."

Barnes asked, "How many guests were expected for luncheon yesterday?"

"Four or five. The luncheon was buffet-style and people were supposed to help themselves, so I don't recall the exact number of people." She frowned thoughtfully. "Let me see, Mr. Gibbons was coming, Mr. and Mrs. Sapington, and I think one or two others. They were all quite stunned to find out he'd been killed, of course. Mind you, that didn't stop them from eating."

"Mr. Sapington stated you insisted the guests go ahead and eat," Witherspoon said. He had no idea why that had popped into his head, but it had.

"Nonsense," she snorted derisively. "I did no such thing. When I went into the dining room to supervise the clearing up, Maud Sapington was right on my heels. We were at school together, Inspector, and Maud delighted in sneering at how I'd come down in the world. But I digress again. Before I could so much as pull the trolley away from the butler's pantry, she grabbed a plate and began filling it with roast beef."

"Did she make any comment or did she just help herself?" Barnes asked curiously. Odd behavior by anyone at a murder scene was always worth noting.

"She looked at me and said, 'There's no reason to let all this food go to waste.'" Mrs. Rothwell snorted again. "Then she stuck her head out the door and called the others to come in and eat. I was amazed. I wasn't fond of Lawrence in the least, none of us were, but it was no longer a social occasion of any sort. But Maud was always like that, pushy and greedy."

Witherspoon nodded sympathetically. "It must have been a very awkward situation for you."

She actually laughed. "It was, but it was also funny. I'm sure the story of the whole lot of themselves eating themselves silly before their host's body was even carted off by the police is already making the rounds. The Sapingtons will hate that. Arnold Sapington is a stickler for the social niceties, which is a bit of an affectation if you ask me, considering he was nothing but a builder's son from Slough. Maud doesn't care what people think of her. She never did."

It was obvious Mrs. Rothwell had no love for Maud Sapington. "I take it you've known Mrs. Sapington for quite some time," Witherspoon said.

"As I said, since we were in school," Mrs. Rothwell replied. "She was a greedy thing back then, too. Which is odd, really; she grew up with everything. Oh, her family weren't aristocrats, but they were rich as Croesus."

"Are the Sapingtons and Mr. Boyd close friends?" the inspector pressed. He wanted to find out if all of yesterday's luncheon guests disliked their host.

"Oh, good lord, no." She laughed again. "Lawrence thought Maud a silly woman and considered her husband a social-climbing upstart. He only invited them for luncheon because Walter Gibbons was going to announce that it was Lawrence who'd won the chairmanship of the Bankers Benevolent Society and not Sapington." Her smile faded. "I told you, Inspector, my cousin had a cruel streak. He wanted to watch Arnold Sapington's face when he heard the news."

Witherspoon noticed that she now referred to the victim as "Lawrence" rather than "Mr. Boyd." But he didn't think that fact had anything to do with his murder. Furthermore, she might have disliked her cousin, but she did have an alibi. "Had Mr. Boyd been worried or unduly concerned about anyone or anything of late?"

"Not that I know about," she replied. "But he'd have hardly confided in me."

"Who would he have spoken with if he had concerns?" Barnes asked.

"No one. Lawrence kept his own counsel. He was a very secretive man, Inspector, in everything. He wouldn't even let anyone see one of his paintings until he was finished with it. He once sacked a gardner for sneaking a peek at an unfinished oil painting."

"So as far as you know, no one had been threatening him or doing anything of late to cause him alarm?" Witherspoon probed.

She shook her head and then glanced at an ornate carriage clock on a small table to her left. "Is this going to take much longer?"

"I think that will be all for now," Witherspoon said. "We appreciate your help in this matter."

Mrs. Rothwell got to her feet. "I don't know that anything I've said will help find who murdered him. If I were you, I'd stay a bit and have a chat with his lawyer. He should be here soon."

"Thank you for your time, Mrs. Rothwell. In the meantime, we're going to question the rest of the staff. I expect you'd like us

to conduct our interviews below stairs. Do you have a space we
might use, perhaps the butler's pantry . . ."

"You can talk to them here." She waved him back to his seat.
"Who do you want me to send up first?"

Witherspoon smiled gratefully. "Could you ask Mr. Leeson to
spare us a few minutes. We've a few more questions for him, and
do let me know when Mr. Boyd's solicitor arrives. I'd like to insure he doesn't leave without speaking with us first."

Betsy stood on the pavement and shivered as a gust of wind
slammed into her. The day had started out bright and sunny so
she'd not bothered with her heavy jacket, just a light lavender
shawl over her dress. But May weather was treacherous, and now
dark clouds scuttled across the sky and the air had that raw heavy
scent of impending rain. She debated going back to the house for
her umbrella and jacket and then decided to risk the deluge. The
worst that could happen was she'd get wet.

She pulled her shawl tighter, crossed the road, and walked into
the greengrocer's. The clerk, a young man with a prominent Adam's
apple and wispy brown hair, was emptying cabbages into a bin.
"I'll be with you in a moment, miss." He put the sack down on the
floor, brushed off his hands, and came toward her.

After surveying all the shops in the area, Betsy had deliberately
picked this one for her first stop. A lone male clerk was always best
when it came to ferreting out information. "A pound of carrots,
please." She gave him a wide smile.

The clerk shifted to one side and reached into the shallow bin
holding carrots. "Would you like them topped?"

"Yes, please." She gave him another dazzling smile. "That's
very kind of you."

He smiled self-consciously as he twisted the green leafy tops
off the carrots, put them on the scale, and then reached back into
the bin for another one to make up a pound.

"A friend of mine works in a household near here," she began.
"But I'm not sure exactly where. I wonder how far away that is."

"I've lived in this area all my life. If you'll tell me the name of
the street, I can probably help," the clerk offered.

"Oh, that's very kind of you. Let's see, what did her last letter
say? I've just moved up from the country and I'd like to call on her.
We're from the same village, you see. It's Laurel Road; yes, that's

the name of the street. I only found out this morning that it's so close by."

"Oh, that's just up the road a bit." He pointed to his left. "Not far at all. You can't miss it."

"Thanks ever so much. I'd like half a pound of those sprouts as well." She knew Mrs. Goodge would be glad of the extra vegetables. "I do hope my friend is still there. She'd written that she was thinking of looking for another position." Betsy stepped a bit closer and lowered her voice. "She didn't like the place very much."

"She'd not have a hard time findin' work," he replied as he dumped sprouts on the scale. "Not these days. Do you know the name of the family she works for?"

"It's not a family. It's a gentleman on his own. A Mr. Boyd."

"Lawrence Boyd, the banker?"

"I believe Emma did say her employer was a banker," Betsy replied. This was going even better than she had hoped.

"Your poor friend's not goin' to be havin' an easy time of it, then," he declared. "Lawrence Boyd was murdered yesterday. It was in the morning papers."

"Murdered! Goodness, that's terrible." Betsy widened her eyes in pretended shock.

"Poor bloke was bashed on the head," the clerk said, repeating the information with obvious relish.

"The papers described how he was killed?" Betsy asked, her voice incredulous. The accounts she'd read this morning hadn't given any details at all.

"Oh, no." He leaned closed. "My mum got it from Mrs. Norton, who works next door to the Boyd house. She overheard the police talkin' about it when they was searching the grounds next to her house. She's got real good ears does Mrs. Norton, so I'm sure she didn't get it wrong."

"Why was the poor man killed?" Betsy asked.

"No one knows yet." He dumped the sprouts on the counter next to the carrots and pulled a sheet of brown paper off the roll. "Would you like anything else, miss?"

"No, that'll be all."

"Mind you, Mr. Boyd wasn't the nicest of people." The clerk slapped the paper down and then shoved the vegetables into the center. "My mum says that's why he never married again. No other woman would have him."

So Boyd was a widower, Betsy thought. That was certainly interesting news. "You mother didn't like Mr. Boyd?"

"Mum hated him. He used to buy from us, but he and Mum got into a dispute over a bill, so he took his business elsewhere." He folded the paper so that it made a nice package. "Mum had to threaten him with the law to get him to pay what he owed. But he finally did."

"He doesn't sound a nice person at all," Betsy agreed. "That's probably why Emma—that's my friend—wanted another position."

"We weren't the only merchant he squabbled with." He pulled a length of string off a roll and deftly twisted it around the packet of vegetables. "The chemists had stopped supplying him and so had the draper's shop over on Thornhill Lane. But I don't think any of the merchants were angry enough to bash the bloke's head in. That's not a particularly useful way of getting your bills paid, is it?"

"I suppose not," Betsy agreed. "Who do you think did kill him, then?"

"I've no idea." He shrugged, and then his gaze moved over Betsy's shoulder. He broke into a wide smile. "Good morning, Miss Devers. It's very nice to see you."

Betsy turned her head and saw a pretty, dark-haired young woman standing at the entrance. She wore clothes very much like Betsy's and had a shopping basket over her arm. "Hello, Mr. Clarkson." The girl smiled warmly at the clerk. "It's nice to see you as well. Have you any rutabagas today. Cook needs them for a stew."

"I've some lovely rutabagas," he replied. Without taking his gaze off the newcomer, he picked up Betsy's packet and handed it to her. "Thank you, miss," he said dismissively.

She handed him the money for the vegetables. Betsy was no fool. She wasn't going to get anything else out of this one, not when his lady love was right in front of him. "Thank you," she said politely as she turned to leave.

He didn't appear to hear her.

Smythe stood in front of the Dirty Duck Pub and hesitated for a moment before pushing the door open and stepping inside. He'd thought long and hard about the wisdom of asking Blimpey Groggins for help, but had decided that there was no point in not using a perfectly good source of information just to salvage his pride. He had plenty of money and he could afford Blimpey's fees, and just because he chose to use him, it didn't mean he couldn't do his own investigating.

Even though it was only fifteen minutes past opening time, the pub was already crowded. Dockworkers, day laborers, tally clerks, and bargemen were two deep at the bar, and there wasn't a single empty seat on the side benches. The tables were full as well, but Blimpey was in his usual spot. A rough-looking man with wild black hair and a scar bisecting his right cheek sat next to him.

Blimpey glanced in Smythe's direction, then leaned over and said something to his companion as Smythe pushed his way through the crowd. As he drew close, the man got up.

"Sorry," Smythe apologized. "I didn't mean to interrupt, but I need to 'ave a quick word with Blimpey."

"After what your lot done for Tommy Odell, I'd gladly give up my seat to you," the man said. "It's rare that people like us get any justice in this old world."

Smythe was dumbstruck. Did the entire world know the inspector's household had kept a pickpocket from hanging for a murder he'd not committed? Blast a Spaniard, this was getting out of hand.

"This is Eddie Blanding. He's Tommy's uncle. He works on a merchant ship and he only got back a few days ago," Blimpey explained quickly.

"Pleased to meet you." Smythe extended his hand and the two men shook.

"If there's ever a favor I can do for you," Eddie said, "you've just to name it. I felt real bad that I wasn't here when Tommy and Edna—that's his mum and my sister—were goin' through their troubles. But I was at sea."

"You weren't to know then," Smythe said easily. "And I appreciate the offer of a favor. Maybe I'll take you up on it one day."

"I'm here for the next three months. Blimpey knows where to find me." Eddie nodded gravely, glanced at Blimpey, and then headed for the door.

Blimpey waved at the barmaid and mouthed "two pints" as Smythe took Eddie's chair.

"Now before you get all het up," Blimpey said, "I didn't say anything to Eddie. It was Tommy and his mum that let the cat out of the bag. But Eddie's a taciturn type; he'll not be speaking out of turn about what your lot is up to."

"That's good," Smythe said. "The fewer people that know what we're about, the better. But then, you know that better than anyone. It wouldn't do you much good if every mother's son was privy to your business."

"That's why I keep my 'ead down and my ears open," he replied. Blimpey was a ginger-haired man of late middle age with a ruddy complexion and a bit of a belly. He'd once been a petty thief. However, as he possessed a phenomenal memory and the ability to pick up bits and pieces of information from a variety of sources, he soon realized he could make far more money selling information than stealing. Blimpey had no stomach for violence or prison, so he changed careers and was now a successful businessman with a vast network of informants. Impoverished noblemen, court clerks, bailiffs, shopgirls, and barmaids fed him a steady stream of facts, gossip, and speculation that he turned into a useful commodity. He sold that commodity to whoever was willing to pay his price. Smythe had been using him for years, but on their last case, it had been Blimpey who had come to them seeking help.

"Not to worry, old sport. Those of us who know the truth can keep our mouths closed." Blimpey broke off as the barmaid brought their pints and put them on the table. "Thanks, love." He waited till she'd moved off before he spoke. "I heard your inspector got that banker's murder."

"That's why I'm here," Smythe replied. He was certain that Blimpey knew as much about the victim as he did. "It's a bit of an odd one."

"Killer tried to make it look like an accident." Blimpey took a quick sip of his beer.

"That's what it looks like." Smythe lifted his pint and took a quick drink. It was a bit early for him, but he didn't wish to offend Blimpey. "Now I need you to find out what you can about Lawrence Boyd."

"Your victim?" Blimpey's eyesbrows shot up. "Is that all? I already know a bit about him. Don't you have any other names for me?"

"That's just it: we're not sure who we ought to be concentratin' on. There were only two people in the house when the murder was done, but Boyd was 'avin' a fancy luncheon that day and the guests turned up before they even carted off the body."

"Just give me the names you've got," Blimpey ordered.

"James Glover—he was Boyd's chief clerk—and there was a young woman, a Miss Eva Clarke. She's one of them typewriter girls. They were the two that were there when it happened."

"Who were the guests?"

"Arnold and Maud Sapington. He's another banker."

"I know who he is," Blimpey said. "Go on."

"And a man named Walter Gibbons. I don't know what he does for a living, but he was there to give Boyd some news about bein' the honorary chairman of the Bankers Benevolent Society."

Blimpey snorted. "There's no such thing as a benevolent banker, but this ought to do for now. Not to worry, I've already got my boys looking into the matter. Boyd had plenty of business rivals; that'll do for a start."

"You said you had some information for me already," Smythe reminded him. "What is it?" He hoped it was something really good. He'd like to show up at today's meeting with some interesting tidbits.

"Your Mr. Boyd wasn't very good at his job," Blimpey said. "He recently loaned a great deal of his bank's money to a mining enterprise called Bagley Hills out in Australia."

"I take it the venture isn't doing too well," Smythe said.

"It's a heap of red sand out in the middle of nowhere." Blimpey laughed. "You've been to the bush, Smythe. You know what it's like. Anyways, Boyd not only invested his bank's money in the thing, but he talked some of the bank's biggest clients into backing a loan for equipment and operating expenses. So not only are some of his clients furious at him, but his general partners aren't too happy."

"How come none of this has been made public?"

"Are you daft, man?" Blimpey laughed cynically. "This isn't the sort of news any bank wants bandied about. They bury this sort of information. I found out because . . . well, it's my job to know these kinds of things, and seein' as how I'm a bit beholdin' to you, I thought I'd pass this on. You might put a word in your inspector's ear to have a good look at the books."

"Thanks, Blimpey. I appreciate it."

Blimpey burped softly. "Oops, that slipped out. Sorry. Nell would have my guts for garters if she heard me belchin' this way."

"How is your good lady?" Smythe asked.

"She's fine. Mind you, a wife does change a man's habits. Time was I could break wind out of either end and not think anything of it, but not now. Nell's always going on about how to behave in public." Blimpey chuckled good naturedly. Then he sobered. "There is one thing I'd like to ask you about. It's more in the way of advice, if you know what I mean."

Smythe raised an eyebrow. "The last time I gave you advice, you ended up married."

"And it was the best bit of advice a man ever got," Blimpey declared. "That's why I'm glad you stopped by today. I need to ask you something else, and frankly, it's not the sort of thing I'd be comfortable askin' anyone else."

"What is it?"

Blimpey took a deep breath. "I told you before that the reason I wanted you and your lot to find Tommy's killer is because I thought Tommy was mine."

"I remember, and I've kept my promise. I've not told anyone. No one knows that Tommy is your son. Your secret is still safe." He took a quick sip of his beer.

"I know I can trust you. That's not what I'm worried about." He sighed heavily and looked down at the tabletop.

"Then what is it?"

"It's Nell. I feel bad about keepin' it from her. I think I should tell her."

Blimpey was still staring at the tabletop, and his voice was so low that Smythe had to lean forward to catch his words. He had no idea how to respond. This was very dangerous territory, so he took the coward's way out and said nothing.

After a long moment, Blimpey raised his head and stared at Smythe. "Well, what should I do? I don't like keepin' this kind of secret from Nell. She's been too good to me and it don't feel right."

"I'm no expert on women," Smythe muttered. "But if keepin' it to yourself makes you feel bad, then maybe you should tell her."

"You really think so?" Blimpey asked hopefully.

"She knows you weren't a saint all these years," he said.

"And she knows the kind of life I led. I never lied to her about how I made my living."

"So, she can hardly be surprised that you'd sowed a wild oat or two, can she?" Smythe pointed out.

"Of course she's got to understand," Blimpey agreed. "Once you get to be our age, you've got a past, and it's not always one you're real proud of, if you know what I mean."

"Blimpey, you're fifteen years older than me."

"I wasn't meanin' you." Blimpey shook his head impatiently. "I meant once you got to be mine and Nell's age. Mind you, you're no spring chicken. What are you, forty?"

"I'm thirty-eight," he said defensively. His age was a bit of a sore subject as Betsy was only twenty-four. It had once been an issue between them, but she'd put a stop to that nonsense.

"Now, now, don't get yourself all het up. I was only makin' a comment. So you think I ought to tell Nell?"

Smythe felt a great deal more confident now that the two of them had discussed it man to man. He also knew he'd not like to keep anything important from Betsy. "Nell's a good woman. I don't think she'd begrudge you spending a bit of time or lolly on your own flesh and blood."

"This will be a big load off my mind." Blimpey grinned broadly. "I like to share everything with my Nell."

"Glad I was able to help." Smythe drained his glass and rose to his feet. "I've got to be goin'. I'll come by in the next day or two. Thanks for the information about Boyd's business ventures. I'll put a flea in the inspector's ear to have a look in that direction."

"Don't be nervous, miss." Inspector Witherspoon gave the red-haired young woman a reassuring smile. "I'm only going to ask you a few questions. What's your name?"

"Lydia White" she replied. "But I wasn't even here when the master was killed, so I don't see what I could tell you."

"Please sit down." The inspector pointed at the chair directly across from him. "I know you weren't here, but it's important we question everyone from the household."

She sat down. "All right, then, what do you want to know?"

"How long have you been employed here, Lydia?" Witherspoon hoped Barnes was having an easier time of it. So far, he'd not learned anything useful from Boyd's servants. Barnes, on the other hand, had gone to the house next door to see if they'd seen or heard anything out of the ordinary.

"A little more than a year, sir," she replied.

Witherspoon nodded. He'd expected that sort of answer. Except for the housekeeper and the butler, virtually the entire staff was relatively new. "Did you like working for Mr. Boyd?"

She hesitated for a second and then said, "I know it's wrong to speak ill of the dead, but I didn't like it at all. Mr. Boyd wasn't very nice to us. Truth is, I was looking for a new position."

"How was he 'not nice'?"

"He never wanted to give us our full afternoon out," she said. "On your free day, you're supposed to be allowed off at noon, but he was always finding little jobs and things for you to do before you could go. It weren't just me; he did it to everyone. He kept a list of who had what afternoon off, and on those days, he'd make Mrs. Rothwell give us these stupid things to do that kept us here for half the afternoon. Last Friday he had poor Mary—she's the upstairs girl—cleaning out the attic before she could get off. She missed her train and didn't get to go home to see her parents."

He'd heard much the same from the others. Boyd wasn't very good to his servants, but from what the inspector had observed, half of London's gentry treated their staff badly. Strange, really, that people who had so much could begrudge those who had so little a few hours of leisure.

"And he wanted me to clean the paint off the floor in his studio on my day out last week," she continued. "The only reason I didn't have my afternoon ruined was because he suddenly decided he had to start workin' on a new painting. He never lets any of us in the studio when he's painting. Doesn't like people to see his work, not that any of us would want to anyway, but that's the only reason I got my day out."

"Did you see Mr. Boyd yesterday before you left for your friend's funeral?"

"No."

"When was the last time you saw him alive?"

"The day before he was murdered. I saw him come out of his study." Lydia grinned, exposing a mouthful of lovely white teeth. "He'd just had an awful row with Mrs. Rothwell and he looked fit to be tied."

"He had a row with Mrs. Rothwell?" Witherspoon repeated.
"How do you know?"

"I heard it," Lydia replied. She looked over her shoulder at the
door to the drawing room. "I don't suppose telling you about it
will make any difference now. We're all goin' to be turfed out now
that he's dead. Mind you, there's plenty of positions about, but I'm
thinkin' about goin' back home and getting a job at the shoe factory. They've just opened up two of them in Nottingham and one's
right close to my home. I don't really like London all that much . . ."

"That sounds perfectly splendid, miss," Witherspoon interrupted. "But could you tell me a bit more about Mrs. Rothwell's
row with Mr. Boyd? Exactly when did this happen?"

"Like I said, the day before he was murdered. It was early of the
morning and the two of them were in Mr. Boyd's study. I'd come
down the back stairs to get my shoes out of the kitchen. They'd
gotten wet in the rain, so I'd left them by the cooker to dry. The
rest of the household was still upstairs; not even Leeson had come
down yet. The house was real quiet, so I could hear everything."
She paused and took a breath. "I'd started back up the stairs when
I heard Mrs. Rothwell shouting loud enough to wake the dead.
Then he'd shout right back at her and then she'd scream at him. It
was awful but it was interesting, too."

"You were on the back stairs," he clarified.

"That's right. The back stairs are just on the other side of the
study," she said.

"Could you hear what they were shouting at each other?"

"There's nothing wrong with my ears, sir; I heard them plain as
I hear you. I sat down on the steps and had a good listen." She giggled. "I know it was wrong, but I couldn't help myself."

"Of course you'd be curious," he agreed. "Do go on."

"Mrs. Rothwell was shouting that she'd trusted him and
now he'd let her down. Mr. Boyd was yelling that it wasn't his fault
and that there were always risks involved. She called him a fool
and an idiot. I thought he was going to sack her, but all he did was
scream that it wasn't his fault and that he had enough worries without her adding to them."

"Then what happened?"

She frowned. "They seemed to realize how loud they were, so
they dropped their voices and I couldn't hear. Then she left the
room. I heard the study door open, so I got up and tiptoed up the

stairs to landing." She smiled self-consciously. "I didn't want her to catch me sitting on the bottom stairs. It would have been obvious I'd been listening."

"Yes, that's very understandable," Witherspoon said softly.

"I was going to go back to my room, but I heard Mr. Boyd come out of the study and come down the hall. Honestly, he looked like he wanted to kill someone."

"You could see him from where you were standing?"

"Oh, yes, I just ducked back on the landing and stood in the shadows. He couldn't see me, but from where I stood I could see him as clear as day. His jaw was set and his face was redder than one of cook's strawberry tarts. He stomped down the hallway past the larders and out the side door. He slammed it as hard as he could, too. Didn't care a toss if he woke anyone else in the house. That's the kind of man he was, Inspector, selfish and mean to the core."

"Do you know where he was going?" Witherspoon asked. "You did say it was very early in the morning."

"Out to his studio," she replied. "When he was workin' on a painting, he liked to go out there for a time before he went into his office, and I know he was in a hurry to get this painting finished. I'd overheard him tell Leeson he needed it finished before the luncheon."

"You're sure you don't remember anything else?" the inspector asked. He'd found that people could often recall a tidbit or two if you pressed them just a bit.

"I might have," Lydia said slowly, her brow furrowed in concentration. "I think I heard her tell him something like, 'You'd better do something to make it right if you know what's good for you.' But they'd already lowered their voices by then so I can't be sure. But that's what it sounded like she was saying."

"You'd better do something to make it right," he repeated. He wondered what that meant.

CHAPTER 5

The rain began in earnest by the time they gathered at Upper Edmonton Gardens for their afternoon meeting. Mrs. Goodge had the table laid and the tea ready as the last one to arrive, Wiggins, walked in the back door.

"It's pourin' out there." He swept off his cap and shrugged out of his coat as he crossed the kitchen to the coat tree. "Cor blimey, I thought it was goin' to crack my head open, it's coming down that 'ard. Where's Fred?"

"He's upstairs under your bed, sound asleep," Mrs. Jeffries replied. More like he'd climbed up on the lad's bed, but she pretended she didn't know that. "There's a towel on the chair by the cooker. Dry yourself off and come have your tea."

"Can I go first?" Luty helped herself to a slice of Mrs. Goodge's warm brown bread. "I think it's only fair considerin' how I've been unable to help much in the last two cases we've had."

"Of course, Luty," Mrs. Jeffries replied. "I don't think anyone would object."

"Thank you." She reached for the butter pot and put a dab on her bread plate. "I didn't think I was goin' to have much luck today considerin' how it started." She frowned as she slathered butter on her bread. "I went to see one of my banker acquaintances, but he turned out to be as useless as teats on a bull . . ." She broke off as series of grunts and gasps erupted from the others. Betsy giggled, Wiggins was holding back a snicker and not doing a very good job of it as it escaped as a series of snorts, Mrs. Goodge had her hand

76

over her mouth to smother a chuckle, and Smythe was laughing so hard his chair was shaking.

"Oh dear," Luty exclaimed. "What did I say . . . uh-oh, I guess you're not supposed to say 'teats on a bull.' "

"It's not generally a phrase one uses in polite company." Hatchet smiled broadly.

"But it is one that's quite useful," Mrs. Goodge declared. "I've known a number of people who fit that description."

"I'm sure it expressed precisely what you meant to say," Mrs. Jeffries agreed. "Do go on with your report."

The others quieted down and Luty continued. "As I was sayin', the banker was useless. The only thing I got out of him was that Lawrence Boyd wasn't well liked. Well Nell's bells, we already knew that. The fellow was murdered, so that means someone sure hated him. Anyways, I didn't let one little setback stop me; I went and paid a visit to my friend Fiona Arburton. Her husband's in banking, and Fiona loves gossip they way most of us love cream cakes. She had plenty to say. When I first got there, I thought I was in for another disappointment as she didn't know much about Boyd exceptin' that he was an artist as well as a banker. Then I happened to mention the names of the people who were due at the luncheon, and she had plenty to say about them."

"Who specifically?" Hatchet asked. He hoped that she'd not come across the same information he'd learned.

"For starters, she was surprised that Mrs. Sapington had agreed to set foot in the Boyd house." Luty paused dramatically. "Maud Sapington hated Lawrence Boyd. It seems Mr. Boyd had jilted Maud twenty years ago and eloped with her sister, Marianna. It was quite a scandal at the time. The wedding had already been announced and the banns read in the local church."

"That poor woman must have been terribly humiliated." Betsy shook her head. She was a bit disappointed that she wasn't the one to tell them that Boyd had once had a wife, but she didn't begrudge Luty her moment of triumph. "I can't say I'd blame her for wanting to kill the man who did that to her. But waiting twenty years is a bit odd, don't you think?"

"I thought Boyd didn't 'ave a wife," Wiggins exclaimed.

"He doesn't now," Luty explained. "Marianna died of scarlet fever a year after she married Boyd. According to what Fiona told me, Boyd didn't even let Maud and her parents know that Marianna was on her deathbed, so they never got to see her before she died."

"I take it there was a rift when Marianna eloped with Boyd?" Mrs. Jeffries said.

"Sure was. Maud and her parents were so furious, they refused to see or speak to the couple. When Marianna died so soon after marryin' him, it was a double blow." Luty shook her head. "Sad, isn't it."

"The family probably thought they had plenty of time to make it up with her," Mrs. Goodge commented. "I've seen situations like that before: families squabble and say terrible things to one another and for a few years no one speaks, then someone swallows their pride and before you know it, all is forgiven. But it seems like in this case they never got the chance."

"I agree with Betsy." Smythe frowned in puzzlement. "Why would Maud Sapington wait twenty years to take her vengeance?"

"We don't know she did, but I certainly think we should continue thinking of her as a suspect," Mrs. Jeffries commented. "That sort of public humiliation could be a powerful motive."

"Maybe it weren't just gettin' jilted," Wiggins suggested. "Maybe she was still mad about not gettin' to say a proper good-bye to her sister when she died."

"That's certainly possible," Mrs. Jeffries said. "It would be helpful if we knew her movements on the morning of the murder."

"I'll 'ave a go at that," Wiggins volunteered.

"That was really about all I learned." Luty grinned. "But I figured it was pretty good. Twenty years might have passed since Maud got left at the altar, but I've known people who could hold grudge for a lot longer than that. Maybe Maud Sapington was just bidin' her time, waiting for a chance to kill him. Maybe yesterday, she got that chance."

"She might have hated Boyd," Mrs. Goodge said, "but I think she got over him well enough. She married Arnold Sapington, and before that, she was engaged to her cousin."

"Why didn't she marry him?" Betsy asked curiously. "Did she break her engagement?"

"No, he died."

"Maud Sapington didn't seem to 'ave much luck when it comes to 'angin' onto a fiancé," Wiggins said. "She let two of 'em get away."

Mrs. Goodge frowned at the footman and continued speaking. "His name was Nicholas Cutlip and he was a distant cousin. But he drowned in an accident, and a year later, Maud married her father's chief clerk, Arnold Sapington."

"So he married the boss's daughter," Smythe said softly. "That's one way to advance your career."

"But just because she was engaged to a fellow that died and married someone else doesn't mean she didn't hate Lawrence Boyd," Luty insisted. She wasn't about to give up her suspect without cause.

"That is very true." Mrs. Jeffries glanced around the table. "And we will most certainly keep her in the forefront of our investigation. Hatchet, would you like to go next?"

"Thank you. I too found out something very interesting. According to my sources in the financial world, the general partners of Boyd's bank weren't very happy with the way Lawrence was managing the business."

"Did they want to sack him?" Wiggins asked eagerly.

Hatchet shook his head. "They couldn't even if they wanted to. Boyd controlled the majority of shares in the bank. But the board could make his life miserable enough that he'd resign and they'd be free to bring in a professional money man."

"What had he done?" Smythe asked.

"He made a substantial number of bad loans," Hatchet replied. "He recommended financing companies that went under and poured money into investments that went sour. One of my sources said the board was concerned that Boyd had gotten so involved in this charity work and his art that he'd completely lost interest in the bank's business."

"Were any of the board members angry enough to kill him?" Luty asked. "That's one way of gettin' shut of someone who's pouring your money down a rat hole—and the fastest, too."

"It's impossible to know precisely how angry any of the other board members might have been." Hatchet shrugged.

"How many people are on the board?" Smythe asked.

"Besides Boyd, there are three others: Evan Kettleworth, John Sawyer, and Harvey Holcomb. Next to Boyd, Sawyer and his family are the largest partners. James Stanford, one of the original partners, died years ago with no heirs."

"Do you think they warrant further investigation?" Mrs. Jeffries asked. "Should I mention their names to the inspector? Drop a few hints so he'll look in that direction?"

"For what it's worth," Smythe said quickly, "my sources told me much the same thing that Hatchet found out."

"Despite what madam says, murder is a rather drastic way of getting rid of an incompetent manager." Hatchet took a sip of tea.

"Not if the incompetent manager owns most of the bank," Luty interjected with a laugh. "But you're right, this isn't the Wild West."

Smythe wasn't so sure, but he'd wait his turn before he spoke.

"Let me have a day or two to see if I can ascertain where the board members were on the day of the murder," Hatchet suggested. He helped himself to a slice of seedcake. "That's the extent of my information, but I shall endeavor to learn more tomorrow."

"I've not found out a lot," Betsy said and then told them the few tidbits she'd gotten from the clerk at the greengrocer's, stretching it out and making more of the conversation than it had really been. She was covering up because she was a bit ashamed. Her attempts to get anything interesting out of the other shopkeepers had been a complete waste of time. All she'd heard was what the greengrocer's clerk had already told her. So she'd gone to the draper's shop he'd mentioned and gotten more interested in the curtains and the tablecloths than in asking useful questions. She'd given herself a stern talking to, tried her best to get something about their victim out of the shopkeeper—a stuck-up old stick of a woman who looked down her nose at Betsy—and gone to the shop next door. But it was a dressmaker's and it had been busy, so she'd sat down to look at the pattern book while she waited for the customers to clear out, and she'd gotten completely carried away. It was too much for any soon-to-be bride to resist. The outfits had been so beautiful—and the wedding dresses! There'd been over half a dozen patterns! "It's not much," she finished, "but I'll get back out there tomorrow and have another go at it."

"Why don't you see what you can learn about Maud Sapington," Mrs. Jeffries suggested. "Ask a few questions in her neighborhood. So far, she's the person who might have had the most personal reason to hate Boyd."

Betsy nodded enthusiastically. "That's a wonderful idea. The only thing the shopkeepers in Boyd's neighborhood want to talk about is what a tight-fisted miser he was."

"Do you remember where the Sapington's live?" Mrs. Jeffries suspected that the maid was having a difficult time concentrating on the case. She didn't really blame her; planning a wedding, even a simple one, was often a strain on a bride.

"It's Mayfair, isn't it?" Betsy frowned in annoyance. She'd forgotten the street address but didn't want to admit it.

"Number 34 Parrington Street," the housekeeper supplied.

"My turn," Smythe said. Without mentioning his source's name, he gave them a quick, concise report on the information Blimpey had given him. "So you see, my source is sayin' the same thing Hatchet heard, that Boyd is muckin' up his job. Only the way my source tells it, it isn't just the general partners that are furious, some of his clients are as well."

"Are there any particular clients that have lost enough to want to take their pound of flesh?" Mrs. Jeffries asked.

"My source is workin' on finding out that very thing," he continued. "Once I hear something, get any names of likely suspects, I'll take a look at what they mighta been doin' on the day Boyd was killed." He knew that Mrs. Jeffries would find a way to mention these new suspects to the inspector. She made certain that every idea, even the ones they'd decided were a bit far-fetched, was dropped into conversation with the inspector. "In the meantime, there's a number of pubs and a hansom stand not far from the Boyd house. I thought I'd have a chat with the drivers and see if any of them remembers takin' any fares to the Boyd house near the time of the murder. See if there was someone other than Glover and the luncheon guests that might have gone there that day."

"So you'd be lookin' for someone who went there between ten forty-five that morning and half past eleven?" Wiggins said. Constable Barnes had told Mrs. Jeffries that based on the statements of Eva Clarke and James Glover, they were sure the murder must have happened during this time frame. "That's a busy neighborhood. You'll 'ave a difficult time sussin' out anything."

"I might get lucky, too." Smythe grinned. "That's happened to us more than once."

"Indeed it has," Mrs. Jeffries added. There were times when she was sure providence had deliberately sent them just the right information they needed to solve the case. But she always believed that

God worked in mysterious ways, and deep in her heart, she knew he didn't like killers running about the streets.

"And you can always pick up a tidbit or two in a pub," Mrs. Goodge declared. "Nothing loosens tongues like gin or beer. Unfortunately, I didn't have many loose tongues in my kitchen today. The only bit I found out was that Lawrence Boyd was very pleased to have beaten out his rivals for the honorary chairmanship of that charity . . ." She broke off, frowning. "What's it called?"

"The Bankers Benevolent Society," Mrs. Jeffries supplied. "But not to worry, you weren't the only one who didn't learn anything useful. I went all the way over to St. Thomas's Hospital to find Dr. Bosworth only to be told he was in Edinburgh at a medical conference."

Dr. Bosworth was another one of their special friends. He'd been involved in one of their earlier cases and had helped them ever since. He'd spent part of his career in San Francisco, where he'd become an expert on gunshot wounds. His observations led him to the conclusion that a thorough examination of both the victim and even the scene of the crime would yield useful clues to the identity of the killer.

Bosworth tried his best to get all the surgeons working with the Metropolitan Police Force to take his methods seriously, but to date, he'd not had much luck. But the household of Upper Edmonton Gardens had great respect for him and his views. He was also very good at getting hold of postmortem reports.

"So I guess that means we'll not find out anything about the postmortem," Smythe muttered. "Blast. That might have been useful in tracking down the kind of weapon that was used."

"When is the good doctor due back?" Hatchet helped himself to another slice of cake.

"Tomorrow," she replied. "And I intend to be sitting outside his office door when he gets to the hospital." She didn't tell the others, but she was sure she'd been followed today. This morning, just as she'd reached the corner and turned onto Holland Road, she'd seen a man step from the vestibule of St. John's Church. She'd thought nothing of it at the time; people frequently came in and out of St. John's. But she'd noticed the man had a long black scarf around his neck, and when she'd gotten off the omnibus at St. Thomas's, she was sure she saw the same fellow getting off as well. She'd recognized the scarf. She'd not seen him board the omnibus, but then she'd not been looking either. She'd told herself it was just a coincidence, that the man had business in that part of town. But when she'd spotted him again on her way home, she thought perhaps it wasn't just her imagination. But she couldn't be sure and she wasn't certain she ought to say anything to the others. They'd already been warned about keeping an eye out for Nivens and his minions, so they wouldn't do anything foolish. No, she'd wait and see if anything odd happened again. She didn't wish to cry wolf, upset the others, and then come to the conclusion that the entire incident was simply a coincidence. And coincidences did happen. She looked at Wiggins. "How did you do today?"

"Pretty poorly." Wiggins sighed. "I 'ad the worst run of luck. I got chased off Laurel Road by the woman I think is Boyd's housekeeper, and then I tried speaking to half a dozen other people in the neighborhood but no one knew anything. Honestly, it's shockin' 'ow little interest some people take in their neighbors. You'd think with a murder right under their noses, they'd be concerned. But no, most of the ones I spoke with didn't give a fig. People are selfish, aren't they. They're only interested in their own little world."

"You just had a run of bad luck," Mrs. Goodge said stoutly.

"I know." He smiled ruefully. "But it was odd, runnin' into so many people that just didn't seem to care a whit. But I'll get back out there tomorrow. I thought I'd try the housemaids at the Boyd house, and then I was thinkin' I might have a chat with someone who works at Miss Clarke's lodgin' house."

Mrs. Jeffries smiled broadly. "That's an excellent idea. You're absolutely correct. We mustn't ignore Miss Clarke. Considering all we've learned of Lawrence Boyd, she might have had reason to want him dead. But don't forget about Maude Sapington. You'll not have time to do everything."

Wiggins had forgotten he'd volunteered to try to trace her movements. "Maybe I ought to put off goin' to Miss Clarke's neighborhood until the day after tomorrow."

"Would you like someone else to try to trace Mrs. Sapington's movements?" the housekeeper suggested. "I could have a go at it."

"No, no," he said quickly. "I can do both. I can put off Miss Clarke's neighborhood until later."

"Good." The housekeeper nodded in approval. "Anything else you'd like to add?"

Wiggins hesitated for a moment. "No, that's all." He'd been tempted to tell them about the man he'd seen when he left the café today, but he decided they'd think he was being silly. It was just a fellow in a flat workman's cap and gray jacket, an ordinary working man. Yet Wiggins had spotted him through the window of the café when he'd been talking to the counter girl; the chap had stood right outside, staring in through the glass. He'd not thought much about the bloke. After all, working men were all over London. Yet he'd seen the man again an hour later, when he'd gone back to have another go at Laurel Road. For some reason, he'd glanced over his shoulder and there the fellow was, less than half a block back. The bloke had slowed then and began staring at the house numbers as he walked, trying to make it seem as though he was looking for an address. But Wiggins knew a trick when he saw one. He'd done that very same thing a number of times. There was something about the chap that put Wiggins on his guard. He didn't care if he was being silly; he'd keep a sharp eye out, and if he spotted this bloke again, he'd tell the others.

Mrs. Jeffries poured two glasses of sherry and handed one to the inspector. "Here you are, sir."

"Thank you, Mrs. Jeffries." He took a sip and sighed with pleasure. "One doesn't wish to become dependent on alcohol, but I must say, this does fill the bill nicely."

"I hardly think you're in danger of becoming dependent, sir." She sat down. "How did the investigation go today, sir?"

"As one would expect," he replied. "The house-to-house didn't yield any results and that was disappointing, though a maid at the house next door reported that she saw someone in a long coat climbing over the fence in their back garden shortly after the fire started."

"You don't think that's significant?" she asked.

"Not really." He smiled faintly. "I'm afraid it's a case of 'crying wolf.' According to the other servants, the girl has a habit of telling tales, so I'm not sure we ought to put much credence in the report."

"That's too bad, sir," Mrs. Jeffries said sympathetically. "You might have had a witness there. Did the girl get a look at his face? If she saw him again, could she recognize him?" She made a mental note to find out the maid's name and address. Maybe this time the girl wasn't crying wolf.

"I'm going to speak to her myself," he said. "But I'm not expecting very much in the way of useful information. But it's important to investigate all clues, even the ones that might be from
unreliable people."

"Were you able to speak to Mr. Boyd's servants?" she pressed.
"I know they weren't in the house when the murder happened, but
they might have seen or noticed something out of the ordinary either before they left yesterday morning or after they returned."

"Actually, one of them told me that the housekeeper had had a
dreadful row with Mr. Boyd the day before the murder," he said
and then relayed the conversation he'd had with the maid.

"Oh dear, that certainly doesn't sound very nice," she commented. "But of course, the housekeeper is the one person who
couldn't have committed the murder. She was with the others at a
funeral."

"But was she?" Witherspoon frowned thoughtfully.

"Do you have reason to believe she didn't go to the funeral?"

"No, but I didn't specifically ask any of the servants if they'd all
been together the whole time."

"But surely someone would have told you if they hadn't," Mrs.
Jeffries pointed out.

"Would they?" He looked doubtful. "Some people think the less
they say to a policeman, the better."

"Yet the maid told you about the row," Mrs. Jeffries observed.
"Surely she'd have mentioned it if Mrs. Rothwell hadn't gone to
the funeral."

"Perhaps." He smiled cynically. "But I didn't specifically ask
that question."

"I see."

"I concentrated on what time they'd all left that morning and
what time they returned. I didn't ask anyone if Mrs. Rothwell had
been absent for part of the time. I must make sure I do ask that
very thing tomorrow. If I've learned one thing, Mrs. Jeffries, it's
that one mustn't ever take anything for granted. Let's be honest
here: there's a goodly number of working people who don't consider the police their friends. They don't ever volunteer information."

"That's true, sir," she replied, though she thought it highly unlikely that all the staff would protect the housekeeper. Besides, the
maid hadn't been shy about telling Witherspoon about the house-

keeper's row with Boyd, so she obviously wasn't trying to protect her. Yet she didn't wish to argue the point with Witherspoon. She didn't want him to have any reason to doubt his abilities or lose confidence in the investigation. "Were you able to get any useful information from Mr. Boyd's bank staff?"

"We spoke to James Glover again, but I suspect I'll have to go back. Merchant banking is quite complicated, and I'm not sure I understand how it works. I wasn't sure what questions I ought to be asking or even if I ought to be looking into his business affairs at all. But I can't ignore it, can I? Someone did murder the fellow."

"Of course you must look into his business," she declared. "As you always say, sir, one mustn't leave any stone unturned when dealing with murder."

"One must be thorough." Witherspoon relaxed a bit. Talking about his cases with Mrs. Jeffries was so very helpful. It clarified his thoughts. "I had a brief word with Boyd's solicitor today, but he wasn't able to tell me anything about who benefits financially from Boyd's death because he says it's dreadfully complicated. I've an appointment to see him tomorrow morning." He yawned. "It's going to be a very busy day, I'm afraid."

"I'm sure you'll manage, sir," she said cheerfully. "You always do."

She continued chatting with him. She listened carefully and made sympathetic noises at the appropriate moment to bolster his spirits and raise his confidence. By the time he was ready to go in and eat his dinner, he'd gotten a great deal of frustration off his chest and she'd found out everything he'd heard and most of what he'd seen that day.

She also managed to slip in an idea or two of her own. Tomorrow, she was certain he'd have a closer look at Boyd's business partners. She rather agreed with Luty on that subject. People did get upset when you were pouring their money down a rat hole, and being murdered for incompetence might be unusual, but she'd bet her quarterly wages that it had happened before.

The next morning, Mrs. Goodge got the others out of her kitchen only moments before her guest arrived. "Come in, Irma," she said as she ushered her in the back door and down the hall. "It's been ages since we've seen one another."

Irma Ballard was a former colleague of Mrs. Goodge. They'd

worked together when Irma had been a lowly scullery maid and Mrs. Goodge the head cook at Lord Melbury's country estate near Reigate. Irma had risen substantially in the world since those days and now owned a small restaurant just off Sloane Street in Belgravia.

"Go right on in and have a seat and we'll have us a nice chat about old times." Mrs. Goodge pointed toward the kitchen table, which was set with a pot of tea and her nice china. A tray of freshly baked hot cross buns was sitting on the counter.

Irma stood in kitchen doorway and surveyed the room. "It's not as big as our old kitchen, is it?"

"No," Mrs. Goodge admitted as she picked up the plate of buns and put them on the table. "But then my employer is only a police inspector, not a peer of the realm." She smiled at her guest.

Irma's hair was completely white, her eyes hazel, and her nose a sharp, hawkish shape. She was dressed in a gray-and-blue striped day dress with a high collar and long, puffy sleeves. Her hat was an elegant blue bonnet with a tiny veil and one small feather on the side. A long string of pearls was visible through the opening of her short blue cloak. She'd either dressed in her best or she'd been very successful in her life. "That's a bit of come down in the world for you, isn't it?" Irma sniffed and pulled a white lace-edged handkerchief from her sleeve.

"Yes, I suppose it is," Mrs. Goodge said cheerfully. "But I'm old and I was lucky to find the position. Not many people want to hire someone my age, and frankly, if I'd not found the inspector, I don't know what I'd have done."

Irma blinked in surprise and then her plain face split in a wide grin. "I expect you'd have done all right. Just the smell of those buns is making my mouth water. I'll warrant you can still hold your own when it comes to cookin' and bakin'."

Mrs. Goodge laughed. It was amazing how a bit of honesty could clear the air. "Then sit yourself down and let's have us a nice old natter. How's your husband?"

"He's even older and crankier than I am." She laughed. "But we're both in good health so we've no reason to complain. Sorry I was a bit stroppy when I first come in, but the truth is, I was ever so surprised to get your note yesterday. Well, I wasn't sure why you wanted me to come by."

Mrs. Goodge used her serving fork to put two buns on Irma's

plate. "I imagine you were surprised. I wanted to see you. It's nice to chat with someone from the old days. So many of the ones we knew are gone now."

"I know just what you mean. Did you hear that Lizzie Drucker died this past winter? She was younger than both of us." Irma picked up a bun and took a bite.

"Oh no." Mrs. Goodge was genuinely distressed. "Lizzie was ever such a nice person."

"It was pneumonia that took her." Irma swallowed her food and reached for her tea. "She'd gone to live with her daughter in Bournemouth, poor thing."

They chatted about old friends and old times, which was precisely the way Mrs. Goodge had planned the conversation. "I understand that Minnie Pratt went to work for some banker. Now what was the name?" The cook trailed off and pretended to concentrate. "Oh, yes, now I remember, a man named Lawrence Boyd. That's right, the man that was just murdered. That's what made me think of her. I do hope Minnie is all right. You remember what a timid little thing she was."

"That can't be right." Irma shook her head. "Minnie left service and went to Birmingham. She got a position as a matron at a girl's school. Which is odd, when you think of it—she could barely read or write. But I do know who you're talking about. That banker lived just around the corner from our restaurant. It's quite a posh area, if I do say so myself."

"My gracious, really? Did he ever eat at your restaurant?" This was going even better than she'd hoped.

"Only once that I know about. He came in with that awful Mr. Gibbons and they had a meal together."

"You knew him by sight?" Mrs. Goodge thought that a bit strange.

"Oh, no, Mr. Gibbons kept mentioning his name. This was only two weeks ago, so I quite recall the incident. They came in and had a meal together, but that awful Mr. Gibbons didn't seem to be enjoying himself at all."

"What's so awful about Mr. Gibbons?"

Irma snorted derisively. "He's one of our regulars, and as such, he thinks he can walk all over people. Honestly, I wish he'd take his business elsewhere. He's just one of those people that have been soured on life, if you know what I mean."

"Maybe something happened to him when he was much younger," Mrs. Goodge suggested.

"Nonsense. He's not the first person to have had a fiancée go off and marry someone else," Irma said briskly. "That's supposedly why he's such a miserable old grouch. At least that's what Adelaide—she helps us do the washing up every night—says about him. Her aunt's been his housekeeper for years, so I expect Adelaide knows a bit about the man. But it seems to me that's just an excuse; some people simply enjoy being disagreeable. By the way, did you know that Harriet Day married a merchant sailor and went to live in one of them heathen countries in the Far East?"

"No, I hadn't heard that," Mrs. Goodge replied. Drat, she'd forgotten what a chatterbox Irma could be.

"Strange that I thought of her, isn't it?" Irma took a quick sip of tea. "But of course I would. We were talking about that cranky Mr. Gibbons, and Harriet was the maid to his fiancée. Now what was her name? Oh, yes, now I remember. She was Marianna Reese. Oh, my gracious, that's right! She married Lawrence Boyd." Irma's jaw dropped as she realized the connections. "Gracious, no wonder Gibbons looked like thunder that night. He was having dinner with the very man who'd stolen his fiancée."

"The Lawrence Boyd who was just murdered?" Mrs. Goodge asked softly. She reached for the teapot. "Do have some more tea."

"I don't want to overstay my welcome," Irma replied. "But honestly, it's lovely to see you and be able to talk about anything I like. When I'm at the restaurant, we've got to be so careful all the time. It does get so wearing, and John does tell me I do go on a bit."

"You don't go on at all." Mrs. Goodge refilled her cup. "It's wonderful to be able to chat with an old friend. Now, tell me more about your Mr. Gibbons and his dinner with Lawrence Boyd."

Inspector Witherspoon and Constable Barnes stepped into the office of Reese and Cutlip, Merchant Bankers. The clerks, all busily working at their desks, looked up one by one. Apparently, the sight of a uniformed policeman in their midst was a bit of a surprise for they all gaped at the two officers. The inspector stepped forward just as a door on the far side of the room opened and an older man appeared. "May I help you," the man asked as he came toward them.

"We would like to see Mr. Sapington," Witherspoon replied.

They had been going to see Boyd's solicitor this morning, but as he'd been unexpectedly called out of town, Witherspoon had decided to speak to Boyd's luncheon guests again.

"Is Mr. Sapington expecting you?" The man regarded them over the top of his spectacles. "I'm Mr. Bateman, Mr. Sapington's chief clerk."

"Mr. Bateman, please ask Mr. Sapington if he can spare us a few moments," Barnes said.

"I can spare you as many moments as you need." Arnold Sapington stood in the open doorway just behind the elderly clerk. He stared at them. "Come in, please."

Witherspoon and Barnes followed him inside. Sapington went back to his desk and sat down. He regarded the policemen steadily. "Why are you here?"

"We'd like to ask you a few more questions," Witherspoon said. He noticed there were two empty chairs right in front of the man's desk.

"I don't see how I can help you." Sapington shrugged. "By the time my wife and I arrived for luncheon, Lawrence, Mr. Boyd, was already dead."

"That's true, sir." Witherspoon tried to think of why he wanted to speak to this person again, but for the life of him, he couldn't quite remember.

"Did you come to your office that day, sir?" Barnes asked. His knees were hurting him something fierce and he hated being kept standing like this.

Sapington's eyebrows rose in surprise. "I was here for a little while. Why? Am I considered a suspect?" He seemed amused by the prospect.

"We're only trying to establish the facts, sir," Barnes replied.

"What time did you leave for your luncheon?" Witherspoon asked. He too didn't like being kept standing. He was certain that Sapington was doing it deliberately.

Sapington thought for a moment. "It was probably eleven o'clock or thereabouts. No, no, wait, I left a bit earlier than that because I had to go to my tailor on Bond Street, then I went home and collected my wife. You know what women are like; it took ages before she was ready, so it must have been half past twelve before we left our house."

"Let me make sure I understand this, sir." Barnes hadn't bothered to take out his notebook; writing while standing up was simply too difficult. He'd just make sure he remembered all the details of Sapington's statement. "You left here a few minutes before eleven, went to your tailors on Bond Street, then went home to collect your wife. By half past twelve you were on your way to Mr. Boyd's. Is that the correct sequence of events?"

Again, Sapington thought for a moment. "It was probably closer to half past ten or ten fifteen when I left here. Frankly, Constable, I wasn't really watching the time." He shrugged. "I had no reason to keep my eye on the clock, so I did what I came in to do and then went about my business."

"Perhaps one of your staff will recall exactly when you left?" Witherspoon suggested.

Sapington laughed. "I imagine they will, Inspector. I'm the boss, so I expect my comings and goings are of some importance to them. When the cats away, the mouse will play. By all means, go ahead and speak to the staff."

Witherspoon smiled faintly. "Thank you, sir. That's very cooperative of you."

"I have nothing to hide," he replied.

"Then I'm sure you won't mind giving us the name of your tailor," Barnes added.

"'E didn't give a toss about his bank," Jeremiah Fitch declared. "All he wanted to do was get 'is name in the papers and paint 'is ruddy pictures. It's a wonder they didn't toss 'im out on 'is ear."

Smythe had spoken to half a dozen people this morning, and this was the first time he'd found anyone who knew anything about the victim or any of their list of suspects. He measured his words carefully. Jeremiah Fitch was half drunk but not so far gone as to be useless. But if he had another pint of the fine ale here in the Gray Goose Pub, it might be a different story altogether. "You ought to know. You worked for Boyd long enough."

"Worked for 'im for ten years, I did." Fitch rubbed his nose. He was a balding man of late middle age with weatherworn skin, blue eyes, and a weak chin. He wore a gray coat two sizes too large for his skinny frame, a dirty gray shirt with a frayed collar, and black trousers held up with an old leather belt. "I used to watch him go into that buildin' 'e called a studio and do 'is paintin'. I'm the one that tore the original windows out and put them big ones in for 'im."

"Why'd you stop workin' for 'im?" Smythe asked.

"I didn't." Fitch shrugged and took another quick sip. "'E just stopped 'avin' work for me. I weren't a proper groundsman or gardner, you see, more like a jack of all trades. I'd do fer 'im whenever 'e needed a bit o' carpentry or somethin' like that done. I used to work in the buildin' trade, I did. Mr. Boyd would 'ave me in whenver 'e needed a stair replaced or windows done or a door to be hung. But the past year, 'e's not done much but paint in that ruddy studio. I don't see how 'e could stand all them hours out there. Cold as a whore's heart in the winter and stifling hot in the summer. It couldn'a been comfortable for him."

"Why not?"

"It were only half finished at best. The last job I did for him was them windows, and I was goin' to do the ceilin' next. But 'e told me not to bother. He said he liked it that way."

"'E sounds a strange bird." Smythe took a quick sip of his beer. "The sort of fellow that had a lot of enemies."

Fitch laughed softly. "That's true. 'E weren't well liked. Odd though, he were right sociable. Always off to charity dos and vying to be the honorary chairman of this and that."

"Snob was he?" Smythe muttered. He really wasn't making any progress at all. This might be interesting general information, but it wasn't going to help them find the killer.

Fitch shook his head. "He were a toff, that's for sure. But it was more like he wanted people to take notice of 'im."

"When was the last time you saw 'im?"

"A day or so before the murder," Fitch replied. "I stopped in to see if he'd changed him mind about pullin' that old ceiling down, but he told me to quit worryin' about it, that it was fine the way it was. Boyd usually didn't talk much to me, but that day he was excited and I was the only one there, so he started chattin' with me like we was old mates. Told me he was goin' to get it this year, that they couldn't give it to someone else and that 'e'd be the one making the speech on the big night."

"What was he on about?"

Fitch's weather-beaten face creased in a frown as he tried to remember more details. Finally, he shook his head. "I don't know that 'e ever said the name of the charity. But he was excited to be beatin' the others out."

"Beating the others out?" Smythe repeated. "What does that mean?"

Fitch grinned broadly. "There was another bunch of bankers up for it as well, and what was really makin' him happy was that he was beatin' them out for the top spot. He didn't give a toss about the benevolent society. He was just happy the other blokes were losin'."

"Benevolent society? Is that the name of the charity?" Smythe asked.

"Yeah, somethin' like that," Fitch replied. He looked down at his now empty pint. "I don't suppose you'd stand me another, would ya?"

Smythe was fairly sure he'd gotten as much information as he was going to get out the fellow, so it didn't matter how drunk he got now. "Sure, you've been right good company." He nodded to the barman. "Another pint for me friend 'ere, please."

Wiggins stopped and stared in the shop window. But instead of actually looking at the beautiful bicycle displayed behind the glass, his eyes darted to the left and the right, trying to see if he really was being followed or if it was all in his mind. He saw nothing on either side except the rush of people going about their business on the busy High Street. Wiggins whirled around and spotted his prey disappearing into a doorway directly across the road from where he stood.

The man was quick but not fast enough, and Wiggins got a good look at him before he dived through the door of the chemist's shop. It was the same man who'd followed him the day before.

Wiggins had to warn the others, had to tell them to be careful. He turned and started back the way he'd just come, but he hadn't taken more than a few steps before he stopped. It was no use going back there now; the others would all be out. Besides, he had a much better idea. He looked over his shoulder. Sure enough, the man had just stepped out of the chemist's shop.

Wiggins made sure the man had spotted him, then he sprinted across the busy road, dodging between a hansom and a water cart. "Watch where you're goin', you silly git," the cart driver yelled as he pulled his horse up, but Wiggins ran on. He looked behind him and saw the fellow charging after him. He tore around the corner and then ducked into a small side street leading to a mews. Oh, yes, this was going to be lots of fun.

CHAPTER 6

Betsy stood in front of the dressmaker's shop and gazed at the traveling dress displayed in the window. The three-quarter-length coat was in a pale green check tweed wool and opened to reveal a matching waistcoat. A white blouse with a high neck and a simple bell skirt in a dark green completed the outfit. It was beautifully tailored, practical, and pretty. Betsy knew it would suit her perfectly. She'd never in her life even thought to own something so lovely, but now, thanks to her beloved fiancé, it was within reach.

Not that she loved Smythe because of his money, quite the contrary; she'd fallen in love with him when she thought him a simple coachman. His wealth had been quite a surprise to her, but one that she'd gotten accustomed to as time passed.

Betsy grasped the door handle and stepped inside the shop. It wouldn't hurt to see how much the outfit cost, she told herself. Besides, she was close to the Sapington house and there was a chance the dressmaker might know something about the household.

The shop was small but elegantly appointed. The walls were painted a soft pale rose, and opposite the door was an Empire-style chaise lounge in pink and white stripes. A maroon rug with a cream fleur-de-lys pattern covered the polished oak floor, and a dark red privacy screen was against the wall at the far end of the shop. A small table with three straight-backed chairs crowded around it stood next to the screen. The top of the table was piled high with pattern books.

A plump, red-haired woman wearing a plain gray dress with a high black collar stood behind the counter. She was winding a length of white lace around a spindle. Shelves filled with bolts of colorful cloth, laces, and ribbons were arranged on the wall behind her.

"May I help you, miss?" The woman put down the spindle and gave Betsy a wide, welcoming smile.

Betsy relaxed a bit. Shops like this one were just a bit daunting to her. When she was on the hunt and looking for clues, she could march into any shop on the face of the earth without so much as a by-your-leave. But when she was here just for herself, it was a little uncomfortable. She wasn't sure what to do or how to act. Growing up, her clothes had been hand-me-downs or bought from a street stall. But she really loved that traveling dress. It would be perfect for anything Smythe might have in mind. "I'm interested in that ladies traveling outfit in the window."

The woman stepped out from behind the counter. "That's a checked Harris tweed. It's a very popular pattern. The material for the jacket and the skirt comes in three different colours: burgundy, blue, or the green that's on the mannequin. With your coloring, I'd recommend the blue. It will look lovely with your eyes."

"But the green is so gorgeous." Betsy smiled in pleasure.

"The blue will be just as pretty, and with eyes like you've got, it will be absolutely perfect on you. I'm Geraldine Billingston, the proprietess. Have you visited us before?"

"No, this is my first time," Betsy replied. "How long would you need to get something like that made up for me?"

"Not long, a week or ten days at the most," she replied. "We'd need to take your measurements and do a fitting. Would that do you?"

"That would be fine." Betsy wondered if she dared ask the price. Perhaps this was the sort of place that simply handed you the bill when you came to collect the dress? Drat, she wished she knew what to do. "Do you do wedding dresses as well?" she blurted.

Geraldine Billingston's brows drew together. "Is it for you, miss?"

"I'm getting married next month."

"And you're just now getting the dress ordered?" She looked absolutely horrified.

"I didn't think it would take very long," Betsy mumbled. "I mean, I wasn't sure what I wanted and I've looked at a few patterns, but I couldn't seem to make up my mind. Don't worry, I've got plenty of money." She knew she was babbling but she couldn't seem to stop herself.

"Gracious, we've not a moment to lose. Step this way, please. We've some pattern books you can look at, but you'll need to pick quickly, and we'll also need to get your measurements taken today." She gave Betsy a gentle shove toward the table.

"I hadn't planned on a really fancy dress," Betsy admitted as she yanked out a chair and flopped down. "But I don't suppose it'll hurt to see what you've got."

The proprietress shoved a pattern book under Betsy's nose and opened it to the pages toward the back. "Here, start with this one. It's one of our most popular."

Betsy gasped in pleasure. The dress was every woman's fantasy: yards of white lace, an orange blossom headpiece with a sheer veil, and a train fit for a queen!

"This is a nice one, too." The proprietress flipped to the next page. "We can make any of these gowns up in Duchesse satin, silk, or even a patterned brocade. I've got the really nice bolts in the back room. I'll go get Emma. She can take your measurements while we're deciding on what you need, and we've plenty of tulle on hand for the veil, so you can get measured for that as well."

But Betsy wasn't listening; she was too busy drooling over the wedding dresses.

Wiggins trotted around the corner and crossed the road toward a tiny bookshop tucked between an ironmonger's and a chemist's. He knew his pursuer was still on his heels, and he was determined to throw him off the scent. The fact that he wasn't learning a ruddy thing about their case or the whereabouts of any of their suspects couldn't be helped. No, the fellow had to be convinced that following him would result in nothing more than a pair of very sore feet.

So far Wiggins had run for a good half mile, cutting through a mews and pretending to chase an omnibus. Then he'd sprinted to a boot shop a mile farther up the road and bought some boot blacker, trotted at a good pace for another half a mile and stopped for sweets at the newsagent's, and then doubled back and ended up here. He hoped the bloke trailing him had a painful stitch in his side and blisters on his feet. Wiggins was as tired as a pup and didn't know how much longer he could keep this up. He stopped long enough to catch his breath and then stepped into the shop.

"Can I help you?" asked an elderly man sitting on a chair behind the counter. He was reading a newspaper.

"Do you have the latest edition of *Whitaker's Almanac*?" Wiggins had been meaning to pick up this year's edition for ages now, but he'd not got around to it. He loved reading almanacs; they were filled with all sorts of useful information.

The clerk pointed to a shelf of books just inside the door. "Right there you are, young man."

"Ta, I didn't see it." Wiggins grabbed the top one off the stack on the shelf, checked the date on the front page to make sure it was the latest edition, and then walked to the counter. He pulled some coins out of his pocket and paid the clerk.

"Will that be all, sir?" The clerk pulled a sheet of brown paper off a stack and began wrapping the book.

Wiggins glanced over his shoulder just as his follower ducked into a doorway across the street. "Do you have a back door out of here?"

"A back door?" The clerk raised his eyebrows. "Well, yes, I do . . ."

"I'll give you a shilling if you'll let me use it when I leave," Wiggins said. He had plenty of money and he had suddenly realized it was almost noon, his feet were killing him, and he was tired of playing chase the fox with this fellow. Apparently, this bloke didn't tire easily, and Wiggins didn't want to be the only one at their afternoon meeting with nothing to report.

The clerk handed him the neatly wrapped book. "Let's see the shilling."

Wiggins reached into his pocket again and pulled out the coin. He handed it over as he took his package.

"It's this way." The clerk waved him around the counter and through a small, narrow hallway into a dim back room. He led him through a maze of old bookcases, boxes of books, and broken chairs, finally stopping in front of a door. He threw the bolt and shoved it open. Wiggins stepped out into the bright sunshine and surveyed his surroundings. He was in a mews. He pulled another coin out of his pocket and handed it to the elderly clerk.

"What's this for?"

"A bit of silence." He grinned. "You know, just in case anyone comes into the shop and starts asking questions."

The old man laughed. "Don't worry, young man. There's been no one in my shop for the last half hour, if you know what I mean."

Wiggins nodded his thanks, turned, and hurried off. With any luck, he might be able to learn something useful before he had to head back to Upper Edmonton Gardens.

"What should we do about the note, sir?" Barnes asked the inspector as they climbed out of a hansom in front of the law offices of Oxley and Gardner. "It sounded a matter of some urgency." He turned away briefly to pay the driver.

"We'll go see the chap right after we finish interviewing the solicitor." Witherspoon pushed his spectacles up his nose, checked that his hat was on straight, and then crossed the pavement to the wide double doors of the office building.

"The bank closes at five, sir," Barnes reminded him as he hurried to catch up. "And I don't have the address of the clerk who sent us the note." He reached the wide, flat steps leading into the office block, surged ahead of the inspector, and grabbed the door handle. "Do you think we ought to send a message to the station and have a police constable go along and get the man's address?"

The inspector shook his head as they entered the building. "No, I don't want to draw too much attention to the clerk. After all, Glover is acting as the general manager for the moment. We don't want the chap put into an awkward position. We've no idea what he has to tell us."

They went down the long corridor toward a door at the far end, and a few minutes later, they were in John Oxley's office. The solicitor to the late Lawrence Boyd sat behind a massive mahogany desk and smiled benignly at the two policemen. "I'm so sorry I had to cancel our first appointment, but it was unavoidable. I do hope it didn't inconvenience you too much."

"We understand, sir." Witherspoon smiled faintly. The solicitor had actually put him off twice, but for the sake of cooperation, he wouldn't correct him. "These things happen. I know you're a very busy man, so we'll not take up any more of your time than necessary. I'm sure you know why we're here."

"You're interested in my late client, Lawrence Boyd." Oxley was a portly, brown-haired man with a full set of side whiskers and bright blue eyes.

"He had a will, I take it?" Witherspoon shifted slightly in his seat. He and Barnes were sitting in two straight-backed chairs and his wasn't very comfortable.

"Of course he had a will," Oxley replied. "He was a very prudent man."

"What can you tell us about the disbursement of his estate?" Witherspoon asked. He didn't like to come right out and ask who benefited from the poor man's death. That sounded so very crass and he'd observed that how one phrased a question often influenced the answer. He wanted facts here and nothing more.

"You mean who might have benefited from Boyd's murder." Oxley smiled slyly.

"Er, uh, yes."

"There's no one person in particular." Oxley's chair creaked as he leaned back. "Lawrence Boyd had no close family. His wife died many years ago and they'd had no children."

"What about his housekeeper?" Barnes asked. "Isn't she a relative?"

"She is, but she inherits very little," Oxley explained. "Hannah Rothwell along with two other of his cousins will each inherit a few hundred pounds. The rest of his estate is very complex. He made a number of bequests to various charities—"

"Was the Bankers Benevolent Society one of them?" Witherspoon interrupted. Solicitors could be just a tad longwinded and it was getting late. He wanted to get back to Boyd's bank and have a word with that clerk.

Oxley nodded. "So you know about that, do you? It was really bad form, but Lawrence would have his way."

"What was bad form, sir?" Barnes looked up from his notebook.

"The way Lawrence behaved." Oxley pursed his lips in disapproval. "I know he really wanted to be named this year's honorary chairman. It was very important to him, but honestly, telling the board of trustees that you're leaving them a rather large sum of money in your will is practically the same as buying the honor."

Barnes didn't see why Oxley was so offended. From his observations, money generally changed hands before honors were awarded. But usually it was done discreetly and diplomatically. "He told them he was leaving them a legacy?"

"Yes, at their meeting last month." Oxley shook his head. "What's more, they weren't the only ones. Lawrence told all of the charities he'd named in his will that he was leaving them money.

The Amateur Artists Guild, the Society for Choral Singing, the Association for the Dramatic Sick Fund, the Royal Academy, the Doodlers Club. There are so many I can't even recall all their names."

Witherspoon's heart sank. He couldn't believe that any charitable institution would actually commit murder to gain a bequest, but considering his experiences as a policeman the past few years, he couldn't discount the notion either. "Wasn't that a bit unusual?"

"Of course it was," Oxley replied. "But Lawrence didn't care. He told me he wanted a monument to himself, something to leave on this earth so the world would know he'd been here."

"Which charity is getting the largest bequest?" Barnes asked. "The Bankers Benevolent Society?"

"Oh no, but they're getting quite a bit, believe me. The charity benefiting the most is the Amateur Artists Guild. Mr. Boyd left them his house and his paintings. The place is to be turned into a permanent exhibition venue for the society providing Boyd's paintings are prominently displayed in the main gallery."

"Main gallery?" Witherspoon repeated.

"Actually, that's currently his drawing room," Oxley explained. "But he's left an enormous amount of money for the rooms to be redone as an art gallery. The upstairs rooms are to be turned into offices and work spaces for young artists. The whole place is to be renamed. It's to be called the 'Lawrence Boyd Memorial Gallery.' I don't know what the local council will say, and I'm quite sure the neighbors will have a fit. In that neighborhood I can't see the residents wanting the general public tromping up and down their street on a daily basis, I can tell you that. But Lawrence didn't care a toss about the difficulties in doing what he wanted. He simply instructed us to do as he directed. I imagine we'll be in court for years over this bequest."

"I should think that would benefit you, sir," Barnes pointed out.

"I beg your pardon?" Oxley glared at the constable.

"You'll be able to charge his estate legal fees as long as the matter is under litigation."

"Are you implying I had anything to do with his death?" Oxley's face began to turn red. "I'll have you know, Constable, I tried to talk him out of doing such a foolish thing with his estate. But would he listen to me? No, he would not, and now he's left a fine mess for us to sort out."

"I'm sure the constable wasn't implying anything," Witherspoon interjected quickly. Ye Gods, if he didn't shut Barnes up they'd have a list of suspects longer than his right arm. Not only were half of the charities in London on the list, but now even the victim's lawyers had a good reason to want him dead. Why couldn't it just be a few greedy relatives? Why did his cases always get so complex? Sometimes he wished he was back in the records room at the Yard. Then he realized he mustn't think that way; for some reason, the good Lord had set this task before him and charged him with serving justice. But still, he wished the good Lord hadn't given him quite so many suspects.

"I should hope not." Oxley gave Barnes one last glare before turning his attention to the inspector. "Some cases are so complex they are simply not worth it, if you take my meaning. We'll earn every farthing of the fees we charge for handling this matter, I can tell you that."

"I'm sure you will, sir," Witherspoon said quickly. "Is there anyone else who is going to benefit under the terms of Mr. Boyd's will?"

Oxley frowned slightly. "There are some minor bequests to various individuals. As I said, he left his housekeeper and two other cousins a small amount of money. He also left the housekeeper one of his paintings. I believe there's a portrait of his late wife he's left to her sister, Maud Sapington. But other than that, everything goes to the various charities. I'll have my clerk give you a list."

"Thank you." Witherspoon smiled gratefully. "When was Mr. Boyd's will actually done?"

Oxley rolled his eyes. "It took ages to get it made up the way he wanted, but we finally got it signed and witnessed last month. I remember because Boyd kept insisting he had to have it completed by the time the trustees of the Benevolent Society had their monthly meeting. We had it ready for him with a day or two to spare."

"I see," Witherspoon replied. "You said that Boyd told all the various charities he was leaving them a bequest, is that correct?"

"That's right," Oxley snorted softly. "Oh, he wasn't crass enough to actually send them a letter or anything like that, but he made sure that when he was out socially and he'd run into a director or trustee from one of them, he'd be sure to mention the fact that he was remembering them in his will."

"He told you he'd done this?" Barnes said incredulously.

"Oh, no, he didn't actually tell me," Oxley replied. "I overheard it for myself. I happened to be standing right behind him at the opera, it was Mozart's *Magic Flute*, very good actually, top drawer if I do say so myself. I'm very fond of music, you know. But I mustn't digress. As I was saying, I happened to be standing right behind him when he ran into the president of the Amateur Artists Guild. I heard Boyd telling him every little detail of the legacy they were going to get when he died. Honestly, I couldn't credit my own ears, but he was speaking so loudly half the people in the lobby heard him. That wasn't the only time he bragged about it. My wife overheard him discussing the matter at the Art Institute dinner just last week. Lawrence Boyd wanted everyone to know which charities were getting his money, so he took every opportunity afforded him to discuss the matter at great length."

"Was it a lot of money?" the inspector asked softly.

Oxley leaned forward eagerly. "There was a great deal, Inspector. The value of the whole estate is over half a million pounds."

"Would you care for another drink?" Hatchet asked his companion, Reginald Manley. They were sitting in the small lounge of the Doodlers Club on a tiny street off Sheridan Square. Manley was a member. The fact that he was drinking with a butler, even though the butler had a net worth ten times Manley's, wouldn't be considered remarkable in any case. The Doodlers Club membership was composed of artists, cartoonists, fine craftsmen, glassblowers, and even a street portrait painter or two. Unlike most London clubs, this one actually required its members to be skilled at something difficult. Of course, the club was housed in an ancient two-story brick building that had a sagging roof, crumbling masonry, and several cracked windows. But the lounge was nicely furnished with comfortable chairs, a decent green wool carpet, and a meeting room that was large enough to use for member exhibits and the occasional lecture. A waiter, who also served as a barman, moved slowly around the room, taking orders or bringing drinks.

"I don't mind if I do." Reginald Manley caught the waiter's attention and then lifted his empty glass. He was a middle-aged man with a full head of black hair, sharp features, and deep-set gray eyes. "This is very kind of you, Hatchet. What is it you want?"

Hatchet took no offense. "You always did get right to the point,

Reggie. I like that about you. You're right, of course; I do want something. Information. If you can help me with anything useful, I'll pay you. As I recall, you always did like money."

Manley laughed, revealing a set of perfect white teeth with exceptionally long incisors. "I'm not the only one who gets right to the point. I could use a few quid. My last few paintings haven't sold, and frankly, I'm getting too old to enchant the ladies much longer. I think I'm actually going to have to get married if I want to keep on eating and having a roof over my head."

Now it was Hatchet's turn to laugh. Manley made more money courting the ladies than he ever did selling his paintings. "Do you have someone in mind?"

"Of course, and despite what you probably think of me, once we're wed I'll be a very good husband. I may not be able to support the lady in question, but I will most certainly stay by her side for the rest of our lives. But that's enough about me. Do you still work for that odd American woman?"

"I do," he replied.

Manley smiled at the waiter as another glass of whiskey was placed on the table in front of him. "Thank you, Derrick. That'll be all. My companion is practically a teetotaler."

"Yes, sir." Derrick shuffled off.

"Do you know someone named Lawrence Boyd?" Hatchet asked.

"I did, but he was murdered a few days ago." Manley took a drink from his glass. "He was a banker who liked to play at being an artist."

"He was no good?"

Manley shrugged. "He painted things people liked to put on their walls, seascapes and pastoral scenes. He was competent but hardly inspired. He exhibited at the Royal Academy most years, which meant, of course that the rest of us were green with envy."

"Did you know him well?" Hatchet asked. He was fairly sure that even if Reggie hadn't known the fellow very well, he'd know the latest gossip about Boyd. Reginald Manley loved gossip more than he loved whiskey.

"We both studied under Trumwell, but that was years ago." Manley grinned. "Since then, we've hardly traveled in the same circles. But I do know that he was a rotten excuse for a human be-

ing. He eloped with Marianna Reese when he was already engaged to her sister and she was engaged to someone else."

Hatchet shifted in his chair. This was old news. He was hoping
Manley might know something else about the victim. "Yes, I'd
heard that."

"It was twenty years or so ago," Manley muttered. "Marianna
Reese was a lovely woman. Boyd did a portrait of her. That's supposedly when they fell in love."

Hatchet glanced at the clock on the far wall. Time was getting
on and he had to start for Upper Edmonton Gardens soon. "Yes,
love does seem to make some people behave in odd ways."

"But that doesn't excuse his behavior. I might be a bit of a cad,
but I don't go after engaged or married women and I limit my dal-
liances to ladies who know precisely what I'm offering. Boyd be-
trayed his best friend and stole the man's fiancée, humiliated his
own fiancée, and then had the gall to hold a grudge against the lot
of them so that when Marianna Reese was dying, he didn't even
let her family know until after the funeral."

"But isn't that all rather ancient history?" Hatchet sipped the
last of his own drink.

"Not really." Manley grinned broadly. "Not when your former
fiancée's husband is now in the running for the same charity post.
From what I understand, Maud Reese Sapington was doing everything short of showing her petticoats to the trustees of the Bankers
Benevolent Society in order to keep Lawrence from getting the position. You can't blame her for hating the man; he not only jilted
her publicly but then he wouldn't let her near her own dying sister. After Marianna's death, Maud asked Boyd for the portrait of
her sister. He wouldn't give it to her. She even offered to pay him
to have a copy made, but he refused. He really was a dreadful
man."

Wiggins was the last to arrive for their afternoon meeting. He
slipped into his chair just as Mrs. Jeffries finished pouring the last
of the steaming cups of tea. "I hope I didn't hold ya up," he apologized, "but I've had the devil's own time this afternoon."

"You're fine, lad," Smythe said. "We've only just sat down."

"Are you all right?" the cook asked. "You're face is as red as one
of my good strawberry tarts."

"I've been runnin'. I 'ad to cut across the garden from the

back gate down near Lady Cannonberry's," Wiggins explained. "I couldn't come down our road, you see. When I got to the corner, I spotted that fellow waitin' for me, but I managed to nip off and go the other way before he saw me."

There was dead silence for a moment, then they all began speaking at once.

"What man?" the cook demanded.

"What on earth are you talking about?" Mrs. Jeffries asked.

"You tell me if someone is threatenin' you," Luty commanded. "I can take care of that for ya."

"Oh, my goodness, Wiggins, are you all right? Did this man hurt you?" Betsy said anxiously.

"We can't have people following you with ill intent." Hatchet shoved away from the table. "Perhaps a quick word is in order."

"Is he still out there?" Smythe rose to his feet.

"Sit down." Mrs. Jeffries had to shout to make herself heard. "Before we do anything, we'd best see what Wiggins has to say." She turned her attention to the footman. "The first order of business is to make sure you're all right."

"I thought I'd shaken 'im off my 'eels, but he must 'ave high tailed it back 'ere when I didn't come out of the bookshop. He was waitin' for me at the corner, but I'm fine. I never let him get close enough to lay hands on me."

"Good. Now, tell us what happened," Mrs. Jeffries instructed calmly. But inside, she was afraid her worst fears were being realized. Someone from their past, someone connected with a killer they'd helped apprehend was coming back to seek vengeance on them. She handed Wiggins a mug of steaming hot tea.

"Ta, Mrs. Jeffries." He helped himself to a spoonful of sugar. "Today wasn't the first time I've seen the bloke," he began. "But I didn't say anything because I thought it was probably just my imagination playin' tricks on me."

"When was the first time you saw him?" Smythe interjected.

"I think it was yesterday morning." Wiggins stirred his tea. "But I can't be sure. I know for certain that he was following me today." He told them the details of his morning and how he'd tried to tire his pursuer out by running all over London and then when that hadn't worked, by sneaking out the rear door of the bookshop. "But I guess I didn't fool the fellow. He was waitin' for me when I got to our street. It was just luck that I spotted him lurkin' about before he happened to see me. I think he works for Inspector Nivens."

"Inspector Nivens?" Mrs. Jeffries wasn't sure she liked that idea any better than her original one. "How do you know?"

Wiggins wasn't sure how to explain this part; he knew it wouldn't make sense, but he had to try. He knew he was right. "He's got a funny look about 'im. Even though he's wearin' a flat cap and an old coat, he looks like he's playin' a part, like it's not real."

"I'm not sure I know what ya mean," Luty muttered. "But you've got good instincts, so let's assume you're right and that the man is workin' for that no good polecat Nivens. What can we do about it?"

"I don't know." Mrs. Jeffries looked at Wiggins. "But it was very clever of you to throw him off the scent, so to speak."

"What are we going to do?" Betsy asked glumly. "We certainly don't need Nivens poking his nose into our business."

"We'll think of something," Mrs. Jeffries said briskly. "For right now, let's get on with our meeting."

"I do 'ave something else to report," Wiggins said eagerly. "I went around to the Sapington neighborhood and I wasn't 'avin' much luck, but then I spotted a street arab and we got to chattin'. He works that area regular like, and people are always usin' him to send messages to their friends or their husbands."

"Had Maud Sapington sent someone a message?" Mrs. Goodge demanded.

"Oh, no, but her next-door neighbor hired the lad to go to Throgmorton Street with a message for her husband, and the lad told me that as he was nippin' off, he spotted Mrs. Sapington slipping out of her house that morning. He noticed because she was the lady of the 'ouse and he claimed she slipped out the servants door like a thief makin' off with the family silver. He said she stopped and looked around, like she didn't want anyone seein' her leave."

"I don't suppose he happened to note the time he saw her," Betsy asked.

" 'E's not got a pocket watch." Wiggins grinned. "But he knew the time because Mrs. Barclay—she's the one that sent him with the message—said it was already half past ten and she needed her husband to have the message by eleven fifteen. But that's all I found out. I'll keep lookin', though, providin' we can think of a way to get rid of that bloke that's stickin' closer to me than my shadow."

"We'll think of something," Mrs. Jeffries said with more confidence than she felt.

"Of course we will," Hatchet said cheerfully. "If no one objects, I should like to go next. I believe you'll find my information rather interesting, especially in light of what young Wiggins just reported."

"We already know that Maud Sapington hated Lawrence Boyd. Besides, I thought you was goin' to try and find out about Boyd's partners and what they was doin' the day of the murder," Luty charged.

"Unfortunately, my source for that information was unavailable today, but I made an appointment to see him tomorrow." Hatchet smiled slyly. "And I must say there's a fact or two about Mrs. Sapington's relationship with the late Lawrence Boyd that you don't know."

Luty snorted faintly but said nothing.

"I had an interesting chat with a friend of mine, a painter. He has a vast amount of knowledge about the London art world." Hatchet told them about his meeting with Reginald Manley. "You can see why I wanted to share this information as quickly as possible." He turned to Luty. "As you pointed out, we know that Maud hated Boyd, but we didn't know she wanted that portrait of her sister he'd painted and that even when she offered to pay to have a copy of it painted, he refused."

"But why would she wait years to kill him in order to get it?" Luty demanded. "And we don't know for sure she's going to get the danged painting. Maybe he's goin' to give it to someone else."

"Madam, madam." Hatchet gave her a pitying smile. "Not everyone has an intemperate nature. You have heard the saying, 'Revenge is a dish best served cold.' Perhaps Mrs. Sapington simply bided her time."

Wiggins nodded his head wisely. "And her waitin' to kill him now does make a bit of sense. He was gettin' all them big honors and such. That's why they was goin' to luncheon at his house, so that Gibbons fellow could announce to everyone that Boyd 'ad gotten to be the chairman of that bankers charity."

"That's a very interesting idea," Mrs. Jeffries interjected. "But let's not get ahead of ourselves. We're still in the early stages of the investigation and we mustn't jump to conclusions."

"That's right," Luty added eagerly. "Let's not jump to conclusions. Maybe the rest of us found out some interestin' bits as well."

"Why don't you go next, Luty," Mrs. Jeffries suggested.

"Why, thank you, I don't mind if I do. I didn't find out too much, but I did learn a little bit more about Hannah Rothwell." Luty paused. "She was supposed to have gone to that funeral, but she might not have actually been there. She met up with the others from Boyd's household when they got back to Paddington Station."

"You mean she doesn't have an alibi?" Mrs. Goodge asked.

"Oh, I wouldn't go so far as to say that," Luty replied. "Hannah Rothwell went with them all the way to the church, but it's one of them small country churches and it was crowded, so they all split up so they could find seats. My source said there was people standing in the aisles and crammed into every bit of space, so she could have actually been there, but the only way to prove it would be to find someone who saw her. There was a funeral reception at the girl's home and Boyd's servants all went to pay their respects to the family, but they weren't together at that point. They'd not sat together, so I think everyone just paid their respects and went to station to get the next train back to London. Remember, they had to be back in time to serve that luncheon, so I think they each of them went to the station and got on the train. Then they met up at Paddington."

"But why would Hannah Rothwell want to kill Lawrence Boyd?" Betsy asked.

Luty shrugged. "She was his kin, but he made her work for her keep. That's got to rankle, and we know she and Boyd had that big ruckus the day before he was murdered. It had to have been about something important."

"We really must find out if she was at that funeral," Mrs. Jeffries remarked. "I'm afraid I might have made a terrible mistake. I should have been more encouraging when Inspector Witherspoon raised the issue."

"You mean our inspector wondered the same thing?" Wiggins said.

"Yes." Mrs. Jeffries nodded. "But it seemed such a strange scenario that I dismissed it out of hand. But I'll make sure to bring it up this evening."

"That's all I found out." Luty settled back in her chair with a smug smile on her lips.

Mrs. Jeffries looked at the Betsy. "Were you able to find out anything about Maud Sapington?" she asked.

"Not really," Betsy admitted. "But I heard a few bits about her husband. It's not much, but he was hoping to get the chairmanship of the Bankers Benevolent Society as well. He's considered a real social climber. His father was actually a builder and wanted him to go into the business with him, but he had other ideas and became an articled clerk when he left grammar school."

"What's wrong with bein' a builder?" Wiggins asked.

"Absolutely nothing," Hatchet explained. "But generally, people from the 'trades' don't end up climbing very high in social status."

"Sapington seems to have managed it," Betsy continued. She'd only found out about Arnold Sapington because she'd brought up Maud's name when she was at the dressmaker's. The seamstress hadn't known anything about Maud, but the little apprentice had come from Slough, the same town as Arnold. "Mind you, my source says the man worked hard for what he's got. He went to grammar school on a scholarship and then came to London and worked his way up at Reese and Cutlip."

"Marryin' the boss's daughter probably helped a bit," Smythe reminded her.

"True and he is the lucky sort," Betsy agreed. "He only got the scholarship because another lad had it but he died, so Arnold got to take his place."

"Looks like he's lucky again," Wiggins laughed. "Now that Boyd's dead, maybe he'll get to be the honorary chairman."

"So I take it none of us were actually able to ascertain all of Maud Sapington's movements on the morning of the murder?" Mrs. Jeffries probed.

"We know she snuck out of her 'ouse," Wiggins said. "But that's all I was able to learn."

"I'll be out again tomorrow," the maid declared.

"Me, too," Wiggins added.

"I 'ad a bit of luck myself," Smythe said. He told them about the drink he'd shared with Jeremiah Fitch. "From what he told me,

Boyd's greatest pleasure in his charitable work was beatin' some-one else out of an honor, especially on this Bankers Benevolent Society. Boyd was an odd bird, wasn't he? From what we've 'eard about him, he didn't have any genuine love for people yet he was bound and determined to do charity work and be recognized for it. It doesn't make a lot of sense, does it?"

"It does if he had an ulterior motive," Mrs. Jeffries replied. "He might have been hoping to eventually get a knighthood or some-thing along those lines. We'll simply have to keep on digging to find out what happened that day."

"Did you see Dr. Bosworth?" Betsy asked eagerly. "Was he able to get his hands on the postmortem report?"

Mrs. Jeffries shook her head. "I spent hours waiting for him, but there was some sort of industrial accident and Dr. Bosworth was in surgery all day. I'll have another go tomorrow."

The time spent wandering the environs of St. Thomas's Hospi-tal hadn't been entirely wasted; she'd had many hours to think about the case. She'd walked up and down the path by the river while she waited to see Dr. Bosworth after surgery; however, even the stiff breeze off the water and the sharp scents of the air hadn't helped her thinking. So far her recalcitrant brain had produced nothing useful about this case. None of the facts they'd learned thus far had formed into any sort of reasonable theory. She was still as much in the dark as she'd been two days ago.

On the other hand, she was quite certain she'd not been fol-lowed today. She glanced at Wiggins and felt a tug of panic. What on earth were they to do? They couldn't continue if their every step was going to be dogged by one of Niven's toadies.

"Mrs. Jeffries, were you through?" Betsy asked. "You've got a worried look on your face. Is everything all right?"

"Oh, sorry, I just got a bit distracted. I'm fine and that was all I had to report." She forced a bright smile. "Does anyone else have anything to report?"

"I've got just a bit to say." Mrs. Goodge had been patiently wait-ing her turn. "An old colleague of mine came around today for morning tea. Her name is Irma Ballard and she's done quite well in the years since I've seen her. She and her husband now own a restaurant just around the corner from one of our suspects."

"That's right handy," Wiggins commented. "Who is it?"

"Walter Gibbons," the cook replied. "He's one of their regular customers. Irma says he's as miserable and mean a soul as she's ever seen."

"Worse than Lawrence Boyd?" Betsy asked. She found that hard to believe.

"It'd be a close race, but so far Gibbons has avoided being murdered." Mrs. Goodge took a deep breath. "Walter Gibbons was Marianna Reese's fiancé before she ran off with Lawrence Boyd."

"Gibbons was engaged to Marianna Reese?" Betsy exclaimed. "And we're just now finding this out?"

"Better late than never," the cook replied. "It all happened years ago, and we were so concerned about Maud Sapington having been jilted by Boyd that none of us thought to ask too many questions about Marianna."

"That's true," the housekeeper said, "but it's often difficult to determine what is important and what isn't, especially when the incident was so long ago." She wondered what else they may have overlooked. She was annoyed with herself because the inspector had specifically mentioned that Gibbons seemed to actively dislike Boyd. She hadn't pursued the matter as carefully as she should have.

"We do the best we can, Mrs. Jeffries. Sometimes we get lucky and we come across a tidbit that's interesting or useful." Mrs. Goodge beamed proudly. She had more to say. "This might have happened years ago, but Irma doesn't think the passage of time has made Gibbons any more forgiving. She says he's as bitter a man as she's ever seen."

"And Gibbons was the one that had to decide who got to be the honorary chairman?" Luty exclaimed. "And he gave it to Boyd? Why? Why would he do that?"

"I don't know," Mrs. Goodge admitted. "But I'm sure there must be a reason."

"Perhaps he wasn't the one who made the decision," Mrs. Jeffries said. "Most charities are run by an administrative board or a set of trustees. Perhaps he had no choice; perhaps he had to give the honor to Boyd. But this at least explains Gibbons attitude about Boyd. Remember, the inspector mentioned that Gibbons made a point of saying it wasn't a social call and he'd not have been there except for the charity business."

"And he wasn't the only one there that day that hated Boyd," Wiggins added. "No wonder the man ended up dead. Seems like everyone who ever crossed his path became his enemy. What a miserable way to live your life."

CHAPTER 7

Witherspoon and Barnes arrived at the bank offices just as the clerks were putting away their ink pots and closing the ledgers. Bingley, a middle-aged man with thinning hair and spectacles, leapt out of his seat and rushed toward them. He gave a nervous glance over his shoulder toward Glover's office. "If you'd like to wait out in the hall, I'll be right with you," he whispered.

Taken aback, Witherspoon gaped at the man, but Barnes grabbed the inspector's elbow and yanked him back through the door. As soon as they were safely out of the bank, Barnes said, "Glover must still be here and Bingley obviously doesn't want to speak in front of him."

Just then the door opened and Bingley slipped out into the hall. He shoved a battered looking brown bowler on his head, looked at the two policeman, and then charged toward the street door. "Come along, gentlemen, we must hurry. There's a café around the corner where we can speak privately. Hurry, hurry. Mr. Glover is right behind me and I don't want to end up losing my position over this." He looked over his shoulder to see if they were following and then increased his pace to a fast trot when he saw they were right on his heels. "Hollinger is going to try to delay him, but I do believe he's already suspicious about me, so please, do come along. You mustn't let him see you."

With Bingley in the lead, they dashed out of the building, around the corner, and up a tiny side road, and then took a quick right that brought them, finally, to a café. Bingley sighed in relief as he sank into a chair facing the window. He took off his hat and placed it on the table in front of him. "Could I have some tea, please?" he asked breathlessly.

"I'll get us all a cup," Barnes offered.

"Do relax a bit and steady yourself," Witherspoon said as he took the chair next to Bingley. "We've plenty of time to hear what you've got to say."

"I hope Mr. Glover didn't see me with you." Bingley wiped the perspiration off his forehead. "He'd sack me for certain."

Witherspoon gave him a few moments to compose himself. "Does he have the authority to dismiss you?" he asked.

Bingley took a deep breath and nodded. "He's temporarily in charge, but you can see from the way he struts about the place that he's fairly sure the position will become permanent."

"Here's your tea, sir." Barnes put a cup of tea in front of the clerk, handed another cup to Witherspoon, and then went back to the counter to get his own. A moment later he slipped into the empty seat facing the inspector.

"Thank you, Constable Barnes," the inspector said. He looked at Bingley. "Why did you want to see us?"

Bingley took a quick sip from his cup. "I saw something today that I thought you ought to know about. One of my duties at the bank is sorting the mail. Usually it's a very simple task. I simply pass out the envelopes that are addressed to individuals directly to them, but the letters that are just addressed to the bank, I open those and pass them along." He paused and took another deep breath. "Today we got a letter that wasn't addressed to anyone, so I opened it. It was from the Metropolitan Police. At first I couldn't understand what it was, then I realized it was some sort of receipt for the files that Mr. Glover took to Mr. Boyd's the day he was killed."

"That would be an evidence receipt, sir," Witherspoon said. "We took the files into evidence and we always issue a receipt to the legal owner. The bank will get them back as soon as I've had a chance to go through them." He knew he ought to have already read the files, but he simply hadn't had time.

"That's not important, Inspector," Bingley replied. "What was important is that one of the files was missing."

"Missing?" Barnes exclaimed. "That's absurd. The Metropolitan Police does not lose evidence."

"I didn't accuse you of losing evidence," Bingley snapped.

"That's why I wanted to speak with you. I'm fairly certain the missing file was stolen before your lot even got there. Mr. Glover took it."

"Oh, sorry," Barnes smiled sheepishly. "Go on Mr. Bingley."

"Thank you," Bingley said waspishly. "The reason I suspect he took it was because I'm fairly certain he's been playing about with the books."

"What, precisely, do you mean by that?" Witherspoon asked.

"It means I think he was stealing from the bank," Bingley said. "You see, the day before Mr. Boyd was murdered I'd sent him a note saying he really ought to take a look at the Pressley file, especially the income and expenditure statements. That's one of Mr. Glover's accounts, and frankly, I've been suspicious for several months now that he's been taking money out of the expenditure account and putting it in his own pocket. But I had no proof until the day before Mr. Boyd's murder." Bingley smiled triumphantly. "I got the receipts you see, and when I went to match them up to the expenditures, I realized the receipts were far less than the ledger amounts. So I sent Mr. Boyd the receipts with a note and told him to take a good look at the file. The next day, Glover gave me a list of files he said Mr. Boyd wished to see and the Pressley file was on the list."

"You're certain that Mr. Glover actually took him that particular file?" Barnes asked.

"Absolutely. I handed it to him myself along with all the others," Bingley answered. "Glover wouldn't have dared show up without it. Mr. Boyd would have sacked him on the spot. He was a very hard man."

"And now it's missing?" Witherspoon clarified.

"Yes, it wasn't on the list I received from your lot," Bingley replied. "And as Glover was bragging to the general partners about how he'd tried to put the fire out before the fire brigade arrived, it all made sense. He didn't fight any fire. He grabbed the file and hid it on his person so that no one would ever see it."

"He did say he was just outside the studio door, sir." Barnes looked at Witherspoon.

"But he said he never went inside," the inspector murmured. "He was frightened of fire."

"Believe me, he's more frightened of going to jail," Bingley said. "And what's more, now he can blame the Metropolitan Police for the missing file. It's worked out rather well for Mr. Glover."

Before the meeting broke up, Wiggins once again asked what he should do about the man who'd been following him.

"Don't worry, lad," Smythe said. "I'll take care of it."

"Smythe, you mustn't put yourself at risk," Mrs. Jeffries cautioned. "Nivens wouldn't hesitate to arrest you or anyone else that gets in his way."

The coachman grinned. "No one's goin' to be arrested," he promised. Under the table, he grabbed Betsy's hand and gave it a reassuring squeeze. "I know what I'm about." He looked back at Wiggins. "Go out tomorrow as usual, lad. I'll take care of the matter."

"What are you goin' to do?" the footman asked eagerly.

"Call in a few favors," he replied cryptically.

Mrs. Jeffries decided that she had to trust that Smythe knew what he was doing. He'd never let her down in the past and she didn't think he was going to start now. "Excellent, then, that's settled. Luty, can you and Hatchet come by early tomorrow morning?"

"Certainly," Hatchet replied. "Is there any special reason?"

"Only that I've a feeling the inspector may have learned quite a bit today," she explained, "and I want to make sure the both of you have the same information as the rest of us."

"We'll be here," Hatchet responded. "Come along, madam. Let's get you home. You've got a dinner engagement with Count Romanov." He ushered Luty toward the back door.

"Let's hope the inspector has plenty to say tonight," Luty called over her shoulder. "We need all the help we kin get."

"Speak for yourself, madam," Hatchet was heard to say just before the door closed. They always left by the back door because Luty insisted on keeping her carriage around the corner. She didn't want the neighbors or the inspector knowing just how often she and Hatchet were visitors to the house.

It was getting dark by the time the inspector got home. "I'm sorry I'm so late," he said as he handed Mrs. Jeffries his bowler. "But it's been an extraordinarily busy day. Er, was there anything interesting in the mail?"

"You received a letter from Lady Cannonberry, sir," Mrs. Jeffries replied. "I put it on your desk." She prayed he wouldn't want to read it yet. She wanted to hear about his day.

"I'll read it after dinner." He smiled happily. "Let's have a glass of sherry."

They went into the drawing room and she poured both of them a glass of Harvey's. "I take it the case is making progress," she said as she took her seat.

"We're learning quite a bit, but I'm not certain I'm making any progress." He took a quick sip. "Honestly, Mrs. Jeffries, I do believe everyone who crossed Lawrence Boyd's path had a reason to want him dead. Everyday my list of suspects gets longer."

"How very inconvenvient, sir," she prompted. She listened carefully as he spoke, occasionally asking a question. By the time he'd finished his sherry, he seemed far more relaxed than when he'd arrived home. He put his glass down, got to his feet, and started for the dining room. "I had better eat my dinner. I don't want to keep the whole household hanging about the kitchen all night."

"That's most considerate of you, sir." She followed him out into the hall. "I'll just go bring it up, sir. It's all ready."

Witherspoon paused by the open dining room door. "Gracious, Mrs. Jeffries, it does so help me to clarify things when I talk them over with you."

"That's very kind of you, sir. I enjoy hearing about your cases."

He went on into the dining room and she went down to the kitchen. She noticed that the coachman was nowhere to be seen. "Has Smythe gone out?"

"Yes, he said he'd be back in an hour or two." Betsy picked up the inspector's dinner tray from the counter and handed it to the housekeeper. "He told me not to worry, but that's not possible. I don't like him being out in the dark."

"Smythe knows how to take care of himself," Mrs. Jeffries said firmly. "So do as he says and stop fretting. He'll be home soon."

Mrs. Jeffries was the last one to go up that night. She made sure the front door was latched properly, picked up her lantern, and made her way up the darkened staircase. She hadn't wanted the others to know, but she was very discouraged about this case. She reached the first floor landing and stopped for a moment to catch her breath. On nights like this, she felt her age. She glanced at the inspector's closed door and went on up the next flight of stairs to her rooms. Opening the door, she slipped inside, put the lantern on the table, and then got ready for bed. But she knew that she wasn't going to be able to sleep, so after she'd changed into her nightclothes, she blew out the flame in the lantern and went to the rocking chair by the window.

Mrs. Jeffries stared out into the night, fixing her gaze at the streetlight across the road. Sometimes, if she simply let her mind go blank, if she deliberately thought of nothing, some sort of pattern about the case would emerge.

Keeping her gaze on the faint glow of the light, she took a deep breath and relaxed her body. Who wanted Lawrence Boyd dead enough to take the risk to murder him? It had to be someone who knew he was going to be alone that morning—but no, she caught herself, that wasn't true. Boyd wasn't alone that day; the typewriter girl, Miss Clarke, was in his study. But maybe the killer didn't know that? She thought back to everything the inspector had mentioned and tried to ascertain who actually knew Miss Clarke was going to be at the house that day. She frowned thoughtfully; she didn't think any of the suspects knew the typewriter girl was going to be there. The servants had all left early that morning, and the guests that were due to come for luncheon wouldn't know anything about Boyd's business arrangements.

Perhaps everyone thought he was alone. But he wasn't and that appeared to be why the killer's plan went so awry. She shifted in her chair and pulled her shawl tighter against her shoulders. But had the murderer actually had a plan, or had the killing been done on the spur of the moment? In her view, the murder itself had been badly bungled, especially if the killer had been counting on the fire getting rid of all the evidence.

And exactly who hated Boyd enough to want him dead? Maud Sapington had reason to hate him, but he'd scandalized her family years ago. Why wait till now to do something about it? If Boyd's clerk was stealing money from one of the accounts, he might risk murder rather than face a prison sentence. The inspector hadn't come right out and said it, but she could tell he didn't believe Glover's story about falling asleep in the drawing room. And what about Boyd leaving all his estate to those charities? It was a peculiar idea, but perhaps there was someone on the board of the Amateur Artists Guild or the Benevolent Bankers Society that thought they might hasten Boyd to his grave and help their cause as well.

She spent another half hour letting the bits and pieces of the case drift in and out of her mind. Finally, she realized she wasn't going to come to any conclusions just yet. She got up and slipped into her bed. But it was hours before her eyes closed in sleep.

The next morning, as the inspector was leaving out the front door, Luty and Hatchet were coming in the back one. They had a quick meeting, and Mrs. Jeffries shared what she'd learned from the inspector. As they broke up to go their separate ways, Mrs. Goodge reminded them to be back by half past four.

"Don't you worry, we'll be here," Luty called over her shoulder as she and Hatchet raced toward the back door.

Wiggins and Mrs. Jeffries had already gone, leaving Betsy and Smythe alone in the hallway. Betsy grabbed Smythe's hand as soon as the door closed behind Hatchet and Mrs. Goodge had disappeared back into the kitchen. "I didn't want to say anything in front of the others, but I picked out a wedding dress yesterday."

"It's about time, lass. I was beginnin' to think you were goin' to walk down the aisle in yer apron and cap," Smythe replied. "And I don't want any sass from you about the cost, either. You just give me the name of the dressmaker's and I'll take care of everythin'. I hope you got some other dresses as well."

Betsy giggled. "I wonder how long you'll be saying things like that after we're married. But yes, I did buy a traveling costume as well. But I felt ever so guilty spending that much money on two dresses!"

Smythe stopped in front of the back door and took her by the shoulders. "We've been over this before, love. I've got more money than either of us can spend and you're to 'ave anything you want. A couple of your dresses won't put me in the poor house."

"I know," she said softly. "But I'm not used to spending like that."

"Well, you'd best get used to it," he said. "I'm goin' to be takin' care of you for the rest of our lives."

"You like taking care of things, don't you." Her smile faded. "Oh, dear, I should have let you go off with Wiggins. I know he's nervous about that man following him."

"I took care of that last night," Smythe replied. He'd made a quick trip to the Dirty Duck Pub and had a word with Blimpey Groggins. "Don't worry about the lad. He'll be fine."

"Should I keep my eyes open, then?" she asked. She was tempted to ask him what he'd done, but she had a feeling she might not like his answer. Mrs. Jeffries was right; she had to learn to stop worrying about him. He could take care of both of them.

"Always keep your eyes open, love," he said, his expression suddenly dead serious. "I couldn't live if something happened to you."

Betsy didn't like the somber mood that had overtaken them both. She forced herself to laugh. "Nothing's going to happen to either of us, and in a few weeks, we're going to be man and wife. I've got to be off. If I don't find out something useful today, I'll never forgive myself."

"You've got time to give us a quick kiss," he insisted. "And then we can leave together. I'll walk you to the omnibus stand." He leaned down and kissed her on the lips.

Betsy moved closer to him and at that very moment, there was a loud knock on the door. She leapt back, stumbling slightly in her haste. Smythe caught her by the shoulders and made sure her stumble didn't turn into a fall. "Are you alright, love?"

"Just startled a bit, that's all." She reached for the door knob as she spoke.

"Hello, Miss Betsy," the butcher's boy gave her a wide smile. He was pulling a huge wicker cart behind him. "I've got your meat order here."

"Mrs. Goodge," Smythe called over his shoulder. "Your lad is here."

"We won't keep you long, Miss Johnston," Witherspoon said to the young maid. "But I do need to ask you a few questions." He and Barnes were at the house next door to the late Lawrence Boyd. The young woman sitting across from them at a rickety table in the butler's pantry was Miss Lorraine Johnston, scullery maid.

"The other copper asked me questions yesterday. I told him what I saw, but then I overheard Letty Wilson tellin' the bloke I told tales." Lorraine's brown eyes narrowed and she cast a withering glance at the closed door of the pantry. She was a thin young woman with pale skin, brown hair, hazel eyes, and slightly protruding front teeth.

"But you're not telling tales, are you?" the inspector said kindly. He noticed her front tooth was chipped.

"I'm tellin' the truth. I know what I saw," she said indignantly. "I don't know why Letty's always makin' up nonsense about me, but I don't tell lies."

"Why don't you tell us what it was that you did see," Barnes suggested. There was a hint of impatience in his tone.

"I saw a fellow climbing over the fence that separates the Boyd property from the mews," she replied. "You can see it as clear as day from the top of the back steps."

"Is that were you were standing?" Witherspoon asked.

Lorraine nodded. "I'd gone outside to get some air. It was so hot in the kitchen I almost couldn't breathe, so I nipped out for a bit of fresh air. I was standing on the top step when a bit of movement caught my eye. When I took a closer look, I saw it was a man climbing over Mr. Boyd's fence."

"What time was this?" Barnes glanced at the inspector. If by chance the girl had seen something, this might give them the time the murder had been committed.

"I don't rightly know." Lorraine shrugged.

"Come now, surely you've some idea," Witherspoon coaxed. He knew he oughtn't to lead the witness, but this might be very important. "Was it just after breakfast?"

"No," she frowned. "I'd done the breakfast dishes much earlier so it was well past that. It was fairly close to lunch. I know that because that's why the kitchen was so boiling hot. The mistress was having a luncheon and cook had both ovens on. I think it was around half past eleven." She nodded to herself. "Yes, that's right. I remember now. I'd looked at the clock just a few minutes before I went out."

Witherspoon wished he'd not pressed the girl. He couldn't tell whether she was telling the truth. "You're certain about this?"

"I said I was, didn't I?" She looked irritated. "Honestly, I don't know why everyone believes Letty and not me. When I saw the man, I ran back to the kitchen to tell the others. Go and ask Annie if you don't believe me. I drug her outside to have a look as well, but by the time we got back out here, the fellow was gone."

"Who is Annie?" Barnes asked.

"She's the tweeny. She'll tell you I'm not makin' it up."

"Can you tell us what the man looked like?" Witherspoon asked.

"Not really. There's a lot of greenery by Mr. Boyd's fence. I just barely saw the top of the fellow's head and shoulders as he nipped over. He had on a flat black cap and what looked like a long black coat."

"You didn't get a good look at the man, but you could tell he was wearing a long coat?" Barnes voice was skeptical.

"That's what I said, isn't it?" Lorraine snapped. "I didn't get a look at his face as the top of the ruddy pine tree kept blocking my view. But I noticed the coat because it blew open as he reached the top of the fence." She got up off the rickety chair she'd been sitting on. "I've got to get back to the kitchen. Cook will have my guts for garters if I don't get them carrots peeled. I've told you what I saw, and you can ask Annie if I didn't come running in to get her when it happened. I tried to tell cook about it, but she's a silly old stick and wouldn't listen to me. I'll admit that sometimes I do tell a bit of a story, but I'm not tellin' one now." She stared defiantly at the two policemen.

"Thank you, Miss Johnston. Your information has been very helpful." Witherspoon smiled kindly at her. "We appreciate your cooperation. Now, could you please send Annie into us?"

She nodded, dropped a quick curtsey, and then hurried out.

"Do you think she's telling the truth?" Barnes glanced at the inspector.

"That's just what I was going to ask you," Witherspoon replied. From behind the closed door, he could hear voices.

"I do," Barnes said softly as the pantry door opened again and another young woman stepped into the room.

"I'm Annie Barker," the girl said. She was tall and slender with light red hair, blue eyes, and a wide mouth. "Lorraine said you wanted to speak to me."

"We do. Please have a seat." Witherspoon gestured at the chair Lorraine had just vacated. "We'll not take much of your time."

Annie sat down in the empty chair and stared expectantly at the two police officers on the other side of the table.

"Do you remember the day Mr. Boyd died?" Witherspoon began.

"It was only a couple of days ago." Annie laughed. "Of course I remember it."

"Did Lorraine come and fetch you that morning and ask you to step outside to see something?" He was careful to avoid saying too much. He wanted only her recollection of the event.

"She come running into the kitchen saying there was a man climbing over Mr. Boyd's fence. So I went outside to have a look with her, but I didn't see anyone," Annie replied.

"Why didn't anyone mention this event to the police constable when he was here?" Barnes asked.

Annie shrugged. "Because no one paid any attention to Lorraine when she come running in; the kitchen was noisy, so she couldn't get anyone to listen to her."

"You listened," Witherspoon pointed out.

"I was in the hallway getting more polish out of the cupboard. Besides, I felt sorry for her. Lorraine likes to natter on a bit too much, so some of the others aren't very nice to her. Frankly, I wasn't sure that she wasn't making something up, but I went outside so her feelings wouldn't be hurt."

"So you've no idea if there actually was a man or not?" the inspector pressed.

"No."

"And Lorraine does sometimes make up stories?"

Annie sighed. "Everyone ignores her. Sometimes she makes things up just to get a bit of attention, if you know what I mean."

"Do you think she's making this up?"

Annie shook her head. "I don't think so. She saw someone climbing over that fence and came running into the kitchen to tell someone about it hours before we knew Mr. Boyd had been murdered."

Betsy spied the young maid coming out the servant's entrance to the Sapington house and instantly changed her plans. The neighborhood shopkeepers could wait. Here was someone who actually lived in the house, and even better, she was dressed for a day out, not for running an errand for the mistress of the house.

The girl started down the street and Betsy hurried after her. She followed her for several blocks, not allowing herself to get too close until the girl halted at the omnibus stop. Betsy walked up and stood next to her. She could see the girl was quite pretty with black hair, blue eyes, and very fair skin.

"Excuse me," Betsy said, "but do you know when the next omnibus is due?"

"The one for the train station is due any minute," the girl replied. "The one for Baker Street isn't due for another half hour."

Betsy wasn't sure how to respond. She wanted to make sure she got on the same one as this girl. But before she had to comment, the girl continued. "I'm goin' to the station. It's my day out and I'm going to visit my gran."

"That's what I'm doing as well." Betsy smiled shyly. "I mean I'm having my day out. Where are you going? That is, if you don't mind my asking."

"I'm going to Reading," she announced. "I'm actually going to get to spend the night with my family. I've some exciting news to tell them and I wanted to do it in person, not by post. Oh look, here comes the omnibus. Where did you say you were going? My name is Margaret Blakley, but everyone calls me Meg. What's yours?"

"I'm Lizzie. Lizzie Thompson." Betsy lied. She mentally calculated how long the train journey would take from London to Reading and back. She was taking a big risk here; she might waste hours and find out nothing. On the other hand, she'd seen the girl coming out of the Sapington house. She had to know something. "Gracious, isn't this a coincidence? I'm going to Reading as well."

"It'll be lovely to have someone to ride with," Meg said eagerly. "I hate taking train journeys on my own." The omnibus pulled up and they clambered on board. "There's two in the back." Meg pointed to the only empty seats in the conveyance.

Betsy pushed her way down the narrow aisle and eased into the seat nearest the window. Meg slid in next to her. "We ought to make the 10:33. My family will be ever so pleased to see me. I've not been home in almost a month."

"Your mistress doesn't allow you an afternoon out every week?" Betsy grabbed the handhold as the omnibus lurched forward.

"She does," Meg replied. "She's a hard enough time keeping staff, what with that stingy husband of hers, so we get our day out. It's just that I've been spending mine in London." She laughed merrily. "That's why I'm going home. I want to tell them I'm engaged. They'll be ever so pleased for me, especially my sister Clara. She used to be in service too until she married Bert and they moved back to Reading to open a shop."

Betsy fought the temptation to mention her own engagement. "Is your fiancé in service with you?"

"Oh, no." Meg shook her head. "Billy works down at the Edgington Arms—that's a pub just up the road from me. His father owns the place, so when we marry, I expect I'll be working there as well. Mind you, it'll be a lot easier than what I'm doin' now."

"What position do you have now?" Betsy was beginning to think this was a mistake. Maybe when they reached the station she could come up with some excuse not to board the train. Yes, that's what she'd do; she'd claim she'd forgotten her mother's medicine or something like that.

"I'm the tweeny." Meg made a face. "It's a miserable job. The mistress is all right, but the master is as tight as two ticks on a fat dog's tail. I've never seen such a miser, and you'd think that him comin' from ordinary people, he'd be a bit more generous. But he's the kind that's only good to himself, not the rest of us."

"That's too bad." Betsy's spirits were sinking by the minute. "Maybe he doesn't have much money to spare."

"Don't be daft. He's a ruddy banker," Meg snorted. "And he's got the first shilling he ever made. He's always goin' on about how he got where he is by hard work and good planning." She snorted again. "But he actually got where he is by marrying a rich man's daughter. Honestly, he's an arrogant pig. He comes down and checks the larders to make sure we're not sneaking food. He's so miserly with the heat in the winter in our part of the house, that one of the maids walked about with bronchitis for two months. Mind you, he had it nice and toasty in his study and the mistress's bedroom. But that's the way he is, tight with us and really extravagant when it comes to him or her. The silly fool tosses out anything that isn't perfect, and his wife is almost as bad. But picking up after their leavings isn't reason enough to stay. Last month Mr. Sapington threw out two good shirts just because the collar was frayed. The footman got his hands on those before I could grab them for my Billy. The month before he tossed out two good pair of trousers, and of course, that little weasel of a footman, George, got to them before anyone else could. I did manage to get hold of one of Mr. Sapington's kerchiefs for me dad. All it had was little stain on the corner. One little stain on his bloomin' handkerchief and Mrs. Sapington tosses it in the bin and orders me to go clear across town to buy him a new batch. And they couldn't be any old kerchiefs, could they? Oh, no, I had to go all the way over to Bond Street to buy those fancy ones that cost the earth. I'll be glad to get out of there, believe me."

"Sapington? Now where have I heard that name before? Was it in the papers recently?" Betsy dangled the bait and hoped Meg would mention the Boyd murder.

Meg didn't appear to have heard her. She continued talking like Betsy wasn't even there. "I told Evelyn—she's the one that had bronchitis—to keep an eye on Mr. Sapington, and the next time he tossed out a perfectly good piece of clothing, I told her to grab it before George could get his hands on it. It's not like he needed the things, either. He sells whatever he gets his hands on at the Saturday market." The omnibus rolled to a stop and half the passengers got off. Moments later, another bunch took their place.

"Oh dear, that isn't very nice," Betsy murmured.

Meg laughed. "That's all right. She beat George to Mr. Sapington's boots and gave them to her brother. George was furious that he'd lost them but he didn't have the nerve to complain. When Evelyn started bragging about how there wasn't anything wrong with them exceptin' for a few stains on the back heel, George got up and stomped out of the butler's pantry. We all had a good laugh."

"The Sapingtons don't sound very nice at all." Betsy craned her neck to look out the passenger window. How much longer before they were at the station?

"They're mean and nasty. He can't be bothered to heat the house properly, but he spends plenty of money trying to impress important people. He and Mrs. Sapington are always entertaining, and it's not because they're sociable or nice. It's so Mr. Sapington can move up in the world. He's always plannin' this or that or something else. That's his favorite activity, making plans. She's a bit nicer, but not by much. Mind you, at least she doesn't watch every bite we eat like he does. The man drives us all mad."

Betsy thought she was going to go mad as well.

Witherspoon and Barnes stood in the drawing room of the Boyd house and waited for Leeson. "Exactly why are we back here, sir?" Barnes asked. "I thought we were going to have a word with Mr. Glover this morning."

"We'll see him soon enough," Witherspoon replied. "But as we were in the neighborhood, I thought it might be a good idea to double-check a few details. I want to make sure that everyone who went to that funeral on the day of the murder can actually verify they were in the church."

The door opened and the butler entered. "You wanted to see me?" He tried to smile but couldn't quite manage it.

"Yes, we've a few more questions to ask you," Witherspoon said.

"I'm glad you're here." Leeson moved toward them. "Mr. Boyd's lawyer, Mr. Oxley, has been badgering me about Mr. Boyd's painting. He says it's got to come back to be inventoried. I told him I wasn't sure who took it in the first place."

"It's been taken into evidence" Barnes said smoothly.

Leeson sighed. "Mr. Oxley has been asking me endless questions about the picture, wanting to know what it was, where it was, or who had it. I don't know how he could have expected me to know anything. Mr. Boyd never let anyone see what he was working on. He kept all his paintings locked in a cupboard or covered with a cloth when he wasn't there."

"Tell Mr. Oxley to contact us," Witherspoon said quickly. "May we sit down, Leeson?"

"Certainly, sir," he gestured toward the chairs and settee. "I'm dreadfully sorry. I'm forgetting my manners."

Witherspoon sat down on a chair while Barnes lowered himself onto the settee, wincing as his backside made contact with the stiff, uncomfortable brocade seat. The constable pulled out his notebook and then looked expectantly at the inspector.

Witherspoon cleared his throat; there was no polite way to ask this question. "Leeson, when you and the other staff members went to Helen Cleminger's funeral, were you all together the entire time?"

Leeson's brows drew together in a puzzled frown. "We couldn't sit together on the train. It was crowded, so we moved about until everyone found a seat. But we all got off at the other end and met up on the station platform."

"Was the funeral close to the station?" Barnes looked up from his notebook.

"No, it was in Helen's village church, which was a mile or so from the station," Leeson replied cautiously. "It was a bit of a walk, but we managed."

"Did you sit together in the church?" Witherspoon continued.

"We couldn't. It's a small church, so everyone just made do with what they could find. The church was very crowded. There were people standing in the aisles and even in the entryway at the back."

The inspector nodded in encouragement. "But you all met up with one another after the service, is that correct?"

Leeson hesitated a fraction too long before he answered the question. "More or less."

"What does that mean?"

"It means most of us were present and accounted for." Leeson looked over his shoulder at the closed door. "Oh dear, I hadn't wanted to say anything, but well, you're going to find out anyway if you question the others." He sighed heavily. "Mrs. Rothwell didn't come to the funeral. When we got to the station, she told me she had some pressing business to take care of and that she had to do it that morning. She told us she'd meet us at the church, but she never came. I know because I was watching for her. She never showed up at poor little Helen's funeral at all. The next time I saw her was on the platform of Paddington Station here in London. And she pretended like she'd come to the funeral and been standing at the back the whole time, but she wasn't. I know because I was standing back there and she never arrived at all."

"But the other servants think she did?" Witherspoon clarified. "Is that what you're telling us?"

"I think several of them have guessed the truth, but no one wants to say anything because we all like Mrs. Rothwell and . . . well, what with Mr. Boyd being murdered, we didn't want you to think she'd done it."

"Why would you think she wanted her cousin dead?" Witherspoon asked.

"Because she had that great row with him," Leeson cried. "The whole house heard her screaming at the man. But she isn't a murderess. Despite her anger, she's a decent, good woman who put up with one humiliation after another from that awful man." He clamped his mouth shut as though he'd said too much.

The inspector said nothing for a long moment and the room was silent save the ticking of the clock. Then he said, "Thank you, Leeson. I know this must have been very difficult for you. Can you please ask Mrs. Rothwell to step inside?"

Leeson stared at him. "I know one shouldn't speak ill of the dead, but Mr. Boyd was not a very nice person. He was an absolutely dreadful human being and none of the staff liked him. But none of us, including Mrs. Rothwell, wished him dead." He turned on his heel and stalked into the hall, closing the door softly behind him.

Barnes glanced at the inspector. "You'd have thought one of them might have shared that information with us a bit earlier," he grumbled.

"They obviously didn't want to get Mrs. Rothwell in trouble," Witherspoon replied. "I'm wondering why she didn't tell us herself. Surely she must have realized that eventually we'd find out she didn't go to the funeral."

"I'll check on train times from St. Albans to Paddington," Barnes muttered. "We'll have to see if she'd have had time to get back here, murder Boyd, hide the weapon, and then get to the platform at Paddington in time to meet the others."

"She would have had time." Witherspoon shook his head. "Mark my words."

There was a soft knock on the door and a second later, Hannah Rothwell stepped inside. "I understand you wish to speak to me again."

"Indeed we do," Witherspoon replied. "Why don't you sit down, Mrs. Rothwell."

"There's no need for me to start acting like a guest, Inspector," she said bluntly. "Leeson told me he's already told you that I didn't go to poor Helen's funeral that day."

"Where did you go?" Witherspoon resisted the urge to stand up. He felt awkward sitting in the presence of a woman.

"I came back to London, but I expect you already know that."

"Mrs. Rothwell, please do sit down. My knee is bothering me terribly and if you insist on standing, I'll have to stand as well."

For a moment, he thought she was going to refuse, but then she walked over and sat down on the chair opposite him. "You're obviously very much a gentleman, Inspector. Is this better?"

"Much, thank you. Now, can you please tell us why you came back to London on the morning that Mr. Boyd was murdered?"

"That's simple. I went to see a solicitor," she replied. "There's one very near the station. I had it all planned. When we got off the train in St. Albans, I told the others to go ahead and I'd meet them at the church. Of course, I had no intention of meeting them. Instead, I took the next train back to London, saw my lawyer, and then got to the station in time to meet them when they came back."

"What's the name of your solicitor?" Barnes glanced up from his notebook.

"Jonathan Lampton. He's a partner at Lampton and Beekins. Their offices are at number 12 Holston Road."

"You told no one where you were going, is that correct?" Witherspoon regarded her quizzically. He wasn't sure what to ask next.

"That's correct."

The inspector blurted out the next question that came to mind. "Why did you want to see a solicitor?"

"I wanted to file a lawsuit, Inspector," she replied. "One generally needs a solicitor to do that."

Barnes asked the next question. "Who were you going to sue?"

"Let's stop dancing about this matter, shall we?" She smiled coolly. "I was going to sue my cousin Lawrence, and the reason I was so secretive about my movements is because I didn't want one of the others inadvertently letting Lawrence know what I was up to. I wanted it to be a surprise."

"A surprise," Witherspoon repeated.

"Oh, yes, Inspector, I wanted to be standing right next to him when he got served with the legal papers. I wanted to see that horrid smug smile wiped off his face when he knew that someone was finally going to take him to task for his negligence and his incompetence. I wanted to be a witness to the anguish it would cause his social-climbing soul to know that he was going to have his name and his professional reputation dragged through the courts. In short, I wanted to watch him suffer the way he'd made so many others suffer."

"I take it you didn't like your cousin very much," the inspector muttered.

"I hated him. He ruined what little life I have left. Wouldn't you hate someone who'd taken away everything you've ever wanted," she replied.

"What time was your appointment?" Barnes shifted slightly in an attempt to keep his backside from going completely numb.

"Ten o'clock."

"What time did you leave Mr. Lampton's office?" Witherspoon asked. He had recovered his equilibrium enough to think straight.

"Half past ten." She laughed. "And yes, I would have had time to get here, kill him, and then make it back to the train station to meet the others. We've very good cab service in this neighborhood. There's a stand just up the road."

"Why were you suing your cousin?" Witherspoon leaned forward slightly.

"I thought you'd have guessed, Inspector. Lawrence was an incompetent fool. He lost all my money," she said. "Money that I'd spent the last ten years saving. It was sitting in a post office account and it was nice and safe. Then Lawrence insisted he could make it earn more for me, that I'd do well if I gave it to him to invest. He harangued me about the matter so often that I finally gave in and let him have it."

"You hadn't wanted him to invest your money?" Barnes asked curiously.

"Oh, no, you see, I'm the real fool here. I should never have given him my money in the first place. I knew he didn't care a fig about financial matters. But I assumed that he had people working for him that did know what they were doing and that my money would be safe. That was a foolish mistake on my part. One that I'll regret until my dying day."

"If you felt it was your mistake in trusting him with your money in the first place, why did you want to sue him?" Witherspoon was almost sure that wasn't the reason. "Were you trying to recover your losses?"

"I've already told you why, Inspector." she smiled again. "I wanted to watch him suffer. That's why I filed suit. Furthermore, I'm going ahead with the lawsuit. I'm going to tie his estate up in court for years."

"But aren't you inheriting something from him?" Barnes asked. He wanted to know if she knew about her legacy.

"Humph. He's left me a few hundred pounds. But that's nothing compared to what I lost. Oh, yes, I know precisely how much he was leaving me. He told me what I'd get when he died. But that's not important to me."

"But Mrs. Rothwell," Witherspoon said softly, "you'll be out of a position soon, so surely even a few hundred pounds would be welcome."

"I don't care, Inspector." Her eyes narrowed and her expression grew fierce. "I want the estate tied up in court. It'll be a cold day in the pits of hell before this place is turned into a memorial to that odious man!"

CHAPTER 8

Dr. Bosworth's office fascinated Mrs. Jeffries even though she'd been there several times. The office was small and rather cramped. Most of the available floor space was taken up by the doctor's desk. Books, papers, and medical instruments were strewn willy-nilly across its top, and in the corner there was a jar of clear liquid with a green, oblong object floating in it. Dim light seeped into the room through the tall window of frosted glass just behind his chair. A glass-fronted bookcase filled with medical volumes stood next to the door, and the only other seat in the room was stacked high with papers and magazines.

Dr. Bosworth, a tall man with red hair and a pale, bony face, lifted the clutter off the chair. "Do sit down, Mrs. Jeffries," he said. He put the papers he was holding on top of the bookcase. "Forgive the mess. I meant to tidy up before you arrived, but the time simply got away from me. Sister said you'd come by yesterday, so I was expecting you."

"I hope I'm not catching you at an inconvenient time." She sat down. "But I am so hoping you can help us."

"It's not an inconvenient time in the least. I'm sorry I wasn't able to break away and see you yesterday." He smiled apologetically as he sat down behind his desk. "The sister said you'd waited most of the day."

"That's quite all right," she replied. "I know you were busy. Industrial accidents are terrible, aren't they? The papers said five people were killed and dozens injured."

"I thought they'd never stop bringing them in." He shook his head. "And the awful part was, the accident was preventable. A pressure gauge on the main boiler wasn't working properly. Can you believe it? The owners couldn't be bothered to make sure their equipment was in decent working order and as a result five people died. Dozens more were mangled by the explosion, and half of them probably won't be able to work again. I wonder when this country will start forcing factory owners to spend some of their precious profits on a few, simple safety precautions." He stopped, smiling ruefully. "You mustn't get me started on that topic, Mrs. Jeffries, otherwise we'll both be here for hours."

"I understand how you feel," she replied. "It does seem utterly senseless. How was your trip to Edinburgh?"

"It was most interesting. There were some fascinating papers presented. But you're not here to hear about the latest surgical techniques for removing the gall bladder." He opened his top drawer, reached inside, and pulled out a flat brown file. "This is the postmortem report on Lawrence Boyd."

Her eyes widened in surprise. "How on earth did you know what I needed? I didn't mention it to anyone when I was here yesterday."

"You didn't need to." He laughed. "When I heard you'd dropped by to see me, I knew it was because your inspector must have gotten a murder case. After that, it was easy to track down the identity of the victim."

"You'd make quite a good detective yourself," she said.

"I'll keep that in mind in case I should ever tire of medicine." He smiled. "The postmortem was done at University College Hospital on Gower Street. Getting a copy of the report wasn't difficult, but I warn you, I haven't had time to go over it as thoroughly as I'd like."

"Do you have time to take another look at it now?" she asked. "They've no idea what the murder weapon might have been."

"Whatever it was, it's probably at the bottom of the Thames by now." Bosworth flipped open the file and began to read.

Mrs. Jeffries sat quietly, giving him a chance to absorb the information in the report. While he read, she thought about the case and about what an odd person the victim had been. He was a rich banker who really didn't care a toss about business and an artist who was more concerned with building monuments to himself than with creating brilliant paintings. The only relationships that interested him were those that reinforced his own sense of importance.

Why he was thoroughly disliked was easy for her to understand. What was difficult to comprehend was why anyone would care enough about the man to murder him. That was what was bothering her about this case. Boyd had been the sort of man people would go out of their way to avoid, not someone who could inspire the kind of personal hatred it took to commit murder. Twenty years ago he jilted his fiancée and stole another man's intended. Mrs. Jeffries imagined that a good number of people had been enraged with him then, but people rarely held onto rage for such a long period of time. Strong emotions tended to dim with the passage of the years. But then again, perhaps she wasn't seeing the entire picture. Perhaps the murder had nothing to do with hatred, but was committed for an entirely different reason. It was quite possible that the chief clerk had committed the murder in the hopes of hiding his thievery. Or maybe the housekeeper had done it; she had been furious at Boyd as well. It was all very confusing. Mrs. Jeffries had the feeling that there was something right in front of her that she simply wasn't seeing.

She was jerked out of her reverie by Dr. Bosworth's voice. "Mrs. Jeffries, are you all right?"

"I'm fine. I'm sorry. I was thinking about the case."

"You were obviously deep in thought. I called your name twice." He smiled widely and closed the file. "I'm afraid the postmortem isn't going to be of much help to you. The attending physician didn't do anything except give a very general description of the wounds. He didn't take any measurements nor did he give a detailed description of the shape."

She was disappointed. She had so hoped he'd see something in the report that could help. "Oh, that is most unfortunate. Finding the murder weapon might be very important. This case isn't going well at all."

"I'm sorry." He shrugged apologetically. "I'd have a look at the body myself, but it's already been released to the undertakers."

"You've no idea what kind of weapon might have been used?" she pressed.

"Mrs. Jeffries, without actually seeing the wounds or reading a good description of the precise size or shape, it's impossible to say. The killer could have used anything: a hammer or a rock, a candlestick, or even a police truncheon. Without knowing the size and shape, I simply can't speculate."

Mrs. Jeffries mentally cursed the incompetence of most police surgeons. "I do wish other police surgeons would avail themselves of your methods. It would make our task so much easier."

"Perhaps one day they will," he replied. "Look, I can't tell you what the weapon was, but I can tell you this much: Boyd died from massive head injuries, and the surgeon wrote that he thought no more than two blows were struck. There's no mention that the skull was particularly thin, so I have to conclude that the blow was struck with a great deal of force."

"Which leads you to what conclusion?" she queried.

"The killer was either very strong or the murder weapon was very heavy." He gave her another apologetic smile. "I wish I could narrow it down further, but that's really the best I can do."

"You've been very helpful." She rose to her feet. "Thank you, Doctor. I appreciate your assistance. I know you're busy, so I won't take up any more of your time."

"It was a pleasure seeing you. Give my best regards to the others in the household." He got up, came out from behind the desk, and went to the door. "I wish I could tell you more, but with the scarcity of detail in the report and not having seen the body, I really mustn't speculate further. But do let me know how it all comes out."

"Let's just hope it all comes out with the right person being arrested for the crime," she said somberly.

Wiggins quickened his steps and dodged around a family huddled together in front of the entrance to Hyde Park. Following people was a lot harder than it looked, but he was determined not to lose his quarry. He glanced over his shoulder again, needing to make sure there was no one hot on his heels. But he saw no sign of the man in a flat workingman's cap nor of anyone else for that matter. He knew he was being overly cautious, but he couldn't help himself. Just the idea that one of Niven's lads had been pursuing him made him half sick to his stomach. But whatever Smythe had done last evening must have worked; he'd not seen hide nor hair of anyone since leaving Upper Edmonton Gardens.

He moved closer to the young woman he'd been trailing for the past ten minutes. She was a tall girl with dark blonde hair tucked into a topknot under a red bonnet that had seen better days. She wore a short gray jacket over a simple green day dress and sturdy black shoes. Under her arm, she'd tucked her umbrella and a small purse. Wiggins had seen her come out of the servant's entrance at the Boyd house this morning, so he was fairly sure she was a housemaid. He knew he should have tried to find out a bit more about Maud Sapington's movements on the morning of the murder, but as he knew Betsy was going over that way, he thought he might have another go at the Boyd servants. No one had really had any contact with them.

She rounded the corner and then slowed her pace. She stopped abruptly, looked around and then pulled open a door and stepped inside. Wiggins couldn't see what kind of establishment she'd gone into, but he hoped it was a café.

He ran up to where he'd seen her disappear. "Oh blast," he muttered aloud. She'd gone into a pub. A ruddy pub! Young girls in service weren't supposed to hang about in pubs on their own. But maybe she wasn't on her own, he thought. Maybe she was meeting her fella. He hoped not. He couldn't have much of a chat with the girl if her bloke was standing there watching them.

Wiggins yanked open the door and went inside. As it was just past opening time, the room wasn't very crowded. All three of the small tables were empty, and there was only one old man on the bench along the side wall. His quarry stood alone on this side of the bar. She was engaged in an intense conversation with the barmaid.

Moving nonchalantly, he ambled up to the bar and stopped a few feet away from where she stood. From behind him, he heard the door open, so he glanced over his shoulder, just to be sure it wasn't the man in the flat cap. But it was just an old woman carrying a shopping basket. She trudged up to the bar and eased in between him and the girl.

"Hello, Mum." The barmaid smiled brightly at the old woman. "Janie and I have been 'avin' a nice old natter. We expected you five minutes ago. Where've you been?"

"It's all right, Mum. Lallie's just pullin' your leg. I only just arrived myself."

Blast, Wiggins thought. It was a ruddy family reunion. He'd never get close enough to the girl to find out anything now. He wondered if he ought to leave.

"Don't you worry about me." The old woman put her basket on the bar. "You just worry about findin' another position. Get somethin' decent like your sister's got. But while you're standin' there, make yourself useful and pour me one."

"Oh, Mum." The barmaid rolled her eyes and then seemed to realize she had a customer. She smiled at Wiggins. "What can I get for you?"

Before he could stop himself, he said, "Please serve the lady first," he bowed at the older woman, "and then the young lady. If you wouldn't think me forward, it would be my pleasure to buy the both of you a libation."

"What's a libation?" the old woman asked.

"He means a drink, Mum." The barmaid stared at him suspiciously.

Wiggins pulled a half crown out of his coat pocket and handed it to the barmaid. "I'd like a pint as well."

She hesitated and then reached for the money. "That's right nice of you. Are you buyin' me one, too?"

"Of course," he replied. He was suddenly very glad the pub wasn't full. The elderly gent propped up on the bench in the corner was watching him avidly. Wiggins had a sudden, horrible thought that perhaps the old fellow worked for Nivens. Then he realized he was being stupid. The man had been sitting there when he'd come in. "It would my pleasure. The three of you remind me of my mum and sisters." He searched their faces carefully, trying to tell by their expressions whether he was being too bold. It wouldn't do him any good if they accepted the drinks and then ignored him.

"I'll have a gin if you don't mind." The barmaid grinned broadly. "My name's Lallie. That's short for Eulalie. And this here's my sister Janie and me mum."

"The name is Mrs. Mull." The old woman grinned. "And if you're buyin', I'll 'ave a gin as well."

"A half pint will do me," Janie replied.

"And what would you like?" Lallie grabbed a half-pint glass from underneath the bar and filled it from the pump.

"A half pint will be fine for me as well." Wiggins wasn't sure what to do next, but his offer hadn't ended in disaster, so he figured he might as well try to see what he could find out. "I don't suppose any of you fine ladies might know of an establishment in need of a fully trained footman, do you?"

"You're lookin' for a position, then?" Mrs. Mull stared at him suspiciously.

"I'm not in desperate need of one just yet," he lied. He didn't like the way the old woman's expression had hardened. He didn't want them thinking he was down and out. "The household I'm currently in is gettin' set to go out to India and they want me to go with 'em. But me mum, she lives over in Stepney, and she wants me to stay. I'd quite like to see one of them strange foreign countries, but I promised Mum I'd have a look around and see about gettin' another position here."

Mrs. Mull relaxed a bit. "No mother wants her children so far away."

"There's nothin' goin' where I work," Janie added. "Our master just died, so we're all goin' to be lookin' for positions ourselves."

Wiggins gaze at her sympathetically. "That's a bit of bad news for ya, isn't it? Won't the mistress of the house keep you on?"

"He weren't married." Janie grinned. "But it weren't really bad news, not for me anyways. I was lookin' for a new position anyways. It wasn't a very nice place to work."

"It was perfectly decent." Mrs. Mull frowned at her daughter. "Your Mr. Boyd was a bit of an old maid, but there's worse employers about. You should hear some of the troubles your father and I have had over the years tryin' to make ends meet. At least your Mr. Boyd fed you decently and you had a roof over your head."

"That's about all we had," Janie muttered.

"It's not nice to speak ill of the dead," Lallie said softly.

"Rubbish," Janie snapped. "Just because he died doesn't make him a better person than he was in life."

Wiggins thought they'd forgotten he was standing here.

"It's still not nice to speak ill of him," Lallie shot back. "He's not here to defend himself."

"That's true, I suppose. He might have been a bit of a tartar, but at least he's not as bad as some."

"Has either of you heard anything about the Sapington household?" Wiggins blurted. He knew this was a dangerous tactic. He didn't want to say too much and give the game away. "I've heard they have a position open."

Janie's jaw dropped in surprise. "I know about them. I'd not go there if I was you. That's about the only household in London worse than Mr. Boyd's."

"What's so awful about it?" Wiggins asked.

"On the day that Mr. Boyd were murdered, our household was set to go to a funeral. But Mr. Boyd had a luncheon planned for one of his silly charities. Do you know that the Sapingtons sent a lad over to find out what was bein' served that day? Bloomin' cheeky."

"Your Mr. Boyd was murdered?" Wiggins pretended to be shocked. "That's terrible."

"I suppose so." Janie took a sip of her drink.

"Why did the Sapingtons want to know what was bein' served?" he asked. "I mean, you're right, that's a bit of cheek. No one's ever come around and asked my mistress what was on the menu when they were 'avin' a do."

Janie stared at him blankly for a few moments, then she shrugged. "The lad said Mr. Sapington had sent him over to make sure shrimp wasn't bein' served. Seems he's got an allergy to shellfish and it'll make 'im deathly ill. But Mrs. Rothwell told the boy it was just going to be a cold luncheon of ham and roast beef because we were all to be gone that morning and nothing was bein' cooked."

"How does that make him the meanest master in London?" Wiggins asked.

"Because when Helen—that's the girl who died, the one whose funeral we all went to on the day Mr. Boyd was done in—when she first got ill and went round to the doctor's, she run into another girl there who had the same thing. They both had bronchitis. She and this girl got to talking and it turns out the girl worked for the Sapingtons and that she'd been ill for over a month. She'd asked Mr. Sapington for an advance on her quarterly wages so she could pay the doctor, and he wouldn't give it to her. The bastard had made her wait till the end of the month. All I can say is even Lawrence Boyd wasn't that mean. When Helen got sick, he gave her an advance right away so she could get seen to!"

"And you remembered Mr. Sapington's name all this time?" Wiggins thought that odd. He rarely recalled the names of people who he'd heard mentioned in casual conversation.

"Only because Helen come back and was tellin' us all about it and Mr. Boyd happened to overhear her. Mr. Boyd never said a word to the likes of us unless it was to scream or scold, but he flopped his big arse down right there in the kitchen and made Helen tell him all the details."

"That's peculiar," Wiggins said.

"Not for Mr. Boyd. A few days later, after Helen had gone home to recover, I heard Mrs. Rothwell tellin' Mr. Leeson that Mr. Boyd was spreadin' the story about Mr. Sapington all over town. It was like he wanted everyone to know that Mr. Sapington was a terrible person."

Smythe pushed through the door of the Dirty Duck and headed for Blimpey's table. He was sitting in his usual spot, but he was hunched over and staring at the tabletop like it was a racing sheet. He glanced up and frowned. "Humph, it's you. I might have known the day wasn't going to get any better."

"What 'ave I done?" Smythe sank down on the stool.

"What have you done?" Blimpey repeated. "What have you done? Let me tell you what you've done: you've given me the worst advice I ever had. Nell's so angry she's not said a kind word to me since I took your bloomin' advice and told her the truth about Tommy and his mum."

Smythe was dumbstruck. He didn't know what to say. "But everything was fine last evening," he blurted. "I saw you less than twelve hours ago and you never said a word."

"Twelve hours ago I hadn't told Nell the truth," Blimpey shot back. "But after you left, I decided it was the right time. Nell was in nice mood and we was havin' a nice natter about the upstairs curtains. So I told her the truth. Well, guess what, Smythe? She wasn't in the least happy about the wild oats I'd sowed in my past."

Smythe grimaced. "Oh Blimpey, I'm sorry. I thought she'd be reasonable."

"And what's more," Blimpey continued, "Tommy's mum is furious at me as well. Seems she liked things the way they were and didn't appreciate the fact that now there's a few people about who know Tommy's my lad and not her dead husband's. Though I can't see that she really thought she was foolin' anyone. Tommy were born eleven months after Angus died."

"But you kept her son from bein' hanged," Smythe protested. He was willing to take the blame for Nell being angry, but he drew the line at Tommy's mum. They'd done her a great favor. "I mean, you come to us . . ."

Blimpey waved him off impatiently. "I know what you meant."

"I'm sorry, Blimpey," Smythe said. "I never meant for this to happen." He would never, ever give anyone advice about women as long as he lived.

"Oh, what's the use?" Blimpey sighed heavily. "I know it's not really your fault. I was goin' to tell Nell the truth all along."

"Then why'd you ask my advice?" Smythe demanded.

"Because if things went wrong, which they did, I'd have you to blame." He grinned broadly.

"I didn't mean for my advice to cause you grief. But remember, you did ask me and all I did was tell you what I thought."

"I know, I know. Like I said, it's not your fault. Besides, Nell will get over it and so will Tommy's good mother." He sighed again. "Edna's just a bit embarrassed, but once she gets past that, she'll be fine. Now, let's get down to business." He caught the barmaid's attention. "Two pints, please."

"What have you got for me?" Smythe was relieved to be moving off this sticky subject.

"Quite a bit, actually." Blimpey leaned forward. "Half of London disliked your Mr. Boyd. Turns out that Maud Sapington loathed him so much, she used her influence to try and get him turfed out of the Amateur Artists Guild, but he fought back by givin' 'em a huge donation, so she wasn't able to do much except sully his reputation."

Smythe nodded. "Yeah, that's what we've found out."

"As for the guests that were comin' to luncheon that day, the one you might want to keep your eye on is Walter Gibbons." He smiled at the barmaid as she brought them their beer. "Thanks, love."

Smythe waited until the barmaid had moved out of earshot before speaking. "What about Gibbons? What did you find out?"

"He hated Boyd," Blimpey replied.

"We know that." Smythe struggled to keep the impatience out of his voice.

"But did you know that he was seen walking down Queens Road in Bayswater around the time of the murder?" Blimpey grinned triumphantly.

"How do you know that?" Smythe asked.

Blimpey shrugged. "It's my business to find out such things.

Not only that, but Gibbons recommended to the board of the
Bankers Benevolent Society that the honorary chairmanship be
given to Arnold Sapington and not Lawrence Boyd."

"But it was Boyd who got it," Smythe pointed out. "How did
that happen?"

"Gibbons was overruled." Blimpey took a quick sip of beer.
"There was quite a dustup at that board meeting. Gibbons told the
other members that if they gave it to Boyd, he'd resign from the
board. They still overruled him and he resigned."

"But he went to Boyd's house that day to tell him the news."

"Did he?" Blimpey shrugged. "Or did he just show up after the
fire to make sure the job was done properly?"

Smythe shook his head. "I don't understand any of this. Are you
sayin' you think Gibbons did the murder?"

"All I'm sayin' is that he was spotted in Boyd's neighborhood at
the time of the killin'."

"He was on his way to luncheon at the Boyd house," Smythe
protested.

"You don't show up for a luncheon an hour and a half early. As
I just said, Gibbons had resigned from the board, so one of the
other board members was goin' to take his place at the luncheon,"
Blimpey explained. "But then Gibbons relented and said he'd do
it. The other board members weren't keen on him doing it, considerin' as he'd just resigned over the matter, but they couldn't stop
him as he'd made his resignation effective for the following day.
Seems to me he was planning on more than just givin' Lawrence
Boyd some good news. Seems to me he was plannin' on a lot more
than that."

Luty stood on the pavement and stared through the window of
Brougham's Fine Art. The elegant establishment catered to the
rich and the powerful. She grabbed the doorknob, gave it a twist,
and stepped inside. She paused just inside the doorway and surveyed the room. Tables covered with colorful brocade runners or
fringed silk shawls were strategically placed to best display the
shops offerings of antique Chinese vases, ornate woodcarvings,
crystal glassware, porcelain statues, and other fine home furnishings.

Opposite the door, a young man with slicked-back hair and
dressed in formal coattails was standing in front of a glass display

case. He was speaking with a well-dressed matron. He glanced at Luty and then immediately turned back to the matron.

The door at the back of the shop opened and a tall, dignified man with iron-gray hair and wearing a pin-striped suit stepped inside. His eyes widened in surprise when he saw Luty by the front door. "Oh, gracious, Mrs. Crookshank, how long have you been here? Gaspar, why haven't you offered Mrs. Crookshank a chair?" He flew down the length of the shop.

"That's all right, Harry." Luty chuckled as the hapless clerk's expression changed from haughty indifference to one of dismay. "Your clerk was helpin' this other lady. I kin wait my turn."

"Nonsense. I'll be pleased to take care of you myself." Harry Brougham took Luty's elbow, shot the hapless Gaspar a dirty look, and then led her to a seat at a small round table near the window. "Gracious, Luty, it's been ages since I've seen you. What can I do for you? Would you care for tea?"

As Luty planned to be back at Upper Edmonton Gardens in an hour, she thought it best to decline. "No thank you, Harry. What I'm really after is a bit of information. I'm hopin' you kin help me."

"But of course." Harry smiled brightly. Mrs. Crookshank was a bit eccentric, but then again, she was an American and they were all a somewhat odd. Still, he'd known her for years and she was an excellent customer.

"I'm tryin' to find out about that banker that was killed. I expect you've heard of him. His name was Lawrence Boyd."

Harry's smile faltered. "I saw something about it in the newspapers. But I don't know that I could be of any help."

"But he was an artist and a banker," Luty said doggedly. "Are you tellin' me you never met the man?"

"Perhaps I might have met him a time or two, but certainly I didn't know him well enough to make any sort of comment about his circumstances." Harry picked a piece of nonexistent lint off the arm of his pin-striped jacket.

"Oh, don't be such an old stick, Harry." Luty poked him in the ribs. "You and I go way back. I remember when you were running a stall out of the East End and pushing stuff you'd bought cheap off widows and orphans."

Harry looked around quickly. "Shh . . . Really, Luty, keep your voice down. That was a long time ago."

"I know. I'm just remindin' you to git off that high horse of yours. This is me you're talking to. Now, can you help me or not?"

Harry Brougham had been a friend of Luty's late husband before he'd gone to America to seek his fortune. They'd renewed their acquaintance when the Crookshanks returned some years later. By then, all of them had been successful. Luty had used Harry's services in redecorating her house in Knightsbridge, and over the years since, she'd also steered thousands of pounds worth of business his way.

Harry glanced over his shoulder and gave Gaspar, who was staring openly at them, a good glare. "Continue helping Mrs. Morgan," he ordered. He turned back to Luty. "Alright, I did know him. But he was a dreadful man and certainly not someone I'm going to remember with any great fondness."

"Now we're gettin' somewhere." Luty grinned. "I knew you had to know the fellow. I ain't looking for a testimonial to the man's character. I just need some information."

Harry's eyes narrowed suspiciously. "Why? Did he lose your money?"

Luty nodded, relieved she didn't have to make up some tale about why she was interested in Lawrence Boyd. "Yep, and I aim to git it back. A friend of mine recommended his bank for a commercial transaction, so instead of goin' to my usual bankers, I went to him. Then I found out the fellow got himself murdered and that don't sit well with me."

"Come now, Luty, pull the other one. This is me, remember? Unless you've completely lost your mind, you wouldn't have given Boyd a farthing. You're far too good a businesswoman to do something that foolish." Harry grinned and leaned closer. "Tell me the real reason you're asking questions and I'll tell you what I know about him."

"You always did drive a hard bargain." Luty laughed. She'd forgotten that under that fake upper-class exterior Harry adopted, there was still the sharp, hungry boy from the mean streets of the East End. He wasn't easily fooled. "All right, I'm trying to find out who might have wanted to murder him."

"Half of London," Harry shot back. "And why do you care? I know he wasn't a friend of yours. Boyd didn't have any friends."

"No, but a friend of mine might be in a lot of trouble soon if the police don't catch the real killer," Luty replied. Her explanation was close enough to have a ring of truth. It wasn't a lie. The inspector might get into difficulties if this case went unsolved and Luty considered him a friend. "So tell me what you know."

Harry shrugged. "I don't know any more than most people who have some connections with both art and commerce in this city. Boyd was an exceptional artist, a miserable businessman, and a dreadful person. He's spent virtually the last ten years pushing himself forward to be head of one committee or another. Honestly, the man positively delighted in building monuments to his name. I heard a rumor that he promised the board of the Amateur Artists Guild his house when he died if they'd elect him to their board. Can you believe such gall?"

Luty nodded. Harry wasn't telling her anything she didn't already know about Boyd. "How about the Sapingtons? Do you know them?"

"You mean Arnold and Maud Sapington?" Harry shook his head. "I've heard of them, of course. But I don't know them. They shop at Coventry's on Regent Street." He sniffed disapprovingly at the mention of his rival's name. "People like to say that Arnold Sapington got where he is by marriage to Maud Reese. He was the chief clerk at Reese and Cutlip when they got married."

"Wasn't she the boss's daughter?"

"She was but I don't think she married Arnold Sapington because she couldn't find anyone else," he replied. "And that's frequently what people say when they hear about a marriage such as hers. I think she married him out of gratitude."

"Gratitude?" Luty repeated. "Why would she be grateful to her father's chief clerk?"

Harry laced his fingers together on the tabletop and stared at her. "Because she'd lost the true love of her life, her cousin Nicholas Cutlip. He drowned in a boating accident just a few weeks before they were to marry. Some say Maud only married Arnold because he'd tried so hard to save the young man."

"Sapington was with him when the accident happened?"

"Yes, they were out rowing. The boat tipped over. According to witnesses, Sapington tried his best to pull the young man to shore, but he couldn't manage it. Nicholas kept going under. It was sad. Sapington is a bit of a social climber but he's no fool, and he's not brought Reese and Cutlip to the edge of bankruptcy."

"Was Boyd's bank at the edge?"

Harry shrugged again. "I've heard the other partners have had to put in some infusions of cash and that there was a movement afoot to oust him from his position. But as Boyd held the most shares, it was going to be difficult to get rid of the fellow."

Luty was getting desperate. She hated the thought of being the only one at their afternoon meeting who hadn't found out anything useful and so far, she'd learned nothing they didn't already know. "What about Walter Gibbons? You heard of him?"

Harry thought for a moment. "The name sound's familiar, but I can't say that I've heard anything about him."

"Did Boyd have any other enemies . . . Oh, of course he did. You've already told me half of London hated him." Luty sighed deeply. "But who hated him enough to want him dead? That's the question."

James Glover stared at the two policemen. "I don't know what you're talking about, Inspector," he finally blustered. "The police have all the files that I took to Mr. Boyd that morning."

"They don't have the Pressley file," the inspector said. He wasn't in the best of humor and he wasn't inclined to beat about the bush with Mr. Glover. After he finished here, he was going to have to go back to the Boyd household, and as he'd already been there once today, he felt a tad foolish. But it was his own fault as he'd forgotten to question Boyd's servants about an interesting idea he and Mrs. Jeffries had discussed over breakfast this morning. Drat, he hated being so forgetful.

"You were the last one to have that file," Barnes added.

Glover glared at the constable and shoved his chair away from the desk. "That's ridiculous. I put those files on the table in Mr. Boyd's studio and that's the last I saw of them."

"Are you sure about that, sir?" Witherspoon pressed. He edged closer to the door, wanting to be at the ready in case Glover should try to bolt. His experiences of the past few years had taught him to be very cautious when he was pressing a suspect, so he'd stationed two constables at the street door. They were under instructions to stop anyone who came running out of the building. Witherspoon sincerely hoped there wasn't a fire. "Are you sure you didn't take it when the fire started?"

Glover's eyes narrowed angrily as a dull red flush crept up his face. "Who told you I'd taken that file?" he demanded. "They're lying."

Barnes pulled a piece of paper out of his pocket. "This is the list that Mr. Boyd sent over by messenger on the morning he died. The file is on the list."

"Where did you get that?" he snapped.

"Mr. Bingley had put it in his desk," Witherspoon replied. "He gave it to me when I was last here. I compared this list to the files we took into evidence. The ones from Mr. Boyd's studio. The Pressley file is missing. Can you explain that?"

Glover took a deep breath. "The only explanation is that the police must have lost it."

"We didn't lose it," Barnes said softly. "But you'd have reason to want it to be lost, wouldn't you?"

"I've no idea what you're talking about." Glover swallowed nervously.

Witherspoon sighed deeply. He hated it when people behaved as if the police were fools. "Mr. Glover, you're not doing yourself any good at all."

"I don't know what you mean." Glover's eyes bulged and he leapt to his feet. "I think you'd better leave. We're very busy and I've a number of important matters to see to this afternoon."

"Sit back down, man," Barnes said wearily. "We're not going anywhere and neither are you. If you like, you can accompany us to the station to help with our inquiries, or we can take care of the matter here. Which is it to be?"

Glover's gaze cut to the door and then back to the two policemen.

Barnes slapped his notebook shut and tucked it back in his pocket. Witherspoon shifted so that his weight was on his good knee. Both men knew that Glover was weighing the odds of running for it.

Suddenly, Glover flopped back into his chair, buried his face in his hands, and started to wail. His pudgy shoulders shook and he started rocking back and forth. "Oh . . . no . . . no . . . no . . ." he cried.

Alarmed, the inspector started toward him, thinking that if he kept chugging back and forth like a demented freight train, he'd topple over and hurt himself. But Barnes was quicker. He darted toward Glover and grabbed his arm. "Mr. Glover, for goodness sake, get hold of yourself."

"I didn't do it," Glover wailed. He raised his eyes to the constable. Tears streaked down his cheeks, his skin was dead white, and the hair around his temples was standing straight up. "I tell you, I didn't do it."

"No one has accused you of anything," Witherspoon said softly.

"But you're going to. I know you are. I've always had rotten luck, and now you're going to think I did it because of that stupid file, but I didn't kill him. I swear, I didn't kill him."

"Why don't you tell us exactly what you did do?" Witherspoon suggested kindly. He sat down and motioned for Barnes to take the chair next to him. He was fairly certain the danger was past and that Glover wouldn't charge for the door.

Barnes relaxed his stance, sat down, and pulled out his notebook. He looked at Glover expectantly.

"I'm not sure where to start." Glover pulled out a handkerchief, blew his nose, wiped his face, and took a deep breath.

"Start from the time you received the note from Mr. Boyd," Witherspoon replied.

"That's as good a place as any, I suppose," Glover said wearily. "As you know, I was here at the office when a street lad popped in with a note from Mr. Boyd. The note instructed me to bring some files to his studio and that I was to stay to luncheon. It told me to come straightaway and that's what I did. When I arrived, he told me to put the files on the table and go tidy myself up. He said there was a bathroom in the hallway I could use."

"According to your original statement, you went into the drawing room and fell asleep," Barnes said, reading from his notebook. "Would you like to amend that statement."

"No, that's what I actually did."

"But Mr. Glover, the furniture in there is horribly uncomfortable," the inspector protested. "I can't imagine anyone falling asleep on the settee or any of the chairs."

"But I did, Inspector. I was exhausted you see. I've not slept much for the past few weeks so I really did nod off. I agree, though; the furniture is dreadful." He smiled weakly. "I was awakened by Miss Clarke's cry of alarm. She'd cried out in some fashion and it startled me. I went out into the hall and saw her running toward the back door. She saw me and yelled that there was a fire in the studio. I told her that I'd go to the studio and for her to go get the fire brigade, that there was a station just around corner. She ran off and I continued on to the studio. There was smoke everywhere, and I could see flames through the window."

"But you went in, didn't you?" Barnes said softly. "You knew this was your one chance, so even though you were frightened of fire, you opened the studio door. Right?"

He nodded. "That's right. The fire wasn't as bad as I'd first thought, and when I went inside, I called out for Mr. Boyd. Then I saw him on the settee. It was obvious he was already dead, so I grabbed the Pressley file, stuck it under my shirt, and stepped back out into the garden."

"How did you know he was dead?" The inspector watched him carefully. He didn't know whether he believed him.

"I just knew," Glover replied. "He was so still. It was dreadful of me, I know, but I didn't care in the least that he was dead. I simply wanted to get that awful file and hide it away so no one could ever, ever see it. But that's silly, isn't it? Whether the file is there or not, the money is still missing."

"Did you know that Mr. Boyd had hired a typewriter girl that morning?" Barnes asked.

Glover shook his head. "Not until I arrived. Mr. Boyd told me to stick my head into the study and make sure she was working. He said it never hurt to keep an eye on people." He laughed bitterly. "He was certainly keeping an eye on me."

"What do you mean by that, sir?" Witherspoon asked.

"He knew what I was doing, Inspector." Glover laughed bitterly. "That's why he asked for the Pressley file."

"What did he know?" Witherspoon pressed.

Glover looked him straight in the eye. "He knew I was embezzling money, Inspector. But that makes me a thief, not a murderer."

CHAPTER 9

It was quite late by the time the inspector and Barnes went back to the Boyd residence. "Barnes, you really ought to go on home," Witherspoon said as they waited for someone to answer the front door. "It's already past five and I'm sure your wife will have your supper on the table soon."

"You said this wouldn't take long, sir, and the missus is used to warmin' up my food." Barnes thought they might be on a fool's errand, but the inspector had been adamant about coming back and speaking to the servants again.

Leeson opened the door and stared at them expressionlessly. "Good afternoon, gentlemen."

"Good afternoon, Leeson. We'd like to have a quick word with the staff. If you'll just tell Mrs. Rothwell we're here—"

"Mrs. Rothwell is at the undertaker's," Leeson interrupted wearily. "She took them Mr. Boyd's clothes so they can prepare him for the funeral tomorrow. After she leaves there, she said she was going to visit a friend. I don't expect her back until later this evening." He pulled the door open wide and stepped back. "But you may as well come inside. Go into the drawing room and I'll send them up."

"Thank you. Can you send up the cook first?" Witherspoon asked. He and Barnes crossed the threshold and stepped into the foyer.

"Yes, Inspector," Leeson replied.

They made their way down the hall and went into the drawing room. Barnes sank down on one of the chairs, wincing as he tried to make himself comfortable. "Why do people buy rubbish like this? The seat is as hard as a blooming rock."

"Some people are more interested in appearance than comfort." Witherspoon remained standing. He wandered over to the wall and gazed up at a painting of a seascape. "Boyd was an artist. Apparently beauty was more important to him than comfort."

"Humph," Barnes snorted and pulled out his notebook. "I'll bet he's got a nice old soft chair tucked away somewhere. I can't see anyone sitting for more than a few minutes on this lot."

The cook appeared in the open doorway. "Leeson says you want to speak to me again," she said. She didn't look pleased by the prospect of another chat with the police.

"We would indeed." Witherspoon smiled at the woman. She stared stonily back at him. "It will only take a few minutes. Why don't you sit down?"

"I'd just as soon stand, sir," she said bluntly. "I've a cake in the oven and I need to get back downstairs. Those girls are useless when it comes to baking and they'll let it burn. Now, what do you want to know?"

Witherspoon hesitated. He wanted to ask this question properly, but he didn't want to lead the witness, so to speak. At breakfast this morning, Mrs. Jeffries had handed him his coffee cup and made a comment about the murder weapon and the fact that the Boyd household was in such a busy, crowded neighborhood. That casual remark got him thinking that the killer must have been taking an awful risk walking about with a bloody weapon hidden on his or her person. Then it had occurred to him that perhaps the weapon hadn't been carried off at all. Instead, after the murder, it might have been cleaned off and put back in its proper place here in the house with no one the wiser.

"Inspector, are you going to speak up or just stand there all day?" the cook said impatiently.

"Sorry." Witherspoon took a deep breath. "When you arrived back from the funeral that day, did you notice anything amiss in your kitchen?"

"Did I notice something amiss?" The cook frowned in confusion. "No. Not really. None of the guests had been down there if that's what you're asking. No, now wait a minute, I tell a lie. Janie complained that someone had moved the sugar hammer. It wasn't in the right drawer."

The inspector glanced at Barnes and then back at the cook. "May we see this hammer, please?"

"You want to see my sugar hammer?" The cook looked at him, her expression incredulous. "Right now?"

"That's right," Witherspoon replied. He walked out to the hall. "I'm sorry to put you to so much trouble, but it is important."

"Well, I never," the cook grumbled, but she followed along after him. Barnes fell in step behind her.

A few minutes later, they were standing in the dimly lit kitchen. The cook pulled open a drawer from the center work table and reached inside. She brought out a huge hammer-like thing with an incredibly large head on it. "It's a big one," she said. "Fourteen inches in length and it's got a nice two-inch metal and wood head. We do a lot of baking and I got tired of using that poxy little thing Mr. Boyd had here, so I insisted that he buy this one. It's made by a firm in Germany. They like sweets in Germany. Now if it's all the same to you, I'll get back to my cake." She handed it to the inspector.

"Thank you." He examined it for a moment and then handed it to Barnes.

The constable looked at it closely, then waited until the cook was fussing about at the stove before he spoke. "This could do it, sir. One blow from something this heavy would kill anyone."

"And the killer could have gotten in and out of the kitchen." The inspector pointed to a door leading to the side yard. "The kitchen was empty and the side door probably unlocked. He or she could easily have crossed down the edge of the garden to the studio without being seen by Miss Clarke. The desk in the study faces the hall door."

"Too bad we don't have any way of knowing for certain," Barnes murmured.

"Perhaps we do." Witherspoon glanced at the cook. She was bending over the open oven door holding a straw. The inspector waited till she'd pulled the cake out, poked the center with the straw, and then examined the tip. He and Barnes watched as she picked up the cake and put it on a stone slab lying on the counter. "Excuse me, Mrs. . . ." He spoke loudly hoping she'd turn and look at him. He'd forgotten her name.

"Yes, what is it?" She frowned irritably.

"After Mr. Boyd's murder, did you use this hammer?"

"I'm not sure I understand what you mean?" The cook's frown deepened.

"Did you use this the day you came back from Helen Cleminger's funeral?" Witherspoon hoped that was clear enough.

"That's a funny thing to inquire about. Why would you want to know something like that?"

"We just do," Barnes interjected, "and we'd be obliged if you'd just answer the question."

"I used it that very afternoon," she snapped. "The others were upset, so I made a nice bread pudding to calm everyone's nerves. Mr. Boyd's guests had made real pigs of themselves, so there wasn't much left for us to eat. Honestly, you'd think a murder right under their very noses might have affected their appetites, but not that lot. There wasn't so much as a crumb of Battenberg cake left."

"I'm sure the pudding was delicious," Witherspoon soothed. "When you pulled the sugar hammer out of the drawer, was it as it always was?" He wasn't certain he'd phrased the question so she would understand what he was asking, but he really didn't want to put words in her mouth.

"I don't understand. What would have been different about it? It's a piece of kitchen equipment. It's not going to grow mold or be any different from one moment to the next."

"You're right, of course." That answered his question. "Thank you. You've been very helpful."

"It was different though," a voice said from behind them.

The two policemen turned around. A young scullery maid was standing in the doorway. She was holding a flat wicker basket filled with carrots and tomatoes. "Don't you remember, Mrs. Milford? I got the hammer out for you and it was in the wrong drawer."

"I already told them that," the cook said.

"But I told you that it was wet as well."

"You'd probably not dried it properly." The cook brushed aside her explanation. "In this damp weather, things don't dry out very quickly."

"But I 'ad dried it properly," the girl insisted. "I always dry everything properly ever since Mr. Boyd raised such a fuss about that Wedgwood platter last month. Remember? He threatened to sack me."

"That's right, he did, didn't he? Now that you mention it, I do recall you sayin' the hammer was wet."

"Had you used the hammer that day before leaving for the funeral?" Barnes asked.

"Oh, yes, I used it that morning."

"And I washed it right afterwards." The maid walked over to the worktable and put down the basket of vegetables. "Everything was washed, dried, and properly put away before we left for the funeral. That hammer was dry as a bone when I put it in the drawer, and what's more, I put it in the right drawer, not the one it was in when we come back that day."

"Thank you, ladies," Witherspoon said. "If anyone needs us, we'll be out in Mr. Boyd's studio. We'd like to have another look around."

They left by the side door, Barnes walking slightly behind the inspector. As soon as they were far enough away not to be overheard, he said, "Do you think it's the weapon, sir?"

"Yes, as a matter of fact I do," the inspector replied. "But even with the statements from the cook and the maid, we can't be absolutely sure." He stepped off the path onto the lawn. "Mind you, if that hammer was used to kill Boyd, it solved a number of problems for the killer."

"All he or she had to do was give it a good wash under the pump and toss it back in a drawer."

They reached the studio. Witherspoon pulled open the door. "I think the killer knew the house was going to be empty. Helen Cleminger's funeral had to have been planned for several days, and I think the murderer knew that the servants would be gone."

Barnes followed Witherspoon into the studio. "That's possible, sir," he said. "But it seems to me the killer couldn't be certain there wasn't going to be someone left home. Boyd wasn't known in the area as a particularly kind or generous master, and there was a good chance he'd have made someone stay that morning. The murderer was taking an awfully big chance."

"Most killers are prepared to take quite large risks to get what they want," Witherspoon replied. "That's one of the reasons we're able to catch them. No matter how much planning a murderer does, something unexpected often happens."

* * *

"I hope you lot have found out something useful today." Mrs. Goodge put a plate of sliced maderia cake down next to the teapot. "My sources have been positively useless. The only thing I heard was some old gossip."

"Not to worry, Mrs. Goodge." Wiggins dropped into his seat and reached for a slice of cake. "There's always tomorrow."

"Let's get started then." Mrs. Jeffries slipped into her place at the head of the table and glanced at the empty chair next to Smythe. "I'm sure Betsy will be here any moment. It's only just gone half past four."

"I'm here, I'm here," Betsy called out as she hurried down the hallway. "I'd have been back on time but that ruddy train was late."

"Train?" Smythe repeated. "Where'd you go that you had to take a train?"

"It's a long story." She took off her hat and jacket, hung them up, and then sat down at the table. "Don't worry, you'll hear all about it, and I'm not even sure what little information I got was worth the trip."

Wiggins grinned broadly. "Sounds like you 'ad an adventure. I did, too. I was in a pub and I ended up buyin' drinks for three ladies. I've never done that before."

"I'm sure we've all quite a bit to report," Mrs. Jeffries interjected. Today was going to be one of those times when she had to keep a firm grip on the meeting if they were to get through everyone's report. "Who would like to go first?"

"If it's all the same to everyone, I've found out an interesting fact or two," Hatchet volunteered. "It's not going to be of much help in finding out who murdered Boyd, but it will eliminate some of our suspects."

"Git on with it," Luty said impatiently. "I don't know why you always have to draw everything out."

"I'm not drawing it out, madam," Hatchet said sarcastically. "I'm merely reciting pertinent facts in a forthright and intelligent manner. Now, if you'll let me continue with my narrative, I'll, as you so succinctly put it, get on with it. As I mentioned at our last meeting, I had an appointment to find out some information about Boyd's partners. As we discussed, they weren't happy with the way he conducted bank business, but I don't think any of them could have killed him." He pulled a slip of paper out of his jacket pocket and began to read. "Evan Kettleworth left for the Continent two weeks ago, Harvey Holcomb is in bed with a case of gout and has been incapacitated since three days before the murder, and John Sawyer was in Leeds negotiating a merger. So, unless they hired the murder done, none of them could have committed the crime."

"It wasn't a hired killing," Smythe said softly. "A professional wouldn't have bothered to try to burn the place down."

"I agree." Mrs. Jeffries looked at Hatchet. "Did your contact have any idea what happens to Boyd's share of the bank?"

Hatchet grinned broadly. "Indeed he did. As Boyd didn't have any direct heirs, the terms and conditions of the charter are such that his shares can only be bought by the other partners."

"You mean it's not part of 'is estate?" Wiggins asked.

"It is, but Boyd didn't have the legal right to will the shares to whoever he wanted. The partnership agreement was originally drawn up to keep the bank private. If a partner dies with no direct heirs, then the other partners must buy those shares at the current market value."

"So Boyd's estate gets paid the value of his shares, but the bank stays in the hands of the partners," Smythe murmured. "Only now there are three partners, not four."

"That's a handy motive for wanting him dead," Betsy said.

"True, but my source also told me that Boyd's partners are going to have to take out loans in order to buy the shares, so it's not likely they were eager to see him dead. It's going to cost them all an arm and a leg. Kettleworth is going to have to mortgage his country estate, and Sawyer is putting up his interest in Stratford's Shipping as collateral for a loan to pay his third of the cost. Harvey Holcomb's got a rich wife, but from what I hear, she doesn't care overly much for his company, so getting the cash for his third out of her isn't going to be very pleasant. No, much as Boyd's partners thought him incompetent, his death is causing them no end of problems."

"Then I suppose we'd best concentrate on our other suspects," Mrs. Jeffries said slowly. But she wasn't going to discount the partners completely. She'd keep an open mind about the situation. "Who would like to go next?"

"I found out a bit about Walter Gibbons," Smythe said. He gave them the information he'd learned from Blimpey without, of course, mentioning Blimpey's name. When he'd finished, he reached for a slice of cake and waited for the others to comment.

"So Boyd caused Gibbons to resign," Hatchet said, his expression thoughtful. "That could bring back a lot of old anger and resentments. Perhaps we ought to have a closer look at Mr. Gibbons."

"And he was seen in the neighborhood before the murder," Mrs. Jeffries said, repeating the coachman's words. "Do we know exactly when he was seen?"

"My source says it was close to the time of the murder, and that means he was in the neighborhood a good hour and a half before the luncheon."

"That doesn't mean anything," Betsy pointed out. "Perhaps he had an errand to run."

"Or perhaps he was murderin' Lawrence Boyd," Luty suggested. "Besides, rich people like him don't do their own errands."

"We'll definitely have a closer look at Mr. Gibbons," Mrs. Jeffries said quickly. "Did any of you find out anything about Maud Sapington's movements?"

"I did," Betsy said.

"I didn't," Wiggins admitted. "But I managed to pick up a few bits and pieces from me own sources. Go on, Betsy. Tell us what you 'eard."

"Thank you." She laughed. "Mrs. Sapington was the reason I had a train journey." She told them about how she'd spotted the maid slipping out of the Sapington household and had followed her. Betsy had developed several tricks to help her recall conversations almost word for word. She paused in the middle of her recitation and brought Meg's face into focus in her own mind. Then she continued. "We already know that Maud Sapington slipped out the house that day by the servant's entrance, but what I found out is that she told her husband she was going to spend the whole morning with the cook, going over menus."

"Wonder why she did that?" Luty frowned. "Surely the woman must have realized that the staff wouldn't hold their tongues for long."

"The staff likes her better than they do him," Betsy continued. "He is a miserable person." She told them about the other details that Meg had shared with her, including how Arnold Sapington's boots had ended up with a hansom driver. "So you see, Maud Sapington could be almost sure that her secret was safe. The servants avoid him like the plague."

"But that still doesn't tell us where she went that morning," Mrs. Jeffries murmured.

"Meg didn't know," Betsy said. "But she felt sorry for Mrs. Sapington. He's a monster. He wouldn't even give that poor maid an advance on her wages so she could go to the doctor."

"I 'eard that story, too," Wiggins said. "Oh, sorry, I didn't mean to interrupt."

"I was through," Betsy said. "Go on."

"Ta, as I was sayin', I 'eard the same story you did, only I 'eard it from one of Lawrence Boyd's servants," Wiggins continued. He told them how he'd followed the girl to a pub and ended up buying drinks for her whole family. He took his time in the telling, taking care to give them all the details. When he'd finished, he reached for his tea. "Seems to me it's a close race, but Sapington is a hair meaner than Boyd was, at least Boyd let poor Helen go to the doctor when she 'ad the bronchitis."

"It didn't do her much good, though," Betsy interjected. "The poor girl still died."

"They both ought to be ashamed of themselves." Luty shook her head in disgust. She was rich, but she treated her servants and anyone else that worked for her decently.

"What did you learn today, madam?" Hatchet inquired innocently.

"Quite a bit, but I was waitin' my turn." She sniffed. "Some of us know our manners."

"That's all right," Wiggins told her. "I was finished."

"Alrighty, then." Luty took a deep breath and told them everything she'd learned from Harry Brougham. "So now we know why Maud married Sapington. He tried to save Nicholas Cutlip and she was real grateful."

"Do women marry out of gratitude?" Smythe asked, his expression skeptical.

Luty shrugged. "My source told me she was very grateful and that Sapington was very persistent."

"She lost one fiancé by being jilted and another one to an untimely death," Betsy added. "I don't imagine she had any romantic notions left. She probably just wanted a good husband."

"But he isn't good. He's a mean piece of work," Wiggins protested. "Why would she want to marry someone like that?"

"By the standards of her class, Sapington is no worse than most," Hatchet said. "Remember what Mrs. Goodge's source said about Gibbons: he's no better. Most wealthy households in this city treat their servants dreadfully, so I don't think either Boyd or Sapington should be singled out as monsters."

"Seems to me the whole system is miserable," Mrs. Goodge muttered. "But that's a discussion for another time." She glanced at Luty. "If you're finished, I'll tell my bit."

"I'm done. It weren't much, but you never know what's goin' to end up bein' important," Luty declared.

"Yours is a sight better than what I found out." The cook sighed. "All I got was some old gossip about Cutlip and Reese. Seems a few years back one of their clerks was arrested for embezzlement."

"That might be important." Wiggins reached for slice of cake.

"Don't be daft, lad." Mrs. Goodge smiled to take the sting out of the words. "It's got nothing to do with Boyd's murder, but I appreciate your tryin' to spare my feelings. I've more sources coming in tomorrow."

Mrs. Jeffries looked at the clock and noted it was well past the hour. "Right then, it's my turn. I finally managed to see Dr. Bosworth and I'm afraid the news isn't very good." She told them what the good doctor had shared with her.

"He couldn't tell you anything?" Luty exclaimed. She'd been counting on Dr. Bosworth for some additional clues.

"He did say that from his reading of the police surgeon's report, the killer must have used a very heavy object to strike the blows or been very strong. Only two blows were actually struck. It's not much, I'm afraid, but he said the report wasn't very extensive. The police surgeon merely ascertained the cause of death and left it at that."

Wiggins shook his head in disgust. "You'd think these ruddy doctors would take care to add a few important details."

"Wiggins, the only police surgeon who does do that is Dr. Bosworth and only because he's made a study of bullet wounds. Most of them simply verify the cause of death," Mrs. Jeffries explained. "We've all gotten a bit spoiled by Dr. Bosworth's willingness to look beyond the obvious."

"Seems to me his methods ought to be used by all police surgeons," the coachman argued. He was a great admirer of Dr. Bosworth.

"I agree and perhaps one day they will." She gazed around the table. "Does anyone have anything else to add?" She waited a moment and then asked her next question. "Were any of you followed?"

"Not me." Wiggins smiled gratefully at the coachman. "Whatever you did, it worked. I didn't see 'ide nor 'air of the bloke in the flat cap, and I was lookin'."

Witherspoon was exhausted when he came in that evening. There were dark circles forming under his eyes, and his spectacles had slid so far down his nose it was a wonder they'd not fallen to the floor. "You look very tired, sir," Mrs. Jeffries said as she hung up his hat. "Would you like to go straight in and have your dinner?"

"Dinner sounds lovely. I am very tired." He gave her a weary smile. "But I insist you pour yourself a glass of sherry and keep me company while I eat. It's been an extraordinary day and I want to tell you about it. That comment you made at breakfast got me to thinking, and well, I don't like to boast, but I think I've deduced what the killer used as a weapon."

"That's most kind of you, sir. You know how I enjoy listening to you talk about your methods. Go on into the dining room and I'll be right up with your tray." She told her conscience to be quiet when it protested that he did look dead on his feet and that she should insist he go up to rest. She hurried down to the kitchen and got his tray.

When she walked into the dining room, he'd poured her a glass of sherry. "Why, thank you, sir," she said nodding at the glass sitting in front of the empty chair next to him. "But I could have done that." She put his tray on the table and began to serve.

"And I can serve myself, Mrs. Jeffries. Do go sit down. I'm sure you're as tired as I am."

She did as she was told. "What happened today, sir?"

Witherspoon spread his serviette on his lap. "Quite a bit, if I do say so myself. As I mentioned a few moments ago, our discussion this morning got me to thinking about the weapon." He told her about he and Barnes stopping in at the Boyd house on their way home and what they'd found out from the cook and the maid. "I'm fairly certain the sugar hammer was the weapon," he finished.

"But would it have been big enough to kill someone?" she asked, thinking of the one downstairs in their own kitchen.

"This was a commercial one from Germany. It's much larger than the kind one usually finds in a household."

"The killer was taking a great risk," she remarked. She wasn't sure what this information might mean. "He or she couldn't be certain the house would be empty that morning." As she spoke, an idea flashed through her mind and then was just as quickly gone.

Witherspoon picked up his fork. "Oh, but I think they were certain," he explained. "After all, Helen Cleminger's death was known in the neighborhood, and I think the killer knew the servants would all go to the service. Boyd lived alone, so there was no one else to worry about, and what's more, Boyd was working at home and had been for several days. From the murderer's point of view, it was a perfect time to commit the crime."

"And the killer couldn't have known about Glover bringing the files or Miss Clarke being in the house," she mused. "Those events all transpired that morning."

"That's absolutely correct." He beamed proudly. "But that's not all that I found out today. As I said, it was most extraordinary." Between bites of shepherd's pie and wilted lettuce salad, the inspector told her about Hannah Rothwell and James Glover.

She listened carefully, occasionally nodding her head in encouragement or making a comment. Finally, when it appeared he was finished, she asked, "Are you going to arrest Glover for embezzlement?" Again, there was another nudge at the corner of her mind, but it was gone before she could grab it.

He shook his head. "Not yet. If he's the killer, I'd rather arrest him on that charge." He took a quick drink of water. "He's free for the moment, but I've got some men watching his flat."

"What about Mrs. Rothwell?" Mrs. Jeffries asked. "Do you have someone watching her?"

"I don't think that's necessary. I put the lads on Glover because he's actually admitted to a crime." He frowned. "He insists he's innocent of murder, but I don't know if I believe him."

"Do you think he admitted to the lesser crime to avoid being arrested for murder?" she asked. It didn't seem to her to be a very clever strategy. Most policemen would already have the man arrested and behind bars. Witherspoon wasn't like other detectives, but she didn't think Glover could possibly have known that fact.

"No, I think he admitted what he'd done because he knew we were on to him." He leaned back in his chair, covered his mouth with his hand, and yawned.

"You're exhausted, sir." Mrs. Jeffries put down her glass and rose to her feet. "I'll ask Wiggins to take Fred for his walk."

Witherspoon smiled gratefully and stood up. "Thank you. I am tired. Good night, Mrs. Jeffries."

"Good night, sir." She stacked the dishes on the tray and went down to the kitchen.

Mrs. Goodge was sitting alone at the table. "Wiggins took Fred out for walkies, Smythe and Betsy went out to the garden, and I'm going to my room. Did you find out a lot from our inspector."

"Yes. We've much to discuss at the morning meeting." She took the tray over to the sink and put it on the counter.

"Leave those. Betsy said she'd clear up when they came back," the cook said.

"No, that's all right. I'll do them. Sometimes doing mundane tasks helps me think. Are you off to bed?" Mrs. Jeffries rolled up her sleeves.

"Yes, good night, then." The cook yawned. "See you in the morning."

Mrs. Jeffries put the dirty crockery in the pan of warm soapy water. She let her mind wander as she began to work. She went over every detail of the case she'd learned thus far, hoping that the little nudges she'd felt when she was speaking with the inspector would come back. But they didn't. By the time she'd put the last dish in the drying rack and was hanging up the tea towels, the others had returned.

Wiggins and Fred went right up to bed, and Smythe went to double-check that all the doors and windows were locked. Betsy frowned at the empty sink. "I was going to finish that," she protested.

"I know, dear." Mrs. Jeffries smiled kindly. "But you've had a very tiring day and I needed something to do to keep my mind occupied. Now go on up to bed. We've a very busy day tomorrow and you're going to need your rest."

"So are you," Betsy smiled gratefully. "But thank you. It was nice for Smythe and me to have a few moments to ourselves. I can't believe we're going to be married in a few weeks." She started for the back stairs. "Tell him I said good night."

"I will." Mrs. Jeffries waited till she heard Betsy's footsteps hit the top landing, and then she went to the cupboard and pulled out two mugs.

She was sitting at the table with two steaming mugs of tea when Smythe came back to the kitchen. He raised his eyebrows. "I take it we're going to have us a natter."

"I thought it would be a good idea," she replied. "Betsy said to tell you good night. She's gone up."

He slipped into the empty chair across from her and she handed him his tea. "I think I know what this is about. You're wantin' to know how I called off Nivens' dogs, right?"

"That's correct." Mrs. Jeffries had thought long and hard about asking him what he'd done to alleviate that problem. "I don't want you to think I'm not grateful for your actions. I am, as is everyone else in the household. But Nigel Nivens is a dangerous enemy, and I don't think it fair that you should have had to deal with the problem on your own."

"I'm not scared of that little popinjay."

"Don't underestimate him," she warned. "You've helped solve enough cases to know full well that a rat will bite when it's cornered. I don't want you harmed by that odious man."

"Don't worry, Mrs. J." Smythe shrugged. "I know what I'm about. All I did was call in a few favors."

"It was more than that, Smythe." She looked him directly in the eye.

He sighed. "I also flashed a bit of cash about."

"What do you mean?" Alarmed, she gaped at him. "Did you bribe someone?"

"'Course not." He grinned. "Blimpey Groggins has got some connections in the Home Office. I 'ad him put some pressure on one of them to get Nivens off our patch, that's all. Blimpey owed us a favor or two."

Relieved, she eyed him speculatively. "That must have cost you a pretty penny."

He grinned. "It was money well spent. Blimpey might 'ave felt beholdin' to us, but gettin' him to put pressure on a Home Office bureaucrat cost."

"You mean you paid him because now he can't use that resource for other tasks." She wanted to make sure she understood.

"That's right. Blimpey said he knew someone that owed him a big favor," he fibbed. Blimpey had actually said he knew someone "he had the goods on," but Smythe didn't want to share that with Mrs. Jeffries. "But he could only get the fellow to pull strings once," he explained. "I was a little annoyed, seein' as how we helped Blimpey with Tommy, but lookin' at it from his point of view, it was costin' him quite a bit. I also had Eddie Blandings come along this morning and watch the back garden gate, just in case Blimpey's sources didn't come through in time."

"Eddie Blanding—that's Tommy Odell's uncle, right?" She thought the name sounded familiar.

"That's right. He was 'appy to do it for us." Smythe took a quick sip of tea. "He said he didn't see anyone larkin' about. Tell me what's got ya so worried?"

Mrs. Jeffries shrugged. "I wouldn't say I was worried, but I am concerned."

"Alright, what are you concerned about?"

"Nivens has his own sources in the Home Office. If he was reprimanded, he'll be furious. He'll also assume it was our inspector who is the cause of his problems."

Smythe shrugged. "He already thinks that. I couldn't just let us be followed about while we were on the hunt, Mrs. Jeffries. I 'ad to do something."

"I'm not being critical, Smythe," she said quickly. "Your actions were absolutely correct. I'm sorry you had to spend your own money, though. That's hardly fair."

"I've got plenty to spare." He waved a hand dismissively. "So don't fret over it. But you're not tellin' me everything."

"We've got to catch this killer," she replied, "and I'm so muddled about the whole matter, I'm afraid we're going to fail."

He looked at her for a long moment and then burst out laughing. "You always feel like that when we're on the hunt."

"I'm glad you find it so funny," she said indignantly. "But I'm quite concerned about the matter."

"Don't be. You'll figure it out; you always do."

"But this time it's imperative the case is solved," she persisted. "If our inspector doesn't bring in the killer soon, Nivens will destroy his career. I can feel it in my bones. The only thing keeping

Witherspoon really safe is that he can solve crimes no one else can deal with and the Home Office knows it."

"And as long as he's got us, our inspector will keep on solvin' them," Smythe said bluntly. He got up, picked up his mug, and grinned down at her. "Stop frettin'. You'll come up with the answer."

"I'm glad you've so much faith in me," she muttered. "Go on up to bed. I'll see to the lamps."

"Are you sure?" He didn't want to leave her sitting in the kitchen and feeling bad about herself. "Honestly, Mrs. Jeffries, you get like this on all our cases and it's always just before you come up with the answer."

She laughed. "Oh, get on with you. I'm fine."

"Good night, Mrs. J," he called as he headed for the back stairs.

Mrs. Jeffries sat in the quiet kitchen and finished her tea. She hoped that Smythe was correct and that she would be able to figure out who murdered Lawrence Boyd. She'd meant what she'd told the coachman: Nivens would ruin their inspector if he was given half a chance. She vowed he wasn't going to get that opportunity. They would solve this case. Someone killed Boyd; someone walked into his studio that morning as big as you please, whacked him on the head, and then tried to burn the place down to hide it was murder. But who?

She got up and took her mug to the sink. Who had a compelling reason to want him dead and also had the means to do the deed? Maud Sapington certainly had no love for Boyd. She'd hated him for years. She didn't have an alibi, either. But why pick that day to finally extract vengeance?

Mrs. Jeffries looked out the window over the sink. She fixed her gaze on the street lamp across the road and let her mind wander. Who else could have wanted Boyd dead? Hannah Rothwell had the most reason to hate him. He'd lost her entire savings. But she claimed she was going to punish him by dragging him into court. What about Walter Gibbons? He was seen on the Queens Road close to the time of the murder. What was he doing there? Could he have been on his way to kill Boyd?

But she couldn't think of the answer to any of these questions. Tomorrow morning, when she told the others the information she'd learned from the inspector, perhaps one of them would see something she'd missed and point her in the right direction. She yawned and picked up the little lamp. As she reached the kitchen door, she paused to give the room a quick look, making sure that all was as it should be and nothing had been left burning. She turned and started for the back stairs. Just as she reached the stairwell, she felt another tug at the back of her mind. But before she could grab hold of the thought and make any sense of the feeling, it was gone.

The next morning, Witherspoon and Barnes once again waited in the parlor of Eva Clarke's lodging house while the maid went to fetch the young woman. "I thought it a good idea to have a follow-up interview with the lady," the inspector said to Barnes. "After all, she was in the house that morning, and now that she's had a few days to get over the shock of murder, perhaps she'll recall something she might have seen or heard."

"I don't see how she could hear much of anything with the noise one of those typewriting machines makes," Barnes muttered.

"I also want to ask her why she wanted Glover to stay that day," Witherspoon said. "Perhaps I'm grasping at straws, but I do believe it's important to understand all these little details, don't you?"

"Indeed I do, sir. Speaking of details, when we leave here, sir, are we going to see Hannah Rothwell's solicitor?" Barnes asked. "It's not far and we still need to confirm her story."

"That's a good idea," Witherspoon replied. "After that, I thought perhaps we might have another word with Walter Gibbons—" He broke off as Eva Clarke came into the room.

"Inspector, Constable." She nodded politely at the two men. "You wanted to speak to me?"

"Yes, it won't take long," Witherspoon replied. He noted that she wore a simple white blouse and black skirt. "I do hope we're not going to make you late for an appointment."

"I've no work today, Inspector." She smiled ruefully. "Do make yourselves comfortable." She sank down on the chair as the policemen settled upon the sofa. "Now, what can I do for you?"

"Miss Clarke, we were told that on the day of the murder, Mr. Glover made a statement that he was going to leave the Boyd house and it was you who prevailed upon him to stay. Is that correct?" the inspector asked.

"That's right," she admitted. "He said he wanted to go back to

the office and tell the staff about Mr. Boyd's death. But I asked him
to please stay."

"Why?" Witherspoon hoped she'd tell him something that
would help him solve this case. The elation of perhaps finding the
murder weapon had passed and he was beginning to feel a bit desperate.

She blushed and looked down at the floor. "I'm ashamed to admit the truth." She raised her head. "But I suppose the truth must
come out."

Witherspoon's spirits soared. She knew something and she was
going to tell him. "The truth generally does. Do go on."

She took a deep breath. "I wanted him to stay so that I could
speak to him privately. Oh, this is most embarrassing, but you've
got to understand, I need every farthing I can earn and the agency
doesn't pay me until the client pays them."

The inspector stared at her blankly. "I'm sorry, I don't understand."

"Mr. Boyd was dead," she explained. "I wanted Mr. Glover to
stay so I could speak to him about making sure the secretarial
agency was paid promptly. Otherwise it might take ages for me to
get my wages. But the situation seemed to get more and more awkward as the hours passed, and frankly, Mr. Glover wasn't very ap-
proachable, so I thought better of saying anything to him. The
poor man was in a dreadful state."

Barnes' eyes narrowed. "Can you be a bit more specific?"

"It's difficult to describe," she said. "But he seemed to be in a
fog. His eyes were unfocused, and if you said something to him,
he took a long time to respond. I know he'd had a terrible shock,
but honestly, so had the rest of us."

"I see," Witherspoon replied. Drat, this wasn't particularly helpful. He'd been hoping she might say something like she'd seen
Glover coming out of the kitchen carrying a sugar hammer.

"I'm not usually so selfish," she said softly. "But I do need my
wages."

"Not to worry, Miss Clarke. Your actions were entirely understandable." Witherspoon smiled kindly. As disappointed as he was
by her information, he felt sorry for her.

"You're very kind." She smiled. "Do you think it would do any
good to speak to Mr. Glover now? Surely he's had enough time to
recover."

"There's a Mr. Bingley that works at the bank and I'd have a word with him if I were you. He's a very understanding man," Barnes suggested. "I've a feeling Mr. Glover is still a bit under the weather."

CHAPTER 10

"We're not doing very well, are we?" the cook said to Mrs. Jeffries. The two women were clearing up after their morning meeting. Mrs. Jeffries had shared the facts she'd learned from Witherspoon with the others. Everyone had pretended to be very pleased with the additional information, but she could tell they were beginning to feel the way she felt, that with every new fact they learned the case was becoming even more muddled.

"I wouldn't say that," Mrs. Jeffries hedged.

"I would," the cook said bluntly. She put the last breakfast dish in the drying rack and reached for a tea towel. "Let's have a sit-down. You need to talk it out, Mrs. Jeffries. You can always think better after a good natter."

"I'm not sure it'll do much good," the housekeeper replied. She put the lid on the jam pot and tucked it into the sideboard. "But it certainly can't hurt."

Mrs. Goodge finished drying her hands, spread the tea towel on the edge of the worktable to dry, and took her seat. "Now, why don't we start with the crime itself. Everyone hated Boyd, but hatin' doesn't necessarily mean you have to kill him. People usually kill in the heat of anger or because they'll get something they want. Who stood to gain anything from his death? That's the question."

"But that's just it." Mrs. Jeffries sat down. "It's almost impossible to tell who's going to benefit. He had no real heirs and he left all his money to various charities. No matter how desperate a charity might be for money, I can't see the trustees of the Amateur

Artists Guild or the Society of Choral Singing sitting down and planning to commit murder to bring in some ready cash."

"True," Mrs. Goodge replied. "But gain isn't just money. Look at Glover: with Boyd dead, he might have thought no one would realize he'd been embezzling from the bank."

"What about Hannah Rothwell?" Mrs. Jeffries asked. "What did she gain?"

The cook thought for a moment. "Nothing. So I think we can strike her off the suspect list."

"But she hated him," Mrs. Jeffries protested. She was suddenly feeling more hopeful about the case. "And perhaps she did murder him in the heat of passion. He'd just lost all her money."

"She'd have done it the day she had the row with him if she'd done it in the heat of the moment," the cook said calmly. "And I don't think she'd have planned it all out and tried to make it look like an accident. She'd have just bashed him in the head and left him layin' in his studio. That's the real crux of the matter, you know. Why did the killer try so hard to make it look like an accident?"

Dumbfounded, Mrs. Jeffries stared at her. "Oh my stars and garters! You're right. I've been looking at this completely backwards." She wasn't surprised by the cook's analytical abilities; she'd always known that Mrs. Goodge was very intelligent. She was stunned because she'd not seen what was right under her very nose. That was the secret to unraveling this mess of a case. "That is the real question: why did the killer want it to look like an accident?"

"Because the killer didn't want a murder investigation. He or she wanted a coroner's inquest with a quick verdict of accidental death," Mrs. Goodge said. "Which makes me lean a bit towards Glover as the murderer; he might well have thought that if Boyd was the only one who was onto his thievery, then by killing him and making it look like an accident, maybe he could get away with it. It's no wonder people don't trust banks," she continued, completely oblivious to the fact that Mrs. Jeffries had gone stock still and was staring off into space with her mouth slightly agape and her eyes as wide as saucers. "Just look at the facts. Cutlip and Reese had an embezzler and so did Boyd's bank! I bet there's more embezzlin' goin' on in banks than there are tea tins in a china cupboard, but they won't tell us about it, will they? Banks don't want you to know they can't keep your money safe, do they? I'm glad my money is in a nice, secure post office account . . . Mrs. Jeffries, are you all right? You look like you've seen a ghost."

"Oh my stars and garters, I've been a fool." The housekeeper shook her head in disgust. "And you are absolutely brilliant."

"Am I?" The cook beamed proudly. "That's nice to know. I've never heard you use that particular expression before and you've used it twice now."

"I heard it in a shop last week." She leapt to her feet and headed for the coat tree. "It's a very useful expression."

"Where are you going?" The cook got up as well. "I thought we were having a nice natter . . ."

"We were and it's made me realize something very important." She grabbed her bonnet and flopped it onto her head. "Oh blast, I've got to go upstairs and get my purse. Mrs. Goodge, can you find out something for me? It's very important."

"Of course," she replied. "What do you need to know?"

"Can you use your resources to find out exactly when the chief clerk at Cutlip and Reese was arrested?"

"What?" Mrs. Goodge wasn't sure she'd heard her correctly. "But that case was years ago."

"I know, but it's important." She started for the back stairs. "I've got to get my purse and then I'm going out. Can you have the information by our afternoon meeting? I ought to be back by then."

"I think so," Mrs. Goodge muttered. But Mrs. Jeffries had disappeared up the back stairs.

She reappeared a few minutes later with a light shawl wrapped around her shoulders and a small purse dangling from her fingers. "If I'm not back by half past four, go ahead without me, but make sure that Luty and Hatchet don't leave before I get back. We may need their connections before this is all over." She took off down the hall toward the back door.

Mrs. Goodge was right on her heels. "I'll try to get that information, but I'm not sure I can find it out on such short notice."

"Yes you can." Mrs. Jeffries turned and gave her a confident smile. "You're very good at tracking down useful information."

"I'll do my best," the cook replied. "But where are you going?"

Mrs. Jeffries laughed and stepped outside. "To take a train ride."

* * *

"Sapington's tailor confirmed he stopped by that morning," Constable Barnes said, reading from his notebook as he and Witherspoon climbed the short flight of steps to New Scotland Yard. "But he was only there to pick up a coat he'd had them repair. The tailor, a Mr. Mowbry, says he was out of the shop by ten minutes past ten."

Witherspoon reached for the handle and pulled open the door. "How close is the shop to Boyd's?"

"It's about thirty minutes on foot." Barnes grinned. "Constable Tucker interviewed the tailor, sir, and he also timed the walk to Boyd's residence. He's very keen is that one and a great admirer of your methods."

They stepped into the lobby. Witherspoon nodded to the constable behind the counter, and Barnes, who knew the man, gave him a jaunty wave as they passed on their way to the staircase.

"It's good that we're tying up all the loose ends." Witherspoon started up the stairs. "As soon as we're finished here, I'd like to have a chat with Mr. Gibbons again, and after that, we'll have another interview with the Sapingtons."

"What about Glover?" Barnes winced as a sharp pain speared through his bad knee. He hated climbing stairs.

"We'll speak to him again, of course, and I'd also like to interview Hannah Rothwell one more time." Witherspoon paused on the landing to catch his breath. Chief Inspector Barrows' office was on the third floor.

"Did the chief inspector say why he wanted to see you, sir?" Barnes asked softly. They started climbing again. The constable was always on the alert when they were summoned to the Yard.

"I think he just wants a report on our progress." Witherspoon took another deep breath. "These stairs are a bit much but we're almost there."

Barnes knew the chief inspector wouldn't have called them in for a progress report; he received daily reports on all homicide cases. Someone was starting to apply pressure to get the case solved. The powers that be at the Home Office were very touchy about homicides. Ever since the police had failed to solve the Ripper murders, they were under constant pressure to solve cases quickly. "Should I wait outside, sir?" he asked as they reached Barrows' office.

"Certainly not." Witherspoon knocked on the door. "You're an investigating officer on the case. Your opinions are most valuable."

"Come in," Barrows called.

They went inside. Barnes stopped just inside the door and stood at attention. Barrows was sitting behind his desk, pouring over an open file. He looked up and nodded brusquely. "Come in, Inspector, Constable."

"Good day, sir," Barnes said politely.

"Good morning, sir," the inspector added.

"Sit down." He waved toward two chairs in front of his desk. The inspector took one and glanced over his shoulder at Barnes, who didn't move but continued standing by the door.

"You, too, Barnes," Barrows ordered. "We're not the army, so take a load off those knees of yours."

"Thank you, sir." Barnes sat down.

Barrows frowned at them. "This isn't going very well, is it?" He poked a finger at the file on his desk. "Are you close to making an arrest?"

Witherspoon shook his head. "No, I'm afraid not."

"Ye gods, man, what's taking so long?" Barrows asked impatiently. "You've got someone right under your nose who had a motive and was right there when it happened. Why aren't you arresting him?"

"I take it you're referring to James Glover," Witherspoon said.

"Who else?" Barrows said sarcastically. "He was there, he had a reason to want Boyd dead, and he's an admitted thief. Why isn't he in custody?"

"I'm not certain he's guilty," Witherspoon replied honestly. "There simply isn't enough evidence to arrest him."

"Not enough evidence," Barrows repeated, his tone incredulous. "Are you serious?"

Barnes cringed inwardly. The inspector had, of course, said the wrong thing. He should have claimed they were looking at other suspects or gathering additional evidence. Instead, he'd simply blurted out the truth.

"I know it appears as if Mr. Glover is guilty," Witherspoon began, "but I've a feeling that he isn't the right person."

Barrows gaped at him for a moment and then sighed heavily. "If it were anyone but you, Witherspoon, I'd pull them off the case.

The Metropolitan Police Force doesn't operate on 'feelings' but on facts."

Barnes knew that wasn't true either. The coppers he knew always operated on their instincts.

"But the fact of the matter is—" Barrows stared hard at the inspector—"your feelings often lead to the truth."

Barnes let out a silent sigh of relief.

"How much longer do you think you'll need?" Barrows continued. "We are under some pressure here. We don't want the newspapers going on one of those "incompetent police" crusades again. We've only just begun to restore public confidence and we don't want to lose it."

Barnes held his breath, praying the inspector would answer correctly.

"I'm not certain, sir," Witherspoon replied. "It's a bit of a muddle."

Barnes winced. Did the man never learn?

"Well you'd better get it unmuddled, Witherspoon," Barrows snapped. "We need an arrest and we need it quickly. Furthermore, I'm a bit annoyed that you went around behind my back to the Home Office. I've always treated you decently. There was no reason you couldn't have come directly to me with your concerns about Inspector Nivens."

Barnes drew back in surprise.

Witherspoon's jaw dropped. "I've no idea what you mean, sir," he said when he'd recovered enough to speak. "But I never complained to anyone about Inspector Nivens, and I certainly didn't go to the Home Office."

Barrows eyed him speculatively. "Someone did. I got very specific orders to reprimand Inspector Nivens for interfering in your investigation."

"I don't know what this is about." Witherspoon leaned forward in his chair. "I haven't seen or spoken to Nivens since this case began. I know we've a bit of an awkward history between us, but if I were going to complain about him, I would come to you. But I didn't because he hasn't interfered at all."

Barnes was fairly sure he knew who'd complained, and he suspected he knew why. Good for them. Maybe a good slap on the wrist would keep Nivens out of their business at least temporarily.

But it also brought a whole host of other problems that Witherspoon wouldn't even acknowledge.

Barrows waved his hand dismissively. "Alright, then, you didn't complain. But do get on with solving this case."

It was clear their meeting was over. Witherspoon and Barnes both stood up.

"I'll do my best, sir," the inspector replied.

"Take another look at Glover." Barrows closed the file. "A criminal is a criminal, and Glover's already admitted to embezzlement. It's not that far a step to murder for a weak man like him."

"Yes, sir." Witherspoon backed toward the door. "I'd planned on interviewing him again this afternoon."

Barnes grabbed the door handle, pulled it open, and edged out into the hall.

"And stay away from Nivens," Barrows called. "You're not the only one with friends in high places."

Neither of them spoke as they trudged back down the stairs and crossed the foyer.

"That wasn't very pleasant," Witherspoon said as they stepped outside.

"And what's coming this way isn't very pleasant either," Barnes said.

Witherspoon spun around just as Nigel Nivens, a scowl on his face, charged across the pavement toward them. Barnes shoved himself in front of Witherspoon and rolled his hands into fists. He might be older, but he'd spent twenty-five years patrolling some of the meanest streets in London.

Two constables who'd been about to enter the building stopped and stared, their gazes fixed on Barnes.

Nivens skidded to a halt and glared at the constable. "Out of my way," he ordered.

"Don't start anything, sir," Barnes said softly. "You'll only end up damaging yourself." His gaze cut to the two policemen on the steps and then back to Nivens. If fisticuffs began, the constables would come running. Barnes knew that as Nivens was loathed by the rank and file while Witherspoon was greatly admired, Nivens would end up with the most bruises. The report about the incident wouldn't do his career aspirations any good, either.

Alarmed, Witherspoon tried to shove past Barnes. "Constable, really, let's be sensible about this. I'm sure Inspector Nivens merely wants to speak to me."

Barnes held his ground.

But Nivens was beyond listening to reason. "Get out of my way, Barnes, or I'll have you tossed off the force for threatening a superior officer. You'll not see a farthing of a pension if you're dismissed for that."

Witherspoon dodged around the constable and came almost nose to nose with Nivens. "If you try that, Inspector, I'll use every resource at my disposal to stop you," he warned. "Constable Barnes is a good and honorable officer, and I won't allow you to try and ruin him. Do you understand?"

"I understand you're both going to be sorry." Nivens began to back away.

Witherspoon stepped closer to him. "Hear me well, Inspector. I think I know why you're upset, and perhaps I'd be upset as well if the situation were reversed. But neither I nor the constable had anything to do with you being reprimanded."

"Then who did?" Niven yelled.

"I don't know and I don't care," the inspector continued calmly. "But if you try to harm either of us, I'll use my considerable resources to establish our rights and probably bankrupt you. You may not know this, but I have a great deal of money, and if need be, I'll spend every penny of it suing you."

Niven's mouth worked but no sound came out. His face was crimson and his eyes bulged. Finally, after sputtering for a few seconds, he turned on his heel and stalked off.

The two constables by the door relaxed their stance and went on inside. Barnes turned to the inspector. "I don't know what to say, sir. It was good of you to defend me like that." His feelings were a bit jumbled. He was the one who usually looked out for the inspector.

Witherspoon waved impatiently. "Don't mention it, Constable. I'm sick to death of Nivens's behavior. I'm tired of the man threatening me and running to the chief with one silly tale after another. Come along. We've much to do today." He started up the road.

"But thank you, sir." Barnes fell into step next to him. "Are we going to interview Gibbons now?"

"Yes, there's a cabstand by the bridge."

Barnes knew they'd better get the case solved quickly. Witherspoon had money, and right now, he had influence. He'd solved over twenty homicides and was the most famous detective on the force, but a failed case could cause him great harm. Nigel Nivens was a dangerous opponent, and he really did have friends in high places. Witherspoon's friends would disappear in the blink of an eye if he stopped solving murders.

"I heard some gossip that Gibbons was seen close to the Boyd residence just about the time of the murder," Witherspoon continued.

"It'll be interesting to find out what he was doing there." Barnes waved at a hansom pulling away from the cabstand by the bridge.

"Otherwise, I'm afraid I might be forced to take another look at Glover." Witherspoon stepped into the cab and slid to the far side.

Barnes gave the driver the address and climbed in next to Witherspoon. He grabbed the handhold as the cab pulled out into traffic.

Walter Gibbons lived in a three-story townhouse in Belgravia. Witherspoon and Barnes were shown into the drawing room to wait while the butler went to see if Mr. Gibbons "was receiving."

"At least he's got some comfortable looking places for a body to sit," Barnes murmured as he surveyed the drawing room.

Witherspoon followed the constable's gaze, and a faint smile creased his lips. The room looked very much like every other upper-class drawing room he'd seen. The top half of the walls were painted pale gold and the bottom paneled in a dark-stained wood. A green velvet sofa with a tufted back and two matching parlor chairs stood in front of the fireplace, and a series of colorful woven carpets of different sizes covered the floors. "Considering Mr. Gibbons demeanor the last time we spoke with him, I don't think we'll be invited to sit down."

"That is correct, Inspector." Walter Gibbons strode into the room. "I hardly consider this a social call. What do you want?" He'd not bothered to put on either his coat or a cravat. His white shirt was unbuttoned at the throat as was the bottom button on his maroon waistcoat.

"We want to ask you some questions, Mr. Gibbons," Barnes replied sharply. "As you so aptly put it, this isn't a social call."

Witherspoon smiled faintly. "Mr. Gibbons, where were you around eleven o'clock on the day Mr. Boyd was murdered?"

Gibbons looked surprised by the question. "I've already made a statement concerning my whereabouts that day," he blustered. He jerked his head toward Barnes. "The constable interviewed me rather extensively."

"But I didn't ask that question," Barnes replied. He could tell that Gibbons was avoiding an answer so he could give himself a moment to think.

"But I'm sure you did." Gibbons walked over to the fireplace and propped his elbow on the mantle. "However, if you want me to repeat myself, I was right here."

"No, you weren't," the inspector said softly. "You were walking on the Queens Road, and that's right behind Mr. Boyd's house. We have witnesses, Mr. Gibbons, so I suggest you tell us the truth." He was bluffing, of course. They'd no witnesses at all, only a bit of unverified gossip his coachman had heard from someone at a pub!

Gibbons straightened up and tugged at his waistcoat. "What of it? It's a free country. I'm not obliged to account for my whereabouts to you."

"That is true," the inspector replied. "You do have rights. Were you once engaged to Marianna Reese?"

Gibbons gaped at him. The color drained out of his face, leaving it virtually as white as his hair. "How dare you. How dare you ask such a personal question! I don't have to answer that."

"We can always ask Mrs. Sapington," Witherspoon said softly. "She was Marianna Reese's sister."

"This topic is none of your business," Gibbons yelled. The color had come back into his flesh and his cheeks were now bright pink.

"I'm afraid it is." Barnes wasn't sure what the inspector was about, but he'd do his part to keep the pressure on Gibbons. Witherspoon had mumbled something about gossip when they were in the hansom, but the street traffic had been so noisy he'd missed part of it. "You can either answer our questions sir, or we can ask your friends and associates."

"Marianna Reese married Lawrence Boyd," Witherspoon continued. He knew this was probably a painful memory and it wasn't in his nature to pry about such an intimate matter, but this was a murder investigation. "She publicly humiliated you by running off with the man who painted her portrait. That is a motive for murder, sir."

"For God's sake, man, why would I wait twenty years to kill the bastard?" Gibbons cried.

"Because you knew that the trustees were going to give Boyd the honorary chairmanship of the Bankers Benevolent Society," Witherpsoon replied. "I believe you're one of the trustees. Isn't that correct?"

"Yes." Gibbons shoulders sagged as some of the bluster went out of him. "I'm on a number of boards, Inspector. What of it?"

"The other trustees overruled your objections about Mr. Boyd, didn't they?"

"Most of them knew what he'd done to me," Gibbons said dully. "But they didn't care. All they were interested in was what he was going to give them."

"You resigned over the matter." Witherspoon was relieved. All of this information had come to him as gossip, but he'd discovered that quite often, the gossipmongers had their facts right. "I imagine that made you very angry."

"Don't be a fool, Inspector." Gibbons trudged to the sofa and flopped down. "I was furious. Absolutely furious. I hated Lawrence Boyd, and my colleagues on the board knew that. I made no secret of my feelings toward the man, but as I've just told you, they didn't care."

"Why did you agree to go to the luncheon if you'd already resigned?" Barnes asked.

"I do my duty, Constable."

Witherspoon suddenly recalled another tidbit he'd heard. "If you loathed Boyd so much, why did you have dinner with him a few weeks ago?"

Gibbons stared at him speculatively. "You're very well informed, Inspector. I think I shall need to reevaluate my opinion of the police."

"Just answer the question, sir," Barnes pressed. His knee was starting to throb again.

"I had dinner with him because he had something I wanted." Gibbons shrugged. "I didn't want to invite him to my home, so I asked him to meet me at a nearby restaurant." He laughed harshly. "He only agreed to meet me because he wanted the chairmanship so badly and he knew I was on the board. Otherwise, he'd not have given me the time of day. He was like that, you know. He was a perfectly odious excuse for a man. He didn't see people as human beings. He only saw them as instruments of his own vanity. I can't imagine what Marianna possibly saw in him."

"You met at the restaurant," the inspector pressed.

"I asked him if I could buy the portrait he'd done of Marianna." Gibbons voice had dropped so low both policemen had to strain forward to hear. "I offered him a great deal of money for it, even though I knew he was rich. Of course, he refused, but I was counting on him doing that. Then I offered him the honorary chairmanship."

"What was Boyd's reaction?" the inspector asked.

"He laughed at me." Gibbons looked down at the floor for a brief moment and then back up at them. "He laughed at me and told me he already had it. At first I didn't believe him, but then I realized he was telling the truth. It was quite shocking, Inspector. I knew the board was leaning toward giving it to Sapington. He's a social-climbing martinet of a fellow, but he'd worked hard for the society over the years and had built up a lot of good will. He lobbied furiously for the position, and I was sure he had it. He was certain as well. You should have seen his face when I told him it was going to Boyd."

"You told Sapington he'd not got it?" Barnes clarified. "Why?"

"Because Boyd had invited him to the luncheon that day and I suspected he'd done it so he could enjoy watching Sapington be humiliated when he learned he'd been passed over. Sapington was certain he was going to get the honor, you see." Gibbons smiled slyly. "I didn't want Sapington to be taken by surprise by the announcement. In other words, I wanted to ruin it for Lawrence Boyd."

"Thank you, sir. This information is most helpful." Witherspoon hoped he could keep it all straight in his head. Gracious, people did do awful things to one another. "But you still need to tell us why you were on the Queens Road that day."

"I was ruining Boyd's big surprise, Inspector." Gibbons laughed. "You see, he'd gotten the honor by agreeing to give the society a huge donation. After I resigned, I came home that night and thought about what to do. The answer was so simple. I sent the other trustees a message asking for an emergency board meeting wherein I rescinded my resignation and informed them I'd double whatever donation Boyd was prepared to make. They agreed to my terms."

Barnes looked surprised. "But hadn't they already told Boyd he had it."

"Yes, but it wasn't official," Gibbons replied. "So we took another vote, and we voted to give the honor to Arnold Sapington. That's why I was on the Queens Road that morning. The society meets at the Promenade Club."

"Which is on the Queens Road," Witherspoon muttered.

"So you see, Inspector, I had no reason to murder Lawrence Boyd." Gibbons rose to his feet, walked over to a walnut secretary by the door, and pulled an envelope out of the top drawer. He waved the envelope at the two policemen. "This was my revenge, and the sweetest part was that he had no idea. The only people who knew were me and the other trustees. For once, Lawrence Boyd wasn't going to get what he wanted, and furthermore, this time, I was going to get to watch him be humiliated."

"My feet are achin' and I ain't learned anything at all today." Luty flopped into her chair, took her bonnet off, and tossed it onto the empty seat next to her. "I hope some of you did better than me."

Mrs. Goodge glanced anxiously toward the back door. Mrs. Jeffries still hadn't returned, and she wasn't sure how long to wait before starting the meeting. Everyone else was here. "Mrs. Jeffries should be here any time now."

"It's already close to five," Betsy said. "We got a late start. Where'd she go?"

"I know I was late gittin' back," Luty apologized. "But my hansom got stuck in an awful traffic jam on the Brompton Road."

"You've no need to apologize," Betsy said quickly. "We were all late. I only got here a couple of minutes before you did, and Wiggins only arrived seconds before me."

"I was 'ere on time," Smythe said smugly.

"And I got caught in the same traffic mess as madam," Hatchet supplied. "That's why I was tardy."

"Let's go ahead and start then." Mrs. Goodge decided to take charge of the meeting. "Mrs. Jeffries told me she might be late getting back, and as to where she's gone, I've no idea. She wouldn't say. Now, who has something to report?"

They all stared at her, their expressions glum.

"Surely one of us must have learned something," the cook exclaimed.

"I did hear a bit of gossip about Maud Sapington," Smythe said. "But I don't know that it's got anything to do with our case."

"Tell it anyways," Luty ordered. "Doesn't seem like the rest of us have much to say."

Smythe hesitated. "My source told me that Maud Sapington is spyin' on her husband. It looks like she's tryin' to catch him out." He broke off, not sure how to say what he meant.

"You mean your source thinks she's tryin' to catch him with another woman?" Wiggins asked eagerly. "Cor blimey, that'd set the cat amongst the pigeon. Does she peek in windows?"

"My source thinks that might be the case," Smythe admitted. Leave it to Wiggins to get to the heart of the matter. "So it doesn't look like her trailin' him has anything to do with Boyd's death. She started sneakin' about and watchin' him days before the murder."

"Did she follow him when he left the house in the evenings?" Betsy asked.

Smythe shrugged. "She might 'ave, but my source just said she were spotted hangin' about the bank neighborhood and trailin' him when he left during the day."

"I'll bet she did it in the evenings as well," Betsy said. She looked pointedly at the coachman. "If he was being untrue to her, she ought to leave him. Marriage should be taken seriously."

"'Course it should, love," Smythe soothed. "But there's two sides to every story. We don't know for sure why she was following him."

"Humph," Betsy snorted delicately. "We do. She's tryin' to catch him out because he's being unfaithful."

The back door opened and Mrs. Jeffries footsteps pounded up the hallway. "I'm here," she called. "I'm so sorry to be late, but the train was late."

"A lot of trains are late these days," Wiggins observed. "Betsy ran into the same trouble the other day."

Mrs. Jeffries tossed her shawl and bonnet onto the pine sideboard as she hurried to the table. "What have I missed?" she asked as she slipped into her chair.

"Not very much." The cook put a cup of tea in front of her. "Smythe has a source that says Mrs. Sapington has taken to following her husband about without his knowledge."

Mrs. Jeffries arched her eyebrow. "Really? Did the source have any idea why she was following him?"

"He's bein' unfaithful," Wiggins snickered. "And she's tryin' to catch him out."

"We don't know that. She might be trailin' him for another reason," Smythe argued. But even to him, the words sounded weak. It was a tale as old as time: marriage vows simply didn't mean much for some people. This close to his own wedding day, he didn't want his beloved thinking all men were like Sapington. He would honor his wedding vows until the day he died.

"Sure she was," Luty added sarcastically. "Maybe she wanted to make sure he had his umbrella with him in case it rained."

"Let's move along, shall we?" The cook looked at the housekeeper. "Are you goin' to tell us where you've been?"

"Of course. I went to Slough." Mrs. Jeffries smiled at their confusion. "I'll explain in a minute. Were you able to get the information we discussed?"

"Yes, I had to send a street arab over to Ida's place with a note." Mrs. Goodge reached into her pocket and took out a slip of paper. "He came back with her answer, but Ida's handwritin' is awful." She squinted at the note. "I think it says it happened twelve years ago."

Mrs. Jeffries nodded. "That fits." She looked at Luty. "Can you find out when Arnold Sapington got the chief clerk's position at Cutlip and Reese?"

"I expect so."

"Can you do it now?"

Luty's eyes widened. "You mean right now?"

"Yes. I think I might have the answer, but it's so odd I daren't say anything until I have a few more facts at hand." Mrs. Jeffries was sure she knew the identity of the murderer, but proving it was going to be almost impossible.

Luty got up. "One of my bankers lives just up the road apiece. He ought to be able to help."

"I'll go with you, madam." Hatchet rose to his feet. "And before you protest, let me remind you that your banker probably isn't home as yet, so you may have to wait for some time. My presence will make it look much more like an eccentric social call . . ."

"Eccentric?" she protested.

"Of course, madam. Barging in late in the afternoon without so much as a calling card is considered eccentric, even by your rather loose standards. At least with me along, people will see that you're not madly rushing about the London streets all alone with the evening approaching."

"Oh, horsefeathers. Come on then. Let's go." Muttering under her breath, Luty headed for the hallway.

"We'll have the information for the meeting tomorrow," Hatchet called over his shoulder. "If madam's banker doesn't know, I've some sources of my own."

"He'll know," Luty yelled.

Mrs. Jeffries looked at Smythe. "I need you to go out as well. Do you think you can find out where Nicholas Cutlip drowned?"

"I'm not sure, but I can try," he said.

"Good, but don't stay out too late. Tomorrow is going to be a busy day for all of us."

"I'll be back as soon as I can," he promised. He dropped a quick kiss on Betsy's forehead and left.

Mrs. Jeffries waited until he was gone and then looked at Betsy. "I'll need you to go out tonight as well. Wiggins, I want you to go with her."

"Me?" Betsy smiled in delight. "What do you want me to do?"

"I want you to go to the Sapington house and have a quick word with Meg."

"The girl I went to Reading with?" Betsy looked confused.

"That's correct. When you speak with her, here's what you need to find out."

Mrs. Jeffries spent the next few minutes giving Betsy and Wiggins their instructions. When the others had all gone, Mrs. Goodge looked at the housekeeper. "Do you know who did it?"

"I'm not sure," Mrs. Jeffries admitted. "It simply doesn't make sense, but on the other hand, it's the only thing that makes sense. Let's just hope they bring me back the answers I need."

Arnold Sapington waved Barnes and Witherspoon into the two chairs in front of his desk. "I hope this won't take long, Inspector. I've a meeting in an hour."

"We'll be as brief as possible," Witherspoon said as he and the constable took their seats.

"Mr. Sapington, can you tell us if you had a meeting with Walter Gibbons prior to seeing him at Mr. Boyd's house on the day of the murder?" the inspector asked. He'd decided to verify Gibbons statement as quickly as possible. If Gibbons statement proved to be true, it would give him one less suspect.

Sapington looked surprised by the question. "I'm not sure what you're asking. I've been acquainted with Mr. Gibbons for a number of years. We've worked together on numerous committees for the Benevolent Society."

"But did you have a meeting recently wherein you discussed who was going to get the honorary chairmanship of the society?" Barnes asked.

Sapington said nothing for a moment. "I suppose you found out about it from Mr. Gibbons. It wasn't my idea. Gibbons contacted me and said we needed to meet. That he had some important information for me."

Witherspoon pushed his spectacles up his nose. "How long ago was this?"

"A week or ten days before the luncheon." Sapington shrugged. "I don't recall the exact date. We met at the Bankers Club one afternoon."

The inspector watched Sapington's face as he asked the next question. "What information did Mr. Gibbons share with you?"

"Come now, Inspector." Sapington's smile was amused. "You already know the answer to that question. Gibbons told me that Boyd was getting the honorary chairmanship of the society. He was very sorry, but there was nothing he could do. Boyd had promised the trustees a rather large donation if they'd give it to him."

"I take it you were disappointed?" Barnes looked up from his notebook.

"Very. I'd worked hard for the society, and by right, the honor should have come to me. But I wasn't surprised. Boyd had a reputation for buying his way through life." Sapington's eyes narrowed. "He's supposed to be this great artist just because he's exhibited at the Royal Academy. But he doesn't get it right. That last painting he was working on was all wrong. It's supposed to be the outside of the Bankers Club, but the color of the bricks is all wrong, the windows are out of proportion, and he's even made a mistake on the color of the cat that hangs around the place. Old Tom's a gray and white tabby, but Boyd painted him black as the ace of spades." He smiled bitterly. "But when you're as rich as Boyd was, people tend to overlook the fact that you've neither talent nor character."

*   *   *

It was very late by the time Mrs. Jeffries picked up the lamp from the table and went up to bed. Smythe had been the last one to come home, and he'd confirmed what she suspected. So had all the others, though Wiggins had said he was fairly sure the hansom driver hadn't believed them for an instant. Apparently, Wiggins wasn't very convincing pretending to be a private inquiry agent, but the driver had been willing to part with the shoes for a price.

Betsy had been elated to be out and about at all. She said Meg had been surprised to see her, but once she'd passed her palm with silver, Meg had told her where to find Evelyn's brother. Mrs. Jeffries sighed and stepped into her room. It was too bad they had to pay for so much information, but sometimes it was the only way. She blew out the light and went to her rocker. Sitting down, she tried to think of a way to present her suspicions to the inspector so that he would come to the same conclusion she had reached. When he'd told her about his "chat" with the chief inspector, she'd been quite alarmed. Barrows was telling him to solve this case and to do it quickly.

He'd been very tired this evening, but over a glass of sherry and a good meal, she'd managed to find out the details of his day. Nothing that she learned from him contradicted the conclusion she'd already reached, but she still had no idea how to prove any of it. Yet something he said nagged at the back of her mind, something about the Royal Academy . . . or perhaps it was the Bankers Club . . . She gave up. Perhaps she'd remember it in the morning.

Mrs. Jeffries got up and got ready for bed. She was sure she wouldn't sleep a wink, but she dozed off as soon as her head hit the pillow.

But she didn't rest easy. In her half-sleep state, images, ideas, and words drifted willy-nilly through her mind. Suddenly, she sat bolt upright. "Oh, my Lord, I've been so foolish. The proof is right there."

CHAPTER 11

Mrs. Jeffries wasn't able to go back to sleep, so she spent the wee hours of the morning going over every detail about the murder. She got up before dawn, went downstairs, and made a full pot of tea. By the time Mrs. Goodge and Samson came into the kitchen, she'd gone over the facts so many times, she knew she had to be right. Nothing else made sense. The only piece of the puzzle that was missing was the detail she'd asked Luty to confirm with her banker.

But that detail wasn't long in coming. Luty started talking about it before she even reached the kitchen. Hatchet was right on her heels. "Arnold Sapington got the chief clerk's position about twelve years ago," she said. "Now are you goin' to tell us what's goin' on or are we goin' to have to guess? You never did say why you went to Slough yesterday."

"She told us last night," Wiggins supplied helpfully. "She went to look up the coroner's inquest."

"Coroner's inquest?" Hatchet repeated. "On who?"

"On a young boy who died accidentally in 1860. He fell and hit his head upon a patch of ice," she explained. "I do apologize for sending you off before I could give you all the details, but time was of the essence just as it is this morning." She looked at the cook. "Is the inspector's tray ready?"

"You can take it up now." Mrs. Goodge handed her a covered tray. "What do you want us to do?"

"What's goin' on?" Luty protested. "Do you know who did it?"

"Yes." Mrs. Jeffries took the tray from the cook. "But we're going to have the devil's own time proving it. Mrs. Goodge can give you the details while I take this up. But I'm going to need Hatchet, Smythe, and Wiggins to be at the ready. If I'm successful with the inspector, they'll need to leave immediately."

"Where will we be going?" Hatchet asked, his expression as eager as a schoolboy's faced with an unexpected day out.

"To the Sapington household." She started for the back stairs. "The inspector may need you if the man tries to bolt. The others will tell you everything."

"Actually, we're in a bit of a muddle ourselves," the cook admitted as Mrs. Jeffries disappeared. "She's got it all straight in her own head, but she's not really explained it properly to us."

"But she's pretty sure the killer is Arnold Sapington," Betsy added.

Upstairs, Mrs. Jeffries paused outside the dining room and took a deep breath. She was going to give the performance of her life. She pushed open the door, stepped inside, and smiled brightly at Witherspoon. "Good morning, sir. I've had Mrs. Goodge make you an especially large breakfast. Considering what you're going to be doing today, it might be hours before you have a chance to eat again."

Witherspoon, who'd been reading the *Times*, looked up at her in confusion. "That was very thoughtful of you. Er, uh, exactly what am I doing today?"

Mrs. Jeffries took the lid off the tray and put his plate in front of him. "You see, I had Mrs. Goodge cook three eggs and two extra rashers of bacon."

"Yes, uh, I see. Mrs. Jeffries, what are you talking about?"

"Come now, sir, stop teasing me." She laughed softly. "You know very well I'm on to your methods. But if you insist, I'll show you just how much I've learned from you the past few years." Still smiling, she paused for a breath. She couldn't tell from his expression whether he believed her, but he certainly looked interested. "You're going to go take a look at the painting you took into evidence from Boyd's studio, and after you've confirmed it's a likeness of the Bankers Club, you're going to take two or perhaps three constables to the Sapington home and arrest Arnold Sapington for the murder of Lawrence Boyd."

"I am?" He blinked. "Uh, er, why am I doing this?"

"Really, sir, you've such a mischievous streak! Now do stop

teasing. You know very well why; you told me yourself last night over dinner. You said that Sapington described the last painting Boyd was working on when you interviewed him yesterday, and well, sir, you'd already mentioned that Boyd's staff had told you several times that Boyd never let anyone see a painting until it was exhibited. I believe you said he'd once sacked a servant for daring to take a little peek."

Understanding dawned in the Witherspoon's eyes. "Of course, of course." He forced himself to laugh. "You are very clever Mrs. Jeffries. You're onto me."

She reached for the toast rack and put it next to his plate. "And then of course, there's the other evidence. It's all very circumstantial, but I do believe you'll find enough to convince a jury. After all, you told me Sapington stopped by his tailor that morning and picked up a coat he'd had them repair."

"And the maid next door saw a man in coat climbing over Boyd's fence at the time of the murder." Witherspoon smiled happily as he began to see the pattern. He picked up his fork and attacked his eggs. "Send Constable Barnes in as soon as he gets here. We've much to do today. And do tell Mrs. Goodge the breakfast is excellent!"

"We've got other evidence as well, sir. Don't forget the shoes," Barnes reminded the inspector as they got out of a hansom in front of the Sapington house. They had discussed the case on the drive over, and Witherspoon had painstakingly gone over the evidence against Sapington. He'd been delighted when Barnes had informed him that Sapington's shoes had been turned over to the police by a good citizen who'd noticed an odd stain on the heel of the shoe and thought it might be important. The brown-paper parcel containing the shoes and the note had shown up at the Ladbroke Grove police station early this morning. Barnes was fairly certain that Mrs. Jeffries was behind it all, but he didn't care; he'd take all the evidence against Sapington that he could get.

"The shoes will be very helpful in court." Witherspoon started up the walkway. "But I'm still a bit unclear as to the man's motive."

"I expect that'll all come out in good time," Barnes replied.

"I certainly hope so. Are the constables at the ready?" Witherspoon asked. They'd reached the front door.

"There's two ready to step up here to guard the door when we go inside and an additional constable at each corner of the street." Barnes reached for the heavy door knocker. He had no doubt that Smythe, Wiggins, and probably that white-haired butler fellow who worked for Mrs. Crookshank were close by.

The second the front door opened, Barnes said, "We'd like to speak to Mr. Sapington."

The butler's eyes widened slightly. "I'll see if Mr. Sapington is receiving. You may step into the foyer and wait."

Barnes shoved past him. "This isn't a social call. Go get your master and be quick about it."

The butler gaped at the two policemen then turned on his heel and strode down the hall, muttering something under his breath. He disappeared behind a set of double-wide doors, and a moment later he stepped back out. He waved the two policemen forward. "This way. Mr. Sapington will see you in his study."

They hurried down the hall. The butler gave them a hard glare and then flung open the doors.

"Thank you," Witherspoon said to him.

"Humph," the butler snorted angrily and marched away.

Sapington, fully dressed in a brown coat, bronze cravat, and pristine white shirt, sat behind a wide mahogany desk. "What do you want, Inspector?" he said.

"We've a few more questions we need to ask you," Witherspoon replied.

"Then ask them and be on your way," he snapped. "You've invaded my office and now my home. This is getting tiresome, and if it persists, I'll have to have a word with your chief."

"That is your right, sir," Witherspoon replied. "By all means, file a complaint. But first I need you to explain something to me. Yesterday, you mentioned that Mr. Boyd's last painting wasn't very good, that the windows were out of proportion and the cat was the wrong color."

"What of it? He wasn't much of a painter despite what everyone said." Sapington drummed his fingers on the desktop.

Out of the corner of his eye, Barnes saw a door on the far side of the room open a crack. He stifled a smile. The staff must really hate Sapington if they were willing to risk getting caught eavesdropping. Whoever it was would get an earful today.

"Can you tell me, sir, when you saw this painting?" Witherspoon asked softly.

Sapington was taken aback. "What?"

"It's a simple question, Mr. Sapington. The inspector wants to know exactly when you saw the painting," Barnes said.

Sapington stopped drumming his fingers. He went very still. "I'm not sure," he finally said. "A few weeks ago, I think."

"Where did you see it?" Witherspoon pressed.

"At his studio, Inspector." Sapington sat up straighter and smiled confidently. "I'd dropped by to see him about a charity project for the society. He showed me the painting."

Witherspoon said nothing for a moment. The room was utterly silent save for the faint ticking of the clock. Finally, he said, "Mr. Sapington, I don't believe you. Lawrence Boyd never allowed anyone to see his work."

"I tell you he showed it to me," Sapington insisted.

"When did he show it to you?" Barnes asked. He noticed the crack was opening a bit wider.

"I don't recall the exact date," Sapington said defensively. "It was a few weeks ago."

"He wasn't working on that painting a few weeks ago. Mr. Boyd was a very fast painter. He only began work on the Bankers Club painting a few days before he was murdered," Witherspoon said. "So you couldn't have seen it a few weeks ago, could you?"

"I refuse to listen to any more of this nonsense." He stood up. "I suggest you leave."

"Certainly, sir." Barnes moved in closer to the desk. "But we'll have to ask you to accompany us to the station to help with our inquiries."

"Help with your inquiries." He laughed harshly. "That means you don't have enough evidence to arrest me, Inspector."

"Oh, but we do, sir." Witherspoon moved up to stand next to Barnes. Sapington was a muscular fellow, and the inspector hoped the constables in the front weren't too far away to hear him if he had to call for assistance. "You see, the only way you could have known what Boyd was painting is if you'd been there the morning he was murdered. Until we took the painting into evidence, there were only two people who had seen it. The killer and the victim. Arnold Sapington, you're under arrest for the murder of Lawrence Boyd."

"You'll never get a conviction on that sort of flimsy evidence," he sneered.

"Yes, they will." Maud Sapington marched into the room. "I'll tell them what I saw that day and they'll believe me."

Arnold Sapington stared at his wife in utter disbelief. "Maud, what are you doing? Shut up this crazy nonsense and send for our solicitor."

"Shut up yourself," she snarled. "My God, you're a monster. But I'll tell them what you did. I'll tell them what I saw. You didn't know that I was following you, did you? You killed him; you killed my Nicholas so you could marry me." Her fingers closed around a china shepherdess figurine. Suddenly, she hurled it toward her husband, but her aim was bad. It missed his head and grazed the inspector's forehead.

The distraction was enough for Sapington; he charged around the desk and hurled himself toward the door. Barnes leapt after him as did a dazed Witherspoon, but it was Maud who got to him first. She threw herself at him, throwing him off balance. She wrapped her arms around his knees as he toppled forward.

"Let go," he yelled.

But Maud recovered faster than her husband and managed to flatten him against the carpet. She then climbed onto his back, balled her hand into a fist, and began punching him in the head. "You monster. You killed him. You killed my Nicholas. I loved him; he was my only love, my one true love. You bastard! And it wasn't as if you even were in love with me. I didn't know for certain until now, until I knew for sure you murdered Boyd. That's what you've always done to get what you want. You murder people, just like you murdered my Nicholas. You pig! You monster!"

"Get off! Get off!" Sapington bucked like a wild horse, but he couldn't dislodge his wife. "You don't know what you're saying."

Witherspoon shoved his spectacles back onto his nose and leapt toward the Sapingtons. Barnes stumbled after him. They reached them at the same time, and each of them grabbed one of her arms. "Drag her off, sir." Barnes had to yell to make himself heard over Arnold Sapington's screams of pain and Maud Sapington's stream of verbal abuse.

Witherspoon hesitated for an instant. He hated treating women roughly, but he knew his duty. He yanked her backward with all his might.

"You didn't think I knew, did you?" Maud yelled. "But I've suspected for months, that you killed my Nicholas, and now I know that you did it. That's why I started following you, ever since you told me about not getting the chairmanship; I knew you'd try something. You wanted that more than anything in the world."

"Shut up, Maud!" He flopped over onto his back and glared at his wife. Both his cheeks were staring to swell and a patch of hair was missing from his temple. "For God's sake, shut up."

Just then, the study doors were flung open and two constables charged into the room. They skidded to a halt at the sight of Sapington lying on the floor while two feet away, Barnes and Witherspoon were restraining Mrs. Sapington, who was on her knees. The sleeve of her elegant lavender dress was hanging off one arm, her hair had come down, and a bruise was already forming on her forehead. Her chest heaved as she sucked in air.

"Please take Mr. Sapington to the station," Witherspoon instructed the constables. He was relieved to see they were both tall, rather burly lads.

"You'll never get a conviction," Sapington snarled. The constables helped him up and led him toward the door, which was now crowded with servants.

"Mrs. Sapington, are you alright?" Witherspoon asked.

"Yes, thank you, if you and the constable could just help me up and onto the sofa. I believe I hurt my ankle when I threw myself at Arnold."

"Oh, dear, we must get you to a physician." The inspector and Barnes helped her gently to her feet.

"Don't worry, Inspector." She smiled wearily as they helped her to the sofa across from the desk. "A sprained ankle is a small price to pay to see him hang. Do sit down, please, and I'll make a proper statement." She smiled at Barnes. "That is what you call it, isn't it?"

"That's right, ma'am." Barnes sat down next to her and took out his little brown notebook.

Witherspoon took out his handkerchief, wiped his forehead, and took a seat opposite her. "Mrs. Sapington, you stated you followed your husband on the morning of the murder. Can you tell us why?"

"Perhaps it would be best if I told you everything," she said.

"That would be best," he agreed.

"A few weeks ago, my husband told me that Walter Gibbons

had let him know he wasn't going to get the honorary chairmanship of the Bankers Benevolent Society," she began. "You have to
understand my husband, Inspector; he never, ever gives up when
he wants something. When I first married him, I considered that
aspect of his character to be most attractive, but after living with
it, I realized that with it was a terrible flaw." She stopped and took
another deep breath. "He's insane. Oh, not the sort of insanity that
justifies what he's done. He understood perfectly what he was doing when he murdered Lawrence, but it's a sickness nonetheless.
He's obsessed with achieving any objective he sets for himself. He
makes plans and draws up lists and ticks them off one by one when
he's accomplished his goal." Her eyes filled with tears. "One of
those goals was marrying me, but you see, I was engaged to a man
named Nicholas Cutlip. I'd known him all my life and I loved him
dearly. He was truly the love of my life." She dabbed at her eyes.
"But he drowned in a boating accident on the Thames. Arnold was
in the boat with him. The boat overturned and they fell out. Arnold
claims he tried to pull Nicholas to shore, and for awhile, I believed
him. I was grateful to him. He'd tried to save my beloved, so when
he kept pressing me, I agreed to marry him." She sighed heavily
and shook her head. "I was past thirty, my first fiancé had jilted
me, and poor Nicholas was dead. Of course, I was easy pickings
as the saying goes."

"From what you said to your husband, I take it you now believe
that he didn't try to save your fiancé?" Witherspoon said gently.

"He killed him," she said dully. "I've suspected for some time
now. That's why when I found out that he wasn't going to get the
chairmanship honor, I started following him. I knew he'd do something awful, and he did." Her eyes filled with tears. "I loathed
Lawrence, but as God is my witness, I'd no idea that Arnold was
going to murder him that day."

Barnes glanced at the inspector and then said, "Had you followed him that morning?"

She nodded. "Yes, I knew we were going to the luncheon that
afternoon and that once Gibbons made the announcement, it would
be official."

"So you thought that if he were going to do something he would
do it then, is that correct?" Witherspoon still couldn't believe
someone would commit murder over a charity honor.

"Yes, my husband prides himself on being such a good planner, such a hard worker, but for most of his life, he's simply been lucky or persistent. He wanted that chairmanship more than anything else in the world."

"But why?" Witherspoon persisted. He desperately needed to understand.

"Because it was the first step to a knighthood." She smiled faintly. "That was his master plan. My husband was the son of a builder from Slough, but he told me once that he knew from the time he was a child that he was destined for greatness. The honorary chairmanship of the Bankers Benevolent Society was very prestigious. The next step would be a seat on one of Her Majesty's committees, and after that, he was certain to get the knighthood."

"So you followed him that day," Barnes pressed. "What did you see?"

"He left his office and went to his tailor on Bond Street. He came out carrying a parcel. I almost lost him on the Brompton Road, because he'd ducked into a mews and put on a huge, great black coat. I recognized the coat. That's how I was able to catch up with him again. I followed him to the Queens Road, and then he cut through a mews and climbed over a fence. But you see, I know the neighborhood quite well. I've spent my whole life in this part of London, and I knew he was going to Boyd's house. I hurried around the block, but it's quite a long one, Inspector, and it took me a good ten minutes to get to Boyd's garden. I got there just in time to see Arnold come out of the studio and then climb back over the fence to the mews."

"What did you do then?" Witherspoon asked.

"I ran," she admitted. "I saw the smoke start billowing out of the window and I heard a scream from inside the main house. So I ran."

"You didn't think you ought to help?" Barnes stared at her incredulously.

"Oh, no, when I heard the scream from the house, I knew someone else had seen the smoke and I assumed that they would raise the alarm. I think one part of me was still hoping that it wasn't too late, that I was wrong about Arnold, that he hadn't committed murder after murder to achieve his own ends." She smiled sadly. "But of course he had."

"Why did you wait until now to tell us what you'd seen that day?" Witherspoon asked. "You'd followed your husband; you must have suspected he'd murdered Boyd that day."

"I should have told you," she admitted. "But the truth is, I rather enjoyed watching Arnold squirm." She smiled. "When he realized you weren't going to give up and that Boyd's death wasn't going to be considered an accident, he got very upset. I've enjoyed that enormously. He can barely eat and he's not slept properly for days. My only complaint is that you caught onto him so quickly. I was hoping I'd get another good week of watching his misery."

"You were right, Mrs. Jeffries," Wiggins said as the men trooped back into the kitchen of Upper Edmonton Gardens. "It was Sapington who done it."

"Did it," Hatchet corrected. "It was Sapington who did it."

"What happened?" Betsy asked eagerly. "Mrs. Jeffries hasn't told us anything."

"I wanted to wait until everyone was here before I discussed the matter," Mrs. Jeffries protested. "Did Sapington go quietly?"

Smythe slipped into his seat and grabbed for Betsy's hand under the table. "He went quietly enough, but not before there was a bit of a dustup in the 'ouse. Maud Sapington was screamin' loud enough to wake the dead."

"I overheard one of the constables sayin' she tried to kill Mr. Sapington," Wiggins added eagerly.

"She tried to kill him?" Mrs. Goodge exclaimed. "Are you sure?"

"We're certain," Hatchet replied as he sat down next to Luty. "We don't know why, but I'm sure the inspector will enlighten us as soon as he comes home. But I, for one, would like to hear how Mrs. Jeffries figured it all out."

"So would the rest of us," Luty agreed.

Mrs. Jeffries laughed softly. "It was actually something Mrs. Goodge said that put me on the right track."

"Me?" The cook looked inordinately pleased. "That's nice to know. What did I say?"

"You mentioned that murder was usually committed in the heat of the moment," Mrs. Jeffries explained, "or because someone gained something from the act. That got me to thinking: there were a lot of people who hated Boyd, but who actually gained anything from his death?"

"But what did Sapington get from it?" Smythe smiled his thanks as Betsy handed him a cup of freshly poured tea.

"He got the honorary chairmanship of the Bankers Benevolent

Society," Mrs. Jeffries reminded him. "And that was very important to him."

"Was it important enough to kill for?" Luty shook her head, her expression incredulous. "That's hard to believe."

"I know. That's one of the reasons it took me so long to understand that it was Sapington even when all the evidence pointed to him being the killer. The motive seemed so absurd. But then I realized that virtually everything Sapington had ever obtained had been because someone had died." She took a quick sip from her cup. "He got a place at the local grammar school because the lad who actually won the scholarship slipped on a patch of ice, cracked his skull, and died. That's why I went to Slough. According to the coroner's inquest, the witness to the accident was none other than young Arnold Sapington."

"You think Sapington murdered the lad?" Mrs. Goodge asked. "But he wasn't more than a child himself."

"But he was a child who knew that a grammar school education could be very useful in getting ahead in life," the housekeeper replied, "and this scholarship was his last opportunity. The other boy's death might have actually been an accident, but even so, I think it planted an idea in young Arnold's mind."

"How many other murders do you reckon he's committed?" Luty asked.

Mrs. Jeffries pursed her lips. "It's impossible to know for sure, but I think he probably murdered Nicholas Cutlip because he wanted to marry Maud Sapington."

"Why does where Cutlip drowned matter?" Smythe asked curiously.

"Because I think Sapington wanted witnesses," she smiled faintly. "I think he had it all planned. He made sure the boat tipped, and when they were chucked in the water, he made sure he got his hands on Cutlip and made it look like he was trying to save the man. In actuality, I suspect he was holding him under. But his goal was to marry Maud, and therefore, he needed witnesses so she would be grateful. From what we've heard, that's precisely what happened."

"But he was takin' a powerful risk." Luty shook her head in disbelief. "You never know what's goin' to happen when you're in the water. It all coulda gone wrong."

"But it didn't," Mrs. Jeffries said thoughtfully. "Sapington had a good run of luck."

"Why'd you want to know about when the chief clerk at Cutlip and Reese was arrested for embezzlement?" Wiggins asked. He thought he understood it all, but it was still a bit muddled.

"Because Sapington got his job." Luty grinned. "And the man protested he was innocent all the way through his trial. That's what my banker told me, and he said there was some rumors that the fella wasn't guilty."

"So Sapington got a place in grammar school because his competition for the scholarship died, got the chief clerk's position because the man who had it was conveniently arrested for embezzlement, and married the boss's daughter because her fiancé drowned and she was grateful to his would-be rescuer," Mrs. Goodge said. "And Sapington was conveniently around when all these things happened."

"That's right," Mrs. Jeffries said. "When we were chatting yesterday, I suddenly realized that Sapington was the only person who'd actually gained something from Boyd's death. All the others merely hated him, but most of our suspects had hated him for years. Why now would they suddenly take any action against him? Then I realized that every opportunity for Sapington had come at the expense of someone else. At first I couldn't credit that anyone would commit murder over a charity honor, but that was the only idea that made sense."

"Meg said that he liked to make plans and was always giving them lists of instructions on how things were to be done," Betsy murmured.

From upstairs, they heard the front door open. Mrs. Jeffries leapt to her feet. "Who can that be? It's far too early for the inspector to come home."

"Yoo-hoo, Mrs. Jeffries," Witherspoon called. They heard his footsteps tramping down the hall and onto the back stairs. "Where is everybody?"

"Goodness, sir, we didn't expect you," the housekeeper said as he came into the kitchen. "As you can see, we've visitors. Luty and Hatchet dropped by for tea."

"And the time just got away from us," Mrs. Goodge added. It was well past morning tea time.

"It's all my fault, Inspector." Luty smiled brightly. "But I heard you had an interestin' case and I wouldn't let them get up and go about their business till I heard every detail. You know how much I admire you."

"As do I, sir," Hatchet added, laying it on a bit thick. "I don't suppose we can prevail upon you to drop a few hints as to the next step in your investigation."

"You're too kind and you give me too much credit. I'm merely a humble public servant doing his duty." Witherspoon beamed with pleasure. "Luckily for you, I am at liberty to discuss the matter. We arrested Arnold Sapington this morning. He's at the station right now being processed. That's why I've come home. I'm desperate for a decent cup of tea and a slice of Mrs.Goodge's delicious brown bread."

"Gracious, sir, do sit down and tell us all about it." Mrs. Jeffries waved him into her spot at the head of the table. "I'll pour your tea."

"And I'll get you some fresh bread, sir," Betsy said. She got up and went to the counter. "Would you like a slice of seedcake as well?"

"That would be lovely," Witherspoon replied. "Of course, after our chat this morning, I'm sure this comes as no surprise to you," he said to Mrs. Jeffries. "But I must admit that even with Barnes and I confirming the subject of the painting, I still wasn't sure we'd enough evidence to arrest the man."

"Really, sir? But you said everyone connected with Boyd commented that he was somewhat obsessive about keeping his work secret until he was ready to exhibit it." She poured a fresh cup of tea from the pot on the table and placed it in front of him.

"That's true," he admitted. "But I'm not sure a jury could be convinced that was enough evidence to hang someone. Furthermore, the only motive we could think of sounded so very peculiar that I didn't think we'd much chance of bringing a case against the fellow, even though I was sure he was guilty. But luck or the Almighty was on our side."

"How so, sir?" Hatchet asked. He knew how important it was that all of them pretend to know as little as possible.

"A good citizen turned the shoes that Sapington wore when he murdered Boyd into the police this morning," Witherspoon explained. "There's a paint stain on the heel. I suspect we'll find that the paint came from the floor of Boyd's studio. Sapington tried to get rid of them by putting them in a dustbin, but one of his own servants fished them out and gave them to her brother. It was only a bit later that the girl realized the shoes might be evidence and prevailed upon her brother to turn them over to the police."

"How very fortunate," Mrs. Jeffries commented.

"'Ow do you know the shoes are 'is?" Wiggins asked. He'd done some reading about the law recently, and he knew that evidence had to be directly linked to the crime if the Crown was to obtain a conviction. "I mean, did the servant actually see him putting the shoes in the dustbin?"

"Oh, yes, she did. But it wouldn't matter if she hadn't. Sapington's shoes are custom-made and his initials are on the inside heel. But the most important thing is Mrs. Sapington is prepared to testify not only that the shoes are his, but also that Sapington was wearing them on the day of the murder." He smiled triumphantly.

"His own wife is going to testify against him!" Luty exclaimed. "Nell's bells, she must hate his guts!"

"She does," Witherspoon replied. "Maud Sapington has been following her husband for days now. She suspected all along that he was going to do something awful." In between bites of bread and seedcake, he told them everything that had transpired at the Sapington house. When he was finished, he glanced at the carriage clock on the sideboard and said, "The real irony is that Sapington didn't have to commit the murder at all. He was actually going to get the chairmanship that he wanted so badly."

"That was a bit of bad luck for Lawrence Boyd," Wiggins commented. "Poor sod."

"Yes, he wasn't a particularly likeable fellow, but he didn't deserve to be murdered." Witherspoon got to his feet. "Goodness, I must get back to the station. We're going to have another go at interviewing Sapington."

"He isn't admitting anything?" Mrs. Jeffries probed.

Witherspoon shook his head. "No, but with Mrs. Sapington's testimony, we'll get a conviction."

"I didn't think a wife could testify against her husband," Mrs. Goodge muttered.

"He won't be her husband much longer. She told us she's going to divorce him, and she does have grounds: he did more or less marry her under false pretenses." The inspector drained his cup. "But she'll have the devil's own time proving it, I'm afraid."

"Can't she just divorce him because he's committed murder?" Wiggins asked. "Seems like that ought to be grounds for getting rid of a husband."

Witherspoon paused. "Actually, I don't think it is. But I'm sure that considering everything she suspects he's done over the years, her solicitors will find grounds. Mrs. Crookshank, Hatchet, it was lovely to see you both. I'll see you very soon, I'm sure. We've Betsy's wedding in just a few weeks."

"Good day, Inspector," Luty called.

"Good day," Hatchet echoed.

As soon as he'd gone, they breathed a collective sigh of relief.

"That was close," Smythe said. "He almost caught us."

Mrs. Jeffries said nothing. She was simply grateful that he hadn't questioned them further about why they were sitting around in the middle of the day.

"But he didn't," Betsy said. She got to her feet. "And I've got a dozen different things to do now that the case is solved." She reached into her pocket, pulled out a slip of paper, and handed it to Luty. "Here's the menu for the wedding breakfast. I finally made up my mind."

"What are we 'avin'?" Wiggins asked eagerly.

"Never you mind, lad," Luty retorted. She got up. "That's a secret. We'd best git on home as well. Like Betsy says, now that the case is solved, we've got us a weddin' to do!"

For the next few days, the household kept their ears open for further news about the Sapington case. But they learned very little they didn't already know, and as the days passed, the case receded into the background of their lives. They all had something much more important to think about now.

Smythe and Betsy's wedding.

The guest list was complete, the banns were read, and the menu, after half a dozen last-minute changes, was finalized. Two weeks before the big day, Smythe took Wiggins to his tailor so the lad could be fitted for a nice new suit to wear when he stood up with the coachman as his best man. He also had a chat with the inspector, and both men had come away satisfied with the conversation.

Mrs. Goodge bought a new lavender dress with a nice mother-of-pearl matching jacket and a lacy jabot cravat. She bought Samson a matching ribbon, but he ran off and hid under the inspector's bed when she tried to put it on him. She made the mistake of leaving the ribbon on her bed, and the next time she saw it, it was shredded to bits.

Mrs. Jeffries decided to wear her navy blue suit with a high-necked white blouse. But she did buy herself a lovely new hat with blue veiling and two white feathers on the side.

The week before the wedding, Betsy worked up the courage to ask the inspector to walk her down the aisle. Witherspoon told her he'd be honored to give her away, and he shyly admitted he'd been hoping she'd ask him.

A few days before the wedding, Betsy's trousseau and wedding dress were finished. They were to be delivered the day before the nuptials. Betsy was superstitious; she didn't want Smythe to get so much as a glimpse of her wedding dress. There wasn't going to be any bad luck for her wedding!

Everything was going as planned except that no matter how hard she cajoled, coaxed, or complained, she couldn't get Smythe to say one word about where they were going to live or even where they were going on their honeymoon.

"Come on, give us a hint." She poked him in the arm. The wedding was two days away and they were sitting at the table having their tea.

"No hints," he said firmly. "If I say too much, you'll suss it out."

"That's because she's smart." Wiggins nodded his head wisely. "But you're even smarter because you got 'er to marry you."

"Why, Wiggins, thank you," Betsy replied. "I think."

Mrs. Jeffries smiled at her brood. She was a bit sad that things were going to change, but she knew it was for the best. These two were madly in love and they needed to be out on their own. The coachman had confided his plan to her, and she thought it had a good chance of succeeding.

There was a loud knock on the front door. Mrs. Jeffries got up. "I wonder who that can be. We're not expecting anyone."

She held her breath as she opened the door, hoping that it wasn't someone needing help with an unsolved murder. Not this close to the wedding. A plump, middle-aged woman with bright red hair stood there. She wore an emerald green day dress with a matching hat and leaned against a green-and-white striped parasol she'd propped on the top step. "Hello, hello," she smiled. "Is this the household of Inspector Witherspoon?"

"Yes, but the inspector isn't here. He's at the station."

"Then I'm at the right place." She pushed forward suddenly, causing Mrs. Jeffries to step back. "Is Smythe 'ere?"

"Smythe?" Mrs. Jeffries repeated. "Yes, he's downstairs."

"Let's go, then, I've not much time. Is it through here?" She started down the hall.

"Excuse me," Mrs. Jeffries said, "but who are you?" She had a bad feeling about this.

"I'm Georgiana Merchant," she replied. "Georgy for short. Is he down there?" They'd reached the back stairs.

"Yes, but why do you wish to see Smythe?" Mrs. Jeffries asked, keeping her voice as low as possible.

But Georgy didn't reply; she simply charged down the stairs. "Smythe, Smythe, are ya down there, darlin'? It's me, Georgy, and we've not much time."

Mrs. Jeffries knew disaster was in the making. She raced after the woman.

Georgy dashed into the kitchen, skidding to a halt as she saw the others grouped around the table. Her wide mouth creased in a smile when she spotted Smythe. "Cor blimey, Smythe, I'll bet this is a surprise for ya, isn't it?"

Smythe, his jaw hanging open, got to his feet.

"Who is that woman?" Betsy got up as well.

"It's Georgy Merchant," he mumbled. "She's a friend from Australia. Blast a Spaniard, Georgy, what are you doin' here?"

"You've got to come with me," Georgy said without preamble. She pulled a slip of yellow paper out of the jacket of her dress. "This telegram come for me today, and we've got to get home. They're wantin' to hang Da for murder, but he's run off to the bush."

"What is she talking about?" Betsy protested. "You can't leave. We're getting married in two days."

"Betsy, let me talk to Georgy outside for a moment and see what's what," Smythe said softly. He took the red-haired woman by the arm and pulled her down the hall toward the back door.

"This can't be happening," Betsy said. But a horrid, hollow feeling settled in the pit of her stomach.

Mrs. Goodge rose from her chair and went to stand next to the maid. "Don't worry, Betsy. Let's see what this is all about before you go to frettin'."

"Cor blimey, this isn't good," Wiggins muttered. He knew some-

thing awful was going to happen. In his experience, when the
women of the house wore these kinds of expressions, a man with
his wits about him would do well to lie low. He wanted to sneak
out and go up to his room, but he felt that might be deserting
Smythe.

Betsy's eyes filled with tears, but she blinked them back.

Mrs. Jeffries saw the anguish on the maid's face and it broke her
heart. Like the others, she knew something dreadful was about to
happen, but she had no idea how to stop it.

The room was quiet except for the ticking of the carriage clock
and the faint sounds of the traffic from the road. Then they heard
the back door open and footsteps come up the hall.

Smythe was alone. He stopped at the doorway; his face was
white and there was a sheen of moisture on his forehead. "Betsy,
love, can you come outside with me for a moment?"

"Is that woman out there?" Betsy demanded.

"No, she's gone." He'd sent Georgy out the garden gate with instructions to find a hansom and bring it around to the front of the
house.

Betsy swallowed the lump in her throat. "You can say whatever
you need to say in front of the others."

He hesitated and then gave in. "I've got to go, love. Georgy's father is accused of murder and he's taken off to the bush."

"Go where?" she yelled. But she knew.

"Back to Australia," he whispered. "Dear God, if it was anyone
but him, I wouldn't leave you for all the world. But I owe him a
debt I can never repay. He saved my life; he kept me from starvin'
and took me in when I was half dead, I'm the only one that can
'elp him now and I've got to go."

"We're getting married in two days," she cried.

"We'll get married as soon as I get back." He moved then, coming to her and taking her by the shoulders. "I promise, love, we'll
get married as soon as I'm back, but I've no choice. I've got to go."

Through her tears, she searched his face and realized that she'd
lost. She pulled away from him. "Go then, but don't expect me to
be waiting when you get back."

"You don't mean that, love," he cried, anguish on his own face.

"I've never been more serious in my life," she retorted. She
didn't care if she was unreasonable, she didn't care if she hurt
him; she knew only that she hurt more than she'd ever hurt in her

life. "If you leave me now, if you put me second and humiliate me like this, I'll never forgive you."

"Betsy, no, you can't mean that," he pleaded.

But she tore away from him and ran for the stairs.

He started after her then stopped. He looked at Mrs. Jeffries. "I've got to go Mrs. J. I've got no choice. If I don't, an innocent man is goin' to hang. There's no time to explain everything and make her understand."

"She doesn't mean what she said, Smythe," Mrs. Jeffries said softly. "She's very upset. What do you want me to do?"

He took a deep breath. "Make sure she picks up her weddin' gown and her trousseau from the dressmaker's, and don't let her do anything foolish like try to run off."

Mrs. Jeffries wasn't sure she could stop her, but she wasn't going to share that with him. "Alright. How long do you think you'll be gone?"

"I'm not certain. It's a good nine weeks out there, and God knows how long it'll take to find him. But I've got to try."

"What's 'e done?" Wiggins asked.

"He's accused of murder, so he's gone off to the bush," Smythe said. "Georgy was here in London visitin' her auntie. She got a telegram late yesterday and started lookin' for me."

"Why do you have to go find him?" Mrs. Goodge asked. She was struggling to hold back tears; watching Betsy's face had broken her heart.

"Because I'm the only one who can," Smythe replied. He started for the stairs. "I'm going to throw a few things in a bag and then I've got to be off. The ship leaves on the evening tide."

He was back downstairs in less than ten minutes. The others, except for Betsy, were waiting to say good-bye at the front door. Mrs. Jeffries had seen a hansom pull up outside. "Your cab is here," she said. "Don't worry. I'll take care of telling the inspector."

"Thank you," Smythe glanced up toward the staircase. "I will be back."

"And I'll make sure Bow and Arrow is properly looked after." Wiggins struggled not to cry. "I promise. I know how much them silly 'orses mean to you, and I'll see that the carriage is taken out regularly." The horses and carriage belonged to Witherspoon, but Smythe had been in charge of them for so long, they felt like his own.

"You just be sure to take care," Mrs. Goodge ordered, her voice rough with suppressed emotion. "I'll not have you getting lost out amongst them heathens, and mind you get back here as quick as you can. I want to wear my new dress to your wedding."

Smythe pulled her close in a hug, embraced Mrs. Jeffries, and shook Wiggin's hand. "I'll be back as soon as I can," he promised.

He pulled open the front door and stepped outside. "Don't let her leave," he said to Mrs. Jeffries. "Promise me she'll be here when I get back."

Mrs. Jeffries hesitated. "I promise. She'll be here."

He turned and went down the stairs to the waiting hansom.

Upstairs, Betsy watched from the window. A cry of pain escaped from her lips as she saw him step into the cab. Dear God, this was her worst nightmare come true. He was going. He was leaving her, and she knew deep in her heart that despite what he said, he was never coming back.

She'd been abandoned before.

She watched the cab until it went around the corner. Betsy moved away from the window and went over to her bed. Dropping to her knees, she reached underneath and pulled out her carpet bag. She blew the light coating of dust off the frame and put it on her bed.

Then she began to pack.

EPILOGUE

Betsy stood under the tree in the communal gardens where she and Smythe had spent so many hours together. The others thought she was still upstairs, nursing her wounds. She'd slipped out when she'd heard them go downstairs for their supper. She turned and looked at the house; her packed carpetbag was at her feet.

She could see the lights from the kitchen, and she knew that they'd all be upset when they found her gone tomorrow morning, but that couldn't be helped. A strangled cry arose in her throat, but she pushed it back, determined to stay strong. She had to go. But Lord, it was so hard. She loved them all so much. They'd become her family.

"He'll die when he gets back and finds you gone," Mrs. Jeffries said softly.

Betsy whirled around as the housekeeper stepped out from behind a row of bushes. "I didn't see you come out."

"I came through the gate," she replied. "Don't leave, Betsy. If you go, you'll break all our hearts."

Betsy burst into tears. She hung her head and sobbed. Mrs. Jeffries hurried over and pulled her into her arms. "I know you've had a terrible shock, but he loves you more than life itself. You have to stay and wait for him to come back."

"But he's not coming back," Betsy cried. "I know it. He doesn't really want to marry me."

"Is that what this is all about?" Mrs. Jeffries kicked at Betsy's carpetbag. "Of course he does. That man would die for you."

"But he left me."

"Only because he had to repay a debt of honor." Mrs. Jeffries looked her directly in the eye. "If he'd refused to go and help save an innocent man, you know you'd think less of him. If you're going to marry Smythe, Betsy, then you've got to trust him." She gave her shoulders a squeeze, turned, and started for the house.

After a moment, Betsy picked up her bag and followed Mrs. Jeffries back inside.

Smythe stared at the lights of Tilbury as the SS *Oroya* pulled away from the dock. He was on the first-class deck, but he could care less about the luxurious furnishings in his quarters. All he could think of was Betsy, of her face as she'd realized he had to go. Blast and damn, this couldn't have happened at a worse time. But he had to go. He'd no choice.

He prayed that Betsy would still be waiting for him when he got back. When he'd boarded, he'd asked one of the seamen how long it would take to get to Sydney. The answer had depressed him. Nine weeks, nine ruddy weeks! If you added a month or two for him to find Tommy Merchant and settle whatever mess he'd gotten into, and then another two months back to England, blast, it would be almost Christmas before he got back.

But Betsy would be there. She had to be. He couldn't lose her now.

MRS. JEFFRIES
AND THE FEAST OF ST. STEPHEN

MRS. JEFFRIES
AND THE FEAST OF ST. STEPHEN

EMILY BRIGHTWELL

BERKLEY PRIME CRIME, NEW YORK

THE BERKLEY PUBLISHING GROUP
Published by the Penguin Group
Penguin Group (USA) Inc.
375 Hudson Street, New York, New York 10014, USA
Penguin Group (Canada), 90 Eglinton Avenue East, Suite 700, Toronto, Ontario M4P 2Y3, Canada (a division of Pearson Penguin Canada Inc.)
Penguin Books Ltd., 80 Strand, London WC2R 0RL, England
Penguin Group Ireland, 25 St. Stephen's Green, Dublin 2, Ireland (a division of Penguin Books Ltd.) Penguin Group (Australia), 250 Camberwell Road, Camberwell, Victoria 3124, Australia (a division of Pearson Australia Group Pty. Ltd.)
Penguin Books India Pvt. Ltd., 11 Community Centre, Panchsheel Park, New Delhi—110 017, India
Penguin Group (NZ), 67 Apollo Drive, Rosedale, North Shore 0745, Auckland, New Zealand (a division of Pearson New Zealand Ltd.)
Penguin Books (South Africa) (Pty.) Ltd., 24 Sturdee Avenue, Rosebank, Johannesburg 2196, South Africa

Penguin Books Ltd., Registered Offices: 80 Strand, London WC2R 0RL, England

This book is an original publication of The Berkley Publishing Group.

ISBN: 978-0-7394-8880-5

PRINTED IN THE UNITED STATES OF AMERICA

*This book is dedicated to
Richard Arguile
with love and thanks for all the years
of support, encouragement, and help.
I couldn't have done it without you!*

MRS. JEFFRIES
AND THE FEAST OF ST. STEPHEN

CHAPTER 1

"I do hope you like this, Stephen." Maria Farringdon smiled as she handed the bottle of Bordeaux to her host. "Of course, it's nowhere near as special as that lovely ruby port we received from you yesterday, but our wine merchant assures us this is very good. I do hope you like it."

"Thank you, dear lady." Stephen Whitfield bowed graciously in acknowledgment of the gift. He glanced at the bottle, and his blue eyes widened as he read the label. Blast, she'd managed to outdo him. He'd no doubt that the choice of such an expensive wine had been her idea, not her husband's. Basil was far too well-bred to have gone to such extravagance. This was only to be expected: women from her background always managed to get it wrong. They simply weren't raised to understand the really important social nuances. "But there was no need for you to go to any trouble."

"Nonsense," Basil Farringdon said. "Of course it was necessary. You send us a wonderful bottle of your special port every year. You go to a great deal of trouble."

"Not really," he replied.

"But you do," Basil countered. "You have it shipped all the way from Portugal, and you cork it yourself. It's about time we reciprocated, don't you think." His wide, chubby face creased in a smile. "Maria chose this just for you."

"And it is much appreciated." Stephen forced a chuckle and glanced at her. She was smiling at him, but he could see that the smile hadn't quite reached her eyes. To annoy her, he took her arm and tugged her gently toward a set of double doors farther down the hall. "Let's go into the drawing room. You two are the first to arrive, but I expect the others will be here shortly." He looked over his shoulder. Flagg, his butler, had returned from hanging up the guests' heavy winter wraps and now hovered discreetly at the front door. "I'd like this opened and brought to the drawing room."

"Yes, sir." Flagg took the bottle and disappeared.

Whitfield held himself ramrod straight as he escorted his guests into the drawing room. The moment they stepped inside the cavernous room, Maria Farringdon pulled her arm out of his grasp and moved quickly toward a blue brocade love seat. Basil followed his wife.

Whitfield walked over to a mahogany sideboard near the fireplace. He grinned at Maria, his expression amused. She'd not liked his taking her arm, but she could hardly object, as he was merely playing the solicitous host. "Would you care for an aperitif, or would you rather wait for the Bordeaux?"

"I'd like a sherry." Maria Farringdon returned his smile with an amused one of her own. She couldn't wait for the evening to progress, for the other guests to arrive. Whitfield was in for a big surprise, and it wouldn't be one that he was expecting, either. He was so conceited, she thought. He really thought himself a great catch. She studied him dispassionately as he lifted the crystal stopper off the top of a decanter. He was a tall, thin man with steel gray hair, a bristling mustache, and a lean, hawkish face that some women considered very handsome. He'd been a widower for years now, and every widow in London had set her cap for him at one time or another. Maria had never understood why; he wasn't that rich, and he certainly wasn't very charming.

She eased her thin backside flush against the back of the seat and braced her feet firmly on the floor. Brocade was a very slippery material, and she wasn't taking any chances of sliding off. She arranged the skirt of her green silk dress and leaned back, preparing to enjoy the spectacle. This was going to be priceless, absolutely priceless. Who would have thought the old fool would actually open it in front of her!

"I'll have sherry as well," Basil Farringdon said as he sat down in the armchair next to the sofa. "Are there many others coming this evening?" he asked.

"It's just a small dinner party," Stephen replied. "Henry will be here—I knew you'd want to see him—and Eliza's invited as well.

She's bringing an acquaintance of hers and, of course, my sister-in-law, Rosalind, will be joining us."

Maria glanced at her husband, and their eyes met. They'd both heard the rumors about Eliza Graham's "acquaintance." Apparently Stephen was the only person in London who was still in the dark.

"Ah, excellent." Stephen looked up from his task as the drawing room door opened and two people, a man and a woman, stepped inside. "You're finally here."

"We're not late, Stephen." The woman smiled as she spoke, but there was just the barest hint of irritation in her tone. Eliza Graham was forty-seven and well past her youth, yet her hair was still a lustrous dark brown and her skin smooth and unlined. Her elegant wine red evening gown rustled softly as she and her companion swept into the room. "The traffic was dreadful, and it took ages for Hugh to find a cab. It appears that everyone has decided to stay in town for the Christmas season."

"Now, now, dear." Hugh Langford let go of her arm. "It didn't take all that long. It just seemed a long time because it's so very cold outside. But at least it has finally stopped raining."

"Does everyone know Hugh?" Eliza stopped and looked around at the other guests.

"I'm afraid I haven't had the pleasure." Basil, who'd risen to his feet when they entered the room, crossed the small space separating them, with his hand extended. "I'm Basil Farringdon, and this is my wife, Maria."

"Sorry, thought you all knew each other," Stephen mumbled from the background. "This is Hugh Langford."

Hugh shook hands and then bowed to Maria. "I'm very pleased to meet you both."

Maria smiled politely and inclined her head in acknowledgment of the introduction. She was quite surprised by the man's appearance. He looked so very average, so very ordinary, not at all like she'd imagined. According to the gossip she'd heard, he was supposedly quite a Lothario and had a string of brokenhearted women in his past. But if she was any judge, Langdon had to be pushing sixty. His hair, though still more brown than gray, was receding from his forehead; he was barely an inch or so taller than average; and beneath his beautifully tailored navy blue evening coat, he had a distinct potbelly. But then again, when you were as rich as Langford, you didn't need to worry overly much about your appearance.

Maria glanced at Stephen just as Langford and Eliza sat down together on the settee opposite her. She saw Stephen's eyes narrow, and a flush crept up his sharp cheekbones. Oh, yes, indeed, tonight was going to be great fun!

"It's going to be cold tonight," Wiggins, the footman, said as he came into the kitchen. He was a good-looking young man with brown hair, round apple cheeks, and a very cheerful disposition.

"It's been cold all week," Mrs. Goodge, the portly, gray-haired cook, said. She put a platter of pork chops on the table.

"Gracious, that's a lot of pork," Mrs. Jeffries, the housekeeper, commented as she slipped into her spot at the head of the table. "I'm surprised that any of us is even hungry after that lovely tea we had at Mrs. Maynard's." The household was eating much later than they usually did because they'd gone to a Christmas tea at their neighbors'.

"There are two extra chops," the cook replied. "The inspector is having dinner at Lady Cannonberry's tonight, but he didn't let me know till I'd already started the chops, so the lad here"—she indicated Wiggins with a nod in his direction—"can eat hearty if he's a mind to."

As there was always plenty of food for the servants in the household of Inspector Gerald Witherspoon, the comment wasn't taken seriously.

"Betsy's the one that needs to eat hearty," Wiggins said, tossing a fast glance in the maid's direction. "She's gettin' as thin as a lamppost."

"I've only lost a pound or two," Betsy muttered. She pushed a lock of blond hair, which had slipped out of her cap, back behind her ear. She knew the others were worried about her, but she was fine, just fine. She wished they'd stop fretting over her. The past six months had been the most miserable of her life, but she was getting over it. "I haven't lost that much weight."

"Yes, you 'ave," Wiggins argued. "And when he gets back and sees how peaked you look, he'll 'ave a fit."

They all knew who "he" was.

"Wiggins, that's Betsy's personal business." Mrs. Goodge cast an anxious glance in the maid's direction.

"It's alright, Mrs. Goodge," Betsy said. "Wiggins is just concerned, that's all. Not to worry, though: I'll eat plenty tonight." She reached for the bowl of boiled potatoes that was next to the chops. "And it won't be because I'm worried about what *he'll* think, either. It'll be because I'm hungry enough to eat a horse." It would be a cold day in the pits of hell before she'd ever be concerned about him again, she told herself as she slapped a huge spoonful of potatoes onto her plate. Besides, one of the painful truths she'd learned this past six months was that time did heal all wounds. Two weeks ago, she'd realized she was looking forward to Christmas. The crowds of shoppers on High Street, the smell of Mrs. Goodge's baking, the decorations in some of the more posh shops—she'd found herself liking all of it. She'd even smiled at a young man getting off the omnibus yesterday. Her heart was definitely on the mend, and what's more, she'd never let it get broken like that again!

Mrs. Jeffries glanced at the cook. Both women were relieved to see Betsy showing a bit of appetite; in truth, the girl had gotten so thin that they were concerned for her health. The housekeeper put a slice of bread onto her own plate and reached for the butter pot. The maid had seemed better lately, but she still wasn't her old self. Perhaps it would be best to avoid personal subjects and instead keep the conversation to Inspector Witherspoon's police business. That always cheered everyone up. "Constable Barnes mentioned that the Collinger case is going to trial next week." She stuck her knife in the pot and scooped out a good chunk of creamy butter. "The inspector will be testifying, of course. I believe he's a bit nervous about it."

"Can't think why," Mrs. Goodge replied. "He's testified lots of times, and he always gets it right."

Witherspoon's latest case, the apprehension of a man who'd murdered an elderly woman during the course of a robbery, had involved very little investigation on any of their parts. Harold Collinger, the killer, had left a trail of evidence so obvious that a two-year-old could have followed it. He'd not only been found with the victim's belongings in his possession, but he'd bragged to his mates down at the pub about doing in the poor woman. Within two days after the discovery of the body, Collinger had been arrested and had confessed.

"Yes, but testifying still makes him a bit uncomfortable," Mrs.

Jeffries commented. Inspector Witherspoon had solved more homicides than anyone in the history of the Metropolitan Police Force. He wasn't quite sure how he'd managed to catch so many killers; it just seemed to happen. And he didn't know why he'd suddenly become such a good detective. How could he, when his entire household went to so much trouble to make sure he was kept firmly in the dark? Gerald Witherspoon, one of nature's true gentlemen, had a great deal of help on each and every one of his cases.

When he "caught a case," as Wiggins so colorfully put it, his household leapt into action: they snooped around the crime scene, they found out what they could about the suspects, and most of all, they learned as much information as possible about the victim. A few trusted friends knew of their activities, but for the most part, they worked hard to be discreet. Each member of the household had their own area of expertise.

Mrs. Goodge was excellent at finding out background information, and she never even had to leave the house to do it; she had a steady stream of delivery boys, gas men, fruit vendors, and tinkers tramping through her kitchen. She plied them with treats and tea as she learned every morsel of gossip there was to be had about both victims and suspects. The elderly cook had served some of the richest families in all England, so if her local sources were no good, she used her connections to her former colleagues to find out what she needed to know.

Betsy was very good at getting facts out of shopkeepers, while Wiggins was quite handy at persuading maids or footmen to reveal all sorts of useful clues. Both of them had become rather skilled at following people as well.

"It wasn't much of a case, was it?" Betsy sighed heavily. "We knew right away who'd done it." She'd been bitterly disappointed when the case had been solved so quickly; she'd been hoping that having a good murder to sink her teeth into might prove a welcome distraction. But instead that stupid killer had confessed, and she'd had nothing to do but her household tasks. It wasn't fair. It had been the first murder they'd had since *he'd* left, and it had turned out to be about as interesting as the boiled potatoes she was trying to choke down.

"Yes, well, it was one of the inspector's less complex murders," the housekeeper replied. She stifled a surge of irritation. Smythe, Betsy's fiancé, had been gone for six months, and despite Betsy's protests that she was fine, the girl could still slide into a good bout of self-pity. It was time for her to buck up and act like a grown woman. For goodness' sake, there were people starving on these very streets of London, people who would love that food heaped on the girl's plate. "Besides, I'm not sure any of us were up to a complicated murder."

"Why wouldn't we be up to it?" Betsy protested. "I was prepared to do my part, and so was Wiggins . . ." She broke off as a loud knocking came from the back door.

"I'll see who it is." Wiggins leapt to his feet and started for the hall. Fred, the household's mongrel dog, who'd been sleeping peacefully on a rug near the warm stove, jumped up and trailed after the footman.

"Cor blimey!" they heard Wiggins exclaim. "Look what the cat's dragged home! What are you knockin' for? You shoulda just walked right in."

"I wasn't sure of my welcome," said a familiar voice.

Betsy got to her feet and stared into the darkened hallway. She'd gone deathly pale. Mrs. Jeffries and Mrs. Goodge stood up as well. The cook looked at the housekeeper, her expression anxious. Both of them glanced at Betsy, but she didn't notice; her entire attention was focused on the footsteps coming down the hall.

Wiggins, followed by a tall, dark-haired man wearing a long, heavy gray coat, came into the kitchen. Dampness glistened on the man's thick black hair. A blue and gray woven scarf hung around his neck, and he pulled off a pair of leather gloves as he walked. His face was red from the cold, and there was a hint of shadow on his high cheekbones and his chin.

"Look who I found," the footman said gleefully. "Isn't it wonderful? He made it home in time for Christmas."

"Hello, Smythe. Welcome home," Mrs. Jeffries said softly.

"Maria, are you all right?" Basil Farringdon whispered in his wife's ear as they walked into the brilliantly lighted dining room for dinner. "You've been staring at Stephen for the last hour."

"That's because he's putting on such a good show," she replied softly. "Did you see his face when he took us all into the morning room to show off that ridiculous Christmas tree? I thought he was going to have an apoplexy attack when Mrs. Graham didn't give it more than a glance."

"Shh . . . He'll hear you." Basil looked over his shoulder at their host. Despite the fact that the butler announced that dinner was served, Whitfield hadn't moved toward the dining room.

"Don't be silly," she whispered. "Right now the only thing he's interested in doing is pouring that Bordeaux down his throat. Honestly, he acts as if he's afraid someone's going to steal it away, and he's glaring at Mr. Langford like he's worried the man's going to run off with his silver."

Whitfield was standing in the open door of the morning room. A Christmas tree blazing with candles and colored ornaments of painted glass, wood, and clay stood in front of the marble fireplace. Two uniformed footmen, one with a bucket of sand at his feet and one with a bucket of water, stood on either side of the mantel. Whitfield held a glass of wine in one hand while with his other he pointed at the evergreen boughs decorating the mantelpiece behind the tree. He was saying something, but the others in the room were paying no attention to him. Eliza Graham was standing in front of the tree, laughing at some quip of Hugh Langford's; Henry Becker, another guest, was laughing as well. Rosalind Murray, Whitfield's sister-in-law, was in the corner of the dining room, gesturing for the butler to begin pouring the wine for the first course.

"More like he's worried Langford's going to run off with Mrs. Graham." Basil chuckled softly, caught himself, and composed his features so that no one could possibly accuse him of actually enjoying himself. For goodness' sake, this was a social obligation, and he must act appropriately.

Whitfield, with one last glare at his guests, turned on his heel and stumbled into the dining room. The others followed suit.

Farringdon waited till everyone had approached the table; then he pulled out the ornate Queen Anne dining chair, seated his wife, and took his own seat.

Hugh Langford seated Eliza Graham and took the chair next to her. Stephen was at the head of the table with Maria on his right and Eliza Graham on his left. Henry Becker was next to Maria. Basil was beside Rosalind Murray.

"It's nice to see you again, Mrs. Murray," Basil said politely.

"It's good to see you, Mr. Farringdon," she replied. She was a tall blond woman in her late fifties. Her complexion was pale, her eyes were blue, and the gray in her hair was quickly overtaking the blond. She wore a lavender silk high-necked evening gown and an anxious smile.

The dining room door opened, and the servants began serving the first course.

"Will you be staying in town for Christmas?" Maria asked Rosalind. She felt very sorry for the poor woman, especially tonight. Eliza Graham's bright beauty made the pale Rosalind look even blander than usual.

"Oh yes, we've no plans to leave town." Rosalind smiled faintly.

"We're thinking of going to Scotland," Hugh interjected. "But Eliza's afraid we'll be trapped up there by bad weather."

Stephen glared at Hugh and gestured for Flagg. He nodded at the glass of white wine next to his soup bowl. "I don't want that." He raised the glass of Bordeaux he'd brought with him to the table. "I want this."

"But the first course is a fish soup," Rosalind protested. "It won't go with Bordeaux."

Whitfield ignored her. "Bring me the bottle. It's in the drawing room," he ordered Flagg. Rosalind gave an almost imperceptible shrug and turned her attention back to the guests.

"I thought we agreed you'd be here for Christmas Eve dinner," Whitfield said accusingly to Eliza. "And for Boxing Day as well."

"Those plans were very tentative," Eliza replied softly. She cast a quick, nervous smile at Langford.

"Ah, yes, Boxing Day. It's actually the Feast of St. Stephen," Henry Becker said to no one in particular. "He was quite an interesting saint. I believe he was stoned to death, or perhaps he was drawn and quartered."

Rosalind frowned at Stephen. "If we're having a full dinner for Christmas Eve, Stephen, you'd best let me know so that I can make arrangements with the cook. The servants have plans as well, you know."

"The servants will do as they are told," he snapped.

Maria Farringdon glanced at her husband, her expression amused. Basil gave her a stern look, then quickly picked up his wineglass to hide his own smile. His good wife was enjoying herself far too much, and truth to tell, so was he. Gracious, this might end in fisticuffs before the evening was out.

"I say, Stephen, this is very good wine." Henry Becker, who was totally oblivious to the undercurrents of tension around the table, put his glass down and smiled at his host. He was a slight man with a narrow chest and a full head of graying hair. A widower of many years, he'd been to school with Stephen and Basil, and desired nothing more than some congenial company, a good dinner, and some decent wine.

"It's French," Stephen replied. He took another long sip from his own drink and then nodded at Flagg, who'd come in with the Bordeaux, to refill his glass. "Mr. Langford, do you like French wine?"

"It depends," Langford replied. He put down his soup spoon and turned his attention to his host. "Some French wine is excellent, but some of it isn't worth drinking."

"Or perhaps some people simply can't appreciate a fine wine." Whitfield paused and took a deep breath. "Not everyone has a refined palate."

Maria Farringdon snickered and tried to cover the noise with a discreet cough. Basil gave her a warning look, but none of the other guests appeared to notice her outburst.

"And some people will drink any old rubbish as long as it has a fancy label on it," Langford replied with an amused smile.

Stephen stared at him for a long moment. "I've an announcement I'd like to make."

"An announcement," Eliza interjected. "What sort of announcement?"

"Why, surely you know." Stephen took another deep breath, wheezing a bit as though he was having trouble getting air. "It's something we've been discussing for several months now."

"Perhaps this isn't the right time," Eliza said with a nervous glance at Hugh. "We ought to discuss the matter further. Nothing has been settled as yet. I told you I needed a bit more time to think the matter over."

"Nonsense." Whitfield coughed. "You've had plenty of time."

Langford looked first at his host and then at Eliza, but he said nothing. He leaned back in his chair and folded his arms over his chest.

"What kind of announcement is it?" Henry asked eagerly.

"A very pleasant one." Stephen could barely choke out the words. His face had turned bright red, and his shoulders slumped forward.

"Stephen, you've gone a funny color." Basil stared at him in concern.

"You're very flushed," Rosalind said. "You've turned red. Have you got a fever?"

Eliza stared at him. "You don't look well at all. I think perhaps you've had too much excitement."

"Are you alright, sir?" Langford unfolded his arms and leaned toward his host, his expression concerned.

But their host wasn't alright. Suddenly his eyes widened, his mouth gaped open, and he sat bolt upright. "Ye gods, you've all turned blue."

"Turned blue," Langford repeated. "Is this some sort of absurd joke?"

Rosalind had risen from her chair. "Stephen, for goodness' sake, what is wrong with you?"

But Stephen didn't seem to hear her. His shoulders began to shake, his hands clenched into fists, and his face contorted as though he was in pain. He clutched at his chest. "The light, the light, what's wrong with the light?" he cried. Then he slumped forward and plunged face-first into his soup bowl.

Eliza screamed, Henry blinked in surprise, Maria's jaw dropped, and Hugh Langford was frozen by shock. Basil rushed to his host, grabbed him by the hair, and yanked his face out of the soup bowl. "Get a doctor," he yelled.

"There's one just across the road," Rosalind Murray said. "Run and fetch Mrs. Winston's new lodger. He's a doctor," she ordered Flagg. "Do it quickly. Mr. Whitfield has taken ill."

"I'm afraid it's too late," Dr. Bosworth said as he straightened up. He turned toward the people crowding around the foot of the dead man's bed. "He's gone."

"I'm Rosalind Murray." A woman stepped away from the others and came toward him. "Stephen was my brother-in-law. I'm sorry we didn't have a chance to introduce ourselves properly, but we were in a hurry to get help for Stephen. I'm so sorry to have called you out when you're not even our doctor, but I remembered my neighbor mentioning that she'd rented rooms to a physician, so when Stephen collapsed, all I could think of was getting you here." She glanced at the body on the bed. "What happened to him? Was it a heart attack?"

Bosworth hesitated a moment. "I'm not sure. Can you tell me what he was doing before he collapsed?"

"We were having dinner." She waved at the crowd around the foot of Stephen's bed. "As you can see, we've guests." She looked at them. "Perhaps you'd all be more comfortable in the drawing room, now that we know Stephen is beyond all hope."

"Are you certain there's nothing we can do to help?" a short, rather chubby fellow asked.

"Not really." Rosalind smiled wanly. "Honestly, perhaps it would be best if you all simply went home. This can't be very pleasant."

There was a general murmur of agreement, and with much shuffling of feet and muttering among themselves, the group headed for the door.

"Just a moment," Bosworth called. There was something very wrong here; he could feel it. But these were wealthy, influential people, so he had to be careful.

The little cluster of guests stopped and stared at him expectantly.

"What's wrong, Doctor?" Rosalind asked. "Why can't they leave?"

"I'd like one of you to tell me exactly what happened before Mr. Whitfield died."

"I can give you that information. There's no need to detain our guests," Rosalind said coolly.

"I'm Maria Farringdon. Stephen said we were all turning blue," a small, slender woman with gray hair supplied. "Then he clutched his chest and fell into his soup bowl. That's when Mrs. Murray yelled for the butler to go get you."

"So he was still alive at that point?" Bosworth pressed. "And you're sure about what he said?"

"Honestly, Doctor, I don't think it's seemly for us to be standing by poor Stephen's bedside, having a discussion of his last moments," Rosalind snapped. "At least let's go into the drawing room."

"Of course I'm sure," Maria replied. "We all heard him quite clearly."

"His face contorted just before he went into the soup," the man standing next to Maria Farringdon volunteered. "Don't forget that."

"And he said there was something wrong with the light," another fellow, this one holding the arm of an attractive older woman, added. "I thought it a very odd remark."

"Doctor, can we please go into the drawing room?" Rosalind Murray pleaded. "This is very unseemly."

"Yes, of course," Bosworth agreed. "But do make sure that no one eats or drinks anything, and I do mean anything."

She stared at him in disbelief. "Doctor, have you gone mad? What on earth are you talking about?"

"I think you'd better call the police," Bosworth replied calmly. "As a matter of fact, I'm going to insist upon it."

"The police!" She gaped at him. "Why do we need the police? Didn't Stephen have a stroke or a heart attack?"

Bosworth could hear the others muttering and exclaiming in surprise, but he ignored them and instead looked back at the body on the bed. "There will have to be an autopsy. Mr. Whitfield may well have had a heart attack, but if he did, it wasn't brought on by anything natural."

"What does that mean?" Rosalind Murray cried. "I don't understand any of this."

"It means I think Mr. Whitfield was poisoned," Bosworth announced. "That's why I don't want anyone eating or drinking anything."

Betsy and Smythe stared at each other across the length of the kitchen. "Hello, Betsy," he said.

"Hello, Smythe," she replied. She wasn't sure what to do or even what she felt. She'd planned and thought about this moment for so long, but now that it was here, she was completely in the dark. She'd practiced dozens of mean, cutting things to say to him when he got back, thought often of how she was going to turn up her nose and pretend he meant nothing to her. But now that he was right here in front of her, she couldn't do it. Despite the fact that he'd left her at the altar (at least in her mind), she found she could do nothing but stand like a silly ninny and drink in the sight of him. "How was your trip?"

"It was fine," he muttered. He felt frozen to the spot.

"Take off your coat and sit down, Smythe," Mrs. Jeffries said briskly. "We're just about ready to eat, and I'm sure you're hungry." She could see that both of them had been struck dumb by the sight of each other. Good. It meant they still loved each other, and she was wise enough to know that where there was love, there was hope that things could be put right.

"Alright." Without taking his eyes off Betsy, Smythe slipped out of his heavy coat, slapped it onto the coat tree in the corner, and made his way to the table.

Mrs. Goodge had already gone to the cupboard for another place setting. She stopped at the cutlery drawer and took out a knife and fork. She put everything down at his usual place at the table next to Betsy and then went back to her own chair. "It's good to have you back, Smythe," she said. "We've missed you."

"I've missed all of you," he replied as he sat down next to his fiancée. "But most of all, I've missed you," he said softly to the woman sitting beside him.

Betsy found she couldn't say anything.

"I'm back to stay," he tried. He wished she'd say something. "And I'll never leave you again."

Still, she simply stared at him.

"Cor blimey, Betsy, aren't you goin' to speak to 'im?" Wiggins exclaimed.

"Wiggins, be quiet," the cook hissed. Though she rather agreed with the lad, this was getting embarrassing. Mind you, she did understand Betsy's point of view. Canceling all those wedding plans hadn't been very pleasant for the poor girl. Even though the household knew that Smythe was coming back, everyone else in the neighborhood had assumed that he'd jilted her and made a run for it. Being the object of pity hadn't been easy for Betsy.

"Say something, Betsy," Smythe pleaded. His worst fears were being realized. He'd been prepared for tears or accusations or even a good screaming match, but this dead silence was devastating. It meant she felt nothing. That she'd locked him out of her heart for good.

"What do you want me to say?" she replied calmly. "Welcome home. Mrs. Jeffries, can you please pass the pork chops?"

Smythe gaped at her for a moment. He glanced at the others, noting that their faces reflected the same shock that he felt sure was mirrored in his own expression. "Is that it, then? Pass the bloomin' pork chops?"

"We've got extra," Wiggins supplied helpfully. "The inspector went to Lady Cannonberry's for dinner, so you can 'ave his chops."

Smythe ignored him. "I've been gone for six months," he cried, "and that's all you've got to say to me? For God's sake, woman, I've spent months slogging about the outback, lookin' for a crazy old man." He couldn't believe she was reacting like this. He'd spent practically every waking moment over the past six months thinking about her, telling himself he'd do whatever it took to fix things between them. He knew he'd done the unforgivable, but it couldn't be helped. He'd owed a debt of honor, and now that he'd paid it, he wanted to get on with his life. But she was acting as if he'd only stepped out to have a drink.

Blast a Spaniard, he'd never understand women. He'd sent letter after letter and received nothing in return. But he'd not minded: he'd told himself that she was hurt and upset, and that he could make it right when he got home.

"That was your choice," Betsy said simply. "May I have the butter pot, please?" she said to Mrs. Goodge.

"Betsy," Mrs. Jeffries said softly. "Perhaps you and Smythe would like to go upstairs and have a discussion in private."

"There's nothing to discuss." Betsy grinned. Now that he was back, she intended to enjoy herself a bit. He owed her for the humiliation of being left at the altar (so to speak) and for the misery of the past six months. She fully intended to forgive him—after all, she loved him more than she loved her own life—but she damned well intended that he suffer a bit before they could patch up their differences.

Smythe's jaw was partially open in shock as he stared at his beloved. But he was saved by a loud knock on the front door from having to think of the right thing to say. He got to his feet. Old habits die hard, and he didn't want the women going to the door after dark.

But Wiggins rose first. "I'll get it. You two keep on talking."

"There's nothing to talk about." Betsy reached for a slice of bread and slathered it with butter. She smiled at Smythe. "You'd better hope that the inspector will give you your old position back—that is, if you're interested in working."

Smythe had been the inspector's coachman before he'd gone to Australia.

Mrs. Jeffries sighed inwardly. She wasn't sure whether she was relieved or annoyed. Smythe was home, and Betsy was obviously going to lead him on a merry chase. She hoped the girl didn't go too far. The coachman adored her, but he had his pride. But then again, Betsy had been the one who'd stayed here and faced all the questions about their "postponed" wedding, so Mrs. Jeffries could understand the lass wanting a bit of her own back.

"I think things are going to be very interesting," Mrs. Goodge muttered in a voice low enough that only the housekeeper could hear her. "But at least we don't have a murder to cope with, so the two of them should be able to work out their differences."

Mrs. Jeffries nodded. She could hear Wiggins speaking to someone upstairs. The voice was very faint, but she thought she recognized it. She heard the front door slam shut, and then Wiggins' footsteps pounding along the hallway and down the back stairs.

"That was Constable Barnes at the door," Wiggins cried as he flew into the kitchen. "I sent him over to Lady Cannonberry's to fetch the inspector."

Everyone went still. There was only one reason that Witherspoon would be called out at this time of the evening.

"We've got us a murder," Wiggins continued. "Leastways, that's what the constable said. Should Smythe and I have a go at followin' them?"

The housekeeper nodded. In the past she'd learned it was wise to send the men along to get a firsthand report, whatever the situation might be.

Smythe, with one final glare at his beloved, was already on his feet. He reached across the table and grabbed a pork chop and a slice of bread. "I'm hungry, so I'll take this to eat on the way."

"We can catch 'em on Holland Park Road," Wiggins said as he hurried toward the coat tree for his cap and jacket.

"Be careful," Mrs. Jeffries warned. "Don't let anyone see you."

"And mind you take your scarf and gloves," Mrs. Goodge said to the footman. "It's cold out there, and I'll not have you catching a chill."

"It's not fair!" Betsy exclaimed. "I've been sitting here twiddlin' my ruddy thumbs for six months, and the minute *he* walks in the back door, we get us a murder."

Wisely, Smythe refrained from saying the words that popped into his head.

Bosworth had a very difficult time convincing the constable to call in his superiors. It was only because he was a police surgeon, albeit in a different district, that the man was persuaded to nip back to the station and call for a detective.

"Dr. Bosworth, have we met before?" Gerald Witherspoon asked politely.

"Yes, actually, we have. On one of your previous cases, I did the postmortem." Bosworth could hardly admit that he'd been to the inspector's house a dozen different times and that he was well acquainted with the inspector's entire household. They frequently asked his advice about the murders Witherspoon investigated.

"Ah, yes, I thought you looked familiar." The inspector nodded. "This is Constable Barnes."

Barnes reached over to shake hands. He was an older man with a craggy face and a headful of iron gray hair. As he was well aware of Bosworth's connection to the household of Upper Edmonton Gardens, his eyes were twinkling with amusement. "It's nice to see you again, Doctor."

"It's nice to see you, too, Constable." Bosworth shook his hand. "I do hope I've not called you both out on a wild-goose chase."

"What happened here, Doctor?" Witherspoon asked.

They were standing in the foyer. Bosworth pointed down the hall. "The owner of this house, Mr. Stephen Whitfield, was suddenly taken ill this evening while dining with friends. I live just across the road; I've just taken rooms with Mrs. Winston. But that's neither here nor there. They sent for me when he took ill, but by the time I arrived, he was dead. I think he's been poisoned."

"Poisoned?" Witherspoon repeated.

"That's correct," Bosworth replied. "The other dinner guests are in there." He nodded toward the closed door of the drawing room. "The servants have all gone back downstairs. The victim's sister-in-law lives here as well. She's very upset, which is quite understandable. But she's raising a bit of a fuss. When the local constable said this was your district, I insisted they send for you."

"I see," the inspector said slowly.

"And knowing your methods as I do, I guessed you'd want to see the body before it was moved any farther." Bosworth turned and started down the hallway. "It's just down here, Inspector."

Witherspoon and Barnes followed after him. They climbed a short flight of stairs to the first floor. A uniformed constable stood by the door. "Good evening." He nodded respectfully. "I've not let anyone in, sir."

"Very good, Constable," Witherspoon said as they stepped into the dead man's room.

Bosworth went to the bedside. "As you can see, the body shows no signs of foul play." He pointed at the corpse. The late Stephen Whitfield stared straight up at the corniced ceiling.

"What led you to believe he'd been murdered?" the inspector asked. He took a deep breath and stepped closer to the bed. He was quite squeamish about corpses, but with no sign of foul play, at least this one wasn't likely to be covered in blood or have other bits of tissue popping out from every orifice. He forced himself to look at the body and then almost sighed aloud with relief.

Except for the open eyes, the fellow might as well have been having a nap.

"I'm not sure," Bosworth mused. "I sensed something was wrong even before I asked the dinner guests what had happened, but of course you're not interested in my private intuition. It was when they told me what he'd said before he collapsed that I began to suspect poison."

"What did he say?" Barnes asked. Actually, he was quite interested in Bosworth's private intuition. Policemen liked facts, but as every good copper knew, you didn't ignore feelings or instincts. Especially not from someone as experienced as Bosworth.

"He said that everyone was turning blue and that there was something wrong with the light. He said it quite clearly before he collapsed."

"And that led you to the conclusion that he'd been poisoned?" Witherspoon pressed. Drat, he had a feeling this was going to be a nasty one. Why couldn't the fellow have just keeled over with a heart attack?

"Yes, I think he ingested a massive dose of foxglove. Seeing blue is one of the symptoms. But we'll know more when the postmortem is done."

"Are you an expert on this?" Barnes asked. "I mean, surely, isn't seeing odd things symptomatic with the man's just having a heart attack? When my uncle died, he claimed he saw fairies dancing on the fireplace mantel. No offense meant, sir, but we do need reasonable grounds to do a postmortem on a body."

"And this is obviously a man of some means and importance," the inspector added. Like Barnes, he didn't want to start a murder investigation unless they had genuine reasons to think the death was a homicide and not an act of God.

Bosworth smiled grimly. "Actually, I am a bit of an authority, though I'm more familiar with death by firearms. I spent several years practicing in the United States, in California. When I was working in San Francisco, we had a case of a landlady who murdered her tenants. They were mostly seamen or miners. She robbed them, you see. None of them was rich, but they usually came into the city just after they'd been paid. This woman had a beautiful garden with the most amazing flowers you've ever seen. She had some spectacularly lovely foxglove flowers. Usually her victims were dead by the time they reached us, but once, I managed to get there before the poor miner actually expired. He kept screaming that everyone had turned blue and that the light had gone strange. When we did the autopsy, we found enough digitalis in his system to kill an elephant. Digitalis comes from foxglove."

"Did you exhume the other bodies?" Barnes asked curiously.

"Only one, and it was full of foxglove as well. The leaves last quite a long time in the stomach."

"And Mr. Whitfield appeared to have the very same symptoms." Witherspoon nodded.

"That's correct," Bosworth replied. "I have a feeling we're going to find lots of foxglove when we open up Mr. Stephen Whitfield."

CHAPTER 2

Inspector Witherspoon and Constable Barnes had taken a hansom to Redcliffe Road in West Brompton. Smythe and Wiggins had rounded the corner just as the two policemen disappeared through the front door of the five-story white stone house. They'd looked about for a suitable place to keep watch, and Smythe had spotted a servants' entrance in a darkened house across the road. So far, their luck had held, and none of the constables going in and out of the murder house had caught so much as a glimpse of them.

"Cor blimey, my feet 'ave gone numb," Wiggins muttered softly. When they stuck their heads up from the stairwell, they had a good view of everything, but most of the time they had to stay hunkered down out of sight. The stone steps were cold, and as the night wore on, it was getting colder and colder.

"Wiggle yer toes," Smythe advised. He glanced at the footman. They were lying on the staircase, keeping their heads just below ground level to avoid being seen. They'd been there well over an hour now, and it was blooming miserable. Both of them kept shifting positions in a vain effort to get comfortable or stay warm.

Smythe moved his big frame into a sitting position on the second stair from the bottom, low enough so that he'd not be seen. Wiggins eased down onto the step above him, cupped his gloved hands around his face, and blew gently. "Cor blimey, I don't know 'ow much longer I can sit 'ere. The chill is seepin' right through my trousers."

"If something doesn't happen soon, we'll go back to Upper Edmonton Gardens," Smythe said. He wondered whether he dared bring up Betsy. He was desperate to know whether she'd said anything about him, about whether she wanted him to come back or whether she still cared about him.

Wiggins stopped his blowing and said, "She still loves you. She's got skinny as a lamppost waitin' for you to come back."

"She never answered my letters," Smythe muttered. Blast a Spaniard, had the lad turned into a mind reader? He wanted to talk about Betsy, but now that her name had come up, he was embarrassed.

"She was angry, Smythe," Wiggins said softly. "And 'urt. When the weddin' was called off . . ."

"It wasn't called off. It was postponed," Smythe hissed.

"Alright, postponed," Wiggins agreed, "but you were the one that left. Betsy 'ad to stay 'ere and answer all the questions. It were 'ard for her. All them pryin' comments and pityin' looks she got. She almost run off, you know, but Mrs. Jeffries stopped her from goin'. Neither of 'em know that I know about it, so don't say anything."

"What happened?" Smythe asked softly. He wasn't sure he really wanted to know. The very idea of Upper Edmonton Gardens without Betsy was too awful to bear.

Wiggins stretched and took a quick look at the house across the road before he spoke. "It were right after you left. We'd been called in to supper, but I'd 'ad to run back upstairs for something. On the way back down, I happened to glance out the window on the top landing, and I saw Betsy standing there in the garden, starin' at the 'ouse. She 'ad on her hat and gloves, and her carpetbag was lying at her feet. I felt awful when I saw her just standing there lookin' so miserable. She's like a sister to me, you know, and I wasn't sure what to do. Just then, Mrs. Jeffries stepped out from behind the bushes and they started talking. They didn't speak for very long. Then Mrs. Jeffries went back to the house. I remember holding my breath, waitin' to see what Betsy was goin' to do. But then she picked up her carpetbag and came on inside. I was so relieved. I hated the thought of her goin', of her leavin' and all of us breakin' apart."

Smythe sighed heavily. He knew exactly what the lad meant. Everyone in Witherspoon's household had ended up there for a variety of reasons, but over the years, the bonds they'd formed had become real and important. They'd become family.

Suddenly they heard the door of the house across the road open. Wiggins stuck his head up. "Someone's comin' out." Moving cautiously, lest they make noise and give themselves away, they flattened themselves back onto the staircase and, lying close together, peeked over the top just in time to see two people, a man and a woman, step outside.

The couple wore formal evening clothes and the man held the woman's arm as they descended the stairs and came out onto the pavement. They paused for a moment, speaking quietly together, before moving off toward Fulham Road.

"I'm goin' to follow 'em and see if I can 'ear what they're sayin,'" Wiggins muttered. But just as he started to get up, the door opened again and another couple came outside. He froze.

Neither he nor Smythe so much as moved a muscle until the footsteps of the second couple had faded as they walked away. "Maybe I should go to the local pub and see who lives in that house," Smythe whispered. "You'll not get the chance to follow anyone, not if people keep comin' out that front door."

Moving cautiously, Wiggins stretched up for another quick look. The first couple had reached the corner, and the man was waving his top hat, probably trying to get a hansom. The second couple had gone the opposite way. The door of the house stayed shut. "Maybe I can follow them." He pointed at the second couple, who were just disappearing around the corner.

"Nah, they've got too much of a head start," Smythe replied. "There's a hansom stand up that way—by the time you reach the corner, they'll be gone. Did you see that pub on the Fulham Road?"

"The one next to the bank?" Wiggins asked.

"That's it." Smythe nodded. "When the inspector and Constable Barnes come out, you come meet me at that pub. We're not 'aving much luck just hidin' here in the dark. At least at the pub we might be able to learn who lives there." Smythe stared across the road. "It's not very well lighted, is it? You'd think a posh neighborhood like this would have better street lighting, and you'd think the house would have decent-sized door lamps. Er, uh, what's the number? I can't read it from this distance."

"It's number nineteen," Wiggins replied, "and we're on Redcliffe Road."

"I know that," Smythe said irritably. "I just couldn't see the number, that's all."

Wiggins could see the number quite clearly. But he held his tongue. Failing eyesight happened to people as they got older, and he didn't think Smythe would take kindly to any reminders that he wasn't as young as he used to be.

"I'm not sure it was a wise idea to let everyone leave," Witherspoon murmured. "But we'd no grounds to force them to remain here. We're not absolutely sure it was even murder."

"We've got their names and addresses, sir," Barnes said patiently. "And they did make statements."

A constable stuck his head into the drawing room. "The wagon is here, sir, and the lads are ready to take him away as soon as you give the command. Are we waiting for the police surgeon?"

"You can take him away," Witherspoon replied. "Dr. Bosworth has volunteered to write the report and do the postmortem. Send word to the station that I've seconded him to our district for this case."

The constable nodded respectfully and left, closing the drawing room door behind him. Witherspoon hoped no one would raise a fuss about his actions. But Dr. Bosworth was a police surgeon, and it seemed foolish to call in someone else just because Bosworth was assigned to another district. "Do you think Dr. Jolyon will object?" he asked Barnes. Dr. Hiram Jolyon was the surgeon assigned to this district.

Barnes shook his head. "Jolyon's a sensible sort. He'll understand that, given the circumstances, it was logical to keep Dr. Bosworth on the case. Besides, I expect he'll appreciate not having to come out on a cold winter night."

The drawing room door was suddenly flung open so hard that it slammed against the doorstop with enough force to rattle the windows. Rosalind Murray flew into the room and charged straight for the two policemen. "This is outrageous!" she cried. "What do you think you're doing?"

"I'm sorry, ma'am," Witherspoon replied. "But we're only doing what is necessary."

"There are police constables in our kitchen." She stopped in front of Witherspoon. Her cheeks were red and her expression furious. "They are taking away food, grabbing every wine bottle in sight, and upsetting the servants. Cook is in tears, and the scullery maids are hiding in the dry larder. What is the meaning of this?"

"I know this is most distressing," Witherspoon said politely. "But we must take as evidence all the food and drink that was served tonight."

"For goodness' sakes, the only one who died was Stephen," Rosalind snapped. "So I hardly think he's been poisoned."

"Nevertheless, we can't risk losing any evidence," the inspector insisted. But what she said was true. No one else had died or even become ill. "Er, was there any one food or beverage that only Mr. Whitfield consumed?"

Rosalind exhaled, unclenched the hand that had been balled into a fist, and closed her eyes for a brief moment as she got herself under control. "He was the only one who drank the Bordeaux that Mrs. Farringdon brought. The bottle is in the dining room." She turned and hurried to the door.

The two policemen were right behind her.

A constable standing at the dining table and pouring the fish soup into a jar stopped and looked up as they burst into the room.

"Carry on with what you were doing, Constable," the inspector said kindly.

"Yes, sir." He went back to pouring the soup.

"Here it is." Rosalind picked up the Bordeaux from the silver tray on the sideboard and handed it to Witherspoon. "Mr. and Mrs. Farringdon brought this to Stephen as a Christmas gift. He insisted it be opened, but he was the only one who drank it. The rest of us had sherry for an aperitif and white wine with our dinner."

Witherspoon noted that the bottle was three-quarters empty. "The Farringdons gave this to Mr. Whitfield tonight?"

Rosalind's eyes widened as she realized the implication behind the question. "I've just said so, Inspector. But if you are implying that either of them had anything to do with Stephen's death, you're mistaken. Basil Farringdon and Stephen were at school together. They've known one another all their lives."

"Our questions aren't meant to implicate anyone," Witherspoon replied. "We're simply trying to ascertain the facts." He was dreadfully tired and quite hungry. He and Ruth had only just started their meal when Barnes had come to fetch him. "Did any of the other guests bring Mr. Whitfield a present?"

"No. The Farringdons brought one only because Stephen took them a bottle of his special ruby port a few days ago. He imports a cask directly from the vineyard and corks it up himself."

"Had he given a bottle of port to any of the other guests?" Barnes asked.

She thought for a moment. "I think he might have given one to Henry Becker. It's a custom he started a few years ago, but he only did it for his old school friends."

"I see," Witherspoon murmured. He'd no idea whether this was useful information.

They could hear bumps and squeaks outside the door as a gurney was wheeled down the hallway.

The color drained out of Rosalind's face. "Oh, dear God, this is dreadful. What are they going to do with Stephen?"

"They're going to take him to a hospital and do a postmortem," Witherspoon said gently. "I'm so sorry. Please don't let it distress you, ma'am. But we must find out if Mr. Whitfield was poisoned and, if he was, if that poison was administered accidentally or on purpose."

"Did Mr. Whitfield have any enemies?" Barnes asked. He thought he might as well start asking the obvious questions. Despite Witherspoon's misgivings, Barnes knew enough about Dr. Bosworth to trust both the man's medical expertise and the fellow's instincts.

"He had no more enemies than anyone else." She winced as the gurney's wheels scraped hard against the stairs.

"What was his occupation?" Witherspoon asked, hoping to distract her from the thuds overhead as the gurney continued its journey to the dead man's bedroom.

"He was an English gentleman," she replied. "In other words, Inspector, he lived off his income and did very little . . ." She broke off and glanced up at the ceiling as the wheels squeaked to a halt in the room upstairs.

"He had no occupation, correct?" Witherspoon clarified. Drat, that meant he wouldn't have business enemies.

"In his youth, he spent a few years running the family estate, but the estate was sold when he married my sister." She turned her attention back to Witherspoon.

"I see." The inspector desperately tried to think of more questions, but his mind had gone completely blank.

They heard a series of knocks and then a low thud from overhead. A moment later, the wheels began squeaking again as the gurney began the trip down.

Rosalind shuddered. "Inspector, is this going to take much longer?"

"No, ma'am, they are almost finished."

They were bringing the body down the stairs. He could hear bumping and scraping against the banister. "I'm sure this evening has been horrible for you," he said to her. "I'm terribly sorry for your loss."

"Stephen wasn't a blood relative, but he was my brother-in-law and I have lived in his household for almost ten years. I've known him since we were children." She looked past Witherspoon, in the direction of the front door.

They could hear the lads moving about in the foyer, opening the front door, and then the ever-present squeak of wheels. Witherspoon made a mental note to have a word with the duty sergeant and ask who was in charge of maintaining the equipment. They really must get that contraption oiled.

Rosalind closed her eyes briefly. "Is there anything else?"

Witherspoon shook his head. "Dr. Bosworth is doing the postmortem tonight, so we'll be in touch tomorrow. If you'd like, I can ask the local constables to keep a special watch over the house."

"That won't be necessary, Inspector." She opened the door and stepped into the hallway. "I'm sure Stephen's death will turn out to be a heart attack or some sort of accident. Now, if you don't mind, I'm going to go upstairs and lie down. This has been an exhausting ordeal."

"Good night, Mrs. Murray. We'll try to be as unobtrusive as possible when we leave."

"Good night, Inspector." Rosalind Murray turned and went toward the stairway.

Witherspoon was reasonably sure that if the victim had been poisoned, it was probably through the wine. But they couldn't be certain, so it took another hour to finish up in the kitchen. An enormous amount of food had been prepared for the dinner party, and finding suitable containers to carry it all off was impossible, so they had to send back to the station for an evidence box. As they left the house, Witherspoon instructed the local constable on patrol to keep an eye on the house.

"What do you think, sir?" Barnes asked as they turned in the direction of the Fulham Road.

"I've no idea what to think," Witherspoon admitted. "Let's hope this Dr. Bosworth knows his business."

"Oh, I think we're safe in that regard, sir," Barnes said softly. He was well aware of Bosworth's help on previous cases, just as he was aware that Witherspoon's entire household had been assisting him from the very beginning. None of them had told him of their involvement; he'd figured it out on his own. "There's a hansom, sir. I'll just go wave it over."

"What are we going to tell the inspector about Smythe?" Mrs. Goodge whispered as soon as Betsy had gone upstairs to make sure the heat was on in Smythe's room.

"We'll tell him the truth—that Smythe finished his business in Australia and came home because he wanted to get here before Christmas," Mrs. Jeffries replied.

When the coachman had left, they'd told Witherspoon that he'd been called away on urgent business. Witherspoon, being the decent man he was, had agreed that the coachman should have his position back when he returned to England. Not that Smythe needed the position—he didn't. He was as rich as sin, but that, like so many other things in Mrs. Jeffries' life, was a secret. Only she—and Betsy, of course—knew about his wealth. It was Smythe's secret to keep, and he'd let the others know in his own good time.

"That's a good idea. It's always best to stay close to the truth if at all possible." Mrs. Goodge sank down onto her chair. "And Betsy's being a right little madam about him coming back. Mind you, I'm not sure I blame her. Canceling all those wedding plans was so humiliating for the lass. But I've never seen her act so cold."

"But she still loves him." Mrs. Jeffries grinned. "That's obvious."

"How is it obvious?" Mrs. Goodge reached down to lift Samson, her huge orange tabby cat, onto her lap. Samson, as was his nature, glared at Mrs. Jeffries and then curled up in a ball on the cook's lap. Wiggins had rescued both Fred and Samson at different times. Fred was exceedingly grateful to have a good home. Samson wasn't. The only person he liked was the cook.

Mrs. Jeffries laughed. "If she didn't love him, she'd have treated him like her long-lost brother. Instead she's as cool as an autumn evening and treating him as casually as if he'd just been gone for an hour or two. That can only mean one thing; she's going to forgive him, but she's going to make him dance a bit before she'll give him as much as a smile."

Mrs. Goodge didn't look convinced. "Are you sure about this? I'm the first to admit, I don't know much about affairs of the heart. We both know that cooks take the 'Mrs.' as a courtesy title whether we've been married or not. I, for one, never had a husband and never wanted one, either. But you have. Did you ever do such a thing to your man?"

"Well, certainly not very often," Mrs. Jeffries admitted. "But even I, on occasion, had my little ways to get my own back. That's all Betsy's doing—getting a bit of her own back."

"But it wasn't Smythe's fault that he had to go," the cook protested. She petted Samson's broad back, and he started to purr.

"No, and Betsy knows that," the housekeeper replied. "But he could have taken her with him, and he didn't."

"He was goin' to the bush."

"Betsy told me she wouldn't have cared. What hurt her the most was that he didn't even ask her to go. He simply said he had a debt of honor, and out the door he went. She was the one who had to face all the neighbors and all our friends. She was the one who had to tell them the wedding had been 'postponed,' and then watch how everyone tried to pretend that was just fine when it was obvious they all believed she'd been jilted."

"But, still, she's been miserable without him," Mrs. Goodge pointed out.

"And he without her, I'm sure. But this is something they must work out for themselves." She got up and began to pace the room. Fred, who was keeping a wary eye on the cat, jumped up from his spot in front of the warm stove and began to pace alongside her.

Betsy, a sack of flour nestled in the crook of one arm and a bowl of brown eggs in the other, came back into the kitchen. "The sugar cone has gone hard as a rock," she said as she made her way to the worktable near the sink. "But it should be fine if you let Wiggins have a go at it with the hammer." She placed the eggs next to the slab of white marble that Mrs. Goodge used for baking, and put the flour down beside the bowl.

"Thank you, Betsy," the cook said softly. Without even being asked, Betsy had brought Mrs. Goodge's ingredients from the dry larder to the kitchen. The maid had done it because she knew it was hard for the cook to move about so easily when her rheumatism was acting up. Betsy understood that, now that they had a murder, Mrs. Goodge had to get her baking done early so she could feed her sources. The lass was too caring and kind, Mrs. Goodge thought sourly. It made it impossible to stay irritated at her!

"Should I make more tea?" Betsy asked. "We'll want to stay up so we can hear all the details."

"That's a very good idea," Mrs. Jeffries murmured. "It's almost midnight and no one is back yet. We may need to split up. I'll take the inspector, and you two see what the lads have found out."

Betsy nodded. "I'll use the big pot. As cold as it is, everyone's going to want something to warm themselves up."

Everyone returned within minutes of one another. Smythe and Wiggins were coming through the back door just as Mrs. Jeffries heard the inspector come in the front. She grabbed a tray they had at the ready and headed up the stairs.

"Mrs. Jeffries, you shouldn't have waited up," Witherspoon said as he hung up his bowler hat. "It's dreadfully late, and you must be exhausted."

"Not as exhausted as you must be, sir," she replied. "It's so cold out tonight. I wanted to make sure you had something hot to warm you up. I thought perhaps you might be hungry, so Mrs. Goodge made some roast beef sandwiches as well. Shall we go into the drawing room?" She didn't want him running up to bed before she had a chance to find out what he'd learned.

"Bless you both for being so thoughtful. I'm famished." He slipped out of his overcoat and hung it on the peg under his hat. Witherspoon hadn't been raised with wealth, so consequently he treated his servants like human beings and was exceedingly grateful when they did anything over and above their normal duties.

As they went down the hall to the drawing room, Mrs. Jeffries said, "I've some other news as well, sir. Smythe has returned." She put the tray down on a table by the door and poured his tea.

"Smythe is back—that's excellent news." He sank into his favorite chair. "It's been difficult for Betsy since he's been gone. What a wonderful Christmas present that must be for her. I'm sure she's delighted he's finally home."

"He took care of his business, sir." Mrs. Jeffries put the inspector's tea on the table next to him, picked up her own cup, and sat down on the settee.

"He's a good man." Witherspoon blew surreptitiously on the hot drink. "Imagine going all the way to Australia to help out an old friend who was in trouble. Well, I'm glad he's back, to be sure. Let him know that as of tomorrow, he's a member of the household again, and he's to have his full wages for this month."

"I'm sure he'll be very pleased to hear that," she replied. As she knew, Smythe donated half his salary to the poor box at St. John's Church and the other half to an orphans' home in the East End. She was certain they'd be happy he was back as well. "I do hope that Lady Cannonberry wasn't too upset by your dinner being interrupted."

He put down his tea and helped himself to a sandwich. "Considering we'd only just sat down to eat when Constable Barnes arrived, she was exceedingly gracious about the matter." He took a quick bite of his food.

"I suppose it must have been sheer luck that the constable was at the station when the call came in," she commented. "Usually he's home in the evenings."

"It was. He'd stayed late at the station to have a Christmas drink with one of his friends. His wife is out of town for a few days." Witherspoon swallowed his food. "The doctor called to the scene when the victim took ill was familiar with my previous cases. He specifically sent the first constable who arrived back to the station to fetch me. Barnes and Constable Kerry were just going out for their drink when the lad reported back, so his evening was interrupted, too—not that Constable Barnes would ever complain, of course. This roast beef is wonderful."

"Who was the doctor?" Mrs. Jeffries asked cautiously. She didn't want to get her hopes up just yet.

"A Dr. Bosworth. He's one of our police surgeons, but he's not assigned to my district. He just happened to have rented rooms across from the victim's house, so he was sent for when the poor man fell ill." Witherspoon took another bite of his sandwich.

Mrs. Jeffries' spirits soared. For once, they'd have almost direct access to evidence from the postmortem. She couldn't believe their luck. "Your methods have become very well-known, sir. I'm sure Dr. Bosworth has heard a great deal about you."

"He's worked on one of my cases," Witherspoon said. "But I can't recall which one it was."

He'd actually worked on virtually all of the inspector's cases, but only one of them in an official capacity. "If this isn't his district, is he the one doing the postmortem?" She held her breath.

"Indeed he is. He's doing it tonight." Witherspoon took another sip of tea.

"And he was the one that thought there might be foul play involved?"

"He's fairly sure the fellow was poisoned."

Mrs. Jeffries raised her eyebrows. "He was able to make a diagnosis so quickly?"

"It was something the victim said before he died that led the doctor to think so." He told her the circumstances leading to Bosworth's suspicions. "So you see, even if it turns out the man was poisoned, we've still no evidence it was murder. It could be accidental."

"Even if it was foxglove that killed him?" she queried gently. She didn't want the inspector clinging to false hope. She trusted Bosworth's instincts. The good doctor had seen too many corpses not to have developed a heightened ability to know when something was wrong. This was a murder, not an accident.

Witherspoon sighed deeply. "I know I'm probably deluding myself, but it is Christmas, and you know what happens at this time of year, especially if the victim is a member of the upper class."

"And I take it that the deceased is one of them?" She smiled sympathetically. She knew exactly what was bothering her inspector.

"Oh, yes—at least, he appears to be a wealthy man. The house is huge, and he has no occupation. According to his sister-in-law, he's an English gentleman, and you know what that means."

"They'll put pressure on you to solve this case as soon as possible. They'll want an arrest by Christmas," she murmured.

He nodded in agreement. "There's no real reason why this season should be any different from any other time of the year, but somehow it always is. Perhaps we'll get lucky, and by tomorrow morning we'll find out that the doctor was mistaken and poor Mr. Whitfield died of a perfectly natural heart attack or stroke."

"Perhaps you will, sir," she said politely, though she didn't for a moment believe it to be true.

Witherspoon helped himself to the last sandwich. "Gracious, I was hungry. I do hope poor Constable Barnes had something at home he could eat. It appears there are quite a number of people who didn't finish their meals tonight." He told her about the inter-rupted dinner party at the Whitfield house.

She questioned him cautiously. By the time she poured the last of the tea, she'd found out the names of the other guests and the information they'd given in their statements. "So it was Mr. and Mrs. Farringdon who'd brought the Bordeaux Whitfield drank?"

"That's correct." Witherspoon covered his mouth as he yawned. "And the Bordeaux was the only thing that he alone consumed. So I had that taken into evidence along with everything else that had been served. I do hope that, if it is poison that killed Whitfield, it was in the Bordeaux. Otherwise, by tomorrow morning, we may have another half-dozen corpses."

Downstairs, Smythe and Wiggins were doing some reporting of their own.

"There were half a dozen people that come out of the 'ouse," Wiggins said around a mouthful of food. "But I daren't follow any of 'em, 'cause that ruddy front door kept opening and I'd no idea 'ow many more of them was coming down those steps. So I just stayed hid until I saw the inspector and Constable Barnes leave. Then I went and met up with Smythe."

"At the pub?" Betsy asked archly. "How very convenient."

"It's not like there's much else open at that time of night," Smythe replied harshly. "And I was only there for a few minutes before they called last orders."

"So you found out nothing?" she asked.

Mrs. Goodge sighed inwardly and hoped this wasn't a sign of things to come. "Smythe, why don't you tell us in your own words what's what?" she asked.

"Thank you, Mrs. Goodge. As it happens, I did find out a bit. The man who died was Stephen Whitfield. The news had already made it to the pub, but no one had any details. I did find out that Whitfield was a widower in his late sixties, rich as sin and courtin' a woman a good twenty years younger."

"I wonder if she was one of the people who come out of the house. They must 'ave been 'aving a dinner party, because they were all in evenin' clothes." Wiggins frowned thoughtfully. "None of them women come out alone, and there was only one of 'em that looked to be youngish. But she was with another bloke."

"I'm sure we'll get the names of the guests from the inspector," the cook said. She'd noticed that Betsy had gone completely silent. That wasn't good, either. "Mrs. Jeffries is upstairs with him now."

Just then they heard her footsteps coming down the back stairs, and a moment later she hurried into the kitchen, carrying a tray of dirty dishes. "Good, you're all still up."

"We want to find out what happened," Betsy said. "Was it a murder?"

"Dr. Bosworth certainly seems to think so." Mrs. Jeffries put the tray down on the counter.

"Our Dr. Bosworth?" Mrs. Goodge asked. "Did it happen in his district?"

Everyone in the household knew that Bosworth had been appointed a police surgeon. It had helped their investigations enormously.

"It wasn't in his district—it was in the inspector's. But Dr. Bosworth had taken rooms just across the street from the victim's house. He was sent for when the man collapsed." She took her usual spot at the head of the table and told them what she'd learned from the inspector.

Tired as they all were, they listened carefully, occasionally asking a question or making a comment. When the housekeeper finished, she leaned back in her chair. "We've the names of the other guests at the dinner party, and we know the man died under suspicious circumstances, but before we go on the hunt, perhaps we'd better wait until we hear whether Dr. Bosworth finds any poison in the man's stomach."

"But we might not find that out until late tomorrow," Betsy protested. "I think we ought to take Dr. Bosworth at his word and start right away."

"What if it's not murder?" Wiggins asked reasonably. "We'd 'ave wasted a lot of time and energy findin' out about people who've done no wrong. That doesn't seem right."

"And just because these people were at the dinner party, that doesn't mean anything, especially if he was poisoned," Mrs. Goodge pointed out. "A poisoner doesn't have to see his victim die. It's not like doin' the deed with a knife or gun. If Stephen Whitfield was poisoned, the killer might have put it in something he ate or drank days before he actually died. Poisons don't always act right away."

"That's true," Betsy agreed. But she wanted to be out of the house. She wanted to be walking the streets and chatting with merchants and grocery clerks so that she wouldn't have to deal with her current problem. "But I don't think it would hurt anything to find out a few bits and pieces about the people who were there last night. Maybe the killer wanted to watch him die and was sitting right there at the dinner table."

"You think one of the Farringdons murdered him?" Mrs. Jeffries asked curiously. It wasn't like Betsy to leap to any sort of conclusions at this stage of the investigation.

"I've no idea. But Whitfield was the only one drinking the Bordeaux wine, and he's the only one who is dead."

"So far," Mrs. Jeffries murmured. "As Mrs. Goodge has pointed out, some poisons don't act right away. The poison might have been in something else, and he simply got a larger, stronger dose than the others."

"I don't think so," Wiggins said. "No one else that come out of the house looked the least bit ill. Betsy's on to something 'ere. The wine was opened as soon as the Farringdons arrived, but Whitfield were the only one drinkin' it. Then it set open for a good while as the guests milled about the place."

"Which means that anyone might have dropped something into it, especially if it looked like Whitfield was the only one drinking it," Smythe said. "Which would mean the killer was definitely wantin' him dead."

"That's right." Betsy grinned triumphantly, then caught herself and composed her features. She didn't want him getting any special smiles. Not yet, at any rate. "So I think we ought to get right on the case. As Mrs. Jeffries said, our inspector is going to have all sorts of pressure on him to get this murder solved before Christmas."

"What about Luty and Hatchet?" Wiggins asked. "Are we goin' to bring them into it before we know for certain?"

Luty Belle Crookshank and her butler, Hatchet, were friends of the household. Luty was a wealthy, eccentric American who'd been a witness in one of their earliest cases. She'd then come to them with a problem of her own to be solved, and ever since, she and her butler had insisted on helping. Unfortunately, due to Luty's illness and her need to travel to America to confer with her American bankers and lawyers, they'd missed several of the inspector's cases, so now they were adamant about being included right from the beginning.

"I think that would be best," Mrs. Jeffries replied. "Right, then. I take it we're all agreed that we ought to proceed with the investigation."

Everyone nodded their assent.

Betsy got up and headed for the stairs. She didn't want to be alone with Smythe. "I best get upstairs. I want to get my chores done bright and early so I can get out and about."

"I'll do a batch of bakin' to feed my sources." The cook got to her feet. "The worst that can happen is, we'll have extra if it turns out not to be a murder, but this time of year, a bit of extra sweets could come in handy."

"Smythe, can you and Wiggins lock up, please?" Mrs. Jeffries said as she followed the maid out to the hall. She understood that Betsy wasn't ready to be alone with her fiancé as yet, and wanted to make it easy on the lass. "Oh, and Wiggins, can you nip over to Luty's as soon as you get up? We'll want them here for our morning meeting."

"I do hope this doesn't turn out to be a waste of your time," Mrs. Jeffries said as she took her place at the table the next morning.

"When will we know for certain whether or not it's murder?" Luty Belle Crookshank asked eagerly. The elderly, gray-haired American wore a maroon day dress with white lace around the collar and cuffs. On her lap was a gray fur muff, and there was a better-than-even chance that inside that muff was a gun: a Colt .45 that Luty called a Peacemaker.

"Wiggins is going to run down to the station to take the inspector's watch to him." Mrs. Jeffries held up the gold pocket watch. She'd lifted it out of Witherspoon's coat earlier that morning. "Dr. Bosworth was doing the postmortem last night, so he ought to have had a report written and sent over to the station by midmorning."

"So when young Wiggins brings the inspector his forgotten pocket watch, he ought to be able to ascertain whether or not the victim was poisoned," Hatchet said. He was a tall, robust man with a headful of white hair, a smooth complexion, and a devotion to Luty Belle that went beyond just serving as a butler. He was also articulate, well educated, and very clever, with his own network of resources gleaned from a past that he didn't care to talk about.

"But the postmortem will only tell us if it's poison, not whether it's murder," Smythe said. He was in a sour mood. He'd tried his best to get Betsy alone so they could talk about their situation, but he'd been stymied at every turn. Last night she'd gone upstairs with Mrs. Jeffries, and this morning he'd waited for ages on the landing for her to come out of her room, only to discover that she was down in the kitchen and had been for hours. He knew she was deliberately keeping him at bay, and it was beginning to make him angry.

"Of course it'll be murder," Mrs. Goodge said. "The man didn't deliberately dose himself with foxglove."

"It could have been that the foxglove was meant for someone else," Betsy pointed out.

"I, for one, am going to proceed as though it's murder and that Stephen Whitfield was the intended victim," the cook said stoutly. "I've got some nice buns rising in the dry larder, a seed cake in the oven, and a set of jam tarts ready to go in as soon as the cake is done."

"Do you have anyone coming through today?" Mrs. Jeffries asked.

"The laundry lad will be here, and there's a butcher's order due to arrive," the cook replied. "But I've sent notes to several of my friends, and I'm sure one of them will be here for early-afternoon tea, so we mustn't have our afternoon meeting until at least half past four. I've got the names of everyone who was at the dinner party, so someone coming through this kitchen ought to know something useful about one of them." Mrs. Goodge understood the value of gossip.

"And I'm off to talk to the local shopkeepers," Betsy announced as she got up. "By now, the fact that Whitfield died should be common knowledge."

"Stephen Whitfield." Luty repeated the name, her expression thoughtful. "I know I've heard that name before."

"He's probably an acquaintance of one of your friends," Hatchet said. "Actually, if no one objects, I think I'll see what I can learn about the Farringdons. They were the ones who brought the Bordeaux."

"And you've heard their names before, haven't you?" Luty charged. She and Hatchet were very competitive when they were on a case. Each of them reveled in finding out more information than the other.

"I may have heard them mentioned in casual conversations," Hatchet admitted. He knew the Farringdons' butler, but he'd die before he'd own up to it in front of Luty.

Luty snorted. "You've got something up your sleeve, but then again"—she grinned—"so do I."

"Excellent. It seems we've all something to do to keep busy until this afternoon." Mrs. Jeffries looked at Smythe. "Would you like to take today to rest? You've had a hard, long journey."

He shook his head and got up. "I'm fine, Mrs. Jeffries. I've got some business of me own to take care of this morning, but I'll be able to get on the hunt by the afternoon." He shot Betsy a quick glance. She was concentrating on doing the buttons on her coat and didn't look up.

"Should I go to the Whitfield 'ouse after I've seen the inspector?" Wiggins asked. "I'll be careful."

"Yes, that's a good idea," the housekeeper said as she got up. "And I'll see if I can get a word or two out of the good doctor. Mind you, if he was up all night doing the postmortem, he might go home instead of to St. Thomas's Hospital."

"Oh dear, it looks as if Dr. Bosworth was correct." Witherspoon frowned and shook his head as he read from the postmortem report open on the desk. He and Constable Barnes were in the enquiries room in the police station on Kings Road. They'd met here instead of at the Ladbroke Grove station because it was closer to the victim's home. As both stations were in Witherspoon's district, it didn't matter which one they used as a base. "It was a massive dose of poison that killed the poor fellow."

"Foxglove?" Barnes asked.

Witherspoon squinted at the writing on the page. "So it appears." He sighed and got to his feet. "Perhaps we'd better go and break the news to his sister-in-law." He reached into his coat pocket for his watch. "Oh dear, I think I've forgotten my watch."

"That's all right, sir. I've got mine," Barnes replied just as a constable appeared in the doorway. Wiggins stood right behind him.

"This lad says he's from the inspector's household," the constable explained.

"He is." Barnes grinned. He knew exactly why Wiggins was

here. "Come in, young Wiggins, and tell us what brings you down here."

"Good morning, Constable Barnes." Wiggins took off his flat cap and bobbed his head respectfully.

"Gracious, Wiggins, is everything alright at home?" Witherspoon was surprised by the apprehension that had gripped him when he'd seen the footman. He'd been on his own for most of his adult life, but in the past few years he'd become very attached to his household, and one of them showing up unexpectedly might be bad news indeed.

"Everything's fine, sir." Wiggins pulled the inspector's watch out of his pocket and handed it to Witherspoon. "You forgot your watch, sir, so Mrs. Jeffries sent me down to make sure you got it. We thought you might need it."

Relief swept through the inspector. "Thank you, Wiggins. That was very thoughtful of you."

"It's a good thing you arrived when you did," Barnes said. "The inspector and I were just on our way out."

"Goin' back to Ladbroke Grove, were you?" Wiggins asked.

"Actually, we're on our way back to the Whitfield residence," Witherspoon said as he tucked his watch into his waistcoat pocket. "The postmortem shows that the poor fellow was poisoned."

"Ah, what a shame, especially at this time of the year." Wiggins popped his cap onto his head and edged toward the door. He'd found out what he needed. They had them a murder.

CHAPTER 3

Wiggins kept his distance from the two policemen. He'd toyed with the idea of going back to Upper Edmonton Gardens and telling them it was definitely a poisoning, but then he'd realized the only person there would be Mrs. Goodge. She'd more or less already decided it was murder, anyway, and what's more, he knew she wouldn't appreciate being interrupted while she was trying to wheedle information out of her sources. So he'd decided to find out what he could from the servants in the Whitfield household. Surely someone would stick his or her nose out today.

He rounded the corner onto Redcliffe Road just as the inspector and Barnes went into the Whitfield house. Wiggins hesitated for a brief moment, then crossed the road, all the while keeping his eye out for a good hiding spot. He considered returning to the same stairwell that he and Smythe had used the night before, but in broad daylight he'd be easily seen. Instead he kept on walking, slowing his pace while he surveyed his surroundings. But today his luck wasn't good. At this time of the morning, there were too many people coming and going for him to be able to duck behind a convenient bush.

This isn't workin', Wiggins thought as he rounded the corner onto Fulham Road. I've come too far afield. In London, two hundred feet could take you out of one neighborhood and into another. He turned on his heel and started back the way he'd come.

"Cor blimey," he muttered as he got to the corner of Redcliffe Road. "Looks like my luck is changin' for the better." A maid was coming up the servants' staircase of number nineteen. She was dressed in a short gray jacket and a brown skirt. Her blond hair was tucked up under a brown bonnet. Wiggins slowed his pace, waiting to see which way she'd go. She paused on the pavement, pulled on a pair of gloves, and then headed straight for him.

"Excuse me, miss, but did you just come out of that house?" Wiggins pointed at the Whitfield residence. He noticed she wasn't a very pretty girl. She had a large, crooked nose and blotchy skin.

For a split second, he was certain she was going to walk right past him, but she finally stopped. She stared at him, the expression in her hazel eyes wary. "Why do ya want to know?"

"Beg pardon for bothering you, miss." He swept off his cap and bobbed his head respectfully. "But I was lookin' for my cousin, and I was told she works in that house."

"What's her name?" the girl asked.

"Joan Smithson," he replied. "I'm hopin' she can help me find a position. I've just come up from Kent, and I'm in need of work."

The girl shrugged and continued on her way. "Then you're out of luck, lad. There's no one by that name where I work."

He fell into step with her and noted that she didn't quicken her pace in an effort to get rid of him. "I was afraid of that." He sighed heavily. "I was told she was in this neighborhood, but no one was sure of her address."

"Close family, are ya?" The girl laughed.

"The truth is, I've only seen my cousin once and wouldn't know her if I passed her on the street." He was pleased that she was still talking to him. "I'm just so desperate for work, I thought I'd try and find her. I don't suppose there's any positions goin' where you work, is there? I'm a fully trained footman."

"No, there's nothing." She pursed her lips. "What's more, there's a good chance that most of us will be out of work ourselves. God, I don't want to go back to that miserable factory job in Leeds. But I may not have a choice."

"You mean your entire household is getting sacked?" He took her elbow as they came to the corner. "That's awful."

She gave him a sharp glance but didn't jerk her arm away. "We're not getting the boot," she said as they stepped off the sidewalk onto the road. "But our master died suddenly, and no one knows what's goin' to happen."

"You mean your mistress won't keep you on? By the way, my name is Harry Carter. What's yours?" He felt guilty lying to the girl, but he'd learned that it was dangerous to give his real name. It wouldn't do for Inspector Witherspoon to accidentally overhear a young maid mentioning him while the inspector was questioning people at the Whitfield house. But nonetheless, he still felt bad because he had to lie to her.

"I'm Rosemary Keller." She bobbed her head.

"I'm pleased to meet you, Miss Keller," he said politely.

"Call me Rosie." She gave him a smile. "It's my day out today."

"You get a whole day out?" Wiggins was determined to keep the information flowing. "No wonder you don't want to lose your position. Most households only give their servants an afternoon out every week."

"That's all we get as well," she explained hastily. "But I missed my afternoon out last week, so Mrs. Murray said I should take a whole day this week."

"What 'appened last week?" he asked. The comings and goings of a housemaid probably had nothing to do with Whitfield's murder, but it was keeping her chatting and she might eventually say something useful.

"The footman quit, so Marie and I—that's the other housemaid— had to help Mr. Whitfield deliver his port to his friends. It took ages, and we were supposed to be back by lunch so I could have my afternoon out, but our hansom got stuck on Oxford Street and it was half past two before we got back to the house. Mrs. Murray promised me I could have the entire day out today if I'd stay and help clean up the mess down in the dry larder. That's where Mr. Whitfield did the corkin', you see. He'd got one of them wine corkers from Germany. But he did make a terrible mess. He broke two bottles and spilled half the cask of port all over the floor before he got it right. We had to scrub the whole room with sand and soap to get the stink out. I can't abide the smell of liquor, can you?"

"I don't drink," he replied. This was a lie, as he did enjoy a beer from time to time. But he'd learned from past experience that people were more likely to confide in you about all sorts of things if they thought you agreed with them. "Er, if your footman quit, isn't his position vacant?"

"It was up until the master died." She snorted derisively. "But like I said, we're all wonderin' if we're goin' to be shown the door.

No one, not even Cook or the butler, seems to know what's goin'
to happen next, not with the way Mr. Whitfield died."

He gave her what he hoped was a sympathetic smile. She was
getting to the heart of the matter now, and he hoped she wasn't on
her way to the countryside to visit family. "Not knowin' is 'ard,
isn't it? Uh, if you don't mind my askin', where are you goin'
now?" Wiggins prayed she wasn't on her way to a railway station
to catch a train.

"Hyde Park," she replied. "I love it there. Even in the winter it's
nice to walk about and breathe some fresh air. Then I'm goin' to
have tea at the Lyons on Oxford Street." She broke off and smiled
self-consciously. "That sounds awful, I know, especially with the
master newly dead."

"No, it doesn't," he assured her. "You've a right to 'ave some
time to yourself, especially if you've been workin' for days on end.
Do you mind if I walk with you a bit of the way?" He was fairly
sure she wouldn't. He had a feeling the girl was rather lonely. "I
might as well go back to my lodgin' house, and it's on the other
side of the park."

"I don't mind." She shrugged.

"I'm sorry you're worried about losin' your position," he said
softly. "Uh, what was so odd about the way your Mr. Whitfield
died?"

She looked around as though she was making sure no one was
near enough to overhear her words. "He was murdered," she whispered. "We've had the police round. They were there last night,
and just before I left, they came back. They're questioning everyone, but I didn't want to miss my day out again, so I slipped out of
the house when the constable took Marie off to the butler's pantry
to ask her some questions."

"Murder!" Wiggins widened his eyes in pretend surprise. "Goodness, how awful."

"It's been terrible."

His hand was still on her arm, and he felt her tremble. For a moment he felt lower than a worm. The poor girl was genuinely distressed by what had happened in her household, and he was leading her on just to get information from her. Then he told himself
that he was helping to catch a killer. But that made him feel only
a little less miserable.

Then she sighed. "But worse things happen at sea, as my old

gran always says," she continued chattily. "And I am getting my day out."

He stopped feeling quite so remorseful. "But even if your master was murdered, won't someone inherit his house, and won't they need a staff?"

"Mr. Whitfield didn't have any close relations except for Mrs. Murray, and she's just a sister-in-law. None of us has any idea who gets his estate. Mind you, he's rich as old King Midas, so whoever gets it all will be havin' a nice Christmas." She giggled. "It won't be Mrs. Murray, either, not from what I overheard the other day."

He took her elbow again as they reached another busy street corner. "What was it that you overheard?" he asked.

"Mrs. Murray, I know this is difficult, but we must ask questions," Witherspoon said. He and Constable Barnes were back in the drawing room of the Whitfield house. The room was substantially different from the way it had been the previous evening. Instead of the huge wreath that had hung over the fireplace, there was now a picture draped in black crepe. Witherspoon assumed the painting was a portrait of the deceased. The candles, the holly, and the evergreen boughs with their bright red ribbons had all been removed as well.

Black crepe was also draped over the tops of the curtains at the windows and over the gold gilt frames of the other paintings on the walls. He wondered how the household had managed to find so much black crepe in such a short period of time. Did they keep it stored in the attic in case someone died? Had they borrowed it from a neighbor? He remembered crepe-hanging from his childhood, but in recent years the custom had died out.

Unlike the room, Rosalind Murray was not draped in black. She wore a high-necked gray dress with green trim on the cuffs and collar.

"I understand that, Inspector, but I've no idea what you expect me to say." She sank down onto the sofa. "I simply can't believe that someone would want to murder Stephen. Are you certain it wasn't an accident?"

"Mrs. Murray, we think the poison was in Mr. Whitfield's wine," Barnes said. "Unless you can think of a reasonable explanation as to how a rather large dose of foxglove accidentally ended up there, then I'm afraid we're going to have to assume it was added deliberately."

"Which would make it murder," she said dully. "I do understand."

"Could you tell us again what happened last night?" Witherspoon asked. "Why was Mr. Whitfield the only person drinking the Bordeaux?" He thought this a very good question.

"Because civilized people don't guzzle Bordeaux before dinner." She sighed. "I'm sorry. I shouldn't have made that comment. Stephen had a perfect right to drink what he liked, but generally before dinner, one has an aperitif, not a full-bodied wine like Bordeaux. The rest of us had sherry. There was going to be wine with dinner, so I've no idea why Stephen made such a spectacle of himself. But the moment he saw the label, he poured it down his throat like a drunk in a gin mill."

"And it was the Farringdons who brought the Bordeaux, correct?" Witherspoon probed.

"I've already told you they were the ones who brought it," she said wearily.

Witherspoon nodded. "Yes, of course you did. I simply wanted to ensure I'd understood you correctly. Can you describe the sequence of events after the wine had been opened?"

"I'm not sure I understand what you're asking." She frowned. "When the Farringdons arrived, I was still upstairs. I assume they handed the bottle to Stephen and he gave it to Flagg, who opened it in the butler's pantry and then brought it back into the drawing room to be served."

Witherspoon smiled slightly. "What I meant to ask was what happened to the wine after it was opened. My understanding was that dinner wasn't served until after eight o'clock and that the guests went into the morning room to look at Mr. Whitfield's Christmas tree. Where was the wine when the guests were moving about?"

"Oh, now I see what you mean." Her pale brows furrowed as she thought about the question. "Let me see, I believe the first time I saw the bottle, it was sitting on a silver tray next to the decanter of sherry in the drawing room." She shook her head. "The next time I recall seeing it was when Stephen asked Flagg to bring it into the dining room."

"So the bottle remained in the drawing room the entire time the guests were milling about and looking at the holiday decorations," Witherspoon pressed. He had a feeling that understanding who may or may not have had access to that wine bottle might be the key to solving this case.

"I think so," she replied.

"Do you recall whether anyone went into the drawing room after you'd all gone into the morning room?" Barnes asked.

She shook her head, dislodging a tendril of hair that fell across her cheek. "At one time or another, everyone left the morning room. Mr. Langdon went back in at one point, and Henry went in because he wanted to have a look out the window to see if it was snowing. I believe Basil left as well. I was in and out several times myself."

"For what reason?" Witherspoon asked. Gracious, when he was a guest in someone's home, he sat politely in the drawing room. What was wrong with these people? Everyone dashing about from room to room was going to make this very difficult, very difficult indeed. Drat.

"For any number of reasons," she snapped. "But if you want a list, I'll be happy to oblige. I checked with Cook to ensure the roast beef wasn't overdone, I asked Flagg to bring up another bottle of sherry to the drawing room, and I had Marie take away a linen serviette."

"In other words, you were down in the kitchen or in the butler's pantry when you weren't in the morning room," Barnes said. "Did you go into the drawing room?"

"Of course I did. I've just told you, I asked Flagg to bring up another bottle of sherry. I'd gone into the drawing room specifically to see how much sherry was left in the decanter."

"When you were in the drawing room, did anyone else come in?" Witherspoon asked softly.

"No, but I was only there for a moment or two."

"After you left the drawing room," Barnes continued, "where did you go first, the kitchen or the butler's pantry?" Like Witherspoon, he knew it was important to get an idea of where everyone was in that crucial hour before the ill-fated dinner.

"I went to see Flagg in the pantry first, and then I went into the kitchen," she replied.

"About how long were you downstairs?" the inspector asked.

"I didn't note the time, Inspector." She crossed her arms over her chest. "But it was probably no more than ten minutes."

"When did you ask the maid to replace the serviette?" the constable inquired. He could tell by her stony expression that she resented this line of questioning.

"Just before we went into the dining room to sit down for dinner." She uncrossed her arms and sat up straighter. "I'd gone in to do a final check that the table was properly set, and noticed that one of the serviettes had a tear in the lace edging. I sent Marie down to the linen cupboard to get another one."

Witherspoon glanced in the direction of the dining room. "Was the dining room door open? I mean, could you see into the morning room?"

"No, you could not. Flagg opened the connecting doors when he announced that dinner was served. I didn't want the guests seeing the preparations."

"We'd like to confirm that with your butler," Barnes murmured. "And we'll need to speak to the other servants as well."

"Speak to whomever you like." She waved her hand dismissively.

"Did Mr. Whitfield have any enemies?' Witherspoon asked. He always felt a bit foolish with this question. Obviously the poor fellow had an enemy; someone had murdered him.

"Not particularly," she replied.

"Had he had any disputes with neighbors or sacked any servants?" Barnes pressed. He didn't see how a neighbor or a disgruntled former employee could poison a bottle of wine, but stranger things had happened, and a good copper covered all the possibilities.

"Stephen most certainly didn't argue with our neighbors, and he didn't run the household—I did. I've never sacked a servant. We've always been very lucky in our staff," she replied.

"How long have you been in the household?" Witherspoon asked.

"Ten years. My sister was Mr. Whitfield's late wife. When my husband died, Stephen invited me to come live with him, as we were both widowed." She looked down at the carpet and then back up to the two policemen. "He needed someone to run his household, and I was alone, so it seemed an ideal solution to both our circumstances."

Witherspoon nodded sympathetically. "I understand there were five dinner guests and the two of you."

"That's correct. There were the Farringdons, Henry Becker, Mrs. Graham, and Mr. Langford. The dinner had been planned for quite a while. Stephen wasn't overly sociable, but he did like to have the occasional dinner party," she explained.

"Was Mr. Whitfield worried or anxious about anything lately—his health, or his finances?" Witherspoon asked. This was always a very delicate matter, but it had to be addressed. The possibility that the victim had deliberately poisoned himself had to be investigated, and the only way to do that was by asking uncomfortable questions. The inspector had noticed that relatives tended to get upset at the very hint of such a thing. Most people would rather deal with a murderer in their midst than consider that a loved one had taken his own life.

"He wasn't worried about anything," she insisted. "Stephen was looking forward to life. He was making plans for the future, he was enjoying himself, and he'd no financial or health worries whatsoever. He was a bit irritated when Mrs. Graham brought Mr. Langford along last night, but that certainly didn't stop him from announcing his plans."

"What sort of plans?" Barnes looked up from his little brown notebook.

"He was going to Italy in the spring." She smiled bitterly. "I think he was going to invite Mrs. Graham to accompany him. But you'll have to ask her that. Stephen didn't confide all his plans to me."

"Then how did you know he was planning a trip?" Witherspoon asked.

"He's been buying travel guides, Inspector. One doesn't usually purchase a *Baedeker's* for central and northern Italy unless one is planning to go there." She sniffed disdainfully.

"Did he show you these guides?" Barnes asked.

"Of course not, but he left them lying about where anyone could see them," she replied.

"Did you ask him anything about his plans for a trip?" Witherspoon queried further.

"Yes, but all he said was that he was thinking of going in the spring. He said his plans weren't definite as yet, but I knew he was lying. He'd already been in touch with his bank to secure letters of credit for the journey."

"Was he in the habit of being secretive?" the inspector asked hopefully.

She sighed heavily and pursed her lips. "I wouldn't say he was secretive, but he didn't like being questioned. He was far too much of a gentleman to make a fuss about it, but he had a way of discouraging one from asking too much of him."

"How did you know about the letters of credit?" Barnes was careful to keep his tone matter-of-fact.

"I saw the instructions he sent to his banker, Constable. He accidentally dropped the letter on the floor of his study, and I picked it up when I went in to find a book. Naturally, I read it." She stared at Barnes defiantly. "But it hardly mattered whether I'd read the instructions or not. Just before he died, Stephen was getting ready to tell all of us about the trip. He actually said he had an announcement to make, but he collapsed before he could say anything more."

Betsy was determined to keep her mind on the task ahead of her. She took a deep breath, banished the mental image of her former fiancé looking at her with those big brown eyes of his, and then pulled open the door of the grocer's shop and stepped inside.

As she'd planned, she was the only customer, so the young man behind the counter gave her his full attention as she approached. Betsy gave him a dazzling smile.

"Good morning, miss, may I help you?" he asked politely. He didn't return her smile.

"I'd like an ounce of cinnamon, please, and a pound of flour," Betsy said. Mrs. Goodge had given her a short list of provisions before Betsy had left that morning.

"Certainly, miss." He turned around to a row of jars on a shelf behind the counter and pulled down a glass container.

"I was wondering if you knew a family named Whitfield in this neighborhood?" she asked. She held up a cream-colored envelope that she'd borrowed from the inspector's study. "I've got a note from my employer for a Mr. Stephen Whitfield, but I've lost the address."

The clerk took the lid off the jar and set it down next to a set of scales on the far end of the counter. "Whitfield, Whitfield . . . the name sounds familiar, but I've no idea where someone of that name might live." He poured a tiny amount of the spice onto the metal basket on one end of the scale.

Betsy forced herself to smile. This wasn't going as she'd planned. Whitfield's name was supposed to magically open the fellow's mouth so that all sorts of useful information tumbled out. "That's alright. I don't know why he didn't simply write the address on the envelope, but instead he put it on a slip of paper and tucked it into my shopping basket. Unfortunately I've lost it." Maybe the address ploy wasn't such a good idea.

He finished measuring her spice, tipped it onto a small square of paper, and then folded it into a snug little package. He turned and went down the length of the counter to a shelf at the other end and pulled down a small sack of flour. He did all of this in total silence.

"Does anyone else work here in your shop?" Betsy asked. "Perhaps someone else would be able to help me."

He shook his head and put the flour next to the packet of cinnamon. "There's only me here."

"Oh dear, I've no idea what to do next." Betsy watched him carefully as he added up what she owed on a slip of brown paper next to the cash box. Playing the damsel in distress usually worked: He might not know Whitfield by name, but this trick usually got her turned in the direction of someone who did know the locals. There was always at least one shopkeeper in every neighborhood who knew everything and everyone. She smiled expectantly, sure he would tell her where she ought to go next.

"Will that be all, miss?" he asked coolly.

Betsy's smile disappeared. "Yes, thank you." She paid for the provisions, tucked them into her basket, and hurried out of the shop. She hoped her luck got better at the next place.

"Who was the first of the dinner guests to arrive?" Barnes asked. He was in the butler's pantry with Flagg. They were sitting opposite each other at a rickety table.

"Mr. and Mrs. Farringdon," Flagg replied.

"And what time did they arrive?"

"It had just gone a few minutes past seven." Flagg picked a nonexistent piece of lint off his jacket sleeve. "Dinner was to be served at eight, but Mr. Whitfield had asked the guests to come early to enjoy the Christmas decorations."

Barnes nodded in encouragement. It was always useful when people volunteered more information than they'd been asked. "I understand the Farringdons brought a bottle of Bordeaux with them. Did you immediately take charge of it?"

"Mr. Whitfield wanted it opened right away, so after I hung up Mr. Farringdon's cloak and Mrs. Farringdon's jacket, I brought the bottle down here, opened it, put it on a silver tray, and took it back upstairs."

"Did you serve the wine?"

"No, he served himself," Flagg replied. "Mr. Whitfield didn't like servants hovering about the room when he had guests. So I put the wine down and went back to my position in the front hall. That way I could be close if he needed me but also available to answer the door as well."

"Were you able to hear if Mr. Whitfield offered any of the Bordeaux to the Farringdons?"

"I'm not sure." Flagg's broad face creased in a worried frown. "Right after the Farringdons arrived, Mrs. Graham and Mr. Langford knocked on the front door and I was busy with them. It took Mrs. Graham ages to get out of her coat and gloves."

Barnes was disappointed. It would have been interesting to find out what the Farringdons might have said when the Bordeaux was offered to them. "When the other guests went inside the drawing room, did you hear if Mr. Whitfield offered them the Bordeaux?"

Flagg stared at him blankly. "Of course I heard. I was standing just out in the hallway. He offered everyone a glass of wine, but they all wanted sherry."

Barnes had no idea whether this line of inquiry was useful, but the inspector had said he wanted a complete accounting of where the bottle had been, from the moment it arrived in the house until it was taken into evidence.

"By that time, Mr. Becker had arrived, but he only wore a top-coat so it took just a few seconds to put it on the coat tree," Flagg continued.

"When did Mrs. Murray go into the drawing room?" Barnes asked.

"I don't know. I don't recall seeing her come down the stairs. But that doesn't mean much: she nips about quietly and could easily have slipped in when I was putting the coats away," Flagg replied.

"When did Mr. Whitfield and his guests leave the drawing room?"

Flagg looked puzzled. "You mean for dinner?'

"I understand that Mr. Whitfield had one of those 'Christmas trees' done up," Barnes explained. "Didn't he take his guests in to see it?"

"Oh, that." Flagg snorted softly. "As soon as everyone had their drink, he took them into the morning room. It was just a pine tree with some painted glass and clay ornaments, some ribbons, and those wretched candles. That caused a bit of a to-do, I'll tell you. One of the footmen actually quit over them silly candles, told me right to my face that he wasn't going to stand there for hours on end and then walked straight out of the house without so much as a by-your-leave. But Mr. Whitfield didn't care what sort of trouble the ruddy tree caused. He thought Mrs. Graham would find the tree amusing, and that was all that mattered to him."

"And did she find it amusing?" the constable pressed.

Flagg shrugged. "I wouldn't know about that, sir."

Barnes decided to leave that line of questioning for another time. "When did your footman leave?"

"It was the day before the dinner party, sir," Flagg explained. "And truth to tell, it wasn't a surprise. Some lads just aren't cut out for service, and Jacob Prine was one of them. He's a nice enough lad, but he hated working as a servant. Twice I cuffed him for talking back to Cook. Full of himself, he was."

"So he just quit and walked out?" Barnes queried. "Where did he go?"

"His uncle owns two very successful pubs, one in Hammersmith and one in Chiswick. He went there. He'd been champing at the bit to get out of here." Flagg leaned across the table. "Actually, I think the boy was a bit scared of the tree. He didn't like fire, and I don't think he wanted to be near all them blazing candles. I didn't much blame him, either."

Barnes wrote down the name in his notebook. Even though the boy had left the day before the murder, it wouldn't hurt to verify his movements. "Where is he likely to have gone? Hammersmith or Chiswick?"

"He'll be at Hammersmith. The Lineman's Tow is the name of the pub."

Barnes decided that they now had a pretty good idea of who

might have had access to the open Bordeaux. Apparently everyone could have slipped in and doctored it with foxglove. But he wasn't through asking questions. He closed his notebook and looked at Flagg. "What sort of person was Mr. Whitfield?"

Flagg was taken aback. "I'm afraid I don't understand your question. It's hardly my place to . . ."

"You're not stupid, Mr. Flagg. Your employer has been murdered, so that means someone wanted him dead. It's our job to find out who that someone might be, and you'll do the late Mr. Whitfield a great service if you're simply honest with me. What sort of man was he?"

Flagg stared at Barnes for a long moment. "He wasn't any worse than most men of his class."

"What does that mean?'

"He wasn't a kind man by any means, but he was fair and he treated us decently." Flagg sighed. "Mind you, we didn't like the way he'd treated Mrs. Murray recently. She deserved better."

"What did he do to her?"

"Ever since he became acquainted with Mrs. Graham, he's pushed Mrs. Murray aside." Flagg sniffed disapprovingly. "Hardly the act of a gentleman."

"Isn't Mrs. Murray his sister-in-law?" Barnes said, taking care to keep his tone casual.

"Oh, yes, but up until he met Mrs. Graham, everyone assumed that Mr. Whitfield and Mrs. Murray would eventually marry. He always promised he'd take care of her, and frankly, unless he settled an allowance on her, I don't think he could have taken care of her and still been married to Mrs. Graham."

"Mr. Whitfield was going to marry Mrs. Graham?" Barnes asked. He wanted to make sure he understood exactly what the man was telling him. "He actually told you this?"

"Not directly." Flagg chuckled. "He was hardly in the habit of discussing his personal business with me, but one does have eyes and ears. Two weeks ago he sent for his solicitor, and then he made an appointment with a jeweler."

"And those actions led you to believe he was going to propose to Mrs. Graham?"

"Those, and the fact that Cook overheard Mrs. Murray and Mr. Whitfield having words on the subject," Flagg replied. "Of course, Cook wouldn't say precisely what she overheard. She does that, you know—pretends that she doesn't like gossip—but she's no better than anyone else." He leaned across the table again. "But she told me that Mrs. Murray and Mr. Whitfield had some very strong words after the solicitor was here last week. Mrs. Murray is a lady; she never raises her voice. But Cook claims she was screaming her head off last week."

"You look dreadfully tired, Dr. Bosworth," Mrs. Jeffries said as she took a chair opposite him. He was sitting behind his desk, his pale skin even paler after a night of hard work. His red hair was mussed and tufts of it were standing on end. There was a faint air of disinfectant about his person. "I'm sorry. I shouldn't have come. This could have waited till later."

"Don't be sorry. I was expecting you'd be here this morning." Bosworth covered his mouth with his hand to hide a yawn. "That's one of the reasons I came to my office—I was fairly sure this would be where you'd look for me. You're here about Stephen Whitfield."

"I am. Was it poison?"

"It was. He had enough foxglove in his stomach to kill an elephant. That's one of the reasons that death occurred so rapidly—he ingested a massive dose," he replied. "Luckily, as the postmortem was done so quickly, the contents of the stomach were still fresh, and I found an enormous amount of crushed leaves."

"And you're certain it was foxglove?" she asked. She wanted to be sure about this fact. Foxglove was a poison anyone would be able to obtain. It grew all over the countryside, especially in the woodlands. If Whitfield had died of some other kind of poison, it might limit the number of people who could reasonably acquire a large enough supply to kill someone.

"I'm sure." He smiled. "I've seen it before."

"And it was in the Bordeaux?"

He nodded. "Correct."

"You had the wine tested?"

"I didn't need to have it tested. I simply poured a bit out, and the foxglove was floating in the wine as clear as day. It's a wonder no one noticed the leaves in the liquid. They were certainly big enough to be seen."

She thought about that for a moment. "That is very odd. If the leaves were that visible, the killer was taking a terrible risk. If

Whitfield had noticed them, he probably wouldn't have drunk the wine."

"Perhaps." Bosworth shrugged. "But perhaps not. The bottle itself is a very dark color, so the leaves couldn't have been seen unless one held it up to a lamp or took it out in strong sunlight for a good look."

"But once the wine was poured into a glass, the leaves should have been spotted," she argued.

"Only if the person drinking the wine bothered to look." Bosworth leaned back in his chair. "Mrs. Jeffries, there are a number of people who are . . . Well, I'm not sure how to put it, but their need for alcoholic beverages is so great, they simply pour down their throats whatever is handed to them. Stephen Whitfield might have been one of those people."

"You mean an alcoholic?" Mrs. Jeffries had heard the word before but wasn't precisely sure this was the correct context. "But aren't those simply people who lie about in gin palaces and end up in the streets?"

"That's generally what happens if you're poor. If you've money, you can avoid ending up in those circumstances," he said. "Take my word for it—it's not just the poor that suffer from this affliction. There are just as many of the wealthy who have the same compulsion to drink; they simply have the means to hide it better. I'm not saying that this has anything to do with Whitfield's murder. I am saying that a craving for alcohol could be the reason he didn't bother to so much as glance at the contents of his cup."

"I see." She nodded in understanding. "Dr. Bosworth, wouldn't a massive dose like that have changed the taste of the wine?"

"Of course it would, but as we just noted, if he was a person with a craving for alcohol, he wouldn't have cared what it tasted like. He'd have been concerned only with getting it down his throat."

"But what if he wasn't one of those sort of people, one of those alcoholics? What if he had no craving? Wouldn't he have noticed that the wine tasted peculiar?"

Bosworth thought for a moment before he spoke. "He certainly should have noticed—unless, of course, he had a limited sense of taste. That could well be the case. He wasn't a young man."

"I'm not young, either, but I can tell if something tastes odd."

"Can you?" He grinned. "Remember, the man was drinking a

full-bodied French red wine, which has a strong flavor in and of it-self. He may well have thought it was supposed to taste as it did, or he might not have had any sense of taste at all. I've half a dozen patients who can't taste food or drink. It's quite a common afflic-tion."

"Really?"

"Yes. The sense of taste is closely allied with the sense of smell. An infection in the sinuses, a blow to the head, a high fever—any or all of those conditions can leave one without the ability to taste or smell much of anything."

"That could explain why Whitfield didn't notice that the wine tasted unusual," she murmured. "Would the foxglove have changed the taste all that much?'

"I've no idea. Most of the people who have ever put the stuff in their mouths are dead. But I expect it would. Most poisons do have a strong taste. Perhaps it's Mother Nature's way of trying to keep us from ingesting things that are likely to kill us."

"With a large dose like the one he had, wouldn't it be obvious that Whitfield had been poisoned and not died of natural causes?" she asked.

Bosworth shook his head. "Unless they'd had some experience with foxglove poisoning, most physicians would assume he'd died of a heart attack. I only thought to look for poisioning because be-fore Whitfield collapsed, he claimed everyone had turned blue. But if he'd collapsed without speaking, considering his age and his general health, even I would have thought it was his heart."

"Then he was lucky you were the one they fetched to attend him," she said with a smile. "Otherwise the killer would have got-ten away with it."

"Your killer may still get away with it," Bosworth warned. "Proving this kind of poisoning won't be easy. Just about anyone in England who can go for a walk in the countryside has access to foxglove."

"But it doesn't grow in the dead of winter."

"It doesn't have to," he replied. "The poison was in the leaves. Your killer probably gathered them this past summer, dried them out, and crushed them to be put in the wine. The poison would still be very, very potent." He raised his hand to try to hide another yawn.

But Mrs. Jeffries was having none of that. She got to her feet. "You must go home and rest. I've taken up too much of your time."

"I'm glad to help," Bosworth replied as he got up. "Do let me know what happens. I do like learning who the culprit is before it comes out in the newspapers."

"If this case is as difficult as I think it might be," she replied, "you may have a long wait."

CHAPTER 4

Smythe pushed his way into the Dirty Duck Pub and hoped that his old source would be open for business. He took a deep breath, inhaling the mingled scents of beer, tobacco, wood smoke, and river. This was one of the things he'd missed the most when he was gone: the smell of home, of London. Seamen, dockworkers, street vendors, day laborers, and locals crowded the bar and filled the benches along the wall; but considering the number of people in the room, it was relatively quiet. The pub might be on the quayside, but Blimpey Groggins, the man he'd come to see and the probable owner of this establishment, kept the rowdies and troublemakers out of the place.

Smythe eased past a bread seller, taking care not to bump her basket. He craned his neck to look past a burly teamster and saw that Blimpey was sitting at his usual table near the fireplace. He was talking with two other men. Smythe hung back a moment. Blimpey looked to be conducting business, and he wouldn't appreciate being interrupted. One of the men wore an old-fashioned black business suit, a silver and maroon cravat, and a shirt so white that it almost hurt your eyes. He appeared to be a banker. The other fellow had on a ragged gray jacket and paint-stained trousers.

Blimpey Groggins had started out in life as a thief. Breaking and entering was his specialty. But he was possessed of a superb memory and soon realized that as he had no stomach for either prison or violence, he could make far more money buying and selling information. He had sources in the Old Bailey, the magistrate courts, the financial centers in the City, the steamship lines, and the insurance companies. He also had an excellent relationship with every thief, con artist, and crook in southern England. His clients ranged from insurance companies wanting to know whether a suspicious fire had been deliberately set, to petty thieves looking for character references on which fence was the most reliable.

But Blimpey had standards. He wouldn't trade in information that caused physical harm to a woman or a child. Smythe had used him a number of times and had found his information very dependable.

The man in the dark suit stood, picked up his top hat from the table, nodded, and left. A moment later, the day laborer rose and walked away as well.

Fearing he wasn't the only one waiting for Blimpey, Smythe pushed his way through the crowd and slipped onto the stool opposite his quarry. "Hello, Blimpey."

"Well, look what the cat dragged in. Welcome back, Smythe." Blimpey grinned. "You're a sight for sore eyes. I was wonderin' if you were goin' to stay away forever." Blimpey was a short, rotund man with ginger-colored hair, a ruddy complexion, and a broad face. Even though he could afford a Bond Street tailor, Blimpey was dressed in his usual outfit of a brown checked suit that had seen better days and a white shirt that was fading to gray. A long red scarf was twined about his neck, and on his head was a dirty porkpie hat.

"Australia's a long ways off, and it takes time to get there and back." Smythe laughed. He was delighted that there was someone who was glad to see him. "My business took a bit longer than I thought. I'm back to stay, though."

"Good. I'll buy you a pint, then." Blimpey waved at the barmaid, held up his glass, and pointed at Smythe.

"That's nice of ya." Smythe sighed heavily. "You're one of the first friendly faces I've seen since I got back." The others at the household had been happy to see him, but they'd all let him know how much he'd hurt Betsy. None of them seemed to take into account how miserable he'd been the whole time he'd been gone.

"I heard you 'ad to postpone your weddin'. I'll bet that didn't make your lady very happy." Blimpey smiled sympathetically.

"From the way some people are actin', it might be permanent," he muttered darkly. He had no doubt that Blimpey knew every little detail of what had happened and why he'd had to go to Australia.

"Are you back at the inspector's?" Blimpey drew back so that the barmaid had room to put the drinks down on the small tabletop. "Thanks, luv."

"I am." Smythe nodded his thanks as well. "But if Betsy and I don't work out our differences properly, I'm not sure I'll stay." The moment the words were out of his mouth, he knew they were true. He couldn't bear to be in the same house with her and know that she'd lost all feeling for him, that she didn't love him.

"You'll work it all out," Blimpey said. "She's just hurt and angry over bein' left that way. It was right humiliatin' for her, you know. My Nell yammered at me about it for a good two weeks after you was gone."

Nell was Blimpey's wife, and as Smythe had had a hand in helping the two of them reach the altar, Blimpey felt it was his duty to give Smythe a bit of assistance with his lady love.

"What was I supposed to do?" Smythe cried. "I had to go and help. The old bastard had saved my life. I'd not have anything to my name if he'd not taken me in and shown me how to survive. I owed him. I couldn't let him just hide out in the bush, not at his age."

"You found him, then?"

" 'Course I did, and hired him a good solicitor. It was plain as the nose on yer face that he was innocent, so the charges were dropped once I let the lawyer take over." Smythe sighed heavily. "Stupid old git, he never shoulda run. But the idea of prison scared him so bad, he took off into the bush, even though he'd not done it."

"And you come back to face a very angry fiancée." Blimpey grinned. "Like I said, Betsy loves you. She'll come around. Don't give up, and don't even think of leavin'. Just let her have her way for now. Let her get a bit of her own back. After all, she was the one that was here in London with all them pityin' stares."

Smythe was getting tired of hearing about how hard Betsy had had it while he was gone. Did people think that tramping out into the bush was a picnic? But he held his tongue.

"You didn't just drop by to ask after my health," Blimpey continued. "What else do ya need?"

"Information." Smythe sipped his beer.

"I heard your inspector caught that toff's murder, the poisonin'."

Smythe stared at him incredulously. "How did you find out he was poisoned? We've not even had that confirmed ourselves yet."

"Don't be daft, man. It's my job to find out these things. My sources told me about it ten minutes after the postmortem report was delivered to the police. Stephen Whitfield was poisoned, all right, and from the amount he had in his stomach, it wasn't an accident."

"Cor blimey, that was bloomin' fast." Smythe laughed. He suddenly felt better, as though everything was going to be all right. "We need to find out who might have wanted Whitfield dead."

"There's always plenty about that want a rich man dead," Blimpey replied. "But I'm guessin' you'd like a bit more information so you can narrow it down a bit."

Smythe nodded. "We think the poison might 'ave been in a bottle of Bordeaux that was brought by one of the other guests."

"That's what the police surgeon said as well," Blimpey replied.

"Did you read the ruddy thing?"

Blimpey shook his head. "Nah, but I knew you were back, and I knew it was the inspector's case, so I knew you'd be along today. I thought you'd appreciate havin' a few pertinent details."

"I do," Smythe said quickly. "Was there anything else in the report I ought to know about?"

"No, just the fact that he was poisoned and that the poison was in the wine he'd drunk earlier. How come your inspector doesn't just arrest the person who gave Whitfield the Bordeaux? Doesn't he think that person is the most likely killer?" Blimpey asked.

"There might have been plenty of time for any of the other guests to have tampered with the bottle."

"Who were the other guests?" Blimpey took a quick sip of his pint.

Smythe repeated the names he'd gotten from Mrs. Jeffries at their meeting early this morning. "Do you know anything about any of them?"

"Not much. Hugh Langford's got a reputation as a bit of a cad, and Basil Farringdon's family is one of the oldest in England. But like most of that class, they have plenty of breeding but wouldn't 'ave had near as much money if he'd not married a bit more."

"So Mrs. Farringdon was the one with the cash?" Smythe took another drink of his beer.

"That's the rumor, but don't take it to the bank just yet, lad," Blimpey replied. "This is only gossip I'm repeatin', not facts. Give me a couple of days and I'll have more than just idle chat to pass on."

"Good, I knew I could rely on you." He drained the remainder of his pint and stood up. "I'll be back in a day or two."

"You goin' off to do some snoopin' on your own?" Blimpey asked casually.

"I thought I'd make the rounds of the pubs in Whitfield's neighborhood and see what I could pick up."

"Try the Crow's Roost. It's just off the Fulham Road," Blimpey suggested. "It's the cheapest pub in that neighborhood and caters mostly to servants and workin' people. Stand a few rounds, and I've no doubt you'll loosen plenty of tongues."

The Farringdons lived on Connaught Street in Mayfair. Witherspoon and Barnes stood on the pavement and stared at the elegant five-story house. The ground-floor level was white stone and the upper floors red brick. The inspector stepped onto the short stone walkway and walked up to the front door. To his right, a flight of steps led down to a tradesmen's entrance. From his vantage point behind the inspector, Barnes could see a kitchen maid peering out the lower window. When his eyes met hers, she dropped the curtain and stepped back. Good. Their presence would be causing plenty of talk in the kitchen now, and that always helped an investigation.

Witherspoon knocked on the door. A few moments later, a woman wearing housekeeper's black peered out at them. "Yes?"

"We'd like to see Mr. and Mrs. Farringdon," Witherspoon said politely.

"They should be expecting us," Barnes added.

The housekeeper glanced over her shoulder and then looked back at them. "Mr. and Mrs. Farringdon are not receiving this morning,"

"This isn't a social call," Witherspoon said bluntly. "It is imperative we speak with them right away."

She hesitated and then opened the door wider. "Come in. I'll tell

Mr. Farringdon you are here and that you insist upon speaking to him."

As they waited, Witherspoon took a look around. A home could tell you a lot about the people who lived in it, and what this home said was that the Farringdons were very, very rich.

The foyer was painted a lush peacock blue, the polished wood floor was covered with an ornate Oriental rug, and the staircase was at least eight feet wide. Next to the stairs was a round claw-foot table covered with a gold fringed shawl and holding a tall blue and white vase with brilliantly colored feathers. Opposite that was a huge oblong mirror set in an intricately carved rosewood frame.

"Looks like they've got plenty of money," Barnes muttered.

"So it would seem," Witherspoon replied. He turned his attention toward the hall as they heard footsteps. It was Basil Farringdon, and he didn't look happy.

"My housekeeper said you insisted on barging in," he said. "This is not a convenient time."

"Murder is rarely convenient for any of us," Witherspoon retorted softly.

Farringdon stopped, and his eyes widened. "Murder! Ye gods, what on earth are you talking about?"

"He's talking about murder, sir," Barnes said. "Surely you expected to see us again."

"I most certainly did not," he retorted.

Barnes eyed him skeptically. "Last night your host died in very unusual circumstances. We did tell you'd we'd be in touch, yet you seem surprised at our presence."

The constable had decided to get this part of the interview over quickly. They didn't have time to play about, and he'd found that the fastest way to get the upper crust to cooperate was to be as blunt and rude as they were.

"Of course I'm surprised," Farringdon snapped. "I thought Stephen had a heart attack."

"But it wasn't a heart attack," Witherspoon said. "And we must ask you a few more questions."

"Why? I've already made a statement." Farringdon had recovered some of his bluster. "That ought to suffice."

"I'm afraid it doesn't sir," Witherspoon said. "Mr. Whitfield was murdered."

"Are you certain?" Farringdon demanded. "Despite that young pup of a doctor's insistence on fetching the police, I assumed Stephen died of natural causes."

"Mr. Whitfield's death wasn't natural," the inspector replied. Gracious, how many ways did they have to repeat this?

Farringdon frowned. "Our sort of people don't get themselves murdered, Inspector. Are you certain it wasn't a heart attack or a stroke?"

Barnes had had enough. "It was murder," he said. His knees were hurting, and it was so warm in here that he could feel sweat beading on the back of his neck.

Farringdon hesitated and then turned and started back the way he'd just come. "Come along to my study, then. It's this way."

"May I have a word with Mrs. Farringdon, sir?" Barnes asked as they followed him down the hallway. "It will take up less of your time that way."

It would also avoid the two of them being interviewed together and verifying each other's statements.

"My wife isn't home," Farringdon replied.

"Is she expected back soon?" Barnes pressed.

"She's shopping, Constable, and as she's no social engagements for today, it might be hours before she comes home." Farringdon pushed through a partly opened door, and the two policemen trailed after him into his study.

Witherspoon squinted as he stepped into the gloomy room. Heavy green curtains were drawn across the windows, blocking the morning light, and the only source of illumination was two small lamps on the desk in the far corner. The walls were painted a pale gray, with dark wood wainscoting along the lower half. Two straight-backed chairs were in front of the desk. A green leather wing chair and a matching sofa were along the far wall.

Farringdon sat down behind the desk and nodded toward the chairs. "You may sit."

"Thank you," Witherspoon replied as he and Barnes sat where their host had indicated. "Mr. Farringdon, we understand you and your wife bought a bottle of Bordeaux wine for Mr. Whitfield. Is that correct?"

Farringdon's eyebrows rose. "That is correct. It was a little Christmas gift."

"Where did you acquire the Bordeaux?" Barnes asked.

Farringdon uncrossed his arms and straightened up. "Presumably it came from our wine merchant. But my wife, not me, is in charge of the household, so you'll need to ask her."

"What's the name of your wine merchant?" Barnes took out his notebook and flipped it open.

"Kerringtons and Stuart," he supplied. "They're in Oxford Street."

"How long had you and Mr. Whitfield known one another?" Witherspoon asked.

Farringdon sighed heavily, as though he was bored. "I don't see what on earth this has to do with his death . . ."

Witherspoon interrupted. "Nevertheless, it's important that you answer all our questions."

Farringdon drew back slightly, as though he was surprised. "All right, then, we've known each other since we were children. Stephen and I were in the same house at school, and we went up to Oxford together."

"So you'd been friends almost all of your lives." The inspector was trying to get him to speak a bit more freely. He'd found that once people began talking, they would frequently reveal all sorts of interesting information.

"I suppose you could say that." Farringdon shrugged. "Of course, once we were both married, we didn't see one another quite as often."

"But you went to his house for a holiday dinner, isn't that correct?" Barnes said. "And you bought him a gift."

"Only because for the past three years he's been sending us a gift," Farringdon replied. "He gives a nice bottle of his special port."

"Did Mr. Whitfield make his own port?" Witherspoon unbuttoned his heavy overcoat. He wished he'd taken it off, as it was hideously warm in the room.

"Gracious, no." Farringdon laughed. "Stephen could no more brew his own wine or spirits than he could captain a ship around the Horn. He had his wine merchant import a cask of port directly from the vineyards of Portugal. He corked it himself and sent us all a bottle."

"And he's been doing this for the past three years?" Barnes asked.

"That's correct. This year, since we were invited to dinner,

Maria insisted we take him a bottle of really good Bordeaux." Farringdon leaned forward. "Stephen considered himself a bit of a connoisseur of both food and wine, but my wife was certain he'd no sense of taste. He and Mrs. Murray came to our autumn ball, and Stephen kept muttering that there was something wrong with the champagne cups and that they tasted off. Of course there wasn't, but Maria fretted over it for days."

Witherspoon smiled slightly. "Were you present when the bottle was actually opened?"

Farringdon thought for a moment. "No, I believe the butler took it off to the pantry to do that. Why are you so interested in that bottle of Bordeaux?"

Barnes wondered what took the fellow so long to ask. "Because the poison that killed Mr. Whitfield was in the bottle you brought."

Farringdon's eyes widened. "That's absurd. That bottle came directly from our wine merchants, and it wasn't open when we handed it to the butler."

"We're not accusing you or your wife of anything," Witherspoon soothed him.

"That's not how the question sounded to me," he snapped. "I take great umbrage at your implication. There was nothing wrong with the wine we brought."

"We're not implying anything." Witherspoon wondered how many times in every murder investigation he ended up saying those words. "We're simply trying to understand the sequence of events as they happened."

"We're trying to establish whether or not the bottle was left unattended at any given moment," Barnes interjected.

Farringdon relaxed a bit. "It was. It was sitting right there in the drawing room, where anyone could have tampered with it."

"Excellent, sir, that's precisely the sort of information we need." Witherspoon nodded encouragingly. "When the butler brought the Bordeaux into the drawing room, were all the other guests present?"

"I think so." He frowned slightly and rubbed his chin. "No, wait, I think that Henry was there, but Mrs. Graham and Mr. Langford arrived at just about the same time Flagg brought the bottle in. Then Mrs. Murray came in . . . Yes, that's right. She was the last to come into the drawing room."

Witherspoon made a mental note to ask Flagg whether he'd put down the tray holding the bottle while he answered the door to let Mrs. Graham and Mr. Langford into the house. He'd also have had to take their outer garments to the cloakroom, leaving the open bottle in either the hall or the foyer. "What happened after all the guests had arrived? Did everyone stay in the drawing room?"

"We had an aperitif, of course. Stephen offered everyone the wine, but the rest of us had sherry. We sat about and chatted for a few minutes, made pleasant conversation; then Stephen led us all into the morning room to see his Christmas tree. It was quite spectacular. It was one of the first I've ever seen in a private home, though I'm told they're becoming popular in some circles these days." Farringdon chuckled. "I'd thought it was households with children that would like that sort of thing, but then again, Stephen was a great admirer of the late Prince Albert, so I expect he felt he was honoring his memory by having the tree. He knew His Highness, you know. Stephen's mother was from Coburg and was a distant cousin to the late prince consort."

"And you all went in together to see this Christmas tree?" Witherspoon pressed. "No one stayed behind in the drawing room?"

"Everyone went," Farringdon said firmly. "Stephen was adamant that we all go. He ushered us into the morning room as if we were a herd of sheep. I don't really blame him: he'd gone to a great deal of trouble and I expect he wanted us to enjoy the sight. As I said, the tree was lovely. Very bright and colorful. Of course there was a footman on duty to ensure that the candles didn't catch anything on fire. I expect the lad blew the candles out when poor Stephen was taken ill. The household did go into a bit of an uproar."

"Did everyone stay in the morning room together?" Witherspoon asked.

"Everyone stayed for a few moments. Then, of course, there was the usual milling-about that happens at social occasions."

"Can you be a bit more specific, sir?" The inspector wanted to get some idea of who had been where at any given moment.

"I don't think so, Inspector. I wasn't really paying attention to everyone's comings and goings."

"Try, sir. It's very important," Barnes urged.

Farringdon frowned in concentration. "Gracious, I don't know that I can recall the exact sequence of who went in and out."

"It was only last night, sir," Witherspoon pressed, his tone just a tad impatient.

"Well, at one point, Mrs. Murray excused herself to have a word with the cook," Farringdon said slowly. "I remember that because she mentioned it to Maria when she excused herself."

"Excellent, that's very good," the inspector encouraged him.

"And Mr. Langford asked if he could help himself to another sherry, so I know that he went into the drawing room. Henry went to the water closet, and I believe Mrs. Graham excused herself to go and fetch another handkerchief from her evening wrap. Oh dear, I honestly don't remember anymore. We were all milling about and chatting. The door opened and closed half a dozen times."

"Did you or Mrs. Farringdon leave the morning room during this period?" Witherspoon was careful to keep his tone very casual as he asked the question.

Farringdon shook his head. "No, we were both there the whole time. We didn't leave the morning room until the butler announced that dinner was being served."

"How long were you in the house before everyone went in to dinner?" Barnes asked. He thought it might be useful to know how long Stephen Whitfield had been drinking poisoned wine.

"We arrived at seven and dinner was served at eight." Farringdon smiled triumphantly. "I do remember that, because the hall clock had just gonged the hour when we went into the dining room."

"And Mr. Whitfield had been drinking the Bordeaux for all that time?" The constable clarified. "He didn't drink sherry or have any other kind of aperitif?"

"Stephen had nothing but the wine. He was drinking steadily the whole time. He must have had three-quarters of the bottle before we even went in to dinner."

Luty Belle charged into the kitchen, unbuttoning her fur-trimmed cloak as she walked. "Sorry we're late, but it ain't my fault." She flopped into her usual spot next to Wiggins. "Blame him." She pointed to her tall, stately, white-haired butler, Hatchet. "If he hadn't insisted we stop and make small talk with Lord Dinsworthy . . ."

"Don't be absurd, madam. You were quite willing to make that stop when you thought Lord Dinsworthy might have some useful information about one of the principals in the case," Hatchet retorted. He pulled out a chair on the other side of the footman and sat down. "You only began making a fuss when you realized that Lord Dinsworthy had absolutely nothing useful to tell us. You were rude to the poor man."

She snorted and slipped her cloak off her shoulders, letting it fall onto the back of her chair. "He was makin' us late, and if you don't make a clean getaway, the man will talk you to death."

"We've only just sat down," Mrs. Jeffries said cheerfully. "And Betsy isn't back yet, either. So we'll give her a few minutes."

Luty and Hatchet had been present at their morning meeting and had gone out to do their investigating with the same set of facts as everyone else. Because of her wealth, Luty had enormous resources in the financial community, while Hatchet had a network of resources of his own.

"She should be here on time," Smythe muttered. He couldn't decide whether to be angry with her or to throw himself at her feet and beg for forgiveness. He'd careened back and forth all day between the two courses of action, and he was dead tired. On top of that, when he'd gone to Howard's stables to see the inspector's horses, Bow and Arrow, they'd acted like they didn't know who he was, either! This was turning into a right miserable homecoming.

"Sometimes you can't 'elp bein' a bit late." Wiggins' mouth watered as he looked at the table. "Cor blimey, Mrs. Goodge, you've outdone yourself. Look at all this; freshly made brown bread, red currant jam, and a madeira cake."

"Why thank you, Wiggins," the cook replied.

"I'm sure Betsy will be here any moment," Mrs. Jeffries said just as they heard the back door open. Betsy, her face flushed with excitement, hurried into the room a moment later. "I'm sorry to be late, but the omnibus took ages getting across the bridge."

"We've not started yet," Mrs. Goodge assured her quickly.

"But as you're here now, we'll get started," Mrs. Jeffries said. "Who would like to begin?" She noticed that Smythe was staring at the tabletop and that Betsy was keeping her gaze on the buttons of her jacket as she undid them.

"If it's all the same to everyone, I'll go ahead and start," Mrs. Goodge volunteered. Considering the way Betsy and Smythe were avoiding even looking at one another, she thought it best to settle right down to business. She paused briefly to see whether anyone objected, and then plunged ahead. "I had a nice chat with one of my sources today, and I did find out a bit about our victim. Stephen

Whitfield's been a widower for over ten years. The gossip I heard is that his sister-in-law, Rosalind Murray, has had her eye on becoming the second Mrs. Whitfield for quite some time now."

Betsy muttered something, but since her chair was scraping the floor, no one except Smythe could actually hear what she said. He wasn't sure, but he thought it sounded like "silly cow," a reference, no doubt, to any woman wanting to marry. He snorted faintly to let Betsy know he was aware of her attitude, and then kept his attention firmly fixed on the cook.

"Why'd she wait ten years?" Wiggins asked as he helped himself to a slice of bread. "I mean, if 'e's been a widower all that time. Poor lady wasn't gettin' any younger."

"My source wasn't certain, but she'd heard rumors that Mrs. Murray would lose an allowance from her husband's family if she remarried."

"So what?" Betsy asked. "If they really loved each other, *nothing* should have kept them apart." She glanced at her fiancé. Smythe narrowed his eyes, but said nothing. "Besides, wasn't Whitfield wealthy?" she continued.

"He's supposed to be." Mrs. Goodge shrugged. "But then again, I also heard that Rosalind Murray was considered quite an adventuress when she was a young woman. She went to India with her brother and only came home because her mother became ill."

"You found out quite a bit about Mrs. Murray," Luty said admiringly.

"She's the only one I heard anything useful about," the cook replied. "And I doubt the facts that the woman was an adventuress in her youth and is good at math are very helpful to our case. Supposedly she used to explain the stock market to her father. But none of my sources knew anything about the Farringdons or the other guests."

"Mine did." Luty chuckled. "I got an earful from my neighbor. Her sister lives in Chelsea, right across the road from Eliza Graham. Mrs. Graham's first husband died three years ago."

"How did he die?" Mrs. Jeffries asked quickly. Their previous investigations had taught them that background details about the suspects in a case were very important.

"Lydia didn't know." Luty shrugged. "But I reckon it won't be too hard to find out something like that. I'll try and track it down before our next meetin'. But let me tell ya what I did find out. Accordin' to all the gossip, Eliza Graham is a sociable sort of person, if you get my meanin'. She didn't wear widow's weeds for the full year after her husband died, and she started goin' out in society, too. That sure caused a few tongues to wag."

"What are widow's weeds?" Wiggins asked.

"Black clothing," the cook explained. "The Americans call mourning clothes 'widow's weeds.' "

"That's right." Luty nodded. "The only other gossip I heard about the woman was that she needs a rich husband. The family of the late Mr. Graham made sure she didn't get much when he died. That's about all I found out today. But I've got several sources lined up to visit tomorrow, so I ought to have something for our afternoon meeting."

"You've done an excellent job, Luty," Mrs. Jeffries said. She turned her attention to Hatchet. "Would you like to go next?"

"Thank you. I would, actually. Unfortunately my day wasn't terribly productive. The source I had hoped to speak with is currently indisposed with a bad cold." Hatchet hoped the Farringdon butler wasn't the malingering type. "The only information I managed to obtain is that Stephen Whitfield spends several weeks every summer at the Thompson Hotel in Dover." He smiled apologetically. "Apparently he's very fond of the gardens, which my sources assure me are rather spectacular."

"At least you found out something," Betsy said. "My day was miserable. I didn't find one shopkeeper that knew anything about Whitfield. Honestly, you'd think the man didn't buy food or drink or anything else. What did the household live on? Air?"

"Maybe Whitfield didn't buy from the local shops," Smythe speculated. He resisted the urge to reach for her hand under the table. "Maybe he buys his provisions elsewhere. There's lots of shopping areas in that part of London."

"I know," she replied glumly. "But people usually shop close to home, so that's where I started. There's another street of shops about half a mile away. Maybe I'll have better luck there tomorrow. Oh, wait a minute—I tell a lie. I did find out something. Whitfield did buy his vegetables at the local greengrocer's, and I found out he didn't care for beets. That's right useful information, isn't it?"

Everyone laughed. Then Mrs. Jeffries said, "Don't worry, Betsy. Tomorrow will be better. I didn't find out all that much myself. But

Dr. Bosworth confirmed that Whitfield had been poisoned." She told them the rest of the details she'd learned from the good doctor. "So at least we know we're on the right track, so to speak," she concluded. "It was most definitely foxglove."

"Cor blimey." Wiggins shook his head. "Anyone who takes a stroll in the country could find that plant, then, couldn't they? The government ought to do something about that. Why, it's a wonder that hundreds of people don't end up poisoned."

"That wouldn't do any good, Wiggins," Luty said quickly. "Even if they ripped up every foxglove plant in the country, there are dozens of other things that are just as deadly. Yew trees, hemlock, horsetail, nightshade—and those are just the ones I can name off the top of my head. If the government tried to get rid of everything that could kill a person, there wouldn't be much countryside left!"

"Don't put anything in your mouth when you're walking in the country. That's my motto," Mrs. Goodge said wisely. "I learned that when I was just a girl."

"In America, we've got even more stuff that can kill ya," Luty added enthusiastically. "Oleander, locoweed, castor beans, mistletoe, rhododendrons, pokeweed, morning glory . . ."

"We've got mistletoe and morning glory here, too," Wiggins interrupted eagerly.

"Obviously there is no shortage of poisonous plants on either side of the Atlantic," Mrs. Jeffries interjected. "But we must get on with our meeting. The inspector might be home soon, and it's important that we hear everyone's report." She looked at Wiggins. "Would you like to go next?"

"I 'ad a bit of luck today," he began. "I met up with a maid from the Whitfield house, and she told me the servants was all scared they'd be lookin' for other positions now that the master was dead."

"Wouldn't the person who inherits the Whitfield house need a staff?" Betsy asked.

"Yeah, but none of them know who is inheritin' the house," the footman replied. "And that's why they're all worried. Up until recently, the servants thought that everything would go to Mrs. Murray, seein' as she's his only relation. But Rosie—that's the maid—she told me that a few weeks back, Whitfield made an appointment to see his solicitor and change his will. He and Mrs. Murray had a huge row about it. They was screamin' at each other so loudly the entire household heard 'em."

"What were they saying?" Mrs. Jeffries prompted.

"Rosie says Mrs. Murray was yelling that she'd given him the best years of her life and she wasn't going to be pushed aside now, and he was screamin' that he was the master and he'd do as he pleased. Then Rosie said it went all quiet-like, but you could hear Mrs. Murray crying. Mr. Whitfield started talkin' nicer to her then . . ."

Mrs. Jeffries interrupted. "Where were they when they were having this conversation? I mean, where in the house? Was it somewhere close enough for Rosie to actually overhear them, or is she just taking a guess on what was said when the shouting ended?"

Wiggins grinned broadly. "I wondered about that, too, but Rosie did overhear 'em. She and one of the tweenies crept up and put their ears to his study door. But it's a ruddy thick door, and all they could hear was him sayin' somethin' like, 'There's only so much I can do with my money, you know that.' Anyways, they'd no idea what those words meant, and frankly I can't figure it out, either."

"It could mean most of his estate is entailed," Hatchet murmured. "But if that's the case, why would he even bother calling in his solicitor?"

"Maybe only the house is entailed," Wiggins suggested. "He might 'ave made investments and such that aren't part of the entailment. Besides, he doesn't have any close relations, so even if his property is entailed, maybe there's no one to get it if it doesn't go to Mrs. Murray."

"In which case I believe the estate goes to the crown," Mrs. Jeffries replied. "But before we come to any conclusions about Whitfield's estate, let's try to find out the facts. Rosie could easily have misinterpreted the argument that happened between Mrs. Murray and Whitfield."

"I might be able to find out a few bits and pieces about Whitfield's estate by our meetin' tomorrow," Luty offered. "I ain't promisin' anything for certain—sometimes it takes a day or two to shake any information out of them closemouthed lawyers—but I can try."

"Anything you can find out would be very useful, Luty." Mrs. Jeffries turned back to the footman. "Is that all you heard?"

"The only other thing I found out is that the servants all like Mrs. Murray," Wiggins said. "And I hope she isn't the killer. Rosie said she's a right decent sort. She doesn't take advantage of the servants. She let Rosie have a whole day out because she missed her afternoon off last week. She'd been 'elpin' Mr. Whitfield deliver his fancy port to all his friends. Then, when they got back to the house, there was such a mess in the kitchen from where he'd been corkin' the liquor, she had to help clean it up."

"Just because Mrs. Murray is kind to servants doesn't mean she didn't kill him," Betsy said. "But I understand how you feel. We always want the killer to be someone mean and nasty. But it doesn't always happen that way, does it? Even decent-seeming people can turn out to be murderers."

"I still 'ope it isn't Mrs. Murray," Wiggins said.

"If everyone else is finished, I'll go next," Smythe said. "I didn't learn much today, but my source did confirm that Whitfield had been poisoned. He also said that Hugh Langford has a reputation as a cad, and that Basil Farringdon is from an old aristocratic family but it's his wife that has the cash."

"You mean he married her for her money?" Mrs. Goodge snorted. "There's a surprise."

Smythe grinned. "Don't be so cynical, Mrs. Goodge. Maybe she married him for his position. I also found out that Henry Becker played whist with Whitfield on Thursday nights. Becker almost always lost."

"Doesn't it take four people for whist?" Mrs. Jeffries asked.

The coachman nodded. "Two other men played as well. One is named Thornton and one is named Rogers."

"You'd have to be a pretty sore loser to murder someone over a whist game," Luty muttered. "But I've seen people get real fed up with always gettin' whipped. It's not much of a motive, but you never know."

"It does seem an unlikely motive," Mrs. Jeffries agreed. "But, as you said, one never knows. We'll have to have a close look at Henry Becker."

"We'd have done so in any case," Hatchet commented. "He was at the dinner party."

"Tomorrow I'm going to make the round of the pubs near the Whitfield house and see what I can pick up," Smythe said.

"That's a very good idea," Mrs. Jeffries said. "And as Hatchet has reminded us, we need to find out what we can about all the guests that were at the Whitfield house."

"I'll have a go at seeing what I can learn about Eliza Graham," Luty volunteered. "I was goin' to find out how her husband died anyways."

"Don't forget that you're going to try and find out what you can about Whitfield's estate," Mrs. Jeffries reminded her. Information about who inherited from the dead man would be very useful.

"I didn't forget," Luty replied. "I can do both."

"And I'll see what my sources know about Henry Becker," Hatchet added. "And perhaps I can manage to learn a thing or two about Hugh Langford."

"I'll suss out the Farringdons' neighborhood," Wiggins said. "Maybe I'll get lucky again and find another housemaid that likes to chat."

"Excellent." Mrs. Jeffries glanced toward the window over the sink. Her sharp ears had picked up the sound of a hansom stopping out front. "That might be the inspector."

Before she could complete the sentence, the others were on the move and getting up. Hatchet grabbed Luty's cloak from the back of her chair and draped it across her shoulders. "We'll stop in tomorrow morning to find out what you've learned from the inspector. Put on your gloves, madam," he ordered as he shoved her toward the back door. "It's cold outside."

Luty grinned and waved as she disappeared down the hallway. Betsy was right on their heels, but she veered off into the dry larder. Wiggins went up the back stairs to finish polishing the sconces on the second-floor landing, and Smythe muttered that he wanted to make a quick trip to Howard's to check on Bow and Arrow.

Mrs. Jeffries looked at the cook. "How long will it be before the inspector's dinner is ready to be served?"

"You've a good hour." Mrs. Goodge grinned. "It'll take that long for the pudding to finish. There's plenty of time for you to find out everything he's done today."

CHAPTER 5

Mrs. Jeffries spent the following morning sorting the contents of the upstairs linen closet. She'd learned a great deal while the inspector had eaten his dinner, and now she needed to think about everything he'd told her. Sometimes keeping her hands busy helped to free up her mind. She'd shared the information with the others this morning during their brief meeting, and everyone except for Mrs. Goodge had gone off to hunt for clues.

Mrs. Jeffries pulled a stack of sheets out of the closet and laid them on the top of the old tea trolley she used for household tasks. This case was still very much a puzzle. From what she'd heard from the inspector, Basil and Maria Farringdon could become suspects, but so far they'd no motive for wanting Whitfield dead. She leaned down and pulled her dusting rag from the second shelf of the trolley, straightened up, and swept the cloth around the inside of the cupboard. She paused as she remembered a tidbit she'd heard from the inspector. Maria Farringdon had been insulted by Whitfield about her champagne cups. But that was hardly a motive for murder, unless the killer was completely unbalanced. Thus far, they'd no evidence that Maria Farringdon was insane.

Rosalind Murray was still very much in the running as a suspect, since she'd had a screaming argument with Whitfield. But as for what it had been about—well, they were still in the dark over that issue. Experience had shown Mrs. Jeffries that information obtained by eavesdropping through heavy doors could easily be misinterpreted. Mrs. Jeffries grunted as she stretched to reach the far corner of the shelf with her cloth.

What about Eliza Graham? Where did she fit into this strange story? On the surface, it appeared that she was now pushing Mrs. Murray aside in Whitfield's affections. Perhaps that might be another reason for taking a second look at Rosalind Murray. The old adages often proved true: Hell hath no fury like a woman scorned. But then again, Mrs. Graham had brought Hugh Langford with her to dinner that night. Mrs. Jeffries had no idea what bearing that might have on the case. Perhaps it meant nothing, and Langford simply happened to be in the wrong place at the wrong time. Such occurrences happened frequently. Or perhaps there was more to his being there than it appeared.

She stepped back and surveyed the inside of the dark cupboard as best she could. It would do. She laid the rag down and put the sheets back into the closet. Reaching into the bowl of dewberry wood chips on the top of the trolley, she picked up a handful and tossed them onto the stack of sheets.

She moved to the next shelf and pulled out the pillowcases. She glanced at the bowl of dewberry chips. There were only half a dozen left. Betsy had told her that this was the last of them. She frowned as she thought of the maid. Betsy was still keeping her distance from Smythe. At breakfast this morning, she'd spoken barely two words to him. Mrs. Jeffries wondered just how much of that sort of behavior he was going to tolerate.

Smythe loved the girl dearly, but he was a proud man. At some point he was going to get tired of waiting for her to forgive him. She hoped that Betsy would come to her senses soon. Smythe's decision to go, honorable and noble as it had been, had hurt her deeply. But he was back now, and that which had been broken could be mended. The human heart was far more malleable than most people realized. Betsy would get over this, and if she didn't, she'd lose a very good man. Men like Smythe didn't grow on trees. Mrs. Jeffries wondered if it might be wise to drop a hint or two in Betsy's direction; then she realized it was really none of her business. The two of them had to work this out for themselves. She sighed heavily. She knew that there was nothing certain in this life but change; yet the thought of Smythe's leaving permanently and their little band's being broken up prematurely filled her with despair. That was one change that didn't have to happen if Smythe and Betsy would sit down like adults and talk to each other.

She finished the dusting, replaced the pillowcases, and tossed in the last of the wood chips. Mrs. Jeffries took off her apron, draped it over the trolley, and then pushed the trolley into the spare room at the end of the hallway. The house was in good order. It was time for her to get out and about.

Mr. Henry Becker lived in a six-story brick house on a short road off the Marylebone High Street. A tall, austere butler opened the door and immediately ushered them inside. "Mr. Becker has been expecting you," the butler said as he led them to the drawing room. "He'd like you to make yourselves comfortable. I'll tell him you're here."

Witherspoon raised his eyebrows. "That's a surprise," he said as soon as the servant had left.

"It is indeed, sir. People of this class usually behave as if they're doing us a favor by even opening the door." Barnes glanced around the opulently furnished room. The ceiling was a good twelve feet high, with an enormous crystal chandelier smack in the middle. A grand piano was in one corner, and a gold gilt harp stood next to it. Gold brocade curtains hung from the three tall windows, and the floor was covered with a green and gold fleur-de-lys-patterned carpet. The same pattern was duplicated in the white and gold wallpaper. Vases of ivy and holly stood on top of all the cabinets and tabletops. Evergreen boughs tied with huge red velvet ribbons lay across the top of the mantelpiece, and tall silver candlesticks, also festooned with red ribbons, stood on each end. "Mr. Becker didn't stint himself on his Christmas decorations."

"Indeed he didn't. The gentleman also appears to enjoy bright colors," Witherspoon murmured as he looked at the Empire-style furniture upholstered in silver, gray, and gold brocade.

The door opened and Henry Becker hurried into the room, a welcoming smile on his face. "Oh, good, you're here. I've been waiting for you." He nodded politely at Witherspoon and Barnes. "I told my man to have you make yourselves comfortable. Do please take a seat. Would either of you care for tea, or perhaps you would prefer coffee?" He gestured toward the sofa, yanked on the bellpull by the door, and then plopped down on a tall wingback chair.

"Thank you, tea would be very nice," Witherspoon replied. He and Barnes sat down. He waited until the constable had taken out his notebook before he started to speak. "I appreciate your seeing

us, Mr. Becker. I know a visit from the police, especially at this
time of the year, isn't very pleasant."

"Nonsense. I find it exciting. I've been looking forward to it."
Becker turned his head as his butler stepped into the room. "Bring
us some tea, please." As soon as the servant left, he turned his attention back to the two policemen. "I must tell you, I was beginning to wonder if you were ever going to come and see me. I'd actually thought perhaps I ought to go alone and see you chaps, but
then you turned up, so all is well."

Witherspoon had never encountered such an eager witness. The
fellow was obviously rich, and at first glance he appeared quite ordinary: average height, darkish hair with a good deal of gray in it,
and very average features. But his eyes sparkled with enthusiasm,
and he'd smiled almost continuously since he'd entered the room.

Perhaps Mr. Becker smiled a bit too much.

The inspector stared at him for a moment before he replied.
"I'm sorry if it appeared we weren't interested in your statement,
Mr. Becker, but we had to wait for the results of the postmortem to
confirm that a crime had actually been committed."

Becker's smile faded, and he pursed his lips. "Yes, I suppose
you do have to wait for official confirmation of some sort, don't
you?"

"We do, sir." The inspector eased back in his seat.

"I quite understand, Inspector. Of course you had to find out if
old Stephen had been poisoned or simply keeled over from natural causes." Becker sighed. "I suppose I ought to be careful in what
I say. Stephen wasn't really that old; we were the same age. We
were at school together. Still, I shouldn't be surprised that it happened."

"Why weren't you surprised, sir?" Barnes asked.

Becker smiled again, though this time his expression was wist-
ful, not eager. "We always lose schoolmates at this time of the
year, so I suppose I've been deluding myself and I really am getting old. I just don't feel any differently than I did when I was a
lad."

"That's most unfortunate, sir," Witherspoon replied. "Losing
old friends is always painful, especially at this festive season."

"It most certainly is." Becker broke off as the butler returned
with their tea. "Put it down on the table, Manley. I'll pour."

"Yes, sir." The servant put the tray down next to Becker and then withdrew, closing the door quietly behind him as he left the room.

Becker picked up the silver pot and poured tea into the three cups. "Do you take sugar, Inspector?"

"Two lumps, please."

"And you, Constable?"

"Three lumps, sir," Barnes replied.

"As I was saying"—Becker handed Witherspoon his tea—"Christmas used to be my favorite time of the year, but now it looks as if I'm going to another funeral come January." He handed Barnes his tea. "Luckily, it's so cold out that one doesn't have to worry about decomposition, does one?"

The inspector glanced at Barnes, and the constable gave a barely perceptible shrug. He, too, thought Becker's conversation more than a little strange.

"They never have the funerals until after the holidays, so I suppose they must store the corpses someplace," Becker continued. "Do they use cellars or some sort of cold storage?"

"I'm not certain," Witherspoon replied.

"There are several places where bodies are kept," Barnes said. "Now that Mr. Whitfield's postmortem is completed, the body will be released to a funeral parlor or an undertaker's establishment. His family will make that decision."

"He didn't really have any family except for Rosalind, and she's only a sister-in-law. Does that count?" Becker asked curiously.

"I don't know," Witherspoon replied. "I imagine his solicitor has all the particulars about his burial."

"I doubt it. I expect Stephen thought he'd live forever," Becker said cheerfully. "His own death is the sort of subject he wouldn't like to think about. Poor Rosalind will probably get stuck making the arrangements."

"Er, uh, Mr. Becker, you said you were at school with Mr. Whitfield," Witherspoon began.

"Right, we were at Eton together. Whitfield and I were in the same house." Becker grinned broadly. "Stephen didn't like school very much, but, then, neither did I."

"Was Basil Farringdon also in your house?" The inspector took a sip of his tea.

"He was. He was quite good at sports, as I recall."

"And you've all been friends ever since?" Barnes asked. He

studied Becker closely, wondering whether the man had a firm grip on all his faculties. In his long years as a policeman, he'd sometimes arrested people who had obviously committed the crime in question, but he'd sensed that, though those people appeared rational, they really weren't. There were simply some poor souls who completely lost their hold on this world and slipped into another one. But Barnes' job was to keep the peace, and though he often felt very sorry for these unfortunate folk, they couldn't be allowed to run around engaging in murder or mayhem. He thought that Becker had the same sort of look in his eyes, almost as if he wasn't quite all there. Still, the man was rich as sin and probably had a ruddy platoon of lawyers at his beck and call, so they'd better take his statement seriously.

"More or less," Becker answered. "We lost touch for a few years when I was traveling, but once I was back in the country, we renewed our acquaintance." He took a sip of his tea. "Actually, now that I think of it, we lost touch for longer than that. I was back in London for ages before I ran into Stephen. Yes, that's right—his wife had just died. We happened to come across each other at a dinner party. I suppose that was when we sort of reacquainted ourselves."

"How long ago was this?" Witherspoon took another sip of tea. It really was excellent.

Becker thought for a moment. "Let me see. His wife died about ten or eleven years ago—yes, that's right." He gave a short bark of a laugh. "Shortly after that, Rosalind moved in to be his housekeeper. That set a few tongues wagging, I can tell you."

"Yes, I'm sure it did," Witherspoon replied. He found this all very interesting, but as it had happened more than a decade ago, he didn't see how old gossip could have any relevance to who might have wanted to murder Whitfield now. "What time did you arrive at the Whitfield house the night of the death?"

"A few minutes past seven," Becker replied. "My hansom pulled up just as the Farringdons were going inside."

"And what time was dinner served?" Barnes asked. They already had that information, but he wanted to confirm as much of Basil Farringdon's statement as possible.

"Eight o'clock. We had drinks first, and then Stephen ushered us into the morning room to have a look at his Christmas tree. It was rather lovely." He broke off and looked around the room. "I'm thinking of having one here next year. I think that corner over by the fireplace would be perfect. Mind you, one does need a footman on duty to make sure the candles don't burn the house down, but we've plenty of footmen here and most of them don't appear to be doing much of anything."

"Yes, I'm sure that would be just the right spot for it," the inspector murmured. "Er, uh, what happened then?"

Becker dragged his gaze away from the proposed spot for next year's Christmas tree and looked at the two policemen. "What happened when?"

"When you were in the morning room looking at the tree," Witherspoon prompted. "What happened at that point in the evening?"

Becker looked confused. "We all stood around and chatted and admired Stephen's tree."

"Perhaps I'm not making myself clear." Witherspoon smiled grimly. "What we need to know is the sequence of events throughout the evening. Could you describe everything that happened from the time you arrived until the moment Mr. Whitfield collapsed?"

Becker's expression brightened. "Of course, of course, that's precisely what you'd need to know. Now give me a moment to think, Inspector. I do want to get this right."

They sipped their tea in silence for a few minutes while Becker gathered his thoughts. Finally he said, "I came in just after the Farringdons, and I must admit I was a bit annoyed."

"Why was that, sir?" Barnes asked. He still couldn't decide whether Becker was just a lonely man who took any and all opportunities to chat, or whether he was a tad unbalanced.

"They'd brought a gift and I hadn't," he admitted. "It was slightly awkward for a few minutes. Stephen was waving about this bottle of Bordeaux, telling me they'd brought it for him, while I stood there empty-handed. Stephen had given me one of his bottles of port. Dreadful stuff—I can't abide it—but I could hardly refuse to take it. Last year I gave it to my next-door neighbor. But he's dead now, so I am rather stuck with the stuff. I suppose it'll sit in my wine cellar till I give it to one of my servants or find some other poor soul to foist it on."

* * *

Wiggins dropped to his knee and pretended to tie his shoe. He was directly across the road from the Farringdon house and he wanted to get the lay of the land, so to speak. He kept his eye on the staircase to the left of the front door—the stairs leading down to the kitchen, the ones the servants used.

"How long does it take to tie a bloomin' shoelace? Get a move on. You're blocking the pavement," a woman's voice said from behind him.

He leapt up and whirled about, coming face-to-face with a middle-aged woman carrying a shopping basket over her arm. "Sorry, ma'am." He doffed his cap respectfully and moved out of her way. "There was a knot in the lace."

She continued onward, but her harsh features relaxed a bit as she passed him. "No harm done, lad."

"Excuse me, ma'am." He hurried after her. "But I'm lookin' for a family named Farringdon. Do you know them?"

"They live just over there." She pointed to the house he'd been watching, and kept walking. "But they're not lookin' for staff."

"Are you sure, ma'am?" he asked. "I heard they've just lost two footmen, and I've references."

"They haven't lost any footmen," she said, slowing her footsteps and turning to look at him. "And I ought to know. I'm well acquainted with their housekeeper."

Wiggins desperately tried to think of a way to keep this woman talking, but as she wasn't a young girl he could flirt with or a young lad he could lure to a teahouse with the promise of a sweet bun, he wasn't certain what to do. "I guess my friend was wrong, then," he finally said. "I'm sorry to have troubled you, ma'am."

"Don't worry, lad. It was no trouble," she replied as she continued walking. "You might try at the Addison house. They live just around the corner at number seven Connaught Square. No, don't bother goin' there—they get their staff from a domestic agency. Are you with an agency?"

"No, ma'am."

"But you have references?" She suddenly stumbled and pitched forward. She threw out her arms in a futile attempt to catch her balance and would have fallen flat on her face if not for Wiggins. He managed to grab her shoulders and pull her back onto her feet.

"Gracious! Thank you, lad." She was panting hard, frightened by losing her footing. "You saved me from taking a nasty fall. That was kind of you"

"Are you all right, ma'am?" He kept his hand on her elbow as he steadied her. "There's a nasty crack in the pavement there. Someone could really hurt themselves. The council ought to do something about that."

She was still panting and had gone quite pale. "Yes, I suppose they should. But I suspect they won't bother until someone breaks a limb and threatens a lawsuit."

Wiggins whipped off his cap. "Excuse me for bein' so bold, ma'am, but you've gone quite white. I think you need a cup of tea to calm your nerves. There's a Lyons teahouse just up the road . . ."

"There's a café around the corner." She pointed back the way she'd come. "Which is a lot cheaper than a Lyons. I'd be pleased to buy you a cup, young man. You're unemployed and you've just saved me from hurting myself. Let's introduce ourselves properly. I'm Matilda Jones. What's your name?"

Wiggins couldn't believe his luck. Ten minutes later, he was sitting across from Mrs. Jones at a window table with a cup of hot tea in front of him. Her shopping basket was on the chair beside her.

"I'm sorry there are no positions available at the Farringdon house," she said. "They treat their servants quite well."

"That's why I wanted a position there," he replied. "I 'eard they're real decent. Mind you, I also 'eard some other strange bits, but I didn't pay any attention, as it was just gossip."

Wiggins was making it up as he went along, hoping she'd supply him with some information. He'd noticed that if you acted as though you knew something, people often felt a need to tell you what they knew or had heard about the same subject.

"If you're referring to that silly rumor about Maria Farringdon poisoning the Whitfield man, it's nonsense." She sniffed disapprovingly. "Mrs. Farringdon wouldn't do such a thing."

"I'm sure you're right, ma'am." He took a quick sip and tried to think of the best way to keep her talking.

"There are far too many people in this world who have nothing better to do than sit around making up outlandish stories and gossiping."

"You're right, ma'am. I shouldn't 'ave even mentioned I'd 'eard rumors about the household," he said quickly.

"The very idea that someone of her class and background would do such a thing is absurd." She paused and took a deep breath. "Of course she's not from the same background as her husband, but according to Mrs. Mulch—she's their housekeeper and my friend—Mrs. Farringdon works very hard to be a credit to Mr. Farringdon. She takes great pains to ensure she observes all the proper social etiquette."

"I'm sure she does."

"Mrs. Farringdon does occasionally take her diligence a bit too far—at least that's what Mrs. Mulch thinks, and I quite agree with her." Mrs. Jones leaned across the table and dropped her voice. "When she goes to a really posh party, she brings home the wine bottles."

"Wine bottles," he repeated.

Mrs. Jones nodded. "She has her footman go around to the kitchen and fetch them for her. Mrs. Mulch says the footmen hate doing it."

"Maybe it's just as well there aren't any positions available with the Farringdons," he said thoughtfully. "I don't think I'd much enjoy doing something like that, either. What does she do with all of 'em?"

Smythe stayed far enough behind Betsy that she wouldn't spot him, but not so far as to lose her completely. There wasn't enough privacy for them at Upper Edmonton Gardens, and he needed to speak to her. They couldn't go on this way. He had to talk to her. He was going to be making the rounds of the pubs in the Whitfield neighborhood again today, and as they weren't open yet, he thought it would be a good time for the two of them to clear the air.

He watched her pull open a door and step into a grocer's shop. Smythe hurried over and stood just outside the window. He peeked inside. The shop was empty of customers, save for Betsy. The clerk was up on a ladder behind the counter, putting tins on the top shelf.

Smythe stepped back. If he could see Betsy, she could see him, too. A few seconds later, he took another look. The clerk had climbed down off the ladder and was talking to Betsy. He was a young man, probably no more than twenty, tall and handsome in a foppish, silly sort of way.

The clerk dusted his hands on the front of his apron and said something to Betsy that made her laugh. She cocked her head co-quettishly and made some comment in reply. Ye gods, Smythe couldn't believe his eyes. How dare she smile at a strange man like that? She was engaged to be married.

The clerk said something else, but Smythe couldn't hear the words. But whatever it was made her laugh again. Then she turned her head in Smythe's direction. He ducked back just in time.

When he looked again, she was smiling at the clerk and chatting as if they were old friends. Didn't the woman have any sense at all? That clerk was leering at her.

Smythe glared at her through the shop window. Now she was laughing again at something else the stupid git said. This was un-believable. There was no mistaking her manner: she was out-and-out flirting. Blast a Spaniard, she was practically a married woman! Here they were engaged, and she was in there carrying on as though she'd set her cap for the man.

Just then she turned, and this time he wasn't quick enough. She saw him. Her eyes widened and her jaw dropped. Then she said something to the clerk, turned, and marched toward the door.

When she stepped outside, she did not look pleased to see Smythe. "Are you following me?"

"I just wanted to talk to you away from the house," he began. "So, yes, I suppose you could say I was following you."

"You were spying on me?" She put her hands on her hips and glared at him.

"No, I was waitin' for you. That's all. But I couldn't 'elp notic-ing you were battin' your eyes at that clerk like you'd set your heart on 'im."

Betsy's mouth gaped. "Set my heart on him? Don't be ridicu-lous. I was trying to find out something useful."

"I'll bet you found out plenty," he shot back. He was hurt, an-gry, and scared. Betsy was a beautiful girl, and any man would want her. What did he have to offer? Just money, and she wasn't interested in that.

"What do you mean? I was doing what I always do." Out of the corner of her eye, she saw the clerk start to move toward the door. A confrontation between an angry fiancé and a gallant young gro-cer's clerk was the last thing she needed. "Come on. If we're go-ing to argue, let's get out of the street to do it. People are staring."

She turned on her heel and started up the road. When he just stood there, she whirled around. "Come on, then. Let's have this out once and for all."

"And where do you propose having this out?" he cried. He was starting to panic. It hadn't occurred to him that she'd force the issue this way. He could tell she wasn't talking only about this petty little incident. He wasn't sure he was ready for this.

"There's a park around the corner," she snapped. "We can talk there. I'm tired of all this. Let's get it out in the open, and we'll each have our say."

She stomped off toward the corner. Smythe hesitated. If he turned and walked the other way, she wouldn't be able to end it for good. But that was the coward's way out, and by all the saints, he wasn't a coward. He hurried after her. Come what may, he'd face it. If she wanted it over, well, he could always go back to Australia.

"What did you think, sir?" Barnes asked as they came out onto Marylebone High Street. He waved at a hansom dropping off a fare farther up the road.

"I think Henry Becker is a bit eccentric, but not strange enough for us to discount his statement. Ah, good, you've got us a cab," Witherspoon said as it pulled up. He climbed in and slid to the far side, leaving room for the constable.

"Elm Park Gardens in Chelsea," Barnes called to the driver. He slipped in beside the inspector. "That was my impression as well, sir. Too bad his statement didn't really contain any information we didn't already know."

"True, but he did confirm Basil Farringdon's account of the evening," Witherspoon said.

"And he also gave us a bit of gossip." Barnes grinned. "That's always useful. Perhaps we'll have as much luck with Mrs. Graham."

"Let's hope the lady is at home." He frowned thoughtfully. "Becker did confirm the idea that any of them could have done it."

"The open bottle was sitting there for almost an hour," Barnes agreed. "It's too bad that so far none of our witnesses remembers exactly who went where at any specific time. But I guess people don't look at their pocket watches or a clock every time someone leaves a room."

"It would be most useful if people did," Witherspoon murmured. "After we finish taking statements, I want to go back to the

Whitfield house and have another go at speaking to the servants. Perhaps one of them noticed if anyone spent any time alone in the drawing room. But then again, even if someone did go in there on his own, that would hardly prove he put the poison in the bottle."

"It might give us a place to start," Barnes said. "So far our best suspect is one of the Farringdons, and neither of them had any reason to want Whitfield dead."

Witherspoon smiled faintly. "Well, Whitfield did make light of Mrs. Farringdon's champagne cups last summer. She might still be a tad annoyed about that. But I hardly think the woman would commit murder over such a trifle."

Barnes laughed. "You never know, sir. Some women take their food and drink very seriously. What I really wonder is how they got the poison into the house. According to the postmortem report, a large amount of crushed leaves were found in the victim. That means the killer had to get them into the house and into the bottle of Bordeaux without anyone noticing. I don't think that would be particularly easy."

"Why not?" Witherspoon asked. "It seems to me that tucking an envelope filled with crushed leaves somewhere on your person would be simple. Then all the killer would need to do would be to wait till there was no one about, and tip the leaves into the bottle."

"An envelope," Barnes said thoughtfully. "I hadn't thought of that. In my mind's eye, I saw the leaves in one of those tiny glass vials or a little wood box. But you're right, of course. An envelope would be the simplest solution."

"And it would be easy to get rid of the remaining evidence," Witherspoon continued enthusiastically. "The killer could simply chuck the envelope into a fireplace or a stove. There would be nothing left for us to find."

"That's a dreary thought, sir," Barnes replied. "The last thing we need on this murder is a clever killer."

As the hansom made its way through the busy West End streets, they discussed what few facts they had so far. As the cab pulled up in front of the Graham house, a drizzle began to fall. Witherspoon turned up his collar and gazed at the four-story redbrick town house as he waited for Barnes to pay the driver. The dwelling was in excellent condition, the door freshly painted a bright blue, the black iron railing in the front free of rust, and the brass lamps brightly polished.

Barnes moved past Witherspoon and banged the heavy brass door knocker.

A few seconds later, a housemaid holding a feather duster opened the door and peered out at them, her expression curious. "Hello."

"We'd like to see Mrs. Graham," Barnes said. But the girl was already opening the door and gesturing for them to come inside.

"The mistress is expecting you," she said. She tucked her feather duster under one arm and motioned for them to follow. "If you'll come this way, please."

Witherspoon barely had time to whip off his bowler before the maid led them down a short hallway to a set of double oak doors.

"It's the police, Mrs. Graham," she announced as she stepped back and gestured for the two men to go inside the room.

Eliza Graham was sitting on a rose-colored sofa. She got to her feet as the policemen entered. "Good day, gentlemen. I've been expecting you." She smiled courteously.

Witherspoon tried not to stare. He'd seen her only last night at the Whitfield house, but he'd been distracted, and frankly the lighting hadn't been very good. She was past the first flush of youth, but she was still a remarkably lovely woman. He felt a surge of guilt as the image of Ruth Cannonberry's sweet smile flashed through his mind. Witherspoon quickly brought his attention back to the matter at hand. "We'll try not to take up too much of your time, Mrs. Graham."

She sank back onto the sofa. "Please sit down. Would you care for some tea?"

"No, thank you, ma'am, though it's most kind of you to offer." Witherspoon sat down on the love seat next to the sofa.

Barnes sat down on a straight-backed upholstered chair and sighed in relief when it was actually comfortable. He glanced around, noting that the room was nicely decorated but lacked the grandiosity of the homes of the truly rich.

Instead of a crystal chandelier, there were wall sconces and hurricane lamps. The oak parquet floor was covered with simple but elegant rugs in rose and cream, and the furniture was good quality without being overblown. Pink muslin curtains hung at the windows, and the walls were painted a clean cream color. The mantel at the far end of the room was covered with knickknacks, and a huge gilt-framed mirror hung directly over the fireplace.

"I assume you've more questions for me," she said. "Though I'm not sure what I can tell you that will be of any use. I've no idea who might have wanted Stephen dead."

Barnes looked up sharply. "How did you know it was murder, ma'am?"

"You wouldn't be here if it wasn't," she replied with a weary smile. "And unlike the others last night, I knew the doctor wouldn't have sent for you if he wasn't fairly sure Stephen had been poisoned."

"Do you know if Mr. Whitfield had any enemies?" Witherspoon cringed inwardly as he did every time he had to ask the silly question.

"If he had enemies, he never discussed the matter with me," she replied.

"Had he been worried or upset about anything recently?" Barnes asked.

"No, I don't think so." She smiled sadly. "Though Stephen wasn't the sort of man to share his troubles. He was a very private person."

"How long have you known Mr. Whitfield?" Witherspoon asked.

"We met a year ago. As a matter of fact, we met at a funeral reception. Odd place to meet someone, I know, but nonetheless, that's where we were introduced. A mutual friend of ours passed away. We were introduced by Basil Farringdon."

"You brought Mr. Langford to the dinner party." Witherspoon hesitated. He hated to be indelicate, but there was no way to ask this sort of question politely. "Yet I understand that Mr. Whitfield had intended to ask you to accompany him to Italy in the spring."

"That's correct," she replied without a trace of embarrassment.

"Was Mr. Whitfield upset when Mr. Langford arrived with you?"

"I'd asked Stephen if I could bring a guest, and he'd told me it was quite alright." She looked down at the floor. "I feel very badly about this whole matter, Inspector. For some reason, Stephen seemed to think we had some kind of understanding between us."

"I take it that wasn't the case," Witherspoon said softly.

"No, it wasn't. He'd proposed to me, and he acted as if we were engaged. But the truth of the matter is that we weren't. I'd never agreed to marry him."

"Had you agreed to go to Italy with Mr. Whitfield in the

spring?" Barnes interjected. "From what we understand, he'd already begun making plans and arranged for a letter of credit with his bank."

"Stephen could be very arrogant. He presumed too much." She shook her head. "He'd badgered me for an answer, but I'd not committed to that trip, nor had I agreed to marry him. We'd only discussed the matter."

"Yet Mr. Whitfield was confident enough of your response that he was preparing to make an announcement of your engagement at dinner that night. Isn't that correct?" Witherspoon pressed. He'd learned that when the questions took off in one specific direction, it was best to follow up.

"He was preparing to make some sort of announcement, Inspector." She smiled coolly. "But I've no idea what it might have been. He died before he could say anything."

"Mrs. Murray is quite certain he was preparing to announce your engagement," the inspector said. Rosalind Murray hadn't actually said any such thing, but she'd certainly implied it.

"She can say whatever she likes, but that doesn't mean it's true."

"Had you specifically told Mr. Whitfield you weren't going to accept his proposal?" Witherspoon asked.

She sighed, glanced down at the floor again, and then looked back up at the two men. "No, and for that I feel awful, especially now that poor Stephen is dead. I was trying to be kind, you see. It was Christmas, and I didn't want to ruin the holiday for him. He was making such a fuss about the season that I simply didn't have the heart to turn him down. I was going to wait until Boxing Day before I told him. That's why I invited Mr. Langford to accompany me to Stephen's dinner party that night. I was hoping that Stephen would take the hint that it was over. But he didn't. He simply acted the fool and kept trying to make his announcement. Oh, I might as well admit it. Rosalind Murray is correct. I do think he was going to announce our engagement, even though I'd not agreed to marry him." She laughed harshly. "Stephen was a great believer in taking matters into his own hands. He once told me that he'd managed to hang on to a great deal of money by taking direct action instead of waiting for life to reward him."

Witherspoon nodded in encouragement. "So his death . . ."

She interrupted. "Saved me a great deal of trouble and embarrassment, Inspector. But as I'd no idea he was going to do something quite so stupid, I could hardly have thought to bring along a supply of poison, could I?"

"We're not accusing you of anything," Witherspoon replied.

"You really ought to ask Rosalind Murray what she thought about Stephen's sudden declaration." Eliza smiled grimly. "She hated me, and what's more, I think she hated Stephen. He'd been playing her for a fool for years, and I think she finally got fed up with him."

"What do you mean?" Barnes looked up from his notebook.

"I mean that if anyone benefits from Stephen's death, it will probably be her. She'll inherit his house, and that's all she needs to live decently."

"You know this for a fact?" Witherspoon glanced at the constable and then back at Eliza Graham.

"Of course I do," she replied. "Why do you think I decided not to marry Stephen?"

"You weren't in love with him?"

She gave a short bark of a laugh. "Love? What's that got to do with marriage?" She waved her arm, gesturing at the room. "Have a good look around, Inspector. My late husband left me very little money. It looks comfortable enough here, but I don't own any of it. It all belongs to my dear departed husband's family, and they let me live here on sufferance. They don't quite have the nerve to face the gossip that would ensue if they actually chucked me out into the street. I have nothing more than a small allowance from his estate, so I've no choice: I must remarry."

"But Mr. Whitfield could have kept you quite decently," Barnes ventured.

"Only as long as he was alive," she said. "And I'm not going through that kind of misery again."

"I'm afraid I don't understand," Witherspoon admitted. "Why wouldn't you inherit Mr. Whitfield's estate if you and he married?"

"Because he doesn't own anything," she explained. "The house is going to Mrs. Murray, and all the income goes back into the annuity. It doesn't pass on to his heirs."

"Annuity? What annuity?" Witherspoon was terribly confused by this turn of events. "But who inherits the annuity? I mean, someone has to inherit it."

She shrugged. "I'm not certain of all the details about the wretched thing. You'll have to speak to Stephen's solicitor."

"Why would Mrs. Murray get the house?" Barnes blurted. He was a bit confused as well.

"Because the house belonged to his late wife's family," Eliza said. "Under the terms of his wife's will, he can live in the house for the remainder of his life, but upon his death, the property goes back to her family. The only one of them left is Rosalind Murray."

"Mrs. Murray inherits the house," the inspector repeated. He wondered why Rosalind Murray hadn't mentioned this fact during their interview.

"That's right." Eliza smiled cynically. "So it seems the person who most directly benefits from Stephen's death is his dear sister-in-law. That's the only reason she agreed to move in and become his housekeeper, you know. She wanted to make sure the place was kept in good order. Everyone thought it was because she was in love with Stephen, but I don't believe that for a moment. She didn't care one whit about him, and she certainly didn't want to be tied down with another marriage."

"So Mr. Whitfield didn't own any property?" Barnes asked. "Is that correct?"

"As far as I know, he only had the house and the income from the annuity," she replied. "The Whitfield family estate was sold when the annuity was created, and that was years and years ago. The only other fact I know about the mess is that Stephen's heirs would receive nothing when he died, and as I've lived with that once before, it'll be a cold day in the pits of Hades before I do it again."

CHAPTER 6

Mrs. Jeffries tightened the ribbons under her chin as a blast of wind almost tugged her bonnet completely off her head. When she was satisfied that her hat was secure, she turned her attention to the Whitfield house, studied it for a moment, and then stepped back behind a lamppost. Even though there were no constables at the front door, she knew the police were lurking about the neighborhood.

She turned and surveyed the street, wondering if there were still constables doing a house-to-house. Then she realized that, due to the nature of the crime, it was unlikely the inspector had wasted police resources on talking to the neighbors. This murder was definitely a domestic crime, so to speak. The killer would hardly have lurked about outside, waiting for an opportunity to sneak in and chuck some foxglove leaves into an open bottle of wine.

The street seemed ordinary enough as people went about their daily business. A few doors up, a housemaid swept the front steps; directly across from where she stood, a young lad was polishing the door lamps. A butcher's van pulled up at the house next door, and Mrs. Jeffries watched as a deliveryman leapt out, opened the back, and pulled out a large wicker basket, which he hefted onto his shoulders. As he started for the servants' entrance, their gazes met and he nodded respectfully. She inclined her head in acknowledgment and then began to walk down the street.

She couldn't linger here all day. She didn't want any of the neighbors peeking out their front windows and noticing an unfamiliar person loitering about the neighborhood. A murder in the area made people nervous. But she wasn't overly disappointed that she had to move on: she hadn't expected to actually talk to anyone from the Whitfield household. She wasn't as skilled as the others at getting information out of strangers, but nonetheless she'd wanted to see where the murder took place.

A blast of wind slammed into her so unexpectedly, she stumbled backward.

"Careful, Mrs. Jeffries. This wind is the very devil," a familiar female voice said.

Just then she felt a hand on her back, steadying her. Mrs. Jeffries whirled about. "Gracious, it's Mrs. Bowden. Goodness, this is a surprise. I haven't seen you in ages. How are you?"

Geraldine Bowden laughed. She was a tall, broad-shouldered woman with blue eyes and graying brown hair. "I'm well, thank you. I've been trying to catch up with you. I saw you on the High Street, coming out of the draper's shop, and followed along, hoping to say hello."

"That was most kind of you." Mrs. Jeffries smiled broadly. She liked Geraldine Bowden. She was a widow who supplemented her late husband's pension by doing a bit of extra cleaning. She worked for the domestic agency that Mrs. Jeffries used when they needed extra help with the heavy spring cleaning. "Are you working in this neighborhood now?" Unless Mrs. Bowden's economic circumstances had changed greatly since they'd last met, she couldn't afford to live in a posh area such as this one.

"Indeed I am. But I'm no longer with the domestic agency," she explained. "I was offered a position as a live-in housekeeper and caretaker. The house is just around the corner. That's one of the reasons I followed you: I was hoping you'd have time for a cup of tea."

Mrs. Jeffries couldn't believe her good fortune. Perhaps this case wasn't going to be as difficult to solve as it first appeared. "That would be wonderful. I should love a cup of tea. It's so very cold out."

"Come along, then, and we'll have a nice long natter." She took Mrs. Jeffries' arm and led her up the road, talking as they walked. "It's quite a grand place," she said as they rounded the corner. "And I never thought I'd be living in such splendor."

Mrs. Jeffries stared at the six-story redbrick house and nodded in agreement. "It's certainly huge. How many staff does it take to keep it in good order?"

"Right now there's just me." Geraldine Bowden pulled a set of keys out of her pocket and charged up the steps to the front door. "Come on inside, and I'll tell you all about how I came to be here."

Ten minutes later, the two women were sitting in the kitchen, and Geraldine Bowden was handing her a cup of steaming tea.

"How long have you been here?" Mrs. Jeffries asked. "And more importantly, how can you possibly run a place this size with no staff?"

"I've been here a little over a year." Mrs. Bowden took the chair opposite her. "And I can run it easily enough, as it stays empty most of the time. The man who owns it travels quite a bit. But he wanted someone to live in and keep an eye on the house. That's why I'm here all on my own. You know what London is like these days. You've got to be on the watch. Turn your back for a second and the silver's gone missing, if you know what I mean. Not like when we were girls. People kept to their own business back then."

"Times aren't as peaceful as they once were," Mrs. Jeffries replied. She didn't agree with that sentiment in the least. London had always been infested with burglars, thieves, and thugs. The only difference between now and when they'd been young was that back then there wasn't nearly as much access to daily newspapers. Nowadays crimes were reported in the press sometimes within hours and always within a day or two of their discovery.

"We had a murder just around the corner from here," Mrs. Bowden continued. "Can you believe it? If murder can happen in a neighborhood as nice as this one, it can happen anywhere." She paused briefly. "Oh, but you probably already know about the murder, don't you? I imagine that you hear about all of them, seein' as how you work for Inspector Witherspoon."

Mrs. Jeffries realized how very unskilled she was at this sort of thing. It was impossible to know whether to answer in the affirmative or whether it would be more effective to say little and give the other person a chance to show off what they knew. "Well . . . he did mention something . . ." she muttered.

"Of course he did," Geraldine continued cheerfully. "Every man likes to talk about his work. My Reggie, God rest his soul, used to go on and on about the factory. I expect your inspector is no different, especially as he hasn't a wife. The Whitfield murder has been the talk of the neighborhood, I can tell you that. He was poisoned at his own dinner party. One minute he was eating his soup, and the next, his face was in it. He died of foxglove poisoning."

"I believe the inspector did mention that as well." Mrs. Jeffries wasn't in the least surprised that details had already gotten out to the locals. In her experience, servants were very efficient when it came to finding out who, what, where, and why. "Are you here on your own right now?"

"Oh, yes, Mr. Owens is traveling." She grinned. "But not to worry. From what I hear, the killer isn't some maniac roaming the streets, looking for people to murder. It was someone Mr. Whitfield knew, someone who was at the dinner party, so I ought to be perfectly safe."

"That's reassuring," Mrs. Jeffries replied.

"Whoever killed Mr. Whitfield didn't just sneak into his house and poison the poor man; it was obviously planned. The poison was in a bottle of wine. Well, no one's given me any wine, and if I found anything to eat or drink on my doorstep, I'd chuck it away."

"Gracious, was the wine simply found on the man's doorstep?"

"Oh, goodness no, it was a gift from one of his dinner guests." Mrs. Bowden laughed. "Mind you, I don't think the Farringdons will be taking any more wine to the parties they attend, not now that poor old Stephen Whitfield keeled over from drinking the bottle they brought as a gift. Everyone says it was the wine that had the poison in it, but I expect you'd know more about that than me, seeing as how you work for the inspector in charge of the case." She eyed Mrs. Jeffries speculatively. "Has he said anything about the murder?"

Mrs. Jeffries believed that to get information, one had to give a bit back. "Of course he's very discreet," she began, "but he did mention that the wine had come from the Farringdons and that it had been a Christmas gift. He also mentioned the Farringdons were the only guests who brought a gift that night. He thought that very odd."

"But it wasn't, you see. The Farringdons had to bring a present," Geraldine protested. "Mr. Whitfield had started sending them one of his bottles of port for Christmas, so they had to show up with something. As to the other guests not bringing anything, well, I'm not surprised. Henry Becker is a bachelor and doesn't have a wife to remind him of his social responsibilities."

"He's never married, then?" she asked. As she wasn't hearing anything she didn't already know about the Farringdons, she was happy to move on to one of the other suspects.

"Oh, no, women of his own class wouldn't have him, and Becker is too much of a snob to consider marrying anyone but his social equal. Not like Basil Farringdon. Mr. Farringdon was quite happy to marry a woman of inferior social status."

"Why wouldn't a woman of his own background have him?" Mrs. Jeffries asked.

Geraldine took a sip of tea. "From the gossip I've heard, there's more than a touch of madness in the Becker family. And it's the bad kind, not the harmless, silly kind, if you get my meaning."

"I'm not sure that I do," Mrs. Jeffries replied.

"There's a bit of violence in the family tree." Geraldine bobbed her head for emphasis. "Years ago, Henry Becker's father stabbed his mother with a carving knife. Pulled it right out of the Christmas goose and stuck it in the poor lady's arm."

"Gracious, that's terrible."

"And all that blood put everyone right off their dinner," Geraldine added. "They had guests, you see. That's how the story got out and everyone heard about the incident. It kept poor Henry from ever having much of a chance to find a wife. His sister, Drusilla, had to go all the way to Canada to find herself a husband. But Henry didn't really like to travel, so he hadn't much hope of finding anyone from his own class that was willing to overlook the fact that they are a half-mad lot."

"But surely one incident years ago . . ."

"Oh it wasn't just one incident," Geraldine interrupted eagerly. "There was terrible gossip about Henry's grandfather as well. Supposedly he was so insane, he was locked in the attic for doing terrible things to the servant girls. People aren't as willing to overlook those sorts of things as they once were, and Henry Becker ended up an old bachelor."

"Perhaps he didn't wish to marry," Mrs. Jeffries murmured.

"Oh, but he did. He proposed to Isadora Hallowell, but even though he'd lots more money, she turned him down and married Stephen Whitfield instead. Rumor has it that she didn't want her children tainted by the madness of the Becker blood. But seein' as how poor Isadora and Stephen never had children anyway, I suppose it turned out not to matter much."

Mrs. Jeffries took another sip of her tea to give herself time to think. She hadn't remembered Geraldine Bowden being such a chatterbox, but then again she'd only ever known the woman in the capacity of employer to employee. "How sad for poor Mr. Becker."

Geraldine nodded in agreement. "It doesn't seem fair. Despite the lunacy that runs in the family, Henry Becker was never violent with anyone, at least not that I have heard."

"Perhaps he was just better at hiding his faults," she replied.

"Perhaps so," Geraldine said. "People can get very clever at hiding their true selves from others, can't they?"

"I suspect that's a characteristic we all have, to some degree or other."

"I certainly do." Geraldine grinned broadly. "Many a time, if I'd said or acted upon my true thoughts, I'd not have had a position. If Mr. Owens actually knew my real opinion of his character, he'd sack me on the spot. Thank goodness he's gone most of the time."

"I take it when he's here he's not very pleasant."

"He's a right old tartar." She laughed. "But like I said, he's gone most of the time, and all in all I can't complain. The work is easy, I live well, and I like the neighborhood."

"And you're very well informed about the locals," Mrs. Jeffries said admiringly. "You seem to know more about the Whitfield household than the police do."

"Only because I have tea every week with Flagg. He's the Whitfield butler. He's a bit sweet on me, but nothing will come of it. If I were to take another husband, I'd lose my Reggie's pension. I don't want to do that. Besides, having tea once is week is nice. Actually putting up with another husband would be something else altogether."

"This isn't a park—it's a cemetery," Smythe yelled at Betsy's back as she charged through the open iron gates of the West of London and Westminister Cemetery.

"The dead won't bother us." She looked over her shoulder at him. "And we'll have a bit of privacy here."

He cast a quick glance around as he tried to keep up with her. Mausoleums, statues, and crypts were scattered amongst the uneven rows of graves. Leafless trees and winter-dead bushes swayed eerily as the wind whipped around them, tossing bits of dried grass and brittle leaves into the air. The raw odor of newly turned earth reached his nostrils, and he saw that at the far end of the nearest row, two men were digging a grave. This wasn't the sort of place he'd have picked to try to talk some sense into Betsy. But then again, he'd not been given a choice.

He increased his pace and came abreast of her. She didn't look at him but instead kept moving straight ahead up the central drive. They walked in silence for a few minutes until Betsy pointed to a small path that veered off to the left. "There's a good spot. Come on, let's have this out."

She marched past a headstone of a tall, sword-wielding angel and a line of gravestones standing straight as soldiers in a field before finally stopping at a squat, stubby granite marker with ornate carving along the sides and a man's face carved in the center.

She turned and stared at him. "Now, what is it you want to say?"

Smythe froze. Now that they were here and alone, he was terrified. Why on earth had he pushed her into this confrontation? Why hadn't he let her work some of her anger off? Everyone had warned him to let her get a bit of her own back, but here he was, home less than three days, and he was pushing to get everything settled between them. At least when she was barely speaking to him, he didn't have to hear that she didn't love him, that she didn't ever want to be with him.

"Well?" she demanded. She folded her arms over her chest. "Has the cat got your tongue? You were in a big enough hurry to interrupt me when I was trying to find out information about our murder, so get on with it."

"We can't go on like this," he mumbled.

"I agree."

Blast a Spaniard, he was an idiot. Why hadn't he let well enough alone? "Uh, what do you want to do about it?"

"Do about what? Your spying on me and taking me to task for giving some poor grocer's clerk an innocent smile?"

"He was leerin' at you."

"Don't be daft. He was just a lad. And what's more, he was giving me some useful information about Rosalind Murray."

"Oh, well, I'm sorry, then. I didn't mean to interrupt you." Smythe looked down at the ground. "I just wanted to speak with you privately."

"About what?"

"About us," he replied. "About our situation."

"What do you want to do?" she asked. "You're the one who claims we can't go on like this."

"You agreed," he pointed out. He was getting very confused.

"Only because I didn't know what you wanted me to say," she replied. "Honestly, Smythe, you dog my heels like you don't trust me, when you're the one that ran off for six months, and now that we're alone, now that we've got a bit of time to ourselves, you're as tongue-tied as a green boy. What do you want to do? Just go ahead and tell me. But be quick about it. We've got a murder to solve, Christmas is coming, and you know how the Home Office gets."

"I want us to be together," he stammered. "I want you to still love me."

"Oh, for God's sake." She turned on her heel and stomped off back the way they'd just come. "Of course I still love you, you idiot. I wouldn't be here if I didn't."

He charged after her. "But—but—but . . ."

She whirled around to face him. For a woman who'd just professed her love, she didn't regard him with a particularly affectionate expression. "Smythe, listen to what I've got to say. I know you think you did the honorable thing when you left me at the altar . . ."

"I didn't leave you at the altar," he yelled.

"You left me only days before our wedding," she shouted. "You might have done the noble thing, and maybe it was even the right course of action, but you humiliated me in front of everyone I care about. Do you know what that's like for someone like me, someone who has always been at the bottom of the heap?"

"You're not at the bottom of anything," he cried. "You're the very best that there is . . ."

She paid no attention to him. "Then you didn't come back for six months . . ."

"I got back as quick as I could," he protested. "Australia's thousands of miles away. You don't get there and back in just a few days . . ."

"Nonetheless," she interrupted again. "You were gone a bloomin' long time." She turned her back to him and continued on.

"Betsy, listen to me," he said.

"I have listened to you," she replied as she stepped out onto the main drive. "And so far you haven't had much to say."

"You know why I had to go," he said.

"I do, and I gave you your time to do what you felt was right. You've got to give me mine." She dashed toward the main gate.

"What does that mean?" he cried as he scrambled after her.

"It means I've got work to do," she called over her shoulder. "We've got us a murder, in case you've forgotten."

He was almost running to keep up with her. For such a small woman, she could sure move fast when she wanted. "I've not forgotten a thing, and I've work to do as well. But this is important." He wasn't sure, but he thought he heard her give a snort of derision. "It *is* important," he persisted. "And you can take a few minutes out of your precious investigation to talk to me."

"I'll be happy to talk to you when you decide what it is you want to say," she retorted.

They reached the front gates just as a funeral procession entered. It was a big one, with six black horses pulling the hearse and half a dozen rows of black-clad mourners walking behind. A long line of carriages followed the mourners.

"But—but . . ." Blast a Spaniard, he did know what he wanted to say, but he could hardly shout it out here and now.

Betsy darted across the road to the other side. "I'll see you back at the house."

Smythe tried to cross after her, but the hearse was too close and he didn't want to spook the horses by dashing out in front of it. "Blast," he muttered. He yanked off his cap and stood respectfully until the cortege passed. By the time the last of the carriages had rumbled by, she was gone.

But he was in excellent spirits as he went out through the gates and onto the Fulham Road. She'd said the only words that really mattered to him. She still loved him, and that was all that counted.

Kerringtons and Stuart, Wine Merchants, was located on the ground floor of a small but very old building in Oxford Street. Witherspoon peeked through the leaded glass of the front window. "There don't seem to be many customers," he said to Barnes. "That ought to make the proprietors a bit more cooperative."

"Let's hope so, sir." Barnes opened the door, and the two men entered. The shop was paneled in dark wood, giving the room a gloomy, cavelike atmosphere. Shelves of wine, the bottles stored on their sides in racks, were lined up along the walls. A clerk in an old-fashioned black frock coat came out from behind the short counter on the far side of the room. Another clerk was at a small table with a well-dressed elderly woman. They were looking at a large open ledger book.

"May I be of assistance?" the clerk asked. He glanced over his shoulder at the closed door behind the counter.

"We'd like to see your manager, please," Witherspoon replied. "I'm Inspector Gerald Witherspoon and this is Constable Barnes."

The fellow gaped at them a moment, as though he'd never heard of such an outlandish request. "I'll see if Mr. Crick is available."

"If Mr. Crick isn't available, then perhaps we could talk with you," Barnes added.

By now the other clerk and the well-dressed matron had given up all pretence of minding their own business and were avidly watching everything.

"Me?" the clerk repeated. He looked quite alarmed by the prospect. "Goodness, no, that would never do. I'll go get Mr. Crick." He turned on his heel and scurried toward the counter.

"Sorry, sir," Barnes murmured. "But it's getting late and we need this information."

"I'm well aware of your 'methods,' Constable." Witherspoon grinned. Barnes was always reminding the inspector that his methods had become quite famous, and it was quite amusing to be able to turn the tables for once. "And I knew exactly what you were about. Most people would rather do anything than speak to the police. Everyone, that is, except Henry Becker."

"He was a strange one, sir," Barnes agreed. "Especially for someone of that class. But then again, perhaps we oughtn't to look a gift horse in the mouth."

The door through which the clerk had disappeared opened and he reappeared, followed by a short, balding man who did not look at all pleased. "I understand you wish to speak to me," he said, directing his attention to the inspector.

"That's correct," Witherspoon replied.

"Come along to my office, then. Let's not stand about out here." Crick waved them toward the open door behind the counter.

A few moments later the two policemen were standing in a tiny office opposite Mr. Crick, who had taken a seat behind a cluttered desk. Witherspoon started to introduce himself.

"My clerk told me who you are." Crick held up his hand. "What is it you want?"

Witherspoon paused for a moment. He couldn't for the life of him understand why so many people were hostile to answering a few simple inquiries. For goodness' sake, this was a murder investigation. Did honest merchants really want murderers running about the city killing people? You'd think that an old, respectable establishment such as this would be very much in favor of law and order. But the inspector could tell from the hostile expression on Crick's face that getting any reasonable information from the fellow was going to be difficult. Drat.

"We want to see your sales records for Mr. Basil Farringdon," Barnes said bluntly.

"Why should I show you my records?" Crick leaned back in his chair and folded his arms over his chest.

"We're investigating a murder, sir," Witherspoon said quickly. He was rather pleased that Barnes had taken a firm stand. "And your sales records might be very important evidence."

"I doubt that," Crick replied. "This is a very old and honorable establishment. My customers aren't the sort of people to be involved with the criminal element. Furthermore, I don't think they would appreciate having their privacy violated."

"Oh, for God's sake, man, you're a wine merchant, not a lawyer," Barnes snapped. "And unless you spend a great deal of time and effort getting to know your customers intimately, then you've no idea whether any of them are criminals or not. So don't waste our time blathering on about privacy. If you don't wish to cooperate, I'm sure we can ask Mr. Farringdon to come here with us and insist that you verify his story. However, I don't think you'll keep him or many of his friends as customers after that. People like Basil Farringdon don't appreciate being inconvenienced by uncooperative shopkeepers."

Crick's mouth opened in surprise, and he sat up straight. "Well, if you put it like that, I shouldn't like to inconvenience Mr. Farringdon. He is a good customer. Uh, what was it you wanted?"

"Can you verify that he and his wife purchased a half case of Locarno—it's a Bordeaux."

"I know what it is, Inspector." Crick turned around and pulled a ledger off the shelf behind him. He opened it up, leafed through the pages, and then nodded. "That is correct. A half case of Locarno, a case of Riesling, and three bottles of cordials were delivered to the Farringdons on the first of November."

"Did they buy Locarno often?" Barnes asked.

Crick shook his head. "This was the first time. Mrs. Farringdon came in and asked me if Locarno was a good Bordeaux. I confirmed that it is very good, and she ordered half a case. She was planning a large party and wanted to make sure she had plenty of good wine on hand."

"No, Samson, you have to stay inside." Mrs. Goodge gently hooked her foot under Samson's fat belly and pushed him away from the back door. "I'm goin' out to feed the birdies, lovey, and you'll frighten them."

Samson leapt off the offending foot, gave the cook a good glare, and then trotted off.

She pulled the door open and stepped outside. She held on to her cap against the strong wind as she crossed the small terrace. Leaves danced in the air, and the branches of the trees and bushes shook as powerful gusts whipped through the garden. She stepped onto the path and headed toward the clearance near the oak trees. As she came around a clump of evergreen trees, she saw a man sitting on the bench, smoking a cigar. He glanced up just then, saw her, and jumped to his feet.

"Sorry, ma'am," he said. He leaned to one side and jabbed the tip of his cigar against the metal armrest of the wooden bench. "I know we're not supposed to bother the residents or use the gardens, but I'm waiting for the foreman to come back and open up number eighteen. I'm one of the workers."

"Not to worry. You're not botherin' me and the birds," she replied. "Just don't let Mrs. Babcock from down the garden see you. What are they doing at number eighteen, knocking those two rooms together into one?"

"Yes, ma'am. It's to be a library, so we're also goin' to be building some shelves." He relaxed his lanky frame a fraction but didn't relight his cigar. "I appreciate you lettin' me stay here. Lots of people woulda run me out, and it's a lot more pleasant back here than it is hangin' about the front. Truth to tell, I've been wanting to have a gander at these gardens," he said.

"Are you interested in flowers and shrubs, then?" she asked, more to keep him talking than anything else. She was always on the lookout for someone who might have a morsel of gossip to pass along, so she was quite happy to keep on chatting with the fellow. He looked a bit rough—his clothes were stained with paint, and the long gray coat he wore had seen better days—but he was a laborer, and no doubt these weren't his Sunday best.

"I am, ma'am." He grinned broadly. Half of his teeth were missing, and the ones he had left were stained and rotten. "You could say I was once in the trade. I used to work as an undergardener."

"Where at?" She reached under her cloak and into her apron pocket. Pulling out the rolled newspaper containing the bread crumbs, she opened it up and tossed them into the air.

"I started out at a nursery in Chelsea and then got a position as an undergardener at the communal gardens just off the Redcliffe Road. Quite posh they were, too, but the residents' association was deadly cheap. They wouldn't pay enough to keep body and soul together. That's one of the reasons I'm now in the building trade and not gardening. A man's got to make a living."

Mrs. Goodge had gone still. Redcliffe Gardens was near the murder house on Redcliffe Road. "How long ago did you work there?"

"It's been more than ten years ago." He smiled ruefully. "And I really loved the work. There's something very satisfying about muckin' about in the earth. But like I said, a man's got to make a living."

"Ten years ago, eh?" Mrs. Goodge silently debated whether he might have any useful information to impart. But then she decided she might as well risk it; she'd not had much luck today with any of her other sources. "That's a long time. Have you been in the building trade ever since you left the communal garden?"

"I have," he replied. "And it's been good to me. Even though I'm just a laborer and not a proper carpenter or joiner, my wages are still better than my cousin Ned's. I tried to get him to leave with me, but he wanted to stay on. Mind you, he's now the head gardener—well, leastways that's what he calls himself, but as he's the only gardener, I reckon it makes no difference."

"Your cousin stayed on working at the communal garden?"

The workman nodded and pulled his coat tighter against a gust of cold wind that rushed past them. "I wish the foreman would hurry up. It's right cold out here."

This was her chance. "Why don't you step into my kitchen," she said, pointing toward the inspector's house, "and I'll fix you a nice hot cup of tea?"

He hesitated. "I don't want to be any trouble."

"It's no trouble at all," she assured him. "I was going to make myself one anyway, and it is dreadfully cold out here."

"That's awfully kind of you, ma'am. Truth to tell, the rest of them have gone to eat, so it might be awhile before we start work again. My name is Lester Parks," he said.

"I'm Mrs. Goodge. Come along, then—it's just over here." She was sure he was hungry as well as cold.

Twenty minutes later, her assumptions proved correct. Lester Parks had eaten two slices of seed cake and three slices of brown bread, and eagerly accepted a third cup of tea. But she'd learned absolutely nothing useful from the fellow. He knew nothing of their victim nor of any of their suspects.

"So you've never heard of Stephen Whitfield?" she demanded. "You're absolutely sure?"

"Never 'eard of the fellow." Lester Parks looked down at his empty plate. "That was a lovely feed, Mrs. Goodge. You're a good baker."

"Or of Basil or Maria Farringdon?" she urged. She didn't want to be the only one with nothing to report this afternoon, and her next source wasn't due here until after the meeting.

"Like I said, I've never heard of them, either."

She glanced at the carriage clock on the pine sideboard. "It's getting on, I'm sure your foreman is back by now."

"Thanks ever so much for the lovely food." He smiled and got to his feet. "I was right hungry."

"What about Henry Becker?" she tried one last time. "Are you certain you've never heard anything about him?"

"Sorry, I wish I knew something, but I don't." He started toward the back door. "Most people don't bother talkin' to the likes of me."

She got up and followed him down the hallway. She'd brought up the murder but had learned nothing; he'd not heard a word, and he certainly hadn't read any newspapers lately. This had been a waste of time.

"Thanks again, Mrs. Goodge." He reached for the door handle. "I'll be able to work this afternoon, and then maybe the foreman will keep me on to help out tomorrow. Truth to tell, I've not eaten in two days, and I was so light-headed from hunger, I wasn't able to do very much this mornin'. Mr. Mayer—he's the foreman—told me that if I couldn't pull my weight, he'd not be needin' me."

That brought her up short. She stared at him as he stood there in the dim light. She realized then that he'd been out in the gardens resting so he'd have the strength to work. He was one of London's desperate poor. He probably spent his wages on gin, hadn't a proper home, and managed to keep body and soul together with only casual labor. Before she'd come to work here, she'd have thought he deserved his fate, that he'd brought his lot in life upon himself by his own actions. She didn't believe that anymore. "I'm glad I was able to help," she said softly. "Wait, let me give you something to take with you." She started back down the hall. The others would just have to do with a little less food for their afternoon tea.

"No, ma'am," he called. "Don't be troublin' yourself. You've been more than kind to me."

But she ignored him and went on into the kitchen. She grabbed the newspaper that was lying on a chair and hurried to the table. Spreading it open, she put in the remainder of the bread and cut two more slices of cake. Then she folded it into a neat parcel and took it back down the hall. He was still at the back door.

"Take this," she instructed as she handed it to him. "You'll be able to work tomorrow if you have food."

He stared at the package and then looked up at her. "Thank you. It's not often that people do me a kindness."

"Get on now. You don't want to lose your position because you're late," she warned, leaning past him and opening the door.

"I did remember something I heard about one of them names you mentioned," he said as he stepped out onto the terrace.

She didn't believe him. He was merely grateful for the food. "Did you now? That's interesting."

"Rosalind Murray," he continued. "That's the one I heard about. Mind you, it weren't much, but she and her husband used to live in a small flat at the top of one of them big houses that backed onto the gardens."

Mrs. Goodge had no idea whether this was true or not, but she'd give him a chance to salvage his pride for accepting the food. "Go on," she urged.

"He died, and the only thing he left her was some shares in a tea plantation out in the Far East. The poor lady had to move in with a relative just to keep a roof over her head."

Everyone was back at Upper Edmonton Gardens in time for their afternoon meeting. Mrs. Jeffries noticed that Betsy and Smythe seemed to be a bit more relaxed with each other. He'd arrived only moments before Betsy, and Mrs. Jeffries had seen the maid smile at him as he helped her off with her jacket. Good, she thought. It was important for these two to straighten out their differences. They loved each other too deeply to let foolish pride and hurt feelings keep them apart.

"Hurry up, everyone," Mrs. Goodge urged. "The rag-and-bone man is due here at five, and I'll want a few minutes with him before I have to start the inspector's dinner. Joseph always has the latest gossip. He does like to talk."

"It's already gone four," Wiggins protested. "What if our meetin' runs late? I've got a few bits to report on, important things that everyone should hear about."

"Joseph only gets to this area every month or so, and if I miss him today, I'll have to wait till the middle of January," the cook replied. "Let's just get on with this."

"I'm sure we'll finish in good time for Mrs. Goodge to meet with her source," Mrs. Jeffries soothed. "Wiggins, as you appear to have heard something of importance, please go first."

"I don't know that it's so important after all, but I did find out that Mrs. Farringdon collects wine bottles." Wiggins was a bit embarrassed that he'd made a fuss. When said aloud, the information he'd heard from Mrs. Jones sounded silly.

"Does she collect any particular kind of wine bottles?" Hatchet asked politely.

"I'm not explaining this right. What I meant to say was that when she goes to a posh party, if she drinks a wine she likes, she makes her servants go around to the kitchen to collect the bottle. She does it because she's workin' 'ard to be a credit to her husband," he explained. He told them about his encounter with Matilda Jones, and her conviction that Maria Farringdon suffered greatly from feelings of inferiority to her husband's social class. "I know it doesn't seem like such a thing could have anything to do with the murder, but sometimes the oddest bits come together when Mrs. Jeffries is sortin' out who the killer might be."

"That's true," the cook agreed. "You never know what's going to come in useful."

"Shall I go next, then?" Betsy asked. When no one objected, she plunged right ahead. "I didn't have a lot of luck, but I did find out that Rosalind Murray is very well liked by the local merchants. Apparently she makes sure all the bills are paid promptly." She broke off and shot Smythe a quick grin. "Unfortunately I was interrupted before I could find out anything else, but tomorrow I'm going back to Whitfield's neighborhood to see what else I can learn. Mrs. Murray does sound a bit too good to be true, and it seems to me she was the one who had the most to lose if he married Mrs. Graham. But it's early days yet, so I'm trying not to come to any conclusions."

"That's very wise of you, Betsy," Mrs. Jeffries said. She couldn't wait to tell them what she heard from Mrs. Bowden.

"Can I go next?" Luty asked. "I'm bustin' to tell my bits."

"Of course." Mrs. Jeffries told herself to be patient.

Luty leaned forward eagerly. "I found out that Eliza Graham's husband died of a heart attack, and what's more, he died when he was alone in the house with just his wife."

"Where were the servants?" Mrs. Goodge asked.

"They were gone. He died while he and his wife were on holiday. They were staying in a rented cottage on the South Coast." Luty grinned. "Mr. Graham's death happened just after supper, after the two servants that did for them had left for the day."

"Was there an inquest?" Mrs. Jeffries asked.

Luty shook her head. "No. His doctor had sent him on holiday because of his health. He suffered from heart trouble. Even his family didn't think his death was suspicious. But in light of what we know about Whitfield's death, I think we ought to keep our eye on her."

"You mean, if she thinks she got away with murder once, she thinks she could do it again?" Smythe reached for another slice of bread.

"It's a possibility," Luty replied.

"But what would be her motive?" Betsy asked. "Why would she want Stephen Whitfield dead?"

"Maybe she stands to inherit from his estate," Wiggins suggested. "After all, we know he was sweet on her."

"He might have been sweet on her, but I don't think she was goin' to inherit anything from the fellow," Luty said. "I did find out a bit about Whitfield's estate, and it's strange."

"What do you mean?" Mrs. Goodge demanded. "How can an estate be strange?"

Luty was a tad embarrassed. Despite her best efforts, she'd found out nothing more than a general rumor about the late Stephen Whitfield's estate. As the others had charged her with finding out whether or not the house was entailed, she felt almost as if she'd failed. "According to my source, Whitfield doesn't have control of any of his property except his personal property."

"Personal property." Wiggins frowned. "Does that mean just his clothes and hairbrushes and that sort of thing?"

"That's pretty much what it means," Luty said. "Everything else is tied up in some sort of annuity fund. My source wasn't real sure, but he said he'd see if he could find out more about the estate, but it might take a day or two. Sorry I couldn't find out other details. I know you was all counting on me . . ."

"That's all right, Luty. You've done very well," Mrs. Jeffries interrupted. "Much better than anyone could expect in such a short period of time."

"I heard the same, madam," Hatchet added smoothly. "There is something odd about the estate, and none of my sources knew what it was, either." He was annoyed that he'd not been able to get in to see his friend, the Farringdons' butler, but the fellow was still ill. But he was supposedly on the mend.

"Let's hope I get lucky tomorrow and my source comes through with something useful," Luty finished.

Mrs. Jeffries looked at Hatchet. "Would you care to go next?"

"I'm afraid I've found out very little," he said. "Unfortunately one of my sources is still very much indisposed, but I'm hoping that is only a temporary condition." He'd die before he'd let Luty know how depressed he was about his contribution to the case thus far.

"I'm sure you'll do better tomorrow." Luty reached over and patted him on the arm. She'd recovered from her feelings of failure. He glared at her.

"In that case, perhaps I ought to tell everyone what I've

learned," Mrs. Jeffries took a deep breath. "While I was out today, I happened to run into Mrs. Bowden . . ."

Mrs. Goodge broke in. "You mean the lady that gives us a hand with heavy spring cleanin'?"

"That's right," Mrs. Jeffries replied. She reached for her teacup, and as she did, she happened to glance toward the kitchen window. She could see the high wheels of a hansom pulling up in front of the house. "Oh dear, I think the inspector is home early." She leapt and dashed across the room.

"But it's not even half past four," Wiggins cried.

"What's he doin' home this early?" Mrs. Goodge complained. "That's goin' to ruin everything. I don't want to have to stop and get supper now. I want to speak to my rag-and-bone man."

"It's the inspector," Mrs. Jeffries hissed over her shoulder.

Luty and Hatchet were already on their feet and heading for the back door. "We'll be back tomorrow morning," Hatchet promised.

"Come for breakfast," Mrs. Goodge offered. "That way we'll have plenty of time for our meeting."

"Isn't that just like a man?" Betsy looked at Smythe. "Always popping up where you least expect them."

CHAPTER 7

The next morning, Luty and Hatchet joined the household for breakfast. While they ate their bacon and eggs, Mrs. Jeffries told them about her encounter with Geraldine Bowden. She also gave them the information she'd learned from Witherspoon the previous evening while he'd eaten his dinner. The house was now quiet and empty, with everyone out about their business.

Mrs. Jeffries glanced around the kitchen. Mrs. Goodge was at the counter, taking the mince tarts she'd baked early this morning off the cooling tray and putting them onto a serving platter. "Your sources are going to be lucky today. Those look delicious. They smell wonderful as well."

"Thank you. I'm hoping these will help loosen a few tongues. I didn't have much luck yesterday," she replied. The morning meeting had been so rushed that she'd not mentioned her garden conversation with Lester Parks.

"Some days are like that." Mrs. Jeffries smiled sympathetically. "No matter how hard we try, we simply don't hear a word about our suspects or our victim."

"I heard something, alright." The cook sighed. "I'm just not sure it's true."

"What was it?"

Mrs. Goodge laid the last tart onto the platter and then looked up. She might as well repeat what he'd told her. The poor fellow deserved at least that much. Besides, it wasn't the sort of tidbit that would do any harm to the case. "My source mentioned that the only thing Rosalind Murray's husband left her when he died was

330

some shares in a tea plantation in the Far East." She shrugged. "But I don't think this source is particularly reliable, and what's more, even if the information was true, I don't see that it has any bearing on Whitfield's murder. But not to worry—I've an old friend coming around this morning, and I'm hoping she'll have something useful."

"I do hope so," Mrs. Jeffries said earnestly. "This case is becoming a bit of a puzzle."

"Aren't they all?"

"Of course they are," Mrs. Jeffries agreed. "But usually by now we have a few more facts to work with."

"What do you mean?" The cook picked up the clean tea towel she'd laid next to the serving platter and draped it over the tarts. "Seems to me we've got lots of information—we know plenty of things."

"But we don't," Mrs. Jeffries argued. "And the things we don't know are important. For instance, we've still no idea who will inherit Whitfield's estate or even if there is an estate to be inherited."

"Luty has got her sources working on that problem." Mrs. Goodge picked up the empty cooling tray and took it over to the sink. "She seemed confident that she'd have an answer for us by this afternoon's meeting."

"But that's not the only issue I'm concerned about. There's something else equally puzzling." Mrs. Jeffries paused and took a deep breath. She wasn't sure she should even voice this concern aloud. "No one seems to have any reason to want Whitfield dead."

That was what really bothered her: there didn't seem to be a reason for Whitfield's murder.

"What about Mrs. Graham?" Mrs. Goodge grabbed a cleaning rag from the rack above the sink and ran it lightly over the surface of the tray. "Seems to me she'd decided to jilt Whitfield and had set her sights on Hugh Langdon. Perhaps when she told Whitfield it was over, he'd threatened to make trouble for her with Langdon."

"But what could Whitfield have done?"

"Perhaps he said he'd tell Langdon that Mrs. Graham had been his mistress and that they were engaged," Mrs. Goodge replied. "Some men would think twice before stealing another man's fiancée."

"But they weren't engaged," Mrs. Jeffries pointed out. "Eliza

Graham was very insistent on that point. She told the inspector she'd never agreed to marry Whitfield."

"True, but we've only her word to go on." The cook grinned. "She could be lying. After all, Whitfield is dead, and by her own admission, his death saved her a lot of trouble and embarrassment."

"That's true," Mrs. Jeffries murmured. "And from what the inspector told us, Mrs. Graham didn't try to hide the fact that she needed to remarry for financial reasons. I guess what I'm concerned about is why she would jilt a known quantity like Whitfield for a man who had a reputation as a bit of a cad."

"Perhaps Mrs. Graham saw Langdon in a different light." The cook slid the tray onto the bottom shelf of the worktable. "Maybe she fell in love. We both know that love makes people do foolish things. Just look at Betsy and Smythe."

"They seem to be a bit easier with one another, don't you think?"

"Yes, I noticed that as well," Mrs. Goodge replied. "And I'm glad of it. All that tension around the table was hard on my nerves. But back to our problem. The inspector said Mrs. Graham knew that the Whitfield estate wouldn't go to her even if she did marry Whitfield. So she'd be no better off married to him than she is now. Maybe she saw Langdon as a safer bet."

"So you're thinking she might have decided she could get Langdon to propose, and when she tried to break off the relationship with Whitfield, he threatened her in some way?"

"That's one possible motive." Mrs. Goodge shrugged. "Whitfield may not have taken kindly to being publicly jilted. Especially as he'd already made plans to go to Italy, called his solicitor to change his will, and told his mistress of many years that it was over."

"When you put it like that, I see what you mean," Mrs. Jeffries replied. "Perhaps Eliza Graham did have a motive. Gossip can sometimes have devastating consequences to women of her class. Who knows what Whitfield might have threatened when she told him the two of them were finished?"

"And Mrs. Murray has a motive as well," the cook said quickly. "Remember the old saying: Hell hath no fury like a woman scorned." There was a loud knock on the back door. "That's probably my friend."

Mrs. Jeffries took the hint and quickly rose to her feet. "I'll leave you to it, then. I've a busy day planned, so I'll see you this afternoon."

Mrs. Goodge waited till Mrs. Jeffries had disappeared up the back steps before she opened the door. She smiled at the small, sparrowlike woman standing on the stoop. "Hello, Emma. It's been a long time. Do come in."

"It has been a long time, hasn't it?" Emma Darnley agreed as she stepped inside. She had gray hair, deep-set brown eyes, and a sharp chin. "I was ever so surprised to get your note. But then I happened to run into Ida Leacock on Oxford Street the other day, and she said you'd been getting in touch with some of your old acquaintances."

"That's right." Mrs. Goodge ushered her guest down the hall toward the kitchen. "How have you been? It was Ida who told me that you'd moved to London."

"I came to London ages ago," Emma replied as they came into the kitchen. She stopped and surveyed the room. "This is very nice, not at all what I expected. Ida mentioned that you worked for a policeman."

"A police inspector," Mrs. Goodge replied.

"Even an inspector couldn't afford a house this size," Emma retorted. She took off her gloves and hat.

"He's private means as well," Mrs. Goodge said. Emma always had said exactly what she thought, and apparently the passage of the years hadn't changed her in the least. Good. "Give me your things and take a seat. I'll brew us a fresh pot of tea. I've some lovely mince tarts. As I recall, you were always fond of mince tarts."

Emma smiled in pleasure. "You remembered that—how very kind of you." She slipped off her coat and handed it to the cook along with her hat and gloves.

"I remember a lot from the old days. It's the present that I have a hard time keeping up with." Mrs. Goodge tucked the gloves inside the hat and laid them on the sideboard, then put the coat on the rack.

"I was surprised to hear you were still working." Emma continued her study of the kitchen as she sat down at the table. Her gaze lingered for a moment on the almost new, very expensive cooker, before moving on to the slab of marble sitting atop the worktable near the sink.

"I've really no choice about it," Mrs. Goodge said. It was a lie: she had saved practically all her salary over the years she'd worked for the inspector, and she now had a tidy sum tucked safely away in a post office account. He was a most generous employer. But she had found she could get far more information out of her old colleagues if they felt just a bit sorry for her. "I've no family to speak of and, well, here I am, still cooking and baking."

Emma dragged her gaze away from the pine sideboard and turned toward the cook. She smiled sympathetically. "I'm lucky. I've got my Neville, and he's his railway pension. I left service some years ago, you know. Right after we had our Lilly."

"That's what I heard," Mrs. Goodge replied. The kettle, which she'd left on to boil, began to whistle. She took it off and poured the water into the waiting teapot. "Was Lilly your only child?"

For the next ten minutes, they chatted about family, old friends, the weather, the season, and how crowded the shops were these days. Then the cook moved in for the kill. "Have you kept in contact with any of the others from the old days?"

"Not really, though I did get a card from Lorraine Brown last summer. Do you remember her? She worked with us at Lord Lattimer's London house."

"I remember her. She was a nice girl."

"She's moved to Dorset to live with her sister."

Mrs. Goodge didn't have a clue who Lorraine Brown might be, but this was the opening she wanted. "Dorset? Are you sure? I heard she ended up working as a housekeeper for that man who was murdered the other day."

"Lorraine Brown hasn't worked in London in years. What on earth are you talking about, Mrs. Goodge?" Emma stared at her curiously.

Mrs. Goodge put the teapot onto the table next to the plate of mince tarts. "Oh dear, I'm getting muddled. It was Helen Brown who worked at the Whitfield house. You don't know Helen. I worked with her years after you and I worked together."

"Murder," Emma muttered. She frowned. "You mean that man who was poisoned at his own dinner party?"

"Yes, that's him. Stephen Whitfield was his name." She put two mince tarts onto a plate and placed it on the table in front of

Emma. "Poor man was murdered in his own home. My inspector has got the case." She'd decided there was no harm in mentioning this information. After all, they were two old women gossiping together, and it would be expected that she'd discuss her employer.

Emma nodded her thanks, picked up her fork, and sliced into the pastry.

Mrs. Goodge poured the tea. "Of course, there were half a dozen people in the house when the fellow was killed, so even though my inspector is an excellent policeman, it'll take a bit of work on his part to get to the bottom of it all."

Emma shoved a bite of the tart into her mouth.

"Mind you, my inspector has solved every case he's ever had," she continued chattily. "So I've no doubt he'll solve this one as well."

"I wonder who was at the dinner party," Emma mumbled as she swallowed her food. "The papers didn't mention any names."

Mrs. Goodge handed her guest a cup of tea. "The respectable papers never give out names in this sort of case. They don't like to embarrass the upper class."

"Really?" Emma asked curiously.

"Oh, yes," Mrs. Goodge assured her. "Whitfield's guests were all like himself—upper-class and wealthy." She rattled off the names of Whitfield's dinner guests and knew she'd struck gold when Emma's narrow face lighted up when Mrs. Goodge mentioned Hugh Langdon's name. That was precisely the reason she'd invited Emma today. She knew of Emma's connection to the Langdon household. She'd learned of it from Ida Leacock and sworn her to secrecy about the whole matter.

"Hugh Langdon," Emma exclaimed. "My niece works as a housemaid for him. But he's not a murderer. He's a decent employer. He treats Mary and the other servants very well—very well indeed."

"Really?" Mrs. Goodge looked doubtful. "I've heard he's something of a cad. You know, with the ladies. Are you sure your niece is safe with a man like that?"

She knew she was risking making Emma angry, but she wanted to get the woman talking, and sometimes people needed a bit of a nudge. A bit of temper often led to a loosening of the tongue.

"Mary's worked there for years. He's never laid a hand on her or on any of the other girls. Honestly, Mrs. Goodge, you shouldn't believe everything you hear." Emma took another bite of her tart.

"You're right, of course. I'm sure he's a decent fellow. It's strange he's never married, though, isn't it?" She sipped her tea.

"He was engaged, but his fiancée died," Emma replied.

"I've never heard that."

"It was years ago," Emma said. "Right after Mary started working for him. He was going to marry a lady named Ellen Bannister. It was a very sad occurrence. She died on a trip to Paris to buy her trousseau."

"That's awful. How did she die?"

"She contracted some kind of fever and was dead before he could bring her back here for medical treatment. You know what they say about French hospitals, don't you? They're dreadful places." Emma nodded knowingly. "But if you ask me, the fact that he was willing to marry someone like her in the first place speaks well of the man."

"What was wrong with her?"

"There was some ugly gossip about her." Emma waved her hand dismissively. "Supposedly she was a tad free with her favors, it you get my meaning. But Mr. Langdon didn't let the opinions of others influence him. He was man enough to ignore the gossip and propose to her."

"That does speak well of him," Mrs. Goodge agreed. "I wonder how he ended up with his current reputation."

Emma shrugged. "I expect it's because he's not been much interested in getting married all these years. According to Mary, he likes women but is always very honest about his intentions. But then again, he's not old money, is he? So he's not as concerned about the social aspect of his situation. He made his fortune all on his own."

"So he's stayed single all these years?" Mrs. Goodge probed.

"Not for much longer, though," Emma replied. "When Mary came around for tea last week, she told me that she was sure he was finally going to do it—he was finally going to get married."

"To Eliza Graham?" Mrs. Goodge asked.

"Yes, that's her name. How did you know?"

"She was one of the people at the dinner party," the cook reminded Emma. "She'd brought Mr. Langdon."

Emma frowned slightly. "Mary said the staff wasn't particularly

happy about her coming in as mistress of the household. Mr. Langdon's always been on the lenient side, but they're all worried
they'll have to work a lot harder if he takes a wife."

Betsy hesitated for a brief moment. The girl she'd been trailing
had stopped and was looking in a shop window at a display of
ladies' gloves. She was a young woman who looked to be in her
early twenties. Her brown hair was neatly tucked up under a gray
and black hat that had seen better days, her black coat wasn't long
enough to completely hide the last two inches of her gray broad-
cloth skirt, and her feet were encased in sturdy but rather ugly
thick black shoes. Betsy had seen her come out of the Farringdon
house and had guessed she was a housemaid.

She sidled up next to the young woman. "Those are lovely. I
wish I could afford a pair like that." She pointed to a pair of black
kid gloves.

For a moment, the girl didn't reply. She kept her gaze on the
gloves; then she turned and looked Betsy directly in the eye.
"You've been following me. Why?"

Betsy blinked in surprise. She thought about denying the charge
and then realized she'd only be making a fool of herself if she did.
The girl's tone had made it clear that she wasn't asking a question;
she was stating a fact. Perhaps it was time to try another tactic.
"You're right. I have been following you. But only because I'm
desperate for a position, and I heard a rumor that your household
might be hiring a scullery maid."

"I'm just a housemaid. I don't do the hiring," she replied. But
her expression had softened.

"No, but you could tell me if there were any positions available
and . . and . . ." Betsy looked down at the pavement.

"And what?' the girl asked softly.

"And put in a good word for me." Betsy sniffed. "I'm sorry. I
know it was wrong, but I'm desperate for work."

"Oh, don't start sniveling on me," the girl said harshly. "Look,
come along and let me buy you a cup of tea."

"You don't 'ave to do that." Betsy slipped easily into the dialect
of her old neighborhood.

"Don't be daft, lass. It's only a cup of tea I'm offering. I've
been out of work myself, and I know what it feels like."

Betsy swiped at her cheeks and lifted her chin. She'd actually made her eyes water. "Thanks ever so much. I'd love a cup of tea. I'm stayin' at a lodgin' house, and I've not had breakfast because it costs extra."

"There's a café just around the corner." The girl started off. "Come along, then. My name is Rachel Webster. What's yours?"

"I'm Polly Johnson," Betsy replied as she trailed after the girl. "And I'm ever so grateful." She always used a false name when she was on the hunt. There was a chance that Inspector Witherspoon might end up interviewing the girl, and you never knew what might or might not be said.

They went into a small workingman's café on the Edgware Road. This late in the morning, there were only two other customers inside and they were sitting at a table by the counter, chatting with the counterwoman. Rachel ordered their tea and motioned for Betsy to take the table by the window.

Betsy sat down in the rickety chair and hoped it wouldn't collapse on her. She glanced toward the counter just as Rachel opened her tiny black change purse. A wave of guilt washed over her as she watched Rachel counting out coins. Even a cup of tea was an expense when you made as little money as maids usually earned. She promised herself she'd find a way to get the money back to the girl.

Rachel picked up their cups and started across the small space. "This ought to warm you up a bit." She put the tea in front of Betsy.

"Thanks ever so much," Betsy replied. She waited until Rachel had sat down before speaking again. "I'm ever so grateful."

"You've already said that," Rachel retorted, but she was smiling.

"I know, but it's so cold out and you're bein' so nice to me. Uh, I hate to ask, but are there any positions available where you work?" she asked. She looked down at the tabletop as she spoke, trying her best to act as if she really was looking for work. She'd already decided that Rachel was no fool, and she'd see through this trick in a heartbeat if Betsy wasn't careful.

Rachel shook her head. "No, and no one's thinkin' of quittin', either. Why did you think there might be? Mrs. Farringdon would never hire off the streets. She always uses an agency."

"That's why I thought there might be a position." Betsy had an answer at the ready. "I'm registered with the Clements agency, but it's been two weeks now and they've not even got me an interview. I was checking in with them yesterday when I overheard the manager give out your address—I mean, the address of the house I saw you come out of this morning. So I went around and waited, hoping that someone would come out and I could find out if there was any positions goin'." She sighed heavily. "But it looks like I wasted my time."

"You really must be desperate," Rachel said.

"I am." Betsy took a sip of her tea. "What's it like there? Are they decent?"

Rachel shrugged. "They're nice enough, I suppose. But the work is hard, and it's been really difficult lately as the ruddy butler's been sick and taken to his bed. That means the housekeeper is takin' on his duties and we're doin' most of her work. But the missus is alright. She's a bit of a stickler for the social niceties, but usually she's alright."

"She sounds very upper-class," Betsy murmured.

"Not really. Her father made a lot of money in trade," Rachel said. "It's Mr. Farringdon that's upper-class. She married up."

"So she had the money and he had the breeding," she murmured. "One of them marriages of convenience, I suppose."

"Then you'd suppose wrong," Rachel said tartly. "They love each other a lot. He's devoted to her, and Mrs. Farringdon works hard to do everything just right. She wants to be a credit to him. Leastways that's what the housekeeper says when she's had a few too many sips from the brandy bottle."

"That's nice—I mean, that they're so devoted like that. Not many couples seem to care that overly much for one another. The master and mistress in my last household hated each other," Betsy said. "That's one of the reasons I'm lookin' for work. Mr. Summers decided that Mrs. Summers didn't need as much help in the house, so he sacked me and the scullery maid." She wasn't sure she ought to be saying so much. It was important to keep the conversation on the Farringdons. "Are they newlyweds?"

"No, they're old. He's in his late sixties and she's not much younger. They've been married for years." Rachel leaned closer. "He saved her life once."

"Really?" Betsy repeated eagerly. She was relieved that Rachel hadn't wanted any additional details about the made-up Summers household. "That sounds ever so romantic. What happened? That is, if you don't mind my asking. I don't mean to be bold, but this sounds like a lovely story."

"You're not bein' bold," Rachel said. "And it is a good story, all the more interestin' because it's true. It happened a few summers back, a year or two before I started workin' for 'em. They'd gone sailing with some friends, and some part of the sail come flying around and knocked Mrs. Farringdon clean overboard."

"My goodness, that's awful," Betsy exclaimed. She wasn't really acting now. "Could Mrs. Farringdon swim?"

Rachel shook her head. "Not a bit. But Mr. Farringdon leapt right in and grabbed hold of her. He held her up until they could pull them both back into the boat. He's not a very strong swimmer, and the sea was rough, but he held her above the water, even though she was scared and strugglin' something fierce. She was thrashin' about so much he ended up with bruises all over his face. But if he'd not done it, if he'd not gone in after her, she'd have drowned."

"That's so wonderful." Betsy sighed prettily. "He must really care for her."

"He does." Rachel smiled.

Betsy wanted to get Rachel talking about the murder. "It must be the most exciting thing that ever happened to them. I mean, almost drowning isn't very nice, but it is an adventure."

"I'm not sure they'd see it that way," Rachel laughed. "Mind you, they were at a dinner party just a few days ago where the host was murdered. So that's a bit of excitement as well."

"Gracious, what happened?" Betsy remembered she was supposed to be cold and hungry, so she took a quick gulp of tea.

"Their host was poisoned right there at the dinner table." Rachel leaned closer again. "The police think the poison was in the wine the Farringdons brought with them to the man's house."

Betsy's eyes widened. "The police think your master and mistress are murderers?"

"Not really." Rachel shook her head. "I overheard Mr. Farringdon tellin' Mrs. Farringdon that the police think anyone could have put the poison in the bottle. But I know they're both upset over all the bother. They didn't much like havin' the police come 'round. Mrs. Farringdon had hysterics when he told her they'd been to the house. She was terribly concerned that the neighbors might have seen."

"I suppose that could be right upsettin' for a lady," Betsy ventured.

Rachel snorted. "Seems to me she ought to be worried about one of them gettin' arrested, not what the neighbors might think because they see a copper goin' up your walkway to the front door."

Betsy gaped at her. Again, she wasn't acting. "Do you think they might have done it?"

"I don't like to think so." Rachel shrugged. "But you never know about people, do you? And I know that Mrs. Farringdon didn't like the man. She didn't want to accept his dinner invitation when it come, but she'd no choice. Still, it's not nice when your host gets murdered with the wine you've brought to the party. Mind you, the wretched stuff Mr. Whitfield used to send to them tasted like it had poison in it; leastways that's what Mrs. Farringdon claimed. She was really annoyed when another bottle of the stuff arrived this Christmas. I thought she was going to have a fit when he brought it by."

"Mr. Whitfield?"

"He's the man who was poisoned," Rachel explained. "He came around to see the Farringdons just a few days before he was murdered. He brought them a bottle of his special port—leastways that's what he called it when he handed her the bottle. He came himself with just a young housemaid helpin' him. He'd brought the port as a Christmas present."

"And Mrs. Farringdon didn't like getting a present?"

"She didn't like him and she didn't like his wine. Last year she called it pigs' swill and poured it down the sink. But when he showed up at the front door, Mrs. Farringdon was polite enough. She said all the right words and acted like she was ever so pleased, but as soon as he'd gone, she grabbed the bottle and took it up to her dayroom."

Hatchet stopped on the top stair of the servants' entrance to the Farringdon house. He took one long last look at Connaught Street to make sure there were no signs of the police. The Farringdon butler was an old friend of his, but even so, he didn't want to be in a position of having to explain his presence here to Inspector Witherspoon. That could get very awkward. But he didn't see any constables patrolling the street on foot, and the road was free of hansom cabs.

He went down the short flight of steps and knocked on the door. Within moments, a young scullery maid stuck her head out. "You're not the butcher's lad," she said.

As he was wearing a full top hat and elegant black greatcoat, he could understand her surprise. "Indeed I am not." He smiled at the surprised girl. "Is Mr. Emery Richards able to receive visitors? I'm an old friend of his."

"I'm not sure. But he seems a bit better today." She pulled the door wider. "Come on in, and I'll see if he feels up to seein' ya."

Hatchet stepped into the hallway. "Thank you."

"You wait here," the girl ordered.

An older woman wearing a white apron and a cook's cap peeked around the corner. "Tell the butcher's lad he's late. I've been waiting for that joint . . ." Her voice trailed off as she spotted Hatchet.

"It's not the butcher's boy," the scullery maid called over her shoulder as she disappeared into a doorway at the far end of the passage. "It's someone to see Richards."

"How do you do, ma'am?" Hatchet swept off his hat and bowed toward the cook.

"Humph." She nodded and went back into the kitchen.

Five minutes passed before the maid stepped back into the hallway. Hatchet spent the time trying to learn as much as possible about the household. He'd been here before, of course, but then he'd been seeking information about people other than the occupants. But without standing at the kitchen door and shouting questions at the staff, he couldn't find out much of anything except that the hallway was freshly painted and the floor cleaned and polished.

"Come on back," the maid called. "He'd like to see ya."

As Hatchet passed the door to the kitchen, half a dozen pairs of eyes watched him curiously. He nodded to them politely, slowed his steps, and tried to observe as many details as possible. But the only things he actually saw were a row of copper molds and a whole shelf full of copper pans. They had very expensive kitchen equipment, but as he already knew the Farringdons were rich, that fact wasn't going to do him any good.

"It's just there." The maid pointed to an open door at the end of the hallway. "He's sitting up. But don't you stay too long, or you'll tire him out."

"Thank you, miss," he replied.

Inside the small butler's pantry, Emery Richards, attired in a long plaid wool bathrobe and slippers, was sitting at a table. A cup of tea was in front of him. He was a small fellow with a headful of gray hair, blue eyes, and a very pale complexion.

He smiled wanly and tried to get up as Hatchet came into the room. "It's so very good of you to come see me, old friend."

"Don't get up, Emery." Hatchet waved him back to his chair. "We've known each other far too long to stand on ceremony. How are you feeling?"

Emery Richards was a friend from the old days, the days when they'd both been wild and young and ready for any adventure. They'd had more courage than sense, and some would even say they'd been incredibly foolish.

Hatchet watched Emery carefully as he crossed the short space. There were only a few people from his past who had known him when he'd been in the grip of the demon rum. Emery Richards was one of them. But his old friend was hardly in a position to judge him or anyone else. Back in those days, Emery had had a few problems of his own.

"I'm getting better. But a few days ago, if you'd asked me that question, I'd have told you I was dying. It certainly felt that way." Emery grinned and pointed at the chair opposite him. "Sit yourself down, man. I've told Daisy to bring tea."

"And I've done just that, Mr. Richards." Daisy, the maid who'd let Hatchet into the house, elbowed the door open and stepped into the pantry. She was carrying a tray. She put it down and unloaded a small china pot, another cup, a cream pitcher, and a sugar bowl. "But you mustn't stay up too long, Mr. Richards. Remember what Doctor said: bronchitis can come back very quickly."

"Thank you, Daisy," Emery said. "I'll not overdo it."

"Should I pour?" she asked.

"That's all right, miss. I'll manage," Hatchet said quickly. He could see that his old friend wasn't as much on the mend as he'd pretended, and Hatchet didn't want to be responsible for a relapse.

"Right, then, I'll just close the door on my way out," Daisy said.

Hatchet poured his tea and then looked at Emery's half-empty cup. "Should I top you off?"

"Nah, I've had so much of the stuff, my bladder feels like it's going to burst," Emery replied. "Are you still working for that crazy American woman?"

"I am indeed."

"You still snooping around in that inspector's murder cases?" Emery shook his head. "I know that's why you've come to see me. Though, in all fairness, you've done your part over the years to keep in touch."

Hatchet laughed. He wasn't in the least concerned that Emery knew the real reason he was here. He'd used Emery as a source on two of the inspector's previous cases and knew the man could keep his own counsel. "You never were one to beat about the bush. I wonder what the Farringdons would think if they knew you as well as I do."

"The old man would have a stroke, and the good wife wouldn't give a toss as long as I did my job properly." He grinned broadly. "They're good people, even if he is a bit of a stick. Now, I don't know how much longer I can sit upright, so why don't you get on with it?"

"Emery, I'm not just here to get information. I want you to know that," Hatchet said softly. "I was concerned when I heard you were ill."

"I know. You've been a good friend over the years."

"As have you." Hatchet picked up his teacup. "What can you tell me about the Farringdons? More specifically, what can you tell me about their relationship to the late Stephen Whitfield?"

"Whitfield and Basil Farringdon went to school together, but they go back even further." He broke off and coughed lightly, covering his mouth with his hand. "Sorry, where was I?"

"Whitfield and Farringdon go back further than their school days?" Hatchet thought that odd. "Are they related?"

"No, but they are in the same tontine, and that was started the year they were born. So I guess you could say they've known each other from birth."

"Tontine?" Hatchet repeated. "Good Lord, I haven't heard of one of those for years. Aren't they illegal?"

"They were outlawed a good while back. I can't remember the exact year. The tontine was started by the parents the year they were all born. There were originally ten of them in it, and as was the custom, they were all close to each other in age," Emery explained. "That was sometime around 1825, well before the government outlawed tontines."

Hatchet thought for a moment. "Why wasn't the tontine disbanded or stopped when they were made illegal?"

"Because none of the principals wanted it to stop." Emery grinned. "They were making too much money off of it. I once heard Mr. Farringdon tell Mrs. Farringdon that when the law banning them was passed, they had their solicitors do something like rename it as a trust or an annuity, but basically the terms didn't change. It's still a tontine. It was a big one as well. Each family chucked in over ten thousand pounds."

"Was the money invested?" Hatchet asked. He wasn't completely sure he understood how a tontine functioned.

"It was, and this investment brought in substantial incomes to the participants, which is, of course, the reason they had it renamed instead of disbanded." He chuckled, which then turned into a cough. "You can see why the government outlawed the practice. Let's face it: That kind of money would tempt a saint, let alone a bunch of impoverished aristocrats living off the yearly dividend."

"Are you alright?" Hatchet put down his cup and started to get up.

Emery waved him back to his seat. "I'm fine. It's just a cough. Don't mind what Daisy says—I'm not on death's door yet. Speaking of which, if you're thinking that Mr. Farringdon murdered Whitfield to get his hands on all of it, think again. He doesn't need the money."

"But I thought you just referred to him as an 'impoverished aristocrat'?" Hatchet pointed out.

"He would be if he hadn't married Mrs. Farringdon. She's the one with the money. She's rich."

"Tell me more about the tontine." He was amazed they'd not learned about this as yet. Then again, most of the people involved probably had no reason to tell the police about it and, thus, show that they had a motive for wanting Whitfield dead.

"What else is there to say?" Emery asked. "The original charter had ten members. From what I've overheard Mr. Farringdon tell Mrs. Farringdon, two or three of them didn't survive childhood, so that got the number of participants down to seven. The money was invested wisely and, as I said, the fund—or annuity, as it's now called—has paid out a handsome dividend over the years. But the real prize will go to the survivor. He'll get everything." He started coughing again. He put his hand over his mouth, his head bobbed with every choking gasp, and it sounded as if his poor lungs were about to explode. Finally, just when Hatchet had made up his mind to call Daisy, the attack subsided.

Emery slumped back against his chair.

Hatchet got up. "You're too ill to continue this. You must get back to bed."

"Don't be stupid," Emery choked out. "This has done me a world of good. I'm so sick of lying in that bed that even your homely face is welcome. Sit your arse back down and tell me what you've been doing."

Hatchet hesitated. As much as he wanted information, he wouldn't get it at the price of his friend's health.

"For God's sake, sit down," Emery ordered. "I'm not dying. It's just a bad cough."

"Are you sure you wouldn't like me to fetch someone?" Hatchet asked. "You sound terrible."

Emery grinned again. "The only reason I'd want you to fetch a doctor is so I could have more of that lovely cough syrup he dispenses so sparingly. But considering my earlier problem with that very substance, I don't think the doctor will oblige me unless I'm literally at death's door, which I'm not. So, as I said, sit your arse down and talk to me."

Hatchet chuckled and did as commanded. He was pleased that Emery had told his doctor about his problem with opium. Years ago Emery, like so many others, had become addicted to the substance. As it was now used in many medicines, Emery had been wise to tell the physician about his earlier predicament. Apparently his doctor had felt there was a chance of his becoming addicted again, and had been very stingy with the cough syrup. But it was awful to see Emery suffering so much. "The madam and I have been quite busy lately," Hatchet said. "Madam especially enjoys playing detective. Being of service has given her a whole new perspective on life. She's the happiest I've ever seen her."

"You're very devoted to her, aren't you?" Emery asked.

"Of course. She saved me. As you know, I was once in the same position as you found yourself, but mine was because of drink, not opium. If it hadn't been for her, I'd have been dead years ago. She found me drunk and starving in an alley in Baltimore, took me home, cleaned me up, and put me to work. I think she liked my accent."

"I was saved by a thief, not a crazy American," Emery replied. "Who would have thought that getting all my money stolen and then finding myself left to rot in a Bangkok jail cell would end up saving me?"

"You never did tell me how you got out of that cell," Hatchet said. He'd have liked to ask more questions about the Farringdons, but he'd learned enough. Now it was time to just talk with an old friend.

"I didn't actually get out." Emery grinned. "The building caught on fire, so they unlocked all the cells and trooped us out into the street. But the guard got into an argument with a street vendor, and when his back was turned, I took off, as did most of the others. I managed to throw myself on the mercy of an Englishman I ran into, and he hid me in his hotel. He was a decent bloke, a former butler to a Scottish lord. He's the one that taught me the trade, you know. He forged a few references so I could get my first position. You know, Hatchet, sometimes in life, you just get lucky."

"I know."

"And today's your lucky day." Emery smiled wanly. "I'm going to tell you the rest of what I know about the tontine."

"You don't need to do that. I'm quite happy simply to sit here and visit with you. I should have come more often to see you."

"I could have gone to see you as well," Emery replied. "All of us get busy with our own lives. Now, what else do you need to know?"

For a moment, Hatchet's mind went blank. Then he thought of something useful. "I've heard a rumor that Stephen Whitfield and Mrs. Farringdon weren't overly fond of one another. Is that true?"

"Whitfield was a dreadful snob. He looked down on Mrs. Farringdon because her family made a fortune in trade." Emery snorted. "Mind you, his family may be old and aristocratic, but he wouldn't have had a pot to piss in without the dividend from the tontine."

Hatchet laughed. "How many people are left in the tontine?"

"There were three, but now that Whitfield is dead, there's only two left: Mr. Farringdon and Henry Becker."

CHAPTER 8

Hugh Langdon lived in a six-story brown brick town house in Bulstrode Street in Marylebone. Witherspoon and Barnes stood inside the entrance while the housekeeper went to fetch Langdon.

As was his habit, Barnes studied the reception hall. Experience had taught him that a man's home could often give you a hint or two about his character. The walls were painted a pale cream; the floor was made of simple, polished oak; and directly opposite him was a wide staircase. A brass umbrella stand and coat tree were the only furniture in the foyer.

Hugh Langdon stepped through a set of double doors farther down the long hallway and motioned them forward. "Good day, Inspector. I've been expecting you. Do come inside, please."

They went into the drawing room. Barnes noted that the walls were painted the same shade as the foyer. A lovely peacock blue and brown carpet covered the wood floor, and blue and cream striped curtains hung at the three tall windows facing the street. Like those in the foyer, the furnishings were simple, attractive, and well crafted. The fittings and the furniture here hadn't been done to impress anyone, but rather to provide comfort for the occupants.

Langdon waved them to a pair of overstuffed chairs. "Please sit down, gentlemen."

"Thank you, Mr. Langdon," Witherspoon responded. "We'll try not to take up too much of your time. We do understand that you've a business to run."

"Would you or the constable care for a cup of tea?" Langdon asked. He sat down on the love seat opposite them.

"No, thank you," Witherspoon replied.

"Then I expect you'd like to get on with your questions." Langdon smiled sardonically. "I'm sure you're busy as well."

"I understand you were only recently introduced to Mr. Whitfield. You met him shortly before you went to dinner at his home," Witherspoon began.

"Actually, that's not quite true," Langdon interrupted smoothly. "I'd met Stephen Whitfield years earlier."

Witherspoon was taken aback. According to their information, the two men had met for the first time only days before the murder. That was one of the reasons they'd left Langdon to be questioned last. Witherspoon had assumed that because Langdon and Whitfield hadn't known each other or had any obvious connections besides their relationships with Eliza Graham, Langdon would be the least likely of all the dinner guests to have wanted Whitfield dead. "I'm afraid I don't understand. Mrs. Graham specifically told us she'd introduced the two of you only a few days before the murder."

"And she was telling the truth. Eliza had no idea that I'd met Whitfield previously, and it seems he'd forgotten our meeting as well," Langdon replied. "I apologize, Inspector. I ought to have mentioned this before, but the truth of the matter is that I met Stephen Whitfield thirty years ago."

"How did you meet?" Barnes reached in his pocket and pulled out his notebook

"We ran into Stephen last week when we were on our way into the Adelphi Theatre."

"No, I meant, how did you meet thirty years ago?" the constable clarified.

"Oh, sorry," Langdon said. "I wanted to become a member of the Bonfire Club. I was very young and trying my best to make my way in this hard old world, and I thought being a member of that particular organization would help me in business."

"And you met Whitfield at the club?" Witherspoon asked.

"Not quite. Whitfield was the chairman of the membership committee. I went to him and asked for a recommendation." Langdon grinned broadly. "Apparently that was the worst possible course of action. Whitfield took great offense that I'd dare approach him—and not only that, he blackballed me from membership in the club."

"That must have made going to his house for dinner a bit awkward," Witherspoon commented.

"Not really. As I said, he hadn't remembered me when we met that night at the theater." Langdon shrugged. "There was no reason why he should—the incident obviously hadn't been particularly important to him."

"Did you join another gentlemen's club?" The inspector watched Langdon's face as he asked the question. He was trying to determine how important membership to this club might have been for Langdon. Being blackballed from a society he was keen to join could be a motive for murder. In Witherspoon's experience, people were capable of holding grudges for a very long time. Old sins cast long shadows.

"No. I knew that if I couldn't get into the Bonfire, none of the other clubs would have me. Word gets about when you've been blackballed. But it was a long time ago, Inspector," Langdon said. "As the saying goes, it's all water under the bridge now."

"On the night you went to dinner at his home, did you inform Mr. Whitfield that you'd met before?" Barnes asked. "Or that he'd blackballed you?"

"Indeed I did." Langdon leaned back and crossed his arms over his chest. "I hadn't planned on mentioning the matter, as I didn't wish to cause Mrs. Graham any embarrassment. After all, I was her escort. Whitfield took us into the morning room to see the Christmas tree he'd had put up, and afterwards, when I'd gone back to the drawing room, he followed me. He said he wanted to have a word with me. But as I found his conversation somewhat objectionable, I'm afraid my good intentions about being polite went right out the window, and I took the opportunity to remind him that we'd met many years earlier." Langdon paused. "He didn't seem pleased by the news."

"Why did you go back to the drawing room?" Barnes asked quickly.

"I wanted to get some fresh air. The smell in the morning room was overpowering. The candles on that tree were blazing away, there was incense burning, and the ladies had doused themselves quite liberally with perfume. When my eyes began to water, I knew it was time to make a graceful exit into another part of the house."

"What did you mean when you said that Whitfield didn't seem

pleased to know you'd met previously? Did he tell you that specifically?" Witherspoon asked.

"He didn't say a word, Inspector. He just stood there, staring at me. But I could tell the news bothered him."

Barnes looked up from his notebook. "How could you tell, sir?"

"It was dead easy," Langdon replied. "You're a policeman, and I'll bet you know what I'm talking about. I'm sure you do it all the time when you're questioning suspects or taking a statement. You're doing it now as we speak. You appear to be making notes, but I can see that you and the inspector are observing me very closely. You see how my expression changes whenever you ask a question, or you watch the way I hold myself when I give you my answers. Very few people are skilled at truly hiding their feelings, and Whitfield was no exception. His face was as easy to read as the front page of the *Times*."

"I imagine it was," Barnes agreed.

"What did you find so objectionable about Whitfield's conversation when he followed you into the drawing room?" Witherspoon asked.

"Everything." Langdon uncrossed his arms and leaned forward. His expression hardened. "He tried to speak to me about Mrs. Graham. But I cut him off. My personal relationships are no one's business but mine."

"Do you know why he'd wish to discuss such a matter with someone he considered a stranger?" Witherspoon asked. Past experience had shown him that matters of the heart were always sensitive subjects.

"He wanted to warn me off her, Inspector. But I wasn't prepared to discuss her with Stephen Whitfield under any circumstances. I may not have been born to an upper-class family, but I am a gentleman when it comes to the women in my life. I certainly wasn't going to stand there and let him denigrate her character because she'd chosen me over him."

"So you knew that Mrs. Graham and Mr. Whitfield had been seeing each other?" Barnes asked.

"Mrs. Graham told me about her relationship with him from the very beginning," he replied. "Furthermore, she also told me he'd presumed that simply because they'd seen one another socially, she was willing to marry him. She wasn't."

"But he had proposed to her," Witherspoon stated.

"True." Langdon smiled sadly. "But Eliza had been candid with him. She'd told him she needed time to think about the matter. Yet even though she'd been honest and hadn't made any promises, she was sure he assumed she was going to consent to marry him."

Barnes said, "How long had you been seeing Mrs. Graham?"

"We met this past summer at a charity ball. We've been seeing one another ever since."

"And you didn't mind that she was still seeing Stephen Whitfield?" Witherspoon stared at him doubtfully. Men who'd made as much money as Hugh Langdon hadn't done so by sharing what they possessed. "You didn't object to that, sir?"

Langdon flushed angrily. "Of course I didn't like it, Inspector. But Mrs. Graham had her reasons for continuing to see him, and frankly, at the time she told me about him, I'd no idea how our relationship might progress. She needs to marry, and as I wasn't willing to commit to such a course of action until very recently, I could hardly object to her continuing a relationship with Whitfield. He had made it perfectly clear that he did want to marry her."

"And apparently you decided you did as well," Barnes murmured. He suddenly felt sorry for Stephen Whitfield. He might have been an arrogant, upper-class twit, but he'd been playing second fiddle for months and hadn't even known it.

"Yes, I did," Langdon declared. "Mrs. Graham and I are very well suited to one another. I proposed to her. That's the reason I wanted to accompany her to the dinner party that night. I wanted her to break it off with Stephen, and I wanted to be there when she did it."

"Yet you refused to discuss her with him when he brought the subject up," Witherspoon reminded him.

"That's right, Inspector." Langdon said. "I did. I wanted Eliza to do the telling. I only wanted to be there in case he got angry or abusive."

"Was there any reason to think he might react badly?" Witherspoon asked.

Langdon's eyes narrowed. "Of course there was. He had quite a bad temper."

"Did Mrs. Graham tell you that?" Barnes looked up from his notebook.

"She did not. I knew about Whitfield's temper from my own experiences with the man."

"But you hadn't seen him in years," the constable argued.

"So what, Constable? A leopard doesn't change his spots just because he's grown a few gray hairs around his snout," Langdon snapped. "Thirty years ago, when I asked him for help in getting into that stupid club, he became so enraged by my temerity, by my even daring to approach him with such a request, that he tried to strike me."

Witherspoon's eyebrows rose. "That is hardly the act of a gentleman."

Langdon sank back against the love seat. "It didn't really matter, Inspector. He was middle-aged, and I was young and fit. I easily avoided his fists and even got in a blow or two of my own."

That's the real reason he blackballed you, Barnes thought. You didn't let him cuff you about and pretend that his kind still rule the world.

"But you can understand why I wanted to be here when she told him it was over between them. I didn't want him taking his anger out on Eliza," Langdon continued. "But as it turned out, I needn't have worried. Before she could speak to him alone, he died."

Smythe whistled as he stepped through the door of the Dirty Duck Pub. Since he and Betsy had their little chat yesterday, life seemed just that bit brighter. They weren't back to normal yet, but they were getting there. He'd not lost her. She still loved him.

He pushed his way through the crowd to Blimpey's table. "Good day, old friend," Smythe said as he slipped onto the stool.

Blimpey grunted a greeting and then waved at the barmaid, caught her attention, and pointed to Smythe.

"What's wrong, Blimpey?" Smythe asked. "You look right miserable."

"I am miserable. Business is terrible." Blimpey snorted. "Half of London is gone to Scotland or Wales or some such other heathen place for Christmas. My sources at three of the busiest police stations are all down with the flu, and my man at the Old Bailey just told me he wants a raise. Can you believe it? Every time you turn around, someone's got their hand in your pocket or they're malingering in bed instead of doing their work properly." He broke off as the barmaid slipped a pint of beer on the table. She gave Smythe a quick grin and then scurried back to the bar.

"People can't 'elp it if they take ill." Smythe picked up his pint.

"And you don't 'ave to give your Old Bailey source a raise. You can always say no."

"He's too good a source to risk." Blimpey frowned. "I've got to give him a raise. Blast it all. No tellin' what he'll be wantin' next year."

"And there is a nasty flu goin' around." Smythe took a quick sip of beer. "So you can't blame your other sources for takin' to their beds."

"Hah! Young people these days will find any reason not to do their jobs," Blimpey cried. "Not like when I was growing up. You didn't take to your bed at the first sign of a sniffle or a bit of a cough."

Smythe put down his glass and stared at his companion. Blimpey kept his head lowered, staring at the tabletop as if it were a treasure map. "What's really wrong? This isn't like you. You've never complained about your sources taking a bit of time to themselves. As a matter of fact, everyone knows you always treat your people decently. That's one of the reasons people work for you— you're good to 'em."

Blimpey said nothing for a moment; then he lifted his chin and looked Smythe in the eye. "Oh, blast it. I'm bein' silly, and I know it. Makin' excuses because I don't want you to think ill of me."

Smythe didn't like the sound of that, but he said nothing.

"The truth of the matter is, I'm a bit embarrassed. I've not got much information for you at all, and from the way my sources are droppin' off, I have grave doubts that I'm going to find out anything useful in the near future."

Blast a Spaniard, Smythe thought. That wasn't what he wanted to hear. "You have nothing for me?"

"I've got a little. But it's not much, and I don't think the information has anything at all to do with your case." Blimpey shrugged apologetically.

In an effort to hide his disappointment, Smythe forced a smile. "Let's 'ear it, then." He'd been counting on learning a few facts from Blimpey, especially as his own snooping had turned up nothing. "Don't concern yourself on whether or not your information is useful. You never know what little fact 'elps solve the case. Who is it about?"

"Rosalind Murray."

Smythe relaxed a bit. "She's one of our stronger suspects. What did you find out about her?"

"I got a tidbit out of one of her servants . . ."

"They always know what's what." Smythe smiled encouragingly.

"Actually, it was someone who used to work for her, a housemaid."

"You mean the maid doesn't work in the household now?" His smile faded.

Blimpey glanced at the fireplace and then back at his pint. "The truth is, the girl left in September . . ."

"September," Smythe interrupted. "But that was months ago. Cor blimey, Whitfield was just killed a few days ago. How could this girl possibly know anything?"

"You said yourself that you don't know until the very end what might or might not be of value, so just drink your pint and have a listen," Blimpey retorted. "I've paid good money for this, so you can at least do me the courtesy of pretendin' you're interested."

Smythe took a deep breath. "Sorry. Go on."

"Rosalind Murray keeps a diary. She's done so for years. My source read this diary."

"And what did it say?" Smythe didn't see how a diary entry from three months before the murder could help, but he'd agreed to listen.

Blimpey eyed him appraisingly. "Your lot is lookin' at everyone who was at dinner the night Whitfield was killed, and wonderin' what their motives might be, right?"

"That's generally what we do. Why?"

"Because I'm thinkin' that, seein' as how the word I got was that Rosalind Murray was supposedly Whitfield's mistress for the past ten years, you're all thinkin' her motive for murderin' him is because he was goin' to jilt her for another woman, right?"

"Are we playin' guessin' games here, or are you goin' to tell me what you found out?" Smythe cried impatiently. He had the horrible feeling they were going to lose another one of their few motives for this murder.

"Alright, alright, hold yer horses. I'm gettin' to it. What I'm tryin' to tell ya is, if that's what you've been thinkin' about Mrs. Murray, you'd be dead wrong. Rosalind Murray wasn't jealous of Stephen Whitfield carryin' on with another woman." Blimpey grinned. "As a matter of fact, according to her own words, she was glad he'd taken up with someone else so she could get on with her own life. She had plans."

Smythe thought for a moment; then he shook his head. "Are you sure your source wasn't lying? This can't be right. We've a witness who claims Mrs. Murray and Whitfield 'ad a terrible row, and it was about him gettin' serious with Mrs. Graham."

"My source has no reason to lie," Blimpey declared.

"Did you pay her?"

"What's that got to do with the price of turnips? I pay all my sources. That's why I'm able to do what I do," Blimpey said indignantly.

Smythe studied his companion for a long moment. A dull red flush had crept up Blimpey's cheeks, and once again he was studying the tabletop as though it could tell him where King Midas' gold was buried. "She came to you after you'd put the word out that you were lookin' for any information about the Whitfield household, didn't she?"

Blimpey nodded. "But she's a good source, Smythe. I made sure of that. I asked about, and she's not a greedy lass who'd make something up for a bit of coin, nor is she one of them kind that lies just to get people to notice her."

"You know your business, Blimpey," Smythe said. "I'm not questionin' that. It's just—this doesn't make sense . . . or does it?"

"You mean you're wonderin' if maybe the dustup between the Murray woman and Whitfield didn't 'ave sod-all to do with him takin' up with the Graham woman? Maybe you just assumed that's what she was goin' on about, because that's what made sense to you."

"That is what I'm startin' to think," Smythe admitted. In which case, he wondered how many of their other assumptions might be wrong.

Blimpey shrugged. "I wouldn't know whether or not there was some misunderstandin' on what the two of 'em were squabblin' about, but I do know what my source reported."

Smythe nodded, his expression thoughtful. "The girl claimed that Mrs. Murray had plans. Did she know what those plans might be?"

"Nah, she only got to read a few pages of the diary before she had to chuck it back when she heard Mrs. Murray comin' up the stairs." He laughed.

"Rosalind Murray was in the house when the girl was readin' her diary?" Smythe asked incredulously. "That was brave of her."

"Not really." Blimpey laughed again. "She'd already given her notice, and claimed that she didn't much care if she got caught. I don't think she liked the Whitfield house very much. But she's not lying—I'm sure of it. She's a good girl."

"Good girl, my foot," Smythe snorted. "She's a slyboots, she is. She read Mrs. Murray's diary. What does that say about her character?"

Blimpey's eyebrows rose. "It says she was curious. Not everyone who started out in service was lucky enough or clever enough to go off to Australia and make a fortune."

"Even when I was just a coachman, I'd never 'ave read someone's private papers," he replied.

"Climb down off your high horse, Smythe." Blimpey plopped his elbows on the rickety table and leaned forward. "Have you forgotten what bein' in service is like for most young girls? They're worked harder than cart horses, abused by their employers, and constantly dodgin' the lecherous advances of the master or his sons. You can't blame them for wantin' to get a little of their own back."

"But Rosalind Murray had a reputation for treatin' staff decently," Smythe said.

"Maybe so, but even the decent employers work most of their servants harder than slaves, begrudge every bite of food they put in their mouths, and treat 'em lower than dirt."

"Not every household is like that," Smythe said defensively. But he was a bit ashamed. Blimpey had a point. "Besides, you was just complainin' about your people takin' to their beds and wantin' more money."

"Yes, but I was just makin' excuses to cover up bein' embarrassed because I'd found out so little," he said smugly. "You said it yourself—I treat my people real well, and I do it because I know what it's like to work my fingers to the bone for not much more than a crust of bread. Most of the prosperous ones in this town don't have any idea what life is really like for workin' people. Euphemia Witherspoon was a decent sort, and your inspector's a good man as well. But neither of them was from the upper class, were they? Neither of them was trained from birth to see the rest of the human race as slaves put here to do their bidding or make their lives easy. You've had it better than most, Smythe, but not everyone is as lucky as you. Not everyone has a chance to get out."

Smythe stared at him for a long moment. "I 'ave 'ad it better than most."

Blimpey blushed. "Sorry, I didn't mean to go on and on. Cor blimey, you probably think I'm soundin' like one of them ruddy Socialists. But sometimes they have a point."

"Yeah, there is some injustice in this old world." Smythe took another sip of his beer. "And most servants do get treated badly."

"My mother was in service," Blimpey said softly. "Her master tossed her out when she got bronchitis and couldn't work anymore. She never even made it 'ome the night she died. She collapsed in the street."

"How old were you?"

"Ten."

"That's 'ard," Smythe said. No wonder Blimpey sounded so bitter.

Blimpey shrugged. "It was. I loved my mum, Smythe. She was a wonderful woman. Despite how little we had, she made sure I got a bit of education. She never knew I did any thievin'. She'd have hated that. But I think she'd have liked how I've turned out."

"You've become a very prosperous businessman," Smythe said quickly. "Your mum would have been very proud."

"Indeed she would have," Blimpey agreed. "I've money in the bank, I've a nice house, and I own quite a bit of property, if I do say so myself."

"You've done very well."

"I've married a good woman and made a decent home for us," he continued. "But you know what she'd have been most proud of?"

"What?"

Blimpey smiled. "Most of all, she'd have been happy I managed to bankrupt the bastard that tossed her into the streets that night."

Barnes pulled open the heavy front door of New Scotland Yard and held it for the inspector. "What time are you seeing Chief Inspector Barrows?" he asked as Witherspoon stepped past him into the reception area. Barnes followed him inside.

"He said that anytime after three o'clock would do." Witherspoon stopped, pulled out his pocket watch, and noted the time. "So we can go right on up. He ought to be in his office." He nodded at the two policemen on duty behind the counter, and headed for the stairs.

"Is the chief expecting a full report, sir?" Barnes asked as they started up.

"Oh, I daresay he's hoping we've got the case solved"— Witherspoon sighed—"and that I'll walk into his office and tell him we're making an arrest today. You know how the powers that be hate having an unsolved murder over Christmas."

They reached the first-floor landing and turned down the long hallway to Barrows' office, which was at the far end. They were halfway down the corridor when the door just ahead of them opened and Inspector Nigel Nivens stepped out. He stopped when he saw them.

Nivens was a man of medium height who was running to fat. He had dark blond hair going gray at the temples; bulging, watery blue eyes; and a thick mustache. He was dressed in a gray-blue checked overcoat open far enough to reveal a dark blue suit and gray sateen waistcoat. A deerstalker hat in the same fabric as the overcoat dangled from his fingers.

"Well, well, if it isn't the fair-haired lads of the Metropolitan Police Department." He sneered. "Here to give the chief an update on your latest case?"

"We're here to make a report," Witherspoon said politely as he swept past. He didn't like being rude, but he was aware that Nigel Nivens didn't like him and probably did in fact hate him. Their encounters this past year had convinced him that Nivens would like nothing better than to see him utterly destroyed.

Nivens slammed the deerstalker onto his head. He hurried after them, his boots pounding heavily against the wooden floor. "You'd better be close to an arrest, Witherspoon," he said in a loud voice. "If you can't get this case solved soon, they're going to give it to someone who will."

Barnes looked behind him and gave Nivens a good glare. Witherspoon ignored the man and kept on walking.

"That means me, Witherspoon," Nivens cried.

Barnes glanced at Witherspoon, but the inspector resolutely kept his gaze straight ahead.

"Did you hear what I said?" Nivens yelled. He was furious at being ignored—especially as some of the doors down the long hallway had opened and a number of policemen were now watching.

Witherspoon reached Barrows' office. He continued ignoring Nivens, lifted his hand, and rapped softly on the door.

Unable to stop himself, Barnes turned. Nivens had halted a few feet away. "Don't worry, sir," the constable said. "You're not going to be overly burdened with additional work. Inspector Witherspoon has this case well in hand. An arrest is imminent."

"Good, glad to hear that." The voice came from behind him and belonged to the chief inspector.

Barnes turned slowly and saw Witherspoon staring at him with an expression of undisguised horror on his face. Chief Inspector Barrows was beaming. Barnes heard a snort from Nivens, who then turned and stomped off. As he moved down the hall, the constables who'd been watching quickly closed their doors and went back to their business.

"Actually," Witherspoon said quickly, "we're making progress, but I'm not sure we're ready to . . ."

"Don't be so modest, Witherspoon. As the good constable said, you've got the case well in hand." Barrows clapped him on the back. "You're always hiding your light under a basket. Come inside and give me a proper report. You, too, Constable." He ushered the two of them into his office and pointed at two chairs in front of his desk. "Take a seat."

"Thank you, sir," Witherspoon began.

"Don't mind anything Inspector Nivens might have said. His nose is more out of joint than usual. He lost a case in court this morning. Two burglars he nabbed were acquitted." Barrows frowned and shook his head in disgust. "Stupid fool should learn to make sure he's got the evidence before he makes an arrest."

Barnes exhaled the breath he was holding and sat down. He knew he should have held his tongue, but he hadn't expected Chief Inspector Barrows to pop out of his ruddy office. "Actually, sir, I spoke a bit too soon."

Barrows looked amused. "Of course you did, Constable. Your words were for Nivens' benefit. I know that. The man gets on my nerves as well, especially when he makes the police look like incompetent fools in front of a judge and jury, but he does have good political connections. But that aside"—he looked at Witherspoon—

"even if you're not close to an arrest, I take it you are making progress."

"Yes, sir, we are. We're working very hard," Witherspoon replied. "But there are some difficulties."

"Difficulties." Barrows frowned as if the word itself was offensive. "What sort of difficulties?"

Witherspoon hesitated. "Unfortunately we've no idea why Mr. Whitfield was murdered. There simply doesn't seem to be any compelling reason for anyone at the dinner party or any member of his household to have wanted him dead."

"The why is the least of it." Barrows waved his hand impatiently. "Are you absolutely certain the killer was one of the dinner guests or someone in the household?"

"Yes, sir." Witherspoon nodded. "The wine he'd been drinking was poisoned."

"I know that. I've read the postmortem report," Barrows replied. "And you've determined that no one from outside the household could have had access to the open bottle?"

"The butler was on duty near the front door, and if an unknown person had come in through the back, they would have had to walk right by the kitchen, which had staff going in and out all evening long," Witherspoon replied. "It's highly unlikely that an outsider could have gotten in, poisoned the wine, and left the premises without being seen."

"And I suppose it's impossible to determine which of the guests might have been alone long enough to have had access to the bottle," Barrows said.

"They were all milling about, sir," Witherspoon replied. "Mr. Whitfield had one of those decorated Christmas trees in the morning room, and all the guests were dashing about everywhere. No one seems able to recall who might have been where at any given moment in time."

"It would only take a second to put the crushed leaves in the wine, sir," Barnes added.

Barrows leaned back, closed his eyes, and rubbed his forehead. "You'd have thought the man would have noticed leaves floating in his bloody glass, wouldn't you?" He opened his eyes and straightened up.

"They were crushed very fine," Witherspoon explained. "And it was nighttime, sir. There were only gas lamps and candles burning. I expect that the leaves were hardly noticeable under those circumstances."

Barnes, trying to make up for his earlier mistake, said, "The witnesses all stated that Whitfield was drinking the wine as fast as he could get it down his throat, sir."

"In other words, he was slogging it back so quickly he'd not have noticed a ruddy rat floating in it." Barrows sighed again. "This is no good. Christmas is less than a week away. Do you have any other leads? Did you get any useful tips from the neighbors or the house-to-house?"

"We didn't do an extensive house-to-house, sir," Witherspoon told him. "It was obvious right from the start that it was an inside job, so to speak. But we did interview the neighbors on each side of the Whitfield house. They neither saw nor heard anything unusual that night. There was no one suspicious lurking about the area, and none of them knew of anyone who might have wished Mr. Whitfield harm."

"Have you questioned the servants in the adjoining houses?" Barrows rubbed his hand over his chin.

"We have, sir. But none of them saw or heard anything unusual, either." Witherspoon glanced at Barnes. The constable gave a barely perceptible shrug. All of this information was in their preliminary report, which was currently open on the desk right in front of the chief.

"Question the Whitfield servants again." Barrows yawned. "They might know more than they were willing to tell the first time around. And have another go at the dinner guests. We've got to get this one solved, and we're running out of time."

"Yes, sir. We intended to speak again to everyone who was there that night," Witherspoon assured him.

"I don't mind telling you, we're getting pressure from the Home Office on this one." Barrows smiled cynically. "They don't like it when a member of the upper class gets murdered. It scares them. Of course, if it had been some poor sod from Stepney that had gotten it in the neck, they'd not be so concerned." He clamped his mouth shut. "Sorry, I didn't mean to go off on a tirade. It just annoys me that the HO seems to think the life of a rich man is worth more than anyone else's."

"I understand how you feel, sir," Witherspoon replied. "I promise you, we'll do our very best."

Barrows nodded and got to his feet. "Keep digging, Inspector, and please, let's try to have an arrest before Christmas if at all possible."

"We'll keep you informed of our progress, sir," Witherspoon said as he and Barnes got to their feet.

Neither policeman said anything until they were out of Barrows' office and almost to the staircase.

"Sorry, sir," Barnes began. "I shouldn't have spoken up when we ran into Inspector Nivens."

"That's quite alright, Constable." Witherspoon smiled faintly. "The chief inspector made it very clear he knew what you were doing."

"Yes, but he still wants an arrest before Christmas," Barnes muttered.

"Only because he's getting pressure from the HO. Poor man. He looks very tired."

"Do you think he's right, sir?" Barnes started down the stairs. "I mean, about the why of a murder being the least important part."

"No." Witherspoon pulled his gloves out of his coat pocket. "With all due respect to him, I think he's dead wrong about that. In my view, once you discover the why, you find the killer. Now, I think if we hurry, we can have a quick interview with Whitfield's solicitor. He's supposed to be back in his office today."

"This has been an inconvenient time for the man to come down with the flu," Barnes said as they reached the bottom of the stairs. He glanced at the clock over the counter behind the duty constables and saw that it was just past four. They'd never make it to the solicitor's offices on Addison Road and then get back to West Brompton in time to speak to the servants before nightfall. "But what about the servants at the Whitfield house, sir? Should we leave them until tomorrow?"

"I think so." Witherspoon pulled open the door and stepped out.

They were lucky enough to find a hansom right away, so despite the heavy traffic over the bridge, the found themselves at the law offices of Runyon & Gable within twenty minutes.

John Runyon had been expecting them. He ushered them both into his office and instructed the young clerk in the outer office to see that they weren't disturbed. "I'm sorry I've been unavailable," he apologized. "My clerk said you'd been here twice before, but I've been ill."

"That's quite alright, sir," Witherspoon replied politely. "I do hope you're feeling better."

"Thank you. I'm on the mend, as they say. Please sit down." Runyon motioned toward two chairs in front of the desk. He was a slender man with bushy eyebrows. Though elderly, he had very clear blue eyes. He was holding a white handkerchief to his nose and blew gently into it as he walked around the desk and took his seat.

"We won't keep you long, sir, but we do have a few questions about your late client Stephen Whitfield," Witherspoon said. He took off his bowler and sat down. The constable took the chair next to him.

"I know why you're here, Inspector." Runyon picked up a pair of spectacles that were lying on top of an open file on his desktop, and put them on. "My client was murdered, and you're trying to determine who might have had reason to want him dead." It was a statement of fact, not a question.

"That is correct, sir. As his solicitor, you're in a position to tell us who benefited the most from his death," Witherspoon said. "We understand that he had made a will."

"Of course he did," Runyon replied. "In the interest of saving time, I've made a list of his bequests. I take it that's what you're most interested in hearing about?"

Witherspoon nodded eagerly. "Indeed."

Runyon looked down at his desk and began to read. "Let's start with the servants first. He left fifty pounds to the cook, Hannah Walker, and a hundred pounds to the butler, Jeremiah Flagg."

"Nothing to the other servants?" Barnes asked.

"No, they'd not been with him long enough to warrant an inheritance." Runyon glanced up at the constable. "The butler and the cook were family servants. They'd been there for years." He picked up the paper and continued reading. "His other bequests are simple enough. He left his gold watch, two sets of sterling silver cuff links, an onyx ring, and his rosewood jewel case to Rosalind Murray, his sister-in-law. All of his clothing is to be sold and the proceeds used to pay for a memorial plaque at St. Stephen's Church in Holcomb Street." Runyon put down the paper, took off his spectacles, and looked at the two policemen. "Is there anything else I can help you with?"

Witherspoon stared at him incredulously. "Is that it? I don't understand. Wasn't he a rich man?"

"As long as he was alive, he was quite well-off," Runyon replied. "But the house belongs to his late wife's family and will now go to Mrs. Murray; he didn't own any other property; and the only company he ever owned stock in went bankrupt twenty years ago."

"What do you mean, as long as he was alive?" Witherspoon asked.

"As long as Mr. Whitfield was alive, he collected an annual dividend from an annuity that was established many years ago."

"What happens to his share of the annuity, then?" Barnes asked. "Who inherits that?"

"No one." Runyon smiled ruefully. "His share of the dividend becomes part of the annuity capital."

"How long ago was this annuity established?" Witherspoon was beginning to understand.

"When Mr. Whitfield was born," Runyon admitted. "In those days, it was referred to as a tontine. There were ten infants on the original charter. Their families each put in ten thousand pounds, and the money was invested—very wisely I might add. Each child, as he grew, was entitled to one-tenth of the total dividend share. Over the years the investment has grown substantially, and the dividends have increased accordingly."

"So as the shareholders died off, the dividends got bigger and bigger," Barnes muttered.

"That is correct," Runyon said.

"But tontines are illegal," Witherspoon sputtered.

"As well they should be." Runyon nodded in agreement. "There hasn't been a tontine established in over fifty years. But this one was established well before that time."

"We heard that Mr. Whitfield recently sent for you," Barnes added. "He was going to change his will. But why would he bother if all he had to leave was a few bits of jewelry?"

"He wanted the jewelry to go to—" Runyon broke off, looked down at the file, and pushed aside the top page. He picked up the one underneath it. "A woman named Eliza Graham. He said they were engaged."

CHAPTER 9

"Good afternoon, madam. We're so pleased you could join us." With a broad smile, Hatchet greeted the last one to appear at their afternoon meeting. He'd been the first to arrive.

Luty stopped just inside the doorway and stared at him. Her eyes narrowed as she took in his bright expression and barely controlled exuberance. He was fairly bouncing in his seat. "You're grinnin' like the cat that got the cream. You found out somethin' important, didn't ya?" She continued across the room, her skirts rustling as she headed for her usual place at the table.

"Everything we learn is important, madam. This is a group effort, so all of our contributions are essential to solving the case. However, I will admit that I've had some modest success today," he replied. He got to his feet and pulled out her chair.

"Humph," Luty snorted as she flopped into her seat. "Then you have to go last. That's only fair, seein' as how my contributions to catchin' this killer ain't amounted to so much as a hill of beans."

"You mustn't think that, Luty," Mrs. Jeffries said quickly. "You always do your share. You've given us lots of facts we couldn't have gotten without you. You know as well as I do that we never learn until the very end what bit of knowledge led us to solve the case."

Luty smiled wanly. "That's nice of ya to say, but some days it's discouragin'. Tryin' to get people to talk today was like pullin' hens' teeth."

Hatchet stared at her sympathetically. She really did look downhearted. "I take it you weren't able to uncover any details about the distribution of Whitfield's estate?"

"Nope, and I didn't find out much of anything else, either. All in all, it was a right waste of my time. I talked to every lawyer I know and even tried bribin' a couple of clerks, but no one knew anything—or if they did, they weren't tellin'."

"Don't be sad." Wiggins reached over and patted her on the arm. "I 'ad a miserable day, too, and I didn't find out anything, either."

"Some days are simply like that," Mrs. Goodge added. She put a plate of scones onto the table, next to the teapot. "If no one objects, I'd like to go first." She paused briefly and then continued. "Yesterday I heard some gossip about Rosalind Murray. Namely, that the only thing she inherited from her husband when he died were some shares in a tea plantation out in the Far East."

"How come you didn't tell us this at our meeting?" Betsy helped herself to a scone.

"If you'll recall, the inspector came home earlier than expected." The cook grinned. "And at breakfast this morning, there wasn't time. Besides, as I've already told Mrs. Jeffries, I'm not all that convinced my source was very dependable, so I wasn't sure I should even mention it at all. But today I did talk to someone quite reliable, and I found out some very interesting facts about Hugh Langdon." She repeated what Emma Darnley had told her, taking care to ensure that she didn't forget any of it.

"So he wasn't the sort the man to be concerned about gossip," Mrs. Jeffries said thoughtfully.

"And it appears that he was going to marry Mrs. Graham," the cook added. "So that means she certainly didn't have a reason to want Whitfield dead. He wasn't a danger to her."

"There's another suspect gone," Betsy muttered.

Mrs. Jeffries looked at her sharply. She'd thought she was the only one to realize the case was going badly.

Hatchet leaned forward, his expression puzzled. "Pardon me, but I don't quite see how you reached that conclusion." He looked from the cook to the housekeeper and then to the maid.

It was Mrs. Jeffries who answered. "Our assumption has been that Eliza Graham's motive might have been that she was afraid Whitfield could somehow stop her marriage to Langdon."

"I don't see 'ow," Wiggins said. He looked as confused as Hatchet.

"Don't be daft, lad," Mrs. Goodge said. "Among many women of her class, even a breath of scandal would be enough to stop a man from proposing. But from what we've now learned about Langdon, he wasn't the sort of man to pay any attention to scandalmongering or rumors."

"But we don't know whether Eliza Graham knew that," Betsy said hopefully. "We don't know that she had any idea he'd ever been engaged. Mrs. Goodge found out because, well, that's the sort of thing we do. But that doesn't mean Langdon told her about his previous fiancée." She glanced at Smythe. "Some men are very secretive about their pasts."

"I wasn't tryin' to hide anything from you," Smythe said defensively. "You never asked me any questions about my past. I'd 'ave told ya anything you wanted to know."

"Of course you would have. But I didn't ask." Betsy turned her attention back to the others. "That's what I'm talking about. Maybe she didn't ask Langdon any questions, either, and perhaps he didn't think his past was any of her business. Or if he did tell her, he might not have said a word about his first fiancée being the object of vicious gossip."

Mrs. Goodge crossed her arms over her chest and stared at the maid. "Come now, Betsy, you don't really believe that, do you? How could she not know about his past? It's true that we make a point of finding out what we can about our suspects, but do you honestly think that Eliza Graham, a woman we know had to marry for money and position, wouldn't find out everything she possibly could about Langdon before she let their relationship get to the point where he'd propose marriage?"

"The inspector said she was quite candid about her circumstances," Mrs. Jeffries added. "And she obviously found out enough about Stephen Whitfield's financial situation to decide he wasn't a particularly good prospect. She knew the house didn't belong to him."

"But she didn't stop seeing him," Wiggins said.

"Why should she?" Mrs. Goodge answered. "Mrs. Graham wasn't getting any younger. I've no doubt she considered Whitfield her fallback position in case Langdon didn't come through with a proposal."

"But she knew that Whitfield didn't even own his house," Smythe said. "Why not just break it off with him altogether?"

"She isn't a fool," Luty said. "Even if she wasn't goin' to marry Whitfield, if it didn't work out with Langdon, Whitfield was her entry into high society."

"Do women really think like that?" Wiggins looked very disturbed. "That sounds right cold'earted."

"She had no other choice," Betsy replied. "It's not as if someone of her class could go out and find work. I suppose that you're all right, though: Mrs. Graham must have known something about his past, and that means she probably knew about his previous engagement." She broke off and grinned at Smythe. "Maybe you and I should have a nice long natter about your past."

Relieved that she could make light of the matter, he laughed. "As soon as this case is solved, you can ask me anything you want."

"Whatever you can say about Mrs. Graham, she didn't try to 'ide what she wanted with her gentlemen," Wiggins said. "She told the inspector she 'ad to marry for money."

"That's true," Betsy murmured. "And if we could find out so easily about Hugh Langdon's past, so could she. It wasn't a secret."

"I expect Eliza Graham knows everything there is to know about the feller," Luty added. "Includin' how much he's worth and whether or not he's got any relatives."

"Were you able to find out anything else?" Mrs. Jeffries asked the cook. She wanted to move the meeting onward, away from any potentially disastrous discussions of what Smythe might or might not have told Betsy about his past. The girl had smiled at her fiancé, but Mrs. Jeffries had seen a flash of pain in her eyes when she said the two of them should have a "nice long natter" about his past.

Mrs. Goodge shook her head. "Not really. Emma spent the rest of our time together talking about her grandchildren. She has six of them, and to hear her tell it, they're all perfect little angels."

"Who would like to go next?" Mrs. Jeffries looked around the table.

"I'll have a go," Betsy offered. "I didn't find out all that much, but I was able to have a cup of tea with a maid from the Farringdon house." She told them about her meeting with Rachel Webster. She paused occasionally in her recitation, casting her mind back to the café and to Rachel's face as she spoke. It was a trick Betsy used to help herself recall information. When she was finished, she was thirsty, so she picked up her cup and took a long sip of tea.

"So Basil Farringdon and his wife are quite devoted to one another," Mrs. Jeffries muttered.

"They must be," Luty said. "Most people are scared of rough water, especially if you ain't a strong swimmer."

"But the important thing you found out is that Maria Farringdon really did hate Whitfield," Mrs. Goodge said. "We ought to have a closer look at her. She's a strange one, she is. Pourin' good port down the sink when she could have sent it into the kitchen to use for cooking, collecting wine bottles . . ."

"She wanted the labels," Betsy said quickly. "Rachel told me that as well. I almost forgot. She mentioned it as we were leaving. She said that one of her responsibilities at the house was steaming the labels off the empty bottles."

"What did she want the labels for?" Wiggins asked.

"Mrs. Farringdon put them in a big book and then made notes at the bottom of the page on what sort of food was served with that particular wine. Rachel said it was hard to get the labels to come off, so they used a teakettle to steam them. But she said that most of the time they ripped in half or fell to bits."

"Why would anyone want wine labels?" Smythe asked. "I could understand wantin' the bottles. You could use them for brewin' peach brandy or summer wine."

"She got the bottles from social events that she'd attended with her husband. Everyone said she worked hard to be a credit to him, and if you'll recall, Mrs. Farringdon didn't grow up knowing anything about wine. I think it was very clever of her to use the labels to figure out the right food to serve with the right wine when she had her own dinner parties," Betsy explained.

"I still think she's a strange one," Mrs. Goodge said. "Mind you, she's not as odd as Henry Becker. He's another one we need to keep our eye on."

"That's all I heard today," Betsy finished.

"I'll go next," Smythe volunteered. "It seems we might be wrong about Rosalind Murray bein' a woman scorned. Accordin' to my source, she was relieved that Whitfield turned his attentions to Mrs. Graham. She had plans of her own and was glad to get him off her 'ands, so to speak."

"But she had a row with him over his engagement," Mrs. Jeffries said. "And when she was telling the inspector about his plans to go to Italy with her, the inspector was sure she seemed a very bitter person."

"But was the argument really over his engagement, or was it over somethin' else? All we know for sure is that the two of them 'ad a right old dustup, but we don't really know what it was about. As for her bein' bitter, lots of people get soured on life. Besides, my source was repeatin' Rosalind Murray's own thoughts and words. She keeps a diary."

"And your source read this diary?" Mrs. Jeffries asked.

"She did. The girl was a real little slyboots, and she wanted to get a bit of her own back." Smythe told them what details he could without revealing how he'd obtained the information.

"That means that as far back as September, she was makin' plans of her own," Luty said speculatively. " 'Course, it could be that one of them plans was killin' Whitfield—that's one way of gettin' rid of him."

"But why wait until now?" Betsy asked reasonably. "She's known for ten years that the house was hers when he died. Why wait until now to kill him? The inspector told Mrs. Jeffries that Mrs. Murray seemed sure Whitfield was going to marry Mrs. Graham. That means she *was* finally getting rid of him."

"Maybe she was scared he was going to toss her into the street," Wiggins suggested helpfully. "It was his 'ouse as long as he lived, right?"

"He couldn't toss her out," the cook replied. "Whitfield's situation is very common. I worked in two places where the same thing happened. A man ends up living in the wife's family home. Usually he's given a lifetime right of residency, but that's all. He has no control over whether other family members can live in the house as well. Believe me, his wife's family will have made sure of that."

"I've no idea what any of this might mean," Mrs. Jeffries murmured. She had a horrid feeling that she was deluding herself. Though she hadn't had time to think about all of this as thoroughly as she'd like, so far it seemed they were losing motives left and right. "But it's getting late, and we've yet to hear from Hatchet." She looked at the coachman. "Were you finished?"

"I was. Let Hatchet 'ave his turn now." Smythe grinned wickedly.

"He's been very patient, even though it's obvious he's bustin' to talk."

"I am indeed quite eager to say my piece." Hatchet took a deep breath and paused dramatically, making sure that he had everyone's undivided attention. "I found out the details about Whitfield's estate." Without mentioning names, he told them everything he'd learned from his old friend Emery Richards.

He took his time in the telling, explaining the complicated nature of the tontine as best he could. When he finished, he leaned back in his seat and waited for the inevitable questions and comments.

"A tontine." Mrs. Jeffries shook her head. "No wonder we had so much trouble finding out about the estate."

"You can bet yer bottom dollar that none of his fancy lawyers talked much about it," Luty added indignantly. "They'd not like those details bein' bandied about, now, would they?"

"But this one was started before the government outlawed 'em,' Wiggins said. "So why was it so 'ard for us to find out? Annuities are legal, and that's what it is now."

"The legal issues aside," Hatchet began, "I expect it was kept quiet because none of them wished to be associated with an institution that essentially gives those involved a reason to be delighted at the death of one of their peers. There's something quite disgusting about the entire idea."

"Their income went up every time one of them died?" Wiggins wanted to make sure he understood the facts. "So tontines were outlawed. But did people really kill each other so they'd be the sole survivor?"

Mrs. Goodge stared at the footman in disbelief. "Knowing what we do about murder, how can you even ask that? Of course people really murdered one another, and for all we know, that may end up being the motive in this case."

"That's right," Hatchet replied. "As I said, there were originally ten members. Three didn't survive childhood, which left seven. Over the years, the others have died off, and now with Whitfield gone, there's only two left."

"Henry Becker and Basil Farringdon," Mrs. Jeffries said.

"And neither of them need the money enough to kill for it," Smythe muttered. "Becker's wealthy, and Farringdon's wife has plenty enough for both of them.'

"Maybe Basil Farringdon was tired of depending on his wife," Betsy speculated. "Maybe he wanted a bit of his own."

Mrs. Jeffries shook her head. "I don't think so, Betsy. He jumped into a rough sea to save her life. If he wanted money of his own, he could have just let her drown."

Inspector Witherspoon was late getting home that evening. Mrs. Jeffries met him at the front door. "Gracious, sir, we were beginning to worry," she said as she reached for his bowler hat.

"I stayed to finish up some reports," he said. He slipped off his overcoat and handed that to her as well. "And there was a dreadful traffic jam just this side of the park."

She hung up his things and looked at him. He appeared very depressed. His face was paler than usual, there were dark circles forming under his eyes, and tufts of his hair were standing straight up. "Are you alright, sir?"

"I'm just tired," he admitted. "I do hope Mrs. Goodge hasn't gone to too much trouble over my dinner. I'm not really hungry."

"It's a simple grill, sir. Pork chops and potatoes. Stewed apples, too." She watched him carefully as she spoke, hoping that he wasn't coming down with that awful flu that was going around. "Shall I bring it up to the dining room?"

"Not yet. I think I'd like a sherry first. Do come along and join me." He led the way down the hall and into the drawing room. Mrs. Jeffries hurried past him and went to the cabinet. He sat down while she poured both of them a glass of sherry.

"Now, sir, tell me what's wrong," she ordered as she handed him his glass.

"It's this case, Mrs. Jeffries." He sighed heavily, sank back into the chair, and took a sip of sherry. "I've no idea what to do next."

"Is that all that's bothering you, sir?" she asked, striving to sound as unconcerned as possible. "I was worried you were coming down with something. There's a terrible flu going around."

"Mrs. Jeffries, I am deadly serious. I think this is going to be the case that I will not be able to resolve. I've no idea who killed Stephen Whitfield, and the more that I learn, the more muddled I get."

As she felt exactly the same way, it was rather difficult for her to dredge up the right words to bolster his confidence. "But that's the way you always feel just before you find the solution, sir," she replied. She hoped the words didn't sound as false to his ears as they did to hers. "It's always the darkest just before the dawn," she continued, "and I've no doubt whatsoever that your inner eye has already seen that one perfect clue that will lead you to the killer."

"Inner eye," he repeated. "I thought you always told me I had an inner voice."

"It's the same thing, sir," she said cheerfully. "It's that part of your mind that takes in the facts, observes the suspects, and then points you in the right direction. I believe some people call the phenomenon 'intuition.' It is a process that hasn't failed you yet, sir, and you must have faith that it won't let you down this time."

"I do hope you're right," he replied earnestly. But he didn't look convinced.

"Did you find out anything useful today, sir?" She sat down on the settee and took a sip from her own glass. In truth, she was also dispirited. Time was marching onward, and she had no idea who had killed Whitfield.

Witherspoon told her about his day. She heard every detail of the meeting with Hugh Langdon, with the chief inspector, and with Whitfield's solicitor. She listened carefully, asked questions at appropriate intervals, and made occasional comments. When he told her about the tontine, she contrived to look surprised. She even managed to hold her tongue when he described his meeting with Inspector Nivens.

The conversation continued when he went into the dining room for his dinner. By the time he'd finished his stewed apples, he was in a much better frame of mind. "I do feel better." He put his serviette on the table and pushed his empty saucer to one side. "A thorough discussion of the facts of the matter always seems to help so very much."

"Perhaps all you needed was a good meal, sir," she murmured. Her own frame of mind hadn't improved one whit.

"Mind you, if I don't make some headway within the next few days, I may ask the chief inspector to turn this case over to someone else," he commented. A yawn escaped him, and he clamped his hand over his mouth. "Good gracious, where did that come from? I must be more tired than I thought." He pushed back the chair and got to his feet.

Alarmed, Mrs. Jeffries leapt up as well. "You're not serious, sir, are you? Who could possibly take over the case? You're the best detective in the Metropolitan Police Force."

"That's very kind of you, Mrs. Jeffries." He smiled wanly. "But despite my past successes, if I can't solve this one, I may not have any choice."

"Surely the chief isn't going to listen to anything Inspector Nivens has to say," she replied.

"Nivens has many friends in the Home Office," Witherspoon said. "But even so, I don't think Chief Inspector Barrows would take me off the case just because of Nivens' machinations. But he can resist only so much pressure to get the wretched thing solved, and if I can't do it, he'll have no choice but to bring in someone else. I'm not going to let it get that far—if I don't make any real progress in the next few days, I'm going to ask that it be assigned to someone else."

"But, sir, that's simply not right. You must give yourself enough time . . ."

"I've had time," he interrupted. "And frankly, I'm no closer to a solution now than I ever was. But I'm dreadfully tired, Mrs. Jeffries. I really must retire. Can you ask Wiggins to take Fred for his walk?"

She knew when to stop. "Certainly, sir. Sleep well."

Later that night, when everyone in the household had gone to their beds, Mrs. Jeffries crept down to the kitchen. She put her lamp on the kitchen table and got a tin of silver polish and two cleaning rags from the bin under the sink. She put her supplies on the table, spread out yesterday's *Times*, and put the polish on top of the pages. Going to the pine sideboard, she knelt down and pulled open the bottom drawer.

Inside were three flat silver trays, each of them wrapped in soft gray flannel drawstring jackets. She grabbed the trays and heaved them out, groaning a little as she felt the strain on her knees. Putting the stack on the table next to the open newspaper, she slipped the first tray out of its jacket and positioned it next to the tin of polish. Then she sat down and picked up a rag.

Mrs. Jeffries knew she'd not be able to sleep, so she hadn't even bothered to try. She'd decided to clean the trays for two very good reasons. Firstly, she hoped a dull, repetitive task would help her mind come up with some idea of how to solve this case; and secondly, Christmas would be here in a few days, and they needed the trays cleaned.

As she went about her task, she tried not to dwell on any details of the case. She wanted her thoughts to wander freely, moving haphazardly from one fact or bit of information to the next. But try as she might, she couldn't stop herself from thinking.

She smeared a gob of polish over the top of the tray and reached for the other cloth. Rosalind Murray had been the strongest suspect, and now it looked as if she'd no motive at all. But there was still the matter of the house. With Whitfield dead, Mrs. Murray could finally get control of it. A house in that neighborhood and of that size was worth a huge amount of money. Perhaps Mrs. Murray's plans had included selling the place and going off on her own. Yes, that made sense, especially if she was afraid that a new, relatively young wife might spur Whitfield on to a long and vigorous life.

Mrs. Jeffries rubbed the cloth along the top of the tray in long, even strokes. But would getting her hands on the family home be enough of a motive for Rosalind Murray? she wondered. That was the question.

"What on earth are you doing?" Mrs. Goodge asked softly.

Startled, Mrs. Jeffries dropped the cloth. "Gracious, Mrs. Goodge, you gave me a fright. I couldn't sleep, so I thought I'd get started on the silver. We do like using it for Christmas."

Mrs. Goodge came into the kitchen. Samson trailed at her heels. She wore a long gray wool robe and a pair of red carpet slippers. "You can't sleep, can you? The case is keeping you awake."

"No, I can't. I don't mind telling you that this one has got me baffled. What's more, I think the inspector is ready to hand it off to someone else," Mrs. Jeffries said. It felt good to confide in someone.

"We'll not let that happen." The cook slid into the seat next to Mrs. Jeffries, pushed her chair back, and then patted her lap. Samson jumped up, glared at Mrs. Jeffries, then curled into a ball and began to purr.

Mrs. Jeffries picked up the polishing cloth and continued her task. "I'm not sure we can stop it. Every time we have a meeting, I learn something that convinces me that no one had a motive for actually wanting the man dead."

"Nonsense." Mrs. Goodge stroked Samson's broad back. "You're only saying that because it's late at night and you're tired. You'll feel differently in the morning."

"No, I won't. We're running out of motives, Mrs. Goodge. After what we heard about Hugh Langdon, you must see that Eliza Graham didn't have a motive. He wouldn't have given a toss about gossip about her, and he wasn't even willing to listen to Whitfield when he tried to discuss her."

"Perhaps she wasn't as sure of him as we think," Mrs. Goodge said. "Perhaps Eliza Graham wasn't . . . Oh, you're right. She's been seeing the man socially for months now, so she must have some idea of his character. Alright, I'll admit that it appears as if she no longer has a motive, but we've plenty of others. I still think that Rosalind Murray might have done it. Despite what plans she may or may not have had, she might have hated him enough to kill him."

"And risk being hung instead of getting on with her life?" Mrs. Jeffries put the rag to one side. "I don't think that's likely."

"What about Henry Becker? There's madness in his family. He might have done it. Perhaps he was tired of always losing at whist. That might be a sufficient motive for an insane person."

"But we don't know that he is insane. True, there's a bit of lunacy in his family, but I expect if you looked hard enough at many families, you'd find evidence of strange or violent behavior. Becker had no motive. We've no evidence that he hated Whitfield, and he certainly doesn't need the money from the tontine."

"Basil Farringdon doesn't seem to need the money, either," Mrs. Goodge murmured, "and they are the only two left in the tontine."

"Which means we can rule that out as a motive." Mrs. Jeffries picked up the flannel jacket and slipped the tray inside.

The cook reached across and pulled the drawstring tight. "You've still got Maria Farringdon as a suspect. She did hate Whitfield."

"But did she hate him enough to kill him?" Mrs. Jeffries shook her head. "I don't think so. Nor do I think that Hugh Langdon had a motive for murdering him, nor did any of Whitfield's servants, either. The killer went to a great deal of trouble to commit this murder."

"But all they had to do was chuck a few leaves into an open bottle of wine," Mrs. Goodge retorted. "That doesn't seem like much effort."

"That part wasn't. But the actual planning of the murder must have been thought out well in advance. This is the middle of winter, so they would have had to plan it months ago, when foxglove was abundant."

"It's not the sort of plant that people bother to grow in greenhouses," Mrs. Goodge agreed.

"Whoever did it must have picked the leaves, dried them, and stored them somewhere for months before they decided to act." She put the lid back on the tin of polish and slapped it into place. There was no point in trying to do the other trays. She'd not be able to concentrate, and she had a feeling that as long as she was in the kitchen, the cook would feel compelled to keep her company. Mrs. Goodge needed her rest. "I just don't see any of our suspects having a motive strong enough to go to all that trouble."

"Someone did," the cook reminded her softly.

"I've thought and thought and thought about everything we've learned," Mrs. Jeffries said. She looked at the cook. "Frankly, I don't see how any living person could have committed this murder."

The next morning, Mrs. Jeffries' spirits hadn't brightened any, but she went to great pains to keep her thoughts from the others. They were all so eager to be out and about—on the hunt, so to speak.

"I thought I'd 'ave a go at talkin' to a servant," Wiggins said as he tucked into a fried egg.

"If you're goin' to the Whitfield house, be careful," Mrs. Goodge warned. "I overheard the inspector mentionin' to Constable Barnes that they were goin' to go there this mornin'."

"Maybe I'll try the Farringdon house or Henry Becker's servants," Wiggins muttered.

"Where are you going, Betsy?" Smythe asked.

Betsy swallowed the bite of toast she'd popped into her mouth. "I haven't been to Becker's neighborhood, either. I thought I might talk to those local shopkeepers."

"What are you goin' to be doin' today, Mrs. Jeffries?" Wiggins asked.

"I thought I'd give the drawing room a good clean," she replied. She caught the cook's eye and nodded almost imperceptibly, letting her know that though she was ready to give up, she wasn't going to say anything to discourage the others. "I find that doing boring, repetitive tasks helps me to think things through, and we're at the point in this investigation where a good think is in order."

But despite everyone's best efforts when they met for their meeting that afternoon, none of them had anything new to report. It was the same the next day and the day after. Wiggins talked to half a dozen housemaids, footmen, and tweenies. He learned nothing. Betsy had chatted up every grocer's clerk, fishmonger, and baker in three different neighborhoods, with equally dismal results, and Smythe had spent so much time in pubs that he declared the smell of beer actually made him half-sick.

Nor had Inspector Witherspoon done any better. He'd questioned the dinner party guests and the Whitfield servants a second time, but none of them had anything to add to their original statements.

But at the brief morning meeting on the fourth day, there was a glimmer of hope. "I know we seem to be hittin' a dry spell, but my friend Hilda Ryker is back in town," Luty announced. "She loves to gossip and always knows what's what in London. I know I'll have something for ya by this afternoon; I just know it."

"I certainly hope so, madam," Hatchet replied. "We've none of us found out anything these past few days, and Christmas is almost upon us."

"That's not true," Mrs. Goodge corrected. "We did find out that Mrs. Murray's late husband did leave her something valuable. That tea plantation he left her shares in has done very well the last few years."

Inspector Witherspoon had found out that bit of information when he'd interviewed Rosalind Murray for the second time. She'd been quite candid about her plans. She was selling everything, including the house, and moving to Canada to start a new life.

"Let's hope you're very successful today," Mrs. Jeffries said to Luty. "And I know the rest of you will find out lots of useful things as well."

Mrs. Goodge waited till everyone had left, and then she turned to the housekeeper. "Are you going to tell them about the inspector, about what he wants to do?"

"I think I should, don't you?"

"Yes. They'll be disappointed, but they'll get over it." She sighed heavily. "Mind you, I do hate the idea of him giving up on a case. Are you sure he was serious?"

"He was deadly serious," Mrs. Jeffries replied. "When I was serving him his breakfast this morning, he made it quite clear that unless he finds another avenue to investigate, he's going to ask Chief Inspector Barrows to give the case to someone else."

"Did he say when he planned on doing this?" the cook asked. She didn't like the idea of quitting, either. But unless they had a miracle, she didn't see that there was much hope.

"The day after tomorrow."

"That's Christmas Eve."

Mrs. Jeffries nodded. "Let's hope that someone comes up with something useful. Otherwise we'll have failed."

"Of course I'm acquainted with Maria Farringdon." Hilda Ryker said to Luty. "She's a very nice woman, much smarter than her husband, but that's only to be expected. Her family actually worked for what they've acquired. Basil Farringdon's family, on the other hand, has managed to fritter away just about everything they ever had, and believe me, they had plenty. The Farringdons once owned a good share of Norfolk. His mother was a cousin to the duke."

"You sure know a lot about 'em," Luty commented. She was sitting in the drawing room of Hilda Ryker's elegant town house on Ridley Square. Hilda and her husband, Neville Ryker, were old friends of Luty's.

When the Rykers weren't traveling, Hilda spent her whole life immersed in the London social whirl. If there was anything worth knowing about any of the guests who'd been at Whitfield's dinner party on the night of the murder, she'd be the person to ask. Luty was determined to have something for their afternoon meeting. Mrs. Jeffries was doing her best to keep everyone's spirits up, but they were all getting discouraged.

"Of course I do." Hilda's long face creased in a grin. "Gossip is one of my favorite activities. I know we're never supposed to admit such a thing, but it's true nonetheless. If you're not interested in other people, you might as well be dead; that's what I always say." She cocked her head to one side and stared at Luty speculatively. "Why are you so interested in the Farringdons? They can't possibly be friends of yours. He's a bore, and she's far too conventional to appreciate you."

Luty wasn't sure whether she was being complimented or insulted, but she found the comment funny nonetheless. She laughed.
"I'm not. I just happened to overhear that they were at the dinner
party where that Whitfield fellow got murdered. I was just curious;
that's all."

"You're always curious about murder." Hilda poured another
cup of tea from the silver pot on the trolley next to her chair.

Luty held her breath. She hadn't expected Hilda to remember
that Luty had come around once before, asking questions about the
murder of Harrison Nye, one of their previous cases. She started
to mutter something inane, but before she could get the words out,
Hilda continued talking.

"I expect it's because you're friends with that police inspector.
I find murder fascinating as well, certainly far more exciting than
conventional gossip." Hilda reached for the sugar tongs and delicately placed a lump into her tea. "Would you care for another
cup?"

"No, thanks. I'm not finished with this one yet."

"But as to Maria Farringdon, I do hope she's not the murderer."
Hilda said. "Despite her being a stickler for convention, I quite
like her. She's very social, so I see her quite frequently. We always
have a nice chat when we run into one another. But, come to think
of it, I haven't seen her since Lady Emmerson's party last September. Of course Neville and I have been gone quite a bit since then.
Neville does so love to travel, but frankly, I always miss London
when we're gone. Foreigners, especially the French, can be so difficult."

"You said she's smart." Luty didn't want Hilda bringing up her
husband. Neville Ryker was Hilda's favorite subject, and once his
name was uttered, getting her to talk about anything else was almost impossible.

"She is," Hilda replied. "Before she married Basil Farringdon,
she helped run her family's business."

Luty wasn't sure how much to press, but on the other hand she
didn't want the woman shutting up, either. Right now she needed
all the information she could get. She started to ask another question, but Hilda hadn't finished.

"And she's observant as well . . ." Hilda's voice trailed off and
her eyes widened. "Oh my goodness, I've just realized something.
It was Stephen Whitfield that Maria was talking about when she

told me about the cheese incident. Do you think I ought to mention it to your inspector friend? Oh dear, I do hope not. Neville wouldn't like me actually talking to a policeman, even one as respectable as your Inspector Witherspoon."

"Why don't you tell me about this here . . . er . . . uh . . . cheese incident? If it's something that ought to be passed on, I'll mention it to him," Luty suggested. She couldn't believe her good fortune. Maybe their luck was changing. "That way, you won't go gettin' Neville upset, but you'll have done your part in seein' that justice is served."

Hilda looked doubtful. "It probably means nothing. I'd have never thought of it if we'd not started talking about Maria Farringdon."

"Well, what was it?" Luty urged. "Go ahead—you can tell me."

"I've only just realized it was Stephen Whitfield that Maria was staring at as she was telling me about it. I knew who he was, of course. Despite his age, and his being a widower, he was considered quite an eligible catch."

"Go on," Luty pressed. "Tell me what happened." She glanced at the ornate baroque clock on the mantelpiece and saw that it was twenty till four. If she could ever get this woman talking sense, she just might make it back to Upper Edmonton Gardens before the meeting ended. "I'm a good listener."

"I feel so silly. It was such a minor incident, and I think I've made too much of it." Hilda smiled weakly.

"Tell me anyway," Luty ordered. She was tired of pussyfooting around.

"All right, if you insist. As I said, it was in September. Neville and I were getting ready to leave. It had been quite a tedious party, really. Not at all amusing. Neville sent for our footman and then went off to get my wrap. Suddenly Maria Farringdon came up and stood next to me. I'd not seen her that evening, so we started to chat—as I said, she's an interesting woman. We both saw Stephen Whitfield across the room. He was speaking to our hostess, and his expression was, well, very earnest if you know what I mean."

Luty wasn't certain she understood, but she didn't want to interrupt.

"He must have been quite rude to Mrs. Farringdon that day," Hilda continued thoughtfully. "She was glaring at him, and then she said, 'He's trying to recover from having made a fool of himself.' "

"You actually heard her say those words?" Luty confirmed.

"Indeed I did." Hilda nodded. "I asked her what she meant, and she turned, looked at me, and laughed. Then she said, 'He might find it amusing to make fun of my champagne cups, but the man obviously can't taste a thing. I just overheard him commending Lady Emmerson on the lovely Stilton she'd had served. Stupid fool. Lady Emmerson won't forgive that faux pas for a good long while.' I don't like cheese, so I had no idea what she was going on about, and I asked her what she meant. She laughed again and said that it hadn't been a Stilton that was served but a Wensleydale. Apparently our hostess had sent all the way to Somerset for the Wensleydale and was annoyed that it wasn't fully appreciated."

Luty struggled to keep from showing her disappointment. This gossip didn't help one whit! They already knew that Maria Farringdon disliked Whitfield. Blast—this had been Luty's last hope. She had nothing to take back to the others.

She was beginning to think they were never going to solve this case.

CHAPTER 10

"Despite all my big talk this mornin', I ain't found out one thing that's goin' to help us much," Luty admitted. She watched the faces of the others around the table as she described her meeting with Hilda Ryker. Every one of them looked as disappointed as Luty felt. When she'd finished, she sat back, folded her hands in her lap, and shrugged. "Sorry I wasn't able to learn anything we didn't already know about Maria Farringdon."

"You did your best, and you mustn't feel badly. Perhaps Wiggins has found out something useful." Mrs. Jeffries looked at him hopefully.

But he shook his head. "I don't think so. Matter of fact, what I did 'ear makes me 'ope the lady isn't the killer. Mrs. Farringdon is a bit of a soft'earted one. She hired a scullery maid back who'd gone off and 'ad a baby. The baby died, and as the girl 'ad no husband, Mrs. Farringdon took pity on her and let her come back to work."

"That would never have happened in my day," Mrs. Goodge murmured. "Back then, if a girl got in trouble, she was let go and it was her hard luck. Thank goodness times have changed for the better." Not only had times changed, but since she'd become a member of this household, the cook's attitudes had changed as well.

Mrs. Jeffries agreed with the sentiment but realized they had now lost their last suspect. She'd been clinging to the belief that perhaps Maria Farringdon's hatred of Whitfield was so fierce that

384

it was the motive for the murder. "Mrs. Farringdon obviously isn't a cruel, callous woman, or she'd have never hired the girl back."

"Which means she probably isn't mean enough to kill Whitfield over a few insults about her food or her background," Smythe said.

"I agree. But that puts us very much at a loss here," Mrs. Jeffries said morosely.

"Because we're now completely out of any genuine suspects," Hatchet said glumly.

"What about Henry Becker?" Wiggins wasn't ready to give up yet. "With Whitfield dead, he'll get a bigger dividend now."

"He's rich as sin already," Luty reminded him. "He can't spend what he's got now, and he might be strange, but we've never heard of him actin' nasty or violent to anyone."

Mrs. Jeffries started to speak and then thought better of it. She looked down at the tabletop. Perhaps she should wait? Perhaps today the inspector would find the clue that pointed them in the right direction. She glanced up and caught Mrs. Goodge looking at her.

The cook's features hardened a fraction. "I think Mrs. Jeffries has something to tell us," she prompted.

Mrs. Jeffries was aware they were all staring at her, waiting for her to say something. She cleared her throat. "I do have something I need to say. You've all realized this case isn't progressing very well at all."

"You don't have any idea who did it?" Wiggins asked plaintively.

"No, I'm afraid I don't."

"Are you sure?" He couldn't quite believe it.

"I'm positive," she replied. "Inspector Witherspoon is at as much of an impasse in the case as we are. A few days ago he told me that if he didn't make progress soon, he was going to ask Chief Inspector Barrows to assign another officer to it."

They all started talking at once.

"That's ridiculous," Hatchet snapped. "Surely the chief inspector will give him more time."

"Cor blimey, there's plenty of time left to get it right," Wiggins complained.

"He's lost his confidence," Mrs. Goodge muttered darkly.

"Oh, no, that's awful. We can't let him give up," Betsy exclaimed.

Mrs. Jeffries held up her hand for silence. "I appreciate and agree with all your sentiments. But unfortunately I don't think he's going to be dissuaded from this course of action. Unless we can come up with more evidence by tomorrow, he's going to see the chief."

They discussed the matter at great length but could come up with no way of stopping the inspector from asking to be taken off the case. Nor did any of them have a clue as to who might have killed Whitfield. Finally they lapsed into silence, which was broken by the clock striking the hour.

"It's five o'clock, madam," Hatchet said to Luty. "We must get home so you'll have time for a short rest before dinner. Lionel Burston and Lady Fenleigh are coming at eight."

"Oh, nells bells, I'd forgotten all about that stupid dinner," Luty muttered as she got to her feet. She looked at Mrs. Jeffries, her eyes hopeful. "Should we be here at our usual time tomorrow?"

Mrs. Jeffries wasn't sure there was anything left for any of them to do. Yet just as she decided to tell them it was no use, she felt a tug at the back of her mind. It was only a wisp of an idea, and it was gone before she could grab it long enough to make sense of anything; but nonetheless it was real, it was there, she felt it. For the first time in this case, her own "inner eye" was opening. Or perhaps she was simply grasping at straws. "Yes, please. We're not going to give up just yet. We've all day tomorrow to continue the hunt."

"Good." Luty beamed approvingly, and even Hatchet seemed satisfied as he helped her with her coat.

As soon as the two of them had gone, Mrs. Goodge went to her room to put on a clean apron, Wiggins took Fred for a short walk, and Mrs. Jeffries went upstairs to finish polishing the furniture in the inspector's study.

Betsy was still at the table, staring straight ahead, her eyes unfocused and her shoulders relaxed. Smythe wasn't sure this was the best time to broach the subject, but as it was the first time he'd been alone with her in days, he wasn't going to waste the opportunity. "Can I talk to you?"

Betsy looked at him. "Someone's bound to come back in a minute or two, so you'd better be quick about it."

"Are we still engaged?" he blurted. That was what he needed to know; that was what had been haunting him since he'd returned. "You said you still loved me, but do you still want to marry me?"

She said nothing for a moment, just stared at him with an expression he couldn't read. Finally she said, "Do you still want to marry me?"

"Of course I do," he cried. "I want to marry you more than anything. You've got to tell me. Not knowin' is tearin' me apart. Are we still goin' to be married?"

As Betsy had predicted, they heard footsteps coming toward the kitchen. "Yes, we're still engaged," she hissed as she got up and began to clear the table. "And if it's all the same to you, we'll keep this to ourselves until after this case is solved."

"It might never be solved." He got up and reached for the nearest dirty plates.

"Then we'll talk about it after Christmas," she replied. She picked up the sugar bowl and the jam pot and walked to the counter.

"Boxing Day, then. We'll make our plans on the Feast of St. Stephen." He followed after her.

"Feast of St. Stephen," Mrs. Goodge repeated as she came into the room. "I've not heard Boxing Day called that in years."

"It was on the notice board outside the church." Smythe ignored Betsy's warning look, put the plates down, grabbed her by the shoulders, and enveloped her in a hug. "We'll sort everything out then."

Mrs. Goodge beamed at them.

Upstairs, Mrs. Jeffries poured a dab of Adam's Furniture Polish onto her rag and rubbed it on the top of the inspector's desk. She moved her hand in a long circular motion, applying the polish evenly over the wood surface as her thoughts began to float free. What was it that had pushed at her earlier? It was an idea or a thought that had bubbled into awareness while they were discussing the case. She cast her mind back to the moment she'd felt the tiny nudge, it had been when . . . when . . . She shook her head. She couldn't recall what was being said when it had happened. Drat.

She finished all the furniture in the study and had moved on to the drawing room when she heard the inspector coming up the front steps. Putting the rag down, she hurried out into the hall, arriving just as Witherspoon stepped inside.

He didn't look good. His face was paler than usual, his glasses had slid completely down his nose, and his bowler was askew.

"Good evening, Mrs. Jeffries," he said politely. He took off his hat and hung it on the coat tree, then began pulling off his gloves.

"Good evening, sir," she replied. "Have you made any progress today?"

He tucked his gloves in his overcoat pocket, shrugged it off, and handed it to her. "Not really. I spent the day going over all the statements and seeing if there is something I might have missed. But honestly, I didn't see anything."

"Don't give up, sir. I'm sure you'll find the solution soon," she said. She hung up his coat. "Are you still going to ask the chief to assign it to someone else?"

"I must. Perhaps a fresh approach is what's needed," he said. "But I did have one bright moment this afternoon. I ran into Lady Cannonberry on Holland Park Road. She's invited me to come early on Christmas day—you know, before the others arrive."

The inspector was having Christmas dinner with Ruth Cannonberry and some of her relations. She was their neighbor and his special friend.

"That's very nice, sir. I'm sure you'll have a lovely time," Mrs. Jeffries replied. "Would you like a sherry before your dinner?"

"Not tonight, Mrs. Jeffries. I'll have my meal and then I think I'll retire for the evening. I don't like to complain, but reading all those statements and going over the postmortem report has given me a dreadful headache."

In the darkness of her room, Mrs. Jeffries lay in bed and stared at the ceiling. She couldn't sleep. Fragments of conversation and bits of gossip from their many meetings played about in her head, jostling for position and trying to get her attention. She didn't want to delude herself, but she was sure her own inner voice was trying to tell her something, trying to show her something that was right under her nose.

Mrs. Jeffries recalled a maid's words that Wiggins had repeated. *"He'd got one of them wine corkers from Germany. But he did make a terrible mess."* Now why had that sprung into her mind?

She rolled onto her side and let her mind drift where it would. Rosalind Murray had already made plans to sell the house. She wondered what the argument between Mrs. Murray and Whitfield had really been about. If she had truly wanted to be rid of him, then it couldn't have been about his relationship with Mrs. Graham.

She closed her eyes and took a deep breath. Whitfield was planning on taking Eliza Graham to Italy in the spring. But she'd already decided not to marry him. Had he suspected she was going to decline his proposal?

"Now it looks as if I'm going to another funeral come January." Those words popped into her mind. Her eyes flew open and she frowned, trying to remember who'd made this statement. It was Inspector Witherspoon, and he'd been repeating Henry Becker's words. She'd lavished so much praise on the inspector about his ability to recall conversations and statements, and he now took great pride in repeating things word for word.

She flopped onto her back again and looked up at the ceiling. She heard the *clip-clop* of horses' hooves outside and the rattle of wheels as a hansom trundled past the house. Finally she drifted off into sleep.

"Last year I gave it to my next-door neighbor. But he's dead now, so I was rather stuck with the stuff." Mrs. Jeffries jerked away as those words rang in her ears. She squinted into the night, trying to think where she'd heard them. Then she remembered. Henry Becker. Once again the inspector had repeated Henry Becker's own words to her.

She sat there for a moment, letting the idea that was forming in her mind strengthen and take shape. Ye gods, it was right under her nose.

She tossed the covers to one side and leapt out of bed. Ten minutes later, she was downstairs putting the kettle on to boil as she came up with a plan. By the time she heard Mrs. Goodge's bedroom door open, she knew what had to be done.

"I thought I heard someone moving about in here. What are you doing up so early?" Mrs. Goodge stood at the doorway. She was still in her nightclothes. Samson was at her feet.

"I couldn't sleep. I've been up for ages. I think I know what happened, but I'm not saying a word until I have a few things confirmed."

"Let me put Samson out." The cook continued down the hall.

Mrs. Jeffries went to the doorway and stuck her head out. "Do you know what a foxglove plant looks like?" she asked.

"Of course I know what it looks like. They grow all over the place." Mrs. Goodge unlocked the top bolt on the back door and opened it, letting in a blast of frigid air. Samson gave a plaintive meow, but the cook used her foot to nudge him gently outside. "Go on now. Go out and do your business."

"Would you know what a winter-dead one looked like?"

"I imagine it just looks like a stalk of weed," Mrs. Goodge called over her shoulder as she closed the door.

"That's what I thought as well." Mrs. Jeffries moved to the stairs.

"Where are you going?"

"Up to get Wiggins and Smythe. They'll need to move quickly today."

Mrs. Goodge started back to the kitchen and was midway down the hall when she heard soft thuds against the back door. "Oh, he couldn't have done his business that quickly," she muttered, but she retraced her steps and opened the door. Samson, a sheen of wet on his fur, shot through the back door and raced toward the kitchen.

By the time Mrs. Jeffries returned to the kitchen, the cook was nowhere to be seen, but the kettle was on the boil. She made the tea while she waited for the others. She put the sugar, milk, and jam on the table, then went into the wet larder for a pot of butter. She'd come back and was starting to slice a loaf of bread when Mrs. Goodge appeared. This time she was fully dressed.

"What's all this about, then?" she demanded as she crossed the room to the worktable. "Here, I'll do that." She took the knife from the housekeeper and commandeered the spot in front of the bread-board. "I heard the others coming down the stairs. Young Wiggins makes enough noise to wake the dead. Let's hope he doesn't wake the inspector this early and have him down asking what we're all doing. You finish making the tea."

Wiggins, his hair on end and his shirttail flapping, came in first, followed by a yawning Smythe. Betsy trailed behind the two men.

"Sorry to get everyone up so early, but you must get out and on the hunt." Mrs. Jeffries put the teapot on the table. "Everyone sit down and listen to what I have to say. Please don't ask me any questions, because I could be dead wrong about my theory. But if I'm right, we've lots to do today."

Mrs. Goodge put the plate of sliced bread next to the butter pot and sat down. "Should we send Wiggins for Luty and Hatchet? They're not due here for another hour at the earliest."

"That won't be necessary." Mrs. Jeffries poured the tea into the cluster of mugs she'd put on the table earlier. "In any case, they can't do their part until later today. But I need these three out and about early." She finished pouring and waved her hand, indicating they were to help themselves.

No one asked any questions. They all knew the housekeeper wouldn't tell them what she suspected until she was certain she was right. For the next few moments, the room was silent as they fixed their tea to their liking, buttered bread, and came fully awake.

"All right, Mrs. J, what is it ya need me to do?" Smythe asked.

She thought for a moment, trying to sort through the best means to confirm her suspicions. There were several ways one could go about this task. She wanted to be as efficient as possible. "Luckily, the inspector isn't due to see the chief until tomorrow, so we're not going to be too badly rushed. But I think I'd like you to go to the communal gardens at the Whitfield house. Find out if there's foxglove growing anywhere in the garden. This time of year it might look like a weed, so perhaps it would be best if you found the gardener or the groundsman and asked him."

"Is that it?" He didn't want to point it out, but he needn't have been awakened at the crack of dawn for such an errand, especially as they weren't pressed for time.

"For the moment." She turned to Wiggins. "Can you find that housemaid you spoke with before, the one that told you about going with Whitfield to deliver his bottles of port to his friends?"

"That'd be dead easy. She should still be at the Whitfield 'ouse."

"Excellent. I want you to find out how many bottles of port were delivered and, more importantly, where."

Wiggins glanced at the clock. "You want me to go now? Isn't it a bit early?"

"That's the best time to try to see the girl without the butler or housekeeper catching you," Mrs. Goodge answered. "It's the young girls that must get up early to light the fires and make the tea. The cook won't come down until eight, so if you hurry, it ought to be just the younger girls up and about the kitchen."

"What about Fred's walkies? Usually the inspector likes me to take 'im out."

"Don't worry, lad—just be off with you," the cook ordered. "We'll take care of Fred's walkies. The exercise will do me good."

"Alright, alright, I'm goin'." Wiggins took a quick sip of his tea, grabbed a slice of bread, smeared some butter on it, and rose to his feet. Smythe had got up as well, and the two of them went over to the coat tree.

"What about me?" Betsy asked.

"Your task is going to be quite difficult." Mrs. Jeffries took a deep breath. She wasn't sure she should even send her on what might turn out to be a fool's errand. "I'm not certain you'll be able to track down this information, but I think it's important that you try. Last year one of Henry Becker's neighbors died. I'll need you to find out the person's name and the circumstances of the death."

Smythe was putting on his coat, but he stopped and started to say something. Betsy gave him a hard stare, and he clamped his mouth shut and started doing up his buttons. He grabbed his scarf and wound it around his neck. "Just be careful," he said to her as he and Wiggins made for the back door.

"Get back as soon as you can," Mrs. Jeffries called after them. She looked at the maid. "I'll understand if you don't wish to . . ."

"Don't be silly." Betsy laughed and pushed away from the table. "I'll find out something, Mrs. Jeffries. Don't you worry. But I've no idea how long it might take."

"Don't spend too much time on it," Mrs. Jeffries said. "I might need you for another task. Try and be back before too late this afternoon."

"I will." Betsy grabbed her long cloak and bonnet, checked the pocket for her gloves, and then hurried toward the back door.

"The house seems awfully quiet this morning," Witherspoon said. He looked up from his plate of bacon and eggs. "Is everything all right?"

"Everything is fine, sir." Mrs. Jeffries smiled brightly. "And you're correct, as usual. The house is quiet. I've sent Wiggins out on errands, Smythe has gone to Howard's to see to the horses in case you should need the carriage over the holidays, and Betsy's gone to Mrs. Crookshank's to borrow a recipe book for Mrs. Goodge." She laughed. "What an excellent detective you are, sir. Most people wouldn't have noticed the change in the atmosphere."

She was deliberately building up his confidence. She'd been dropping hints about her idea since he'd come downstairs, but so far she had no indication that she'd made any progress.

He beamed in delight. "You're giving me far too much credit, Mrs. Jeffries. Though, I will admit, a good night's sleep has restored my spirits a bit." The door knocker sounded. He broke off and gazed toward the front of the house. "I do believe that's Constable Barnes' knock. It's most distinctive."

As Barnes was expected, this was hardly brilliant detective work, but Mrs. Jeffries nodded in appreciation as she went out to the hall. She flung open the door, but before Barnes could open his mouth, she grabbed his arm and pulled him into the foyer. "Constable, I don't mean to be rude, but you must listen to me. You've got to get the inspector to question Maria Farringdon again. It's vitally important. Ask her to show you the bottle of ruby port that she received from Whitfield."

As the constable was well aware of Mrs. Jeffries' activities and had only the highest regard for her intelligence and abilities, he didn't waste time with needless questions. "What if she claims she tossed it into the dustbin?"

"It was a Christmas gift. She won't have done that." Mrs. Jeffries cast an anxious glance down the hall. "If she sticks to her guns over the matter, ask to speak to her servants. She'll know good and well that if she had really chucked out the wine, one of them would have fished it from the trash and kept it."

"Is that Constable Barnes?" Witherspoon called.

Barnes nodded that he understood. "It is indeed, sir, and I've come with some unsettling news," he announced as he stepped into the dining room.

Mrs. Jeffries followed him, but she stopped just inside the doorway.

"Unsettling news?" Witherspoon repeated. He half rose from his chair. "Egads, what is it now? What's wrong?"

"The chief inspector wants to see you this afternoon," Barnes said.

"But our appointment was for tomorrow morning." The inspector sank back to his seat.

"He changed it to today, sir. I stopped in at Ladbroke-Grove station on my way here. Griffiths had just come back from headquarters with a message from the chief. You're to go in at half past four today, sir." Barnes pursed his lips. "Griffiths thought Inspector Nivens might have something to do with this. The constable saw him coming out of the chief's office, lookin' right pleased with himself."

Witherspoon sighed and then shrugged. "I suppose it's just as well. There's no point in postponing the inevitable. But I will admit that after thinking about the matter, I had come up with some other ideas about the case."

"But you're not seeing the chief until late this afternoon," Mrs. Jeffries said. "You've still time to go to the Farringdon house."

He stared at her blankly, and she realized that even though she'd been dropping hints ever since he'd come downstairs, she'd not mentioned Maria Farringdon. "Oh, come now, sir. You know I'm on to your methods," she said hastily. "We've spent the last half hour talking about Whitfield's Christmas port. Of course you're going to want to speak to her again."

"Yes, I suppose I should." He still looked confused.

"I'm glad we're going back, sir," Barnes added. "I've wondered what she did with her bottle as well."

Smythe got back before either Betsy or Wiggins. Luty and Hatchet had been there but were already gone after having been given their assignments. When Smythe came into the kitchen, Mrs. Goodge was rolling out puff pastry and Mrs. Jeffries was pacing back and forth. She stopped in front of the sideboard.

"There's not a bit of foxglove anywhere in the communal garden," he reported. He expected her to be disappointed, but she merely nodded as though this was what she'd anticipated hearing. "You don't seem surprised."

"I was hoping you'd find it there. I didn't want to have to send you all the way to Dover."

"Dover?" he repeated.

"Specifically, I want you to go to the Thompson Hotel and see if there's any growing in their gardens." She looked over her shoulder at the carriage clock on the sideboard shelf. "It's already nine. Can you get to Dover and back here by half past three?"

He thought for a moment. "I should be able to manage. Why? I thought we weren't pressed for time on this one."

"We weren't, but we are now," Mrs. Jeffries answered. "The inspector's been ordered to report to the chief inspector at half past four today. If we don't have something useful on this murder by then, he's going to be pulled off it."

"And the case will probably be given to Inspector Nivens," Mrs. Goodge added. "We can't have that. Nivens is so desperate to make a name for himself and make our inspector look bad that he'll arrest the first person he lays eyes on."

Mrs. Jeffries nodded in agreement. "I couldn't have put it better myself."

"Blast a Spaniard," Smythe muttered. "I'd better get moving, then. I'll be back by half past. Don't worry—I'll not let you down."

"Why are you here again, Inspector?" Basil Farringdon narrowed his eyes, glaring at the two policemen standing in his drawing room. "This is the third time you've disturbed my household. It's becoming tiresome, and I'll not have it. If you don't leave immediately, I'll be filing a formal complaint with your superiors."

Witherspoon squared his shoulders and met Farringdon's gaze. "You may do as you see fit, sir. But a murder has been committed, and if I might remind you, you and your wife were the ones who brought the means of the murder into Mr. Whitfield's home."

Farringdon's jaw dropped. "How dare you . . . ?"

"I'm doing my job, sir," the inspector interrupted. "Now if you'll ask your wife to join us, we'll ask our questions and get out of your home."

"I'm right here, Inspector." Maria Farringdon appeared in the doorway. She stared at Witherspoon with undisguised hostility, crossed the room, and stood next to her husband.

"Good day, ma'am," the inspector began.

"Let's dispense with the social niceties, shall we?" she said coldly. "Just ask your questions and be on your way."

"You don't have to answer them," Basil said to her. "I'm going to make a complaint."

"We'd like to see the bottle of ruby port that Mr. Whitfield brought you," Barnes blurted.

She didn't answer. She simply stood there, staring at them. But Witherspoon noticed that her face had gone paler, and the hand at her side had suddenly balled into a fist.

"I've no idea where it is," she finally said.

"Oh for goodness' sake, Maria, show them the wretched thing

so they'll leave. I'm sure Richards put it in the wine rack in the butler's pantry." Basil Farringdon glanced at his wife and then moved toward the bellpull beside the door. "I'll just call him."

"Richards was ill the day Stephen came," she said quickly. "So I didn't give it to him to take to the cellar."

Farringdon stopped. "What did you do with it?"

"I chucked it in the dustbin," she said. "I'm sorry, Basil. I know he was a close friend of yours, but I couldn't abide that dreadful stuff. So I threw it away." She looked at the two policemen and smiled confidently. "I'm sorry, Inspector, but I can't show you the bottle. It's gone."

"May we speak to your servants, then?" Barnes asked quickly.

Panic flashed across her face, but she caught herself. "No, you may not. I'd like you to leave."

"We'll leave if you insist, Mrs. Farringdon," Witherspoon replied somberly. "But we will take every one one of your servants with us."

"This is an outrage," Basil blustered. "What on earth are you talking about? You've no right to barge in here, bully us about, and then threaten to take my household God knows where . . ."

"We'd simply be asking them to accompany us to the station to help with our inquiries," Barnes added smoothly.

"It's alright, dear." Maria moved to her husband and took his hand. "Calm yourself. You know what the doctor said about getting overly excited."

He stared at her in confusion for a moment before the realization dawned that she knew more than she'd told him. "For God's sake, Maria," he whispered. "What is going on?"

"I didn't kill him." She looked directly into her husband's eyes as she spoke. "I promise you that."

"Of course you didn't. I know you're not capable of such an act." He seemed to have forgotten that he and his wife weren't alone. "But what's happening? You must tell me."

"Just listen, dear." She took a deep breath and turned to Witherspoon. "How did you discover what I'd done?"

As he still wasn't certain, he tried to be as noncommittal as possible. "It wasn't difficult to figure out, ma'am. But it would be helpful if you'd explain why you did it."

"I wanted to prove a point, Inspector. It's as simple as that."

"I still don't quite see . . ." He let his voice trail off, hoping she'd say a bit more.

"Stephen Whitfield was a dreadful man," she said harshly. "He made it obvious that he thought my husband had married beneath him."

"Maria." Basil put his arm around her shoulders and pulled her close. "Don't say such a thing."

"But it's true, dear—that's what he thought," she continued. "He was always insulting me in nasty little ways. At the summer fete, he pretended that my champagne cups were off, and at a dinner party last Christmas he complained that the wine I served didn't go with the fish course, when I know it did. So I wanted to show the whole world that his opinion was worthless, that he couldn't tell the difference between a ruby port and a Bordeaux." She paused. "When he gave me the port, I took it up to my room and pasted the label from the Locarno on top of his handwritten label. I save labels, you know. That's how I know the wine I served with the turbot was perfect. Lady Emmerson had served the same combination at one of her dinners."

"Maria, why didn't you tell me?" Basil looked at her. "If I'd known how he made you feel, I'd have made sure we avoided him. I'd never have accepted his dinner invitations."

"Don't be silly, darling." She smiled wanly. "You'd known him all your life. We were part of the same social circles, so it would have been impossible to avoid him. That's why I did it, you see. I wanted to teach him a lesson once and for all. I wanted to let him know that I could fight back. When he drank his own port that night, thinking he was drinking an expensive French wine, I was delighted. Once I saw him pouring it down his throat like a drunken sailor, I decided to tell everyone over dessert what I'd done. I was going to pretend it was a jest, something I'd done that was playful and festive. But he'd know the truth. He'd know I'd done it to show everyone that his opinions about food and wine were worthless." She gave a disappointed sigh. "But I never got the opportunity. He collapsed before we'd even finished the first course."

"Why didn't you tell us this?" Witherspoon asked.

"Are you serious, Inspector? I couldn't possibly confess to playing a nasty trick on a man who died at his own dinner party. How would that look? Then when I found out he'd been murdered, I was even less inclined to admit what I'd done."

Witherspoon wasn't certain what this development in the investigation meant, but he was beginning to have the glimmer of an idea. "So the bottle was never opened while in your possession here?"

"Of course not. That was the whole point of the exercise, to prove that he couldn't tell one wine from another. I simply put my label on top of his and gave it back to him. I had a bad moment when Basil handed over the bottle. Stephen stared at it for such a long time that I was sure he was on to me, but I needn't have worried. He was simply playing the exuberant host by pretending to be so touched by our gift."

"Maria, he was touched," Basil chided.

"Don't be silly. He was annoyed that we'd turned up with a better wine than that miserable port he gave to all his friends." She stepped away from her husband. "But even though the port was dreadful, Stephen had done a good job with the corking, so the bottle looked as if it came from a winery and not someone's cellar."

"I see," the inspector murmured. "What would you have done if he'd not drunk the wine in front of you?"

"My original plan was to ask him later how he enjoyed it," she replied. "If he said it was wonderful, which I hoped he would, I was going to tell him it wasn't a Bordeaux, but a port. The two don't taste at all alike, Inspector, and he'd have been terribly upset that I knew his little secret. Then I was going to spread the story all over town."

"What if he'd noticed the difference?" Witherspoon asked.

"But I knew he wouldn't, Inspector. That was the whole point. He had no sense of taste or smell, yet he acted as if he was a connoisseur."

"I see." Witherspoon didn't see at all. It seemed a silly and pointless trick.

"Frankly, I was amazed that none of your people discovered the truth. The police have had the bottle in their possession since the night it happened, Inspector. But then again, I did do a very good job of pasting the label in place," she said with a proud smile.

*　*　*

"The hard part was gettin' the names of all the tontine members out of that clerk." Luty chuckled and tossed her muff onto the table. "Once we had that, the rest was easy."

"It wasn't the least bit difficult once you started waving money about. I found it shocking that the clerk was so easily bribed." Hatchet pulled out her chair, seated her, and slipped into the seat next to her.

"You bribed a clerk?" Wiggins asked. He was grinning.

"It seemed the fastest way," Luty admitted. She glanced around the table. "Should I wait for Smythe before I start?"

"No, go ahead," Mrs. Jeffries replied. "We can't delay any longer. It's almost half past three."

"I'll tell it fast, then." Luty pulled a folded paper out of her muff and opened it. "There were seven charter members of the tontine who survived to adulthood. One of them died a long time ago of scarlet fever, two of them are still alive, and the other four died within the last four years." She began to read. "Whitfield just died. Last January, Jeremy McDevitt died of heart failure. Two years ago, also in January, Harold Stumps had a heart attack that killed him. And guess what—three years ago Martha Slade passed on of natural causes." She looked up at the rest of the group. "The clerk couldn't find out how she'd died, just that it was considered a natural death. The fourth one, Mr. Augustus Bromston-Brown, died four years ago, but he died in February."

"What killed him?" Mrs. Goodge asked.

"Same as most of the others—he had some sort of heart trouble." Luty put the paper on the table and looked at Mrs. Jeffries. "Does this help any?"

"Very much so, Luty," she replied. "And you have my sincerest thanks. You and Hatchet had a very difficult task, and you did it efficiently and quickly. I'm sorry you had to spend your money to bribe the clerk at Runyon's office . . ."

"Oh, I've done that kind of thing lots of times," Luty admitted. "So no thanks are needed. And I've got plenty of money. I don't mind spendin' some of it to catch a killer. I just hope that what we've learned helps."

"It does, but so far most of our evidence is circumstantial," Mrs. Jeffries said. She looked at Wiggins. "Were you successful?"

"Rosie was a bit surprised to see me, but I told 'er I was workin' for a private inquiry agency, and she was willin' to answer my questions." He smiled self-consciously. "She told me that when she helped Whitfield deliver the port, they only went to two houses—the Farringdons' and Henry Becker's. She said she didn't understand how he could have made such a mess in the cellar—he only corked up two bottles of the port."

"Very good. You've done well." She turned to Betsy. "I know your task wasn't easy, either."

Betsy laughed. "It wasn't hard, Mrs. Jeffries. I went into the local greengrocer's and asked if . . . Well, never mind how I found out. The fact is that Henry Becker has only had one neighbor who has died in the past year or so, and that was the poor man that lived next door. His name was Hiram Bates, he was fifty-eight, and he had a heart attack last January . . . Oh, my goodness, another one."

"There seems to be a rash of heart attack deaths in January," Hatchet said thoughtfully.

"It's Christmas that kills 'em," Mrs. Goodge declared. "All that rich food."

"I don't think it's rich food." Luty eyed Mrs. Jeffries speculatively.

"No, it isn't." Mrs. Jeffries cast an anxious glance at the clock. "But we don't have time to discuss this now. We've a decision to make." She took a deep breath. "We must stop Inspector Witherspoon from meeting with Chief Inspector Barrows. I'd hoped Smythe would be here by now—he may have the final piece of the puzzle, the final proof of my idea. But we can't wait any longer . . ." She trailed off as she heard the back door flung open, then the sound of steps pounding up the hallway.

Startled out of a nice nap, Fred leapt up and began barking. Samson, who'd been curled on Mrs. Goodge's lap, shot up, hissed, and ran for the safety of the cook's quarters.

"Easy, boy, it's just me," Smythe said to the dog as he charged into the room. He looked first to make sure Betsy was there and then focused his attention on Mrs. Jeffries. "There's foxglove in the hotel gardens, and what's more, I've got a witness that saw him collecting it last summer. One of the gardeners remembers him. They had words when the gardener asked him to stop pulling the leaves off the flowers."

"The gardener was sure it was him?" she pressed.

"Oh, yes." Smythe grinned broadly. "They knew him well. He's been going there every August for four years now."

"Who did they know?" Mrs. Goodge demanded. "Who are we talking about? I'm confused."

"Stephen Whitfield," Mrs. Jeffries said softly. "He's our murderer."

CHAPTER 11

"But he's the one that's dead," the cook cried. "How can he be the killer?"

"I'll explain later," Mrs. Jeffries replied. "Right now we must stop Inspector Witherspoon from meeting with Barrows." She turned to Smythe. "How long will it take you to get to New Scotland Yard?"

"This time of day, it'll be 'ard findin' an empty hansom," he began.

"The carriage is right outside," Luty interrupted. "We can take ya."

"And our coachman is an expert at finding alternate routes to avoid traffic," Hatchet added.

"Go and get him," Mrs. Jeffries instructed. "Tell him we've an emergency here at home, and he must come at once."

Smythe didn't move. "I'm not questionin' your decision, Mrs. Jeffries, but what's the rush here? Even if our inspector sees the chief and gets taken off the case, that'll not change the facts of the matter. Whitfield will still be the killer. We'll still be able to prove it."

"You don't understand. If Nivens gets it, he'll be the one in charge, and he'll never accept evidence he doesn't find for himself." She looked at the clock again. "And unless Whitfield took a terrible risk this time, which I'm not certain he did, we'll have no way of proving we're correct except with circumstantial evidence." There was one final item that might prove her theory correct, but she wasn't certain Whitfield had been desperate enough to actually poison both men.

"Nivens is out to make a name for himself," Mrs. Goodge pointed out impatiently. "He'll not be concerned with justice, and he's got enough political friends to make sure none of the evidence we find ever sees the light of day." She understood how the world worked.

"Let's go," Luty ordered. "We can just about make it in time if we hurry."

The three of them turned and rushed toward the hall. Smythe skidded to a halt at the kitchen doorway. "What kind of emergency is it to be?"

Mrs. Jeffries said the first thing that popped into her head. "Tell him that he must come home straightaway. Tell him that Mrs. Goodge has collapsed."

The hansom pulled up in front of the tall redbrick building that housed the headquarters of the Metropolitan Police. They climbed out, and Barnes stopped to pay the driver. A cold wind blew off the river, and Witherspoon grabbed his bowler to keep it from flying off as he rushed across the short cobblestone yard to the front door. The constable was right on his heels.

They went inside, nodded a greeting at the two policemen behind the counter, and started for the staircase. Barnes slowed his steps and glanced over his shoulder, hoping to see another hansom pull up and a member of the inspector's household leaping out. He knew that once this case was handed over to Nivens, any hope of justice would go right out the window. But he saw nothing except a few pedestrians, their heads bowed against the strong winds as they hurried toward the bridge.

"I think you ought to tell the chief we've made progress, sir," Barnes suggested. "You found out about Mrs. Farringdon's little trick. It's only a matter of time before you solve it, sir."

Witherspoon started up the steps. "I don't think that matters now. Unless I can walk into Barrows' office and tell him we're going to be making an arrest, he's going to take me off the case. I don't think he's any choice in the matter."

"That's not fair, sir," Barnes protested. "No one can solve a homicide in less than a fortnight."

"We've done it before, Constable," Witherspoon reminded him.

"But it's a pity to lose it now. I'm beginning to have an idea about what might . . . Oh well, it can't be helped. Nivens wants this case, and he has powerful political friends."

They'd reached the first floor. The inspector started down the long hallway, walking briskly with his shoulders back and his spine straight. Barnes followed at a more sedate pace, his mind working frantically to find a way out of the situation. Like the inspector, he, too, had an idea about the murder of Stephen Whitfield, and he didn't want to see the truth buried under Nivens' incompetence or, even worse, watch an innocent person be arrested.

But try as he might, he couldn't come up with one single fact that might keep them from losing the case. Barnes sighed heavily as they neared the end of the corridor.

Barrows' office door was shut, but just then the one opposite it opened, and Inspector Nigel Nivens stepped into the hallway. He nodded curtly. "Witherspoon, Barnes. The chief is expecting us. He said he'd be free in a few minutes."

"Thank you, Inspector Nivens," Witherspoon said politely.

"You couldn't solve this one, could you?" Nivens gave them a smug smile. "It appears you're not quite as brilliant as you think."

"I've never claimed to be brilliant," the inspector said softly. "But I have had a decent record of homicide convictions."

"Humph." Nivens snorted and cast a quick glance at Barrows' door. "You've had help, and you've been damned lucky."

Witherspoon said nothing.

"We're very close to solving it, sir," Barnes said. "And that's what I'm going to tell the chief. All we need is a bit more time."

"Constable Barnes," Witherspoon warned.

"Time." Nivens sneered. "You've had over a week. You're not getting another minute on this case. I've seen to that."

Barnes was momentarily distracted by the sound of footsteps pounding up the staircase. He looked down the corridor.

The door to Barrows' office opened, and the chief inspector appeared. "I wasn't aware you were in charge of reassigning cases," Barrows said.

Barnes jerked his head around. Barrows stood just inside his office, frowning at Inspector Nivens.

"But of course I'm not, Chief Inspector." Nivens' smile was strained. "That's your responsibility. I was merely jesting with the constable here. My little joke, as it were."

Barrows didn't smile back. He simply pulled his door open wider and gestured for them to come inside.

Three people suddenly appeared at the top of the staircase. Barnes sagged in relief as Smythe, Hatchet, and Mrs. Crookshank charged down the hallway, oblivious to the racket their pounding steps made against the wood floor.

"What on earth is that?" Barrows asked. He moved past Witherspoon and Nivens, both of whom had already stepped into his office, and stuck his head out.

"It's the inspector's coachman," Barnes replied.

"Who are those other people?" the chief demanded.

"Friends." The constable moved toward the rapidly approaching figures. "Is something wrong?" he called.

"The inspector's got to come home right away." Smythe tried to catch his breath. He smiled apologetically in the direction of the frowning chief. "Mrs. Goodge has collapsed and might be dying."

"Oh, my good gracious." Witherspoon pushed past Nivens and Barrows. "What happened?"

"Witherspoon, what is this?" Nivens had followed him out. "What kind of trick are you trying to pull now?"

"Sorry to interrupt, Inspector, Chief Inspector." Hatchet took off his top hat and bowed politely. "But Mrs. Goodge has taken seriously ill, and you must come at once. Luckily, the madam and I happened to be there when the unfortunate incident occurred, so we were able to bring Smythe along to fetch you."

"We'll take ya back in our coach," Luty added. "You come along now—there's no time to waste. She might not last much longer."

"Oh dear, this is horrid. Poor Mrs. Goodge." Witherspoon turned to the chief. "I'm dreadfully sorry, sir, but I must go home. My household is very dear to me."

"Of course you must go, Witherspoon." Barrows glanced at Nivens. "This can wait until tomorrow."

"Now, just a minute. It's a trick," Nivens yelled. "They're all in on it."

"We'd better hurry." Witherspoon clamped his bowler onto his head and started off. "I do hope it's not too late."

"You come along, too, Constable," Hatchet said as they turned to go. "We've plenty of room in the carriage, and you live out that way."

"Thank you," Barnes said as he fell into step behind them. "That would be very helpful."

"You're not going to let them get away with this, are you?" Nivens protested.

"Inspector Nivens." Barrows' voice was harsh. "Be careful what you say. Slandering a fellow officer is a serious offense and will not be tolerated."

"But it's a trick, I tell you, a trick. Tomorrow morning he's going to walk into your office and claim he's solved the murder."

Barnes sincerely hoped that would be the case.

"What do I do when the inspector gets here?" Mrs. Goodge asked worriedly. She wasn't one to complain, but she had no idea what they expected of her.

"Lie on the floor and pretend you're at death's door," Wiggins suggested.

"Lie on the floor?" she repeated. "Are you mad? It's too cold. I can look ill sittin' in my usual seat."

"But it would look better if you was lying there." He pointed to a spot in front of the worktable. "Make it more real-like."

"Mrs. Goodge can be resting in her chair," the housekeeper interjected, "and she isn't at death's door. She simply fainted, and she feels much better now. But I do think a nice warm blanket around her shoulders would be appropriate."

"I'll run fetch one," Betsy offered.

"There's a nice plaid traveling rug on the foot of my bed," the cook said. "Get that one."

Mrs. Jeffries waited till Betsy had come back and draped the brown and gold wrap over the cook's shoulder's before she continued with her instructions. "When he arrives, try to follow my lead. I'm not certain our plan will work, but as it's the only one we have, we must do our best." She'd already told them about the hints she'd dropped into the inspector's ear this morning. "Let's hope that I was correct in my assumption about Maria Farringdon, and that when he interviewed her today, she admitted what she'd done." She silently prayed that her own reasoning had been correct in this matter, but after putting all the facts together, she'd come to the conclusion that it was the only way Whitfield's death made any sense.

They heard the sound of a carriage pulling up outside. "Get ready, everyone," Mrs. Jeffries warned. "He's here."

Moments later, Witherspoon and the others raced into the kitchen. "Is she all right?" He charged toward her. "How bad is it? Has the doctor been here?"

"I'm fine, Inspector." Mrs. Goodge raised her gaze to meet his. "I do feel such a fool, collapsing the way I did. I'm so sorry you were disturbed."

"Please don't concern yourself with that, Mrs. Goodge. You're more important than a meeting." He dropped to his knees next to her chair.

Mrs. Jeffries saw that his face was pale and his mouth so white it looked as if the blood had drained all the way to his toes. A pang of guilt shot through her as she realized her ruse had frightened him badly. She vowed she'd make this up to him somehow. But justice was a harsh mistress, and she couldn't risk an innocent person's being arrested.

"Thank you, sir." Mrs. Goodge's lips trembled. "You're very kind. But I'm truly feeling much better. It was just a faint."

"But you must see the doctor," he insisted.

"Oh, no, sir, that wouldn't do at all." Her voice caught, as though she were trying hard not to cry. "Doctors frighten me. I'm fine, truly fine. It was just a faint."

"But you might be very ill," he pressed.

"I'll see a doctor if it happens again," she said.

"I think that's a splendid compromise," Mrs. Jeffries said hastily. She was impressed by the cook's acting ability. She was doing a superb job. "I do think it was just a faint, sir. Mrs. Goodge got up very early this morning to finish her Christmas baking, and she didn't eat breakfast."

"That's right, sir—I didn't eat breakfast, and when you get to be my age, you shouldn't miss your meals." Mrs. Goodge gave him a weak smile. "I'll not make that mistake again, sir. Honestly, now that I've had something to eat and drink, I feel much better."

Witherspoon rose slowly to his feet. "Alright, then, I'll respect your wishes. But you must promise me you'll see a doctor if this happens again."

"Oh, I will, sir. I truly will."

"You should take it easy for the next few days," he instructed.

"Thank you, sir, and again, I'm sorry to have interrupted your work."

"Speaking of which, sir, did you see Mrs. Farringdon today?" Mrs. Jeffries asked. She was painfully aware of everyone watching her, waiting for her to take the lead.

"We did. She admitted that she'd pasted one of her wine labels onto the bottle of port that Whitfield gave them as a Christmas gift," he replied. He seemed unaware that he had a kitchen full of people staring at him. "It was most extraordinary, but it does reaffirm my idea."

"It's more than just an idea, sir," she said with a wide smile. "I'm sure the chief inspector was delighted when you told him you'd solved the case."

"Solved the case," Witherspoon repeated.

"Now, sir, don't be modest," she laughed.

"That's your problem, sir," Barnes added quickly. "You're far too modest. Not at all like that Inspector Nivens—he's always braggin' about his arrests. Now, sir, I know you probably don't want to speak too much about it until you've thought it through the way you always do. But seein' as how it's Christmas, maybe you can give us just a hint on how you came up with your idea."

"Oh, please, Inspector," Luty cried. "Do tell. We love hearing about your work." She grabbed Hatchet's arm and yanked him toward the table. He recovered in time to pull out her chair before taking his own seat.

"I think you're ever so clever, Inspector." Betsy stared at him in admiration. "Most people could never take just a few facts and put them together to catch the killer the way you can, sir."

"Well, er, uh, once I realized that none of the other dinner guests had any real motive for wanting Whitfield dead, I had to . . . uh, look at the crime from an entirely different perspective."

"Was that when you figured it out?" Mrs. Goodge asked. She knew good and well that it had been Mrs. Jeffries' hints that had put that particular notion in the inspector's head. She was glad he remembered it.

"Well, certainly, that was a part of my reasoning," he replied.

"And today when Mrs. Farringdon admitted what she'd done, and that the Bordeaux was actually the bottle of port he'd given her, is that when you realized that with Basil Farringdon dead, there were only Becker and Whitfield left in the tontine?" Barnes said.

"Yes, er, that did occur to me," Witherspoon said eagerly. "That's precisely what I thought. Port is a man's drink, so I was certain it was meant for Mr. Farringdon, not his wife." The picture in his mind was becoming clearer by the minute. He suddenly understood what his inner voice had been trying to tell him since he'd come down to breakfast this morning. "Of course, proving all this is going to be very difficult."

"You'll find a way, sir," Smythe said.

"We could always press for an exhumation order on the other tontine members who have died in the past few years," Barnes suggested. He was fairly certain he now understood what had happened. "As you said, sir, it seemed that every January, Becker and Whitfield met at a funeral of an old friend. I'll warrant that most of those funerals were tontine members and that all of them had received one of Whitfield's Christmas bottles."

"Yes, I suppose we could do that." Witherspoon frowned in confusion as a dozen different courses of action whirled about in his brain. "But I'm not sure we'd get such an order. The courts are generally very opposed to digging someone up, especially on this kind of evidence. It's all circumstantial."

"Don't tease us, sir." Mrs. Jeffries laughed gaily. "That's not the only trick you have up your sleeve. Before you even ask for any sort of order, you're going to test the bottle of port that Whitfield sent to Becker. Am I right?"

"Yes, yes, you are," he cried. "And how did you know I was going to do that?"

"Because Whitfield was still planning on taking Mrs. Graham to Italy," she said. "And as he'd proposed and she'd not given him an affirmative answer, he took matters into his own hands."

"Go on." Witherspoon adopted the pose of a schoolmaster questioning a clever student.

"Have you ever seen the like?" Luty said in a voice just loud enough for the inspector to hear. "He's smarter than that Sherlock Holmes character." She hoped she wasn't overdoing it too much.

"Aha, I see you want me to show that I've been paying close attention to your methods," Mrs. Jeffries replied. "Well, sir, I shan't disappoint you. According to Mrs. Graham's own words, she needs to marry for financial reasons. As she'd not agreed to Whitfield's marriage proposal, he realized that she'd probably been able to ascertain his true financial situation and understood that marriage to him wouldn't give her what she wanted: lifelong security in the manner to which she was accustomed to living. Am I correct so far?"

He nodded.

"Therefore Whitfield concluded that the only way he could have her as his wife was to obtain money of his own, not simply an annuity that went back into the tontine pot upon his death." She paused. "As there were only three of them left, Whitfield decided that this year, he'd kill off Farringdon and Becker both."

"Which would mean that he got it all," Wiggins exclaimed. "Only he didn't count on Mrs. Farringdon sendin' 'is own poisoned wine back to 'im."

"That's correct, Wiggins." Witherspoon nodded in satisfaction. He was so proud of his household. He'd truly taught them to love justice. "And therefore, if my theory is correct, Becker's bottle should contain poison as well."

"That should be easy enough to check, sir," Barnes said. "All we have to do is have a good look and see if there's any leaves floatin' about in it."

"For a minute there, I thought we were doomed." Luty slumped down in her chair. "I was wonderin' if he was ever gonna catch on." She motioned for Hatchet to pass her the plate of apple tarts Mrs. Goodge had put out for their tea.

"I was fairly sure he'd understand," Mrs. Jeffries replied. "Inspector Witherspoon is no fool. He can add two and two and come up with four as easily as I can."

"But what if, when he gets to Becker's house this evening, the port doesn't have any poison in it?" Betsy asked. "What will we do then?"

"Oh, I shouldn't worry about that." Mrs. Jeffries smiled confidently. "Even if there isn't anything in Becker's port, we've still come up with enough evidence for the inspector to make a good case that the killer was Whitfield."

"What got you thinking that it might be him?" Hatchet helped himself to another tart.

"The realization that none of our other suspects had any genuine reasons for wanting him dead. I began to think I was looking at the whole matter the wrong way," she explained. "Once I learned about the tontine and that there were only three surviving members left, two of whom were already wealthy, I remember thinking that if it had been one of them who had died, then Whitfield would be the perfect suspect." That wasn't entirely true, but she could think of no other way to describe how it had all come together in that one bright moment of insight in the wee hours before dawn.

"And once you started down that path, then there was plenty of evidence that it had to be him." Mrs. Goodge bobbed her head for emphasis.

"We already knew that every January one of Whitfield's friends died," Mrs. Jeffries continued. "So I asked myself if these friends might have been other members of the tontine. Since we established that"—she gave Luty and Hatchet a quick, grateful smile— "then, even if Becker's port is free of foxglove, I imagine it will be easy to find out if these poor souls received a bottle of Whitfield's Christmas port."

"And every time one of them died, Whitfield's dividend went up," Smythe muttered.

"Once we found out that Maria Farringdon collected wine labels, then it made sense." Mrs. Jeffries raised her hand over her mouth to cover a yawn. "Oh dear, I am sorry."

Luty laughed and got up from the table. "Not to worry. We've got to be on our way. There's a Christmas ball at Henley House, and I've got to put in an appearance. But you let us know about Becker's port."

It was half past ten by the time Witherspoon came home that night. Mrs. Jeffries didn't even need to ask any questions—despite the late hour, he was grinning like a schoolboy. "The foxglove was there." He paused by the bottom stair. "You could see the crumbled leaves floating in the bottle. Whitfield was so confident he wouldn't be caught, he didn't even try to cover his tracks."

"Whitfield was arrogant, sir. He'd gotten away with it so many other times, perhaps he thought he'd never be caught. Did Mr. Becker realize what you were doing?"

Witherspoon sighed. "He did. I felt sorry for the poor man. He considered Whitfield a friend. I don't think he has many friends." He started up the staircase. "Once I've handed in my report to the chief inspector tomorrow, we can put this matter to rest and enjoy

our Christmas." He continued onward, but when he reached the
first-floor landing, he stopped and looked back at her. "I do hope
that Inspector Nivens doesn't raise too much of a fuss when he
finds out the case has been solved."

But of course he did.

Christmas Eve was wet and cold. Witherspoon shook the rain off
his bowler as he and Barnes walked down the hallway.

"He's here, sir," Barnes warned softly.

Nivens stood in the corridor outside Barrows' office. His eyes
narrowed angrily as they approached. "I hope you're prepared to
give up, Witherspoon," he warned. "I don't think the chief inspector is willing to put up with any more shenanigans out of you."

"Good morning, Inspector," Witherspoon responded politely.
He moved past him to the office door, raised his hand, and gave a
quiet knock. Barnes ignored Nivens completely.

"Come in," Barrows called.

Witherspoon twisted the knob and, as the door opened, Nivens
shoved past him into the room. The other two followed.

Barrows looked up from the report he'd been reading and
frowned. "Inspector Nivens, what is all this? You weren't invited
to this meeting."

"I've a right to be here. You promised me this case."

Barrows stared at him a long moment. "The case has been
solved. The inspector's report is right here." He tapped the pages
on his desk. "So you've wasted time, which could have been properly used in keeping the peace, to come along and try to tell me
how to do my job. I most certainly did not promise you this case.
I said that if Inspector Witherspoon didn't solve it, I'd consider
passing it along to you."

"My apologies, sir. I must have misunderstood you," Nivens
replied coolly. "But as I'm here, may I ask who is being arrested
for the Whitfield murder?"

Barrows pretended to think about it for a few seconds. He
couldn't allow Nivens' insubordination to go unchallenged, but
now that he'd reestablished his authority, he was inclined to be reasonable. Besides, he wasn't a fool. Nivens did have powerful
friends. "No one is being arrested. Stephen Whitfield died by his
own hand."

Nivens gaped at him in shock. "Are you saying the man committed suicide at his own dinner party? That's absurd."

Barrows looked at Witherspoon. "Would you care to explain?"

"Whitfield didn't deliberately take his own life. He was trying to murder Basil Farringdon. But Mrs. Farringdon played a rather odd trick on Whitfield—pasted a different label on the bottle and sent it back to him unopened. He drank it and died."

"How on earth did you reach that ridiculous conclusion?" Nivens snapped. He glared at Barrows. "This is just another one of his tricks. Now he even wants to take credit for the cases he couldn't solve. Are you going to let him get away with this?"

"Inspector Nivens, I've been more than patient with you." Barrows rose from his chair. "You are insubordinate, sir. If I say the case has been solved, then the bloody case has been solved. Now get out of here before I bring you up on formal charges."

Nivens' mouth opened and closed. Then he turned on his heel and stomped to the door. He banged his shoulder into Barnes as he shoved past, muttering to himself. He marched out the door, slamming it hard behind him.

"Gracious, sir, that was most unpleasant," Witherspoon said. "I am sorry that this case has caused you so much trouble. Inspector Nivens will be going straight to the Home Office."

"Let him do his worst." Barrows shrugged. "The man is an incompetent bully. Half of his arrests either result in acquittals or are tossed out of court. If he runs to his political pals and complains about what I've done, he'll be in for a nasty surprise. I've some weapons of my own I can use to defend myself and the department. Don't concern yourself on my account, Inspector." He tapped the report again. "You've done an excellent job here, and it was a very complex case."

"Thank you, sir." Witherspoon flushed in pleasure. "But of course it was a team effort. Constable Barnes and many other policemen worked very hard to help bring this matter to a close."

"I appreciate the fact that you got me the report so early this morning," Barrows continued. "I don't mind admitting, I had to read through it twice to make sure I understood how all the pieces came together. Whitfield was a fool and a murderer, but in the end he got what he deserved." He closed the report and looked Witherspoon directly in the eye. "It's a pity we can't go public with any of this. It looks as if your record is going to be a bit tarnished. Publicly, this must appear as if you couldn't solve this one."

"That's quite alright, sir," the inspector replied. "I understand."

Several years earlier there had been a series of unsolved murders in the East End, which had seriously undermined public trust in the Metropolitan Police Force. Jack the Ripper, as the press referred to the unknown killer, had never been caught. But as time passed, public confidence in the police had returned. If the true facts of this case were to come out, that faith could once again be shattered.

Witherspoon's report suggested quite strongly that Whitfield had murdered at least four people and he'd gotten away with it. The police hadn't had a clue that the crimes had even taken place.

"Have you had confirmation that it was foxglove leaves in the bottle you obtained from Henry Becker's residence?" Barrows asked. "We might as well get all the loose ends tied up nice and neat."

"Yes, sir. We stopped in at the station on the way here. There was poison in the bottle."

"I'm surprised we got confirmation so quickly." Barrows looked puzzled. "Surely a chemist or botanist couldn't have been found on such short notice."

"We fed it to some rats," Barnes answered. "When I walked into the station last night with Becker's bottle, they'd just caught some rodents. As rats will usually eat or drink anything, I suggested we see if the rats would drink the port. There were three of them, sir. So we poured out a bit of it in the top of a Cadbury cocoa tin and put it in the rat catcher's box. Two of them were dead this morning and the third was lying on his side, panting hard. He's probably dead by now, too. The cocoa lid was empty. As the rats looked healthy enough last night, we're pretty sure it was the poison that killed them."

"Ye gods, are you serious?" Barrows exclaimed. "How fiendishly clever."

"Thank you, sir." Barnes smiled proudly. "We are having the port properly analyzed. But as we were in a hurry for an answer, this seemed a sensible course of action."

Christmas Day dawned clear and cold. They all went to church in the morning, and then Inspector Witherspoon crossed the gardens to Lady Cannonberry's. He didn't come home until late that night.

The staff had their Christmas dinner in the kitchen, and afterward they exchanged presents, sang songs, and played games. Neighborhood friends dropped by with bottles of sherry, tins of chocolate, and even a fruit basket. Everyone ate too much, drank too much, and thoroughly enjoyed themselves.

On Boxing Day, they received their Christmas boxes from Witherspoon, and then he left to spend another day with Lady Cannonberry. The household was having guests of their own.

Luty and Hatchet, their arms laden with presents, arrived at noon, and Dr. Bosworth, who'd also been invited to share the day with them, had appeared twenty minutes later.

"I understand the Whitfield case has been resolved," he said as he handed Mrs. Jeffries his hat and coat. "You must tell me what happened. No one's been arrested for the murder."

They took turns telling him the details, and by the time they were ready to eat, he'd heard everything. Bosworth stared at them in amazement and then sat down in the chair next to Hatchet. "This was a most unusual case. It's truly a wonder that you solved it at all."

"Thank you," Mrs. Jeffries replied on behalf of all of them. "Would you care to say the blessing?" she asked.

"I would be delighted."

Everyone bowed their heads as he said grace.

When the doctor had finished and they'd all said a hearty "amen," Wiggins exclaimed, "Cor blimey, this is an even bigger feast than yesterday. Look at all this food."

"It's the Feast of St. Stephen," Mrs. Goodge said. "And I think it's only fitting that we're all here together, celebratin'. As the good doctor said, it's truly a wonder we solved this case at all."

"We'd be right miserable if we hadn't," Smythe murmured. He reached for Betsy's hand under the table and was relieved that she didn't pull away from him.

"But we did solve it." Luty raised her glass of beer. "And if you ask me, it's because we're the smartest bunch of detectives on this side of the river."

Everyone laughed and began to help themselves. As they ate, they discussed the case, gossiped, told jokes, and had a rollicking good time. The weather brightened that afternoon, so everyone went out into the garden for some fresh air.

Wiggins tossed sticks, which Fred felt honor bound to chase.

Mrs. Goodge decided it was too cold, so she went back inside for a nap. Hatchet declared that Luty had had enough excitement, so they took their leave.

Smythe grabbed Betsy's hand and pulled her toward the kitchen door. "Come on. You promised we could have our talk today."

"But what if someone comes in?" Betsy protested.

"Mrs. Jeffries and Dr. Bosworth are discussing the size of bullet holes." He pointed at the two of them, who were seated on a bench near the big oak. "They'll be talkin' about it for hours."

"Where's Wiggins?"

"He's takin' Fred for a walk." Smythe gently urged her across the terrace and into the house.

The kitchen was very quiet, the only sound the ticking of the clock. Betsy took her usual chair, but Smythe, instead of taking the seat next to her, slipped into the spot directly across from her. He wanted to be able to watch her face.

Neither of them said a word for what seemed a very long time. Finally he cleared his throat and began, "You said you were still willin' to marry me."

"I did."

He was scared to ask the next question, but he had to. "Uh, when would we want to have the wedding?"

Betsy cocked her head to one side and crossed her arms over her chest. She'd thought hard about this matter, and she'd come to a decision. "Well, I'd not like it to be too soon. I'm still a bit raw about what happened."

"Alright, I can understand your feelin's about that," he replied.

"And this time, seein' as our last plans didn't work out the way we'd hoped, I'd like it to be a bit smaller."

He wasn't sure he understood. "What does that mean?"

"It means I want a much smaller wedding." She uncrossed her arms. "I don't want a wedding breakfast, and I don't want a lot of fuss and bother. We can get the banns read and then have a quiet wedding with just the household and a few close friends." She wasn't going to risk being humiliated in front of the whole world again.

A rush of anger surged through him, but as he watched her face, the temper vanished as quickly as it had come. He suddenly understood that she was afraid. Her words had sounded strong and confident, but he could see fear and pain in her eyes.

"Betsy, I love you more than anything in this world, and I'm sorry I hurt you. I'll marry you any way that you want. But know this—I'll never, ever leave you again."

"What if someone from your past shows up and they need you?" she asked. Her eyes misted with tears, but she blinked to keep them back.

"Then I'll take you with me," he replied. "I should have taken you with me to Australia. I should have at least asked and given you the choice. I'll not make that mistake again."

Once more she was silent. She looked away and took a deep breath. When she turned back to him, she was grinning from ear to ear. "That's what I've been waiting to hear ever since you got back. That I come first, that you'll never push me aside again."

"I didn't push you aside before."

"But it felt like you had," she said.

"I'm so sorry, love. I'll never hurt you again," he promised.

"Sure you will." She grinned. "We're going to be man and wife. Even the most devoted couples hurt each other from time to time. But just don't ever put me second again. Don't ever push me aside."

"I'll never push you aside." He leapt up and raced around the table.

Laughing, she got up, and he grabbed her, lifted her up over his head, and whirled her about the kitchen. "You've made me the happiest man in the world," he cried. "When, when are we going to wed?"

"Put me down," she giggled. "Someone will come."

Several of them were already there. Mrs. Jeffries and Dr. Bosworth were hovering in the doorway.

"Tell me when first," he demanded.

She'd thought about that, too. "I think I'd like to marry in the autumn. October is a good month."

"October it is, then," he cried.

"Cor blimey, what's goin' on?" Wiggins pushed past Mrs. Jeffries and the doctor. "Are we dancin', then?"

It was Betsy who answered. "I'm going to be a bride again."

"I like celebrations and parties. We gonna 'ave a big one?"

Smythe lowered her to the floor and waited for her to reply. She looked at the three people in the doorway. "Oh, yes, it's going to be a wonderful wedding. I'm going to invite everyone we know."

She reached for his hand. "And this time, if you try to leave me at the altar, I'll hunt you down and skin you alive."

He was humbled by the trust she'd just given him. "I promise you, love—I'll never leave you again."

"And if he does, I'll 'elp ya hunt him down," Wiggins offered.